1826: SPRING

Book 1 of 5

Philip G. Brown

Swanford United Books

Copyright © MMXXIII Philip G. Brown

All rights reserved

No part of this book may be reproduced in any written, electronic, mechanical, recording or photocopying form, or stored in a retrieval system without the express permission of the author. The exception is in the case of brief quotations embodied in critical articles or reviews.

Although every precaution has been taken to verify the accuracy of the information contained herein, the author and publisher assume no responsibility for any errors or omissions.

Except for those in the public domain, all characters and events in this book are fictitious. Any similarity between actual persons, living or dead, is purely coincidental.

Published by Swanford United Books
Please contact:
swanfordunited@aol.com

ISBN 978-0-9932461-8-0

CONTENTS

Title Page
Copyright
Preface
Chapter One — 1
Chapter Two — 10
Chapter Three — 16
Chapter Four — 32
Chapter Five — 47
Chapter Six — 56
Chapter Seven — 67
Chapter Eight — 76
Chapter Nine — 85
Chapter Ten — 98
Chapter Eleven — 109
Chapter Twelve — 123
Chapter Thirteen — 135
Chapter Fourteen — 148
Chapter Fifteen — 157
Chapter Sixteen — 167
Chapter Seventeen — 174

Chapter Eighteen	184
Chapter Nineteen	196
Chapter Twenty	207
Chapter Twenty-One	221
Chapter Twenty-Two	241
Chapter Twenty-Three	254
Chapter Twenty-Four	266
Chapter Twenty-Five	281
Dramatis Personae	294
A Map of Albion	313
A Map of Europa	314
A Royal Family Tree	315
Acknowledgement	317
There Are Five Books In this Series	319

Preface

Consider, if you will, the eight planets: Moon, Mercury, Venus, Sol, Mars, Thanatos, Jupiter and Saturn, revolving in the celestial sphere around our own world. Imagine now the cold, silent orb of Thanatos alone. Would our history be any different if that melancholic influence were missing?

Ramon Llull, Tractatus novus de astronomia, 1297

Chapter One

Blotwell in Knots

Monday 3rd April 1826

Freddy Hall stepped out of the front door of the Sailor's Yarn Inn and found the day warming nicely, with the sun rising into a clear blue sky. The old yew tree in the churchyard of All Souls across the road seemed never to change, but on the village green next door the grass was already in need of a scything, despite the regular attention of Zebedee Tring, the local dog's body. Freddy was on his way to Seekings School, almost two miles distant from the village of Linbury in the county of Dorsetshire on the southern coast of Albion, where he had lived for the whole of his thirteen and three-quarter years.

"Good morning, Freddy, is Farmer Stadden's bull chasing you?"

Freddy looked to his left to see the widow, Mrs Sophie Pattle, standing, broom in hand, on the doorstep of her cottage which doubled as the corner shop. Despite its modest size, Sophie kept it well stocked with everything from tobacco products to gobstoppers. It was a favourite haunt of the boys from the school, who would spend their pocket money on an illicit ounce of shag, a bottle of dandelion and burdock, made to a secret recipe, or a bag of homemade ginger biscuits.

"Hello, Mrs Pattle," answered Freddy with a smile. "In a hurry. Start of the summer term…"

"More haste, less speed, young man."

Freddy nodded politely but didn't slacken his pace. After

the disappointments of the Lenten term, he had set forth with an unusual determination in his stride. It was the day he was going to prove, with the help of his best friend Harry East, that he had been hard done by in his studies and didn't deserve the warning Mr Tallow, his housemaster, had given him.

'Unless things markedly improve, you will be kept back for a second year in the shell class.' The old man had seemed half-asleep when he had intoned the words after reading the report from Mr Hooke, the teacher of natural philosophy. "Do you really want to be classed among the new boys, the dimwits and the *couldn't-care-lessers,* Hall?" Mr Tallow had added, his head trembling slightly.

Freddy had ground his teeth then and was grinding them again at the thought of the injustice he had been forced to endure.

Soon he had passed the village boundary stone and was striding out down the New Coach Road, his heels sending up white powdery dust which coated his shoes and the bottom of his regulation black flannel trousers.

Freddy paused where the road came nearest to the sheer cliff edge, to look out over the sea. He smiled to himself. There had been a report in the *John Bull* newspaper that the Silesian fleet had been sighted in the Channel, but he hadn't believed it when he read it and he believed it even less now.

'Warmongers' was how his dad described those who reported this kind of news story, of which there had been many during the last twelve months.

The sea was as flat as a mill pond. Freddy could hear a faint *sssh* as the tide rolled in, out of sight, over the shingle and sandy beach below.

Freddy breathed in the salt-laden air then started off again, quickening his pace until he was trotting. Seekings came into sight as the road continued to descend to near sea-level.

In no time at all, Freddy had reached the ivy-clad gatehouse which was the headmaster's residence. As usual the caretaker, Mr Hawlings, was standing at the tall wrought-iron gates ready to greet the day boys, collect the post and turn away any unwelcome visitors.

"Making an early start on your first day back, Freddy Hall?" he said.

Mr Hawlings was an occasional visitor to the Sailor's Yarn and had known Freddy before he became a pupil at the school.

"Good morning, Mr Hawlings," said Freddy, taking a surreptitious glance over the bewhiskered man's shoulder at the big clock set high above the main entrance to the school. It was only 8.25 a.m. – fifteen minutes earlier than his usual time of arrival. "I was in a hurry..."

"Are you still in a hurry?" asked the old caretaker. "Your friend won't be here for another twenty minutes yet."

"Not really," Freddy answered ruefully. "I guess I outdid myself this morning."

"Mmm, well, in that case why don't you take a short walk down the drive and see if you can spot anything unusual?"

Freddy was never quite sure what to make of Mr Hawlings. He seemed mysterious, almost otherworldly, and to know a lot more than he let on. It was part of school folklore that the old caretaker was something of a wise man, maybe even a wizard, though no evidence for this conjecture had ever come forth. Perhaps it was partly due to the oat-coloured smock he always wore with attached hood, which he called a kaftan.

"Never fear, I'll keep a lookout for Master East's arrival, so you won't miss him."

"I'll probably hear the post horn anyway," answered Freddy.

Harry East lived in the village of Larkstone, just over the border in the county of Hampshire, twenty-five miles from Linbury and thus twenty-three from the school. Each day, he hitched a lift on the mail coach which arrived promptly at the gates at 8.45 a.m.

Mr Hawlings smiled. "You might indeed, and then again

there's a strangeness in the air this morning..."

Another peculiar thing for the caretaker to say. Feeling as if this was yet another test for him, Freddy entered the school grounds at a snail's pace, looking left and right between the trees that lined the driveway. He wanted to impress Mr Hawlings with his acuity, knowing rightly that he had a reputation for overlooking the obvious.

"Boy! I say, you, boy!"

The voice came from the deep shadows inside the wooded area to his left. Freddy stared hard; he thought he recognised the high-pitched warble, but at first couldn't make out where it had arisen from. Then behind a thicket of laurel he glimpsed a flash of white.

"Yes, you, boy – come here."

Freddy didn't like to be ordered about and called 'a boy', especially in the superior tone used by this individual. But his curiosity and the words of Mr Hawlings drove him to push through the shrubbery.

Simon Blotwell had only been at Seekings for two terms and already he was the most hated boy in the school. His reputation as a milksop – and, worse, a sneak, a snitch, a shirker and downright blackguard – had spread from the shell to the upper sixth. Now here he was, lashed to the trunk of a tree by coil upon coil of ship's rope, which didn't manage to conceal the fact that he was entirely naked.

Freddy chuckled.

"Untie me, there's a good fellow," said Blotwell, still managing to sound patronisingly superior.

"Why should I?" answered Freddy, standing with hands on hips, wondering if this was the unusual sighting that Mr Hawlings had alluded to.

"Because there's a knot sticking into the small of my back and it's getting uncomfortable."

Freddy had to concede that the school sneak was managing to remain largely unruffled by his experience. "What's it worth?" he asked, though he had already decided that he would at least untie the rope.

"I'm expecting a cake next week from Auntie Millicent and you can come to my study on the Wednesday afternoon for a slice, if you like."

The idea had a certain appeal to Freddy, who felt his mouth watering. "Why have you got a study? Shell boys are supposed to sleep in the dorm."

"Auntie Millicent knows Dr Butler and sent him a letter telling him how sensitive I am."

Freddy huffed. "So, it's just plain favouritism?"

"Yes," answered Blotwell with a condescending smile. "Are you going to untie me or not?"

Freddy felt like saying 'not', but instead he walked round the tree to inspect the knot. "Who tied you up?"

"The rough boys."

"You mean Stalky & Co, don't you?"

"How did you know?"

"This is their style, especially leaving your clothes neatly folded by your feet. What did you do to deserve their attention?"

Blotwell gave a gleeful smile. "Cheeseman had sent me on a mission to catch them smoking and I'd been hiding in Coneycop Spinney for three days after school, with no success. Then on Saturday I decided to follow Beetle Kipling all the way to Linbury where he went into the Widow Pattle's, looking very cagey, so I knew he was up to no good. Then I tracked him back to the Spinney where I discovered them puffing away on briar pipes in a brushwood den. Of course, I immediately reported them, and on Sunday Cheeseman gave Corkran and M'Turk six of the best and Kipling ten for supplying."

If Simon Blotwell was the most hated figure at Seekings, then Alfred Mayhew Cheeseman ran him a close second. He was the captain of School House and had his eye on the all-school captaincy when Theodore Oldham ascended to the peerage on his eighteenth birthday, which also happened to be the last day but one of the summer term.

"If you ask me, you got off lightly," said Freddy. "I'd have thrown you into the lagoon and let you drown."

"I can swim," said Blotwell.

"Did Auntie Millicent teach you?"

Freddy wasn't usually very good at sarcasm, but for some reason this struck home. Blotwell went bright red and took on a shifty look. "Actually, no..." he stuttered.

Pleased that he'd got one over on Cheeseman's toady, Freddy, still with some reluctance, pulled at the knot, which surrendered immediately. The rope fell away from Blotwell like an uncoiling snake.

"Well, there's a sight!"

The voice made Freddy jump, even though he instantly recognised it as that of his best friend.

"Scud, what are you doing here?"

"I might say the same about you – loitering in the woods with a naked boy."

"Shut up."

Harry East laughed heartily. "Blotwell, you miserable wretch, put some clothes on and stop showing off your goose pimples."

"Has the mail coach arrived?" asked Freddy. "I didn't hear the post horn."

"Well, obviously it's arrived because I'm here, aren't I? But I'm afraid the postilion has a sore throat today and failed to blow."

"Was Mr Hawlings still at the gate?"

"Of course he was. Collection of the Monday mail sack is an advanced ritual for the old duffer."

Harry was one of the few boys who was dismissive of the caretaker, which irritated Freddy. He didn't seem to notice that the man had depth.

"Scud, you are a ninny," said Freddy.

"Why do you call him Scud?" asked Blotwell, who was now half-dressed in an off-white union suit and socks, one of which hung off the end of his foot.

"Because he can run like the wind, dunce," answered Freddy.

"Hurry up and get your uniform on," said Harry, "or we'll be late for prayers."

"At Blotwell Manor, I have a dresser," said Blotwell.

"Now, why doesn't that surprise me?" Harry chortled. "Anyway, Federico, why are you helping this scoundrel?"

"He's offered me cake," said Freddy, adding pointedly, "in his *study* on Wednesday afternoon."

"Oh well, count me in on that!" exclaimed Harry. "What sort of cake, Blotwell?"

"A light sponge sprinkled with icing sugar and filled with raspberry jam and buttercream," answered Blotwell with relish. "Mrs Strout, Auntie Millicent's cook, makes the most delicious sponge imaginable." He looked down his long nose. "But I only invited Freddy."

Freddy noted that Blotwell had called him by his first name, which he thought was a bit of a cheek, but he remained silent on the matter for now.

Harry put on a threatening posture. "Blotwell, if you don't invite me for cake in your study, I shall take this length of rope and hang you by your skinny neck from that overhanging branch."

"As you please," Simon replied haughtily, buttoning his black morning coat.

The school bell began to toll, rung as always by Mr Topliss, who climbed up a narrow staircase from his rooms in the tower to the belfry. It was 8.55 a.m. and they had five minutes to get to assembly in the Great Hall.

"You know, with all this business, I'd almost forgotten about you-know-what," said Freddy as they began a quick march to the entrance.

"Have no fear, Scud is here. I'll reveal all at luncheon."

"What are you going to reveal?" asked Blotwell, adjusting his oversize collar.

"Mind your own business," retorted Harry. "You'll only go

sneaking to Cheeseman about anything I say."

"I can keep a secret," answered Blotwell.

"Yes, like a sieve can hold water," said Harry.

"Why do you sneak for Cheeseman?" asked Freddy.

"He offered to protect me from the rough boys," replied Blotwell with a smile.

Harry guffawed. "Hasn't done you much good then, has it? All tied up in your birthday suit."

"He doesn't care about you, Blotwell, he's just using you," said Freddy.

"Fweddy, Hawwy, wait for me!" a voice chirruped.

"Oh, it's that common little boy from the lighthouse," said Blotwell.

"He's not common," said Freddy, turning to face the newcomer. "Good morning, Francis, and how are you this morning?"

Frank Kennedy trotted up to them, his satchel high on his back. "Don't call me Fwancis, Fweddy Hall, I'm Fwank."

"That's right, you two, start the new term exactly like you ended the last one," said Harry.

Frank was ten years old, the youngest and smallest boy at the school. His dad was the lighthouse keeper at Clifftop House, which stood on a high promontory overlooking the Albion Channel. A day boy like Freddy and Harry, the money for his schooling had come from a scholarship fund at Trinity House.

"Little boy, why do you speak like that?" asked Blotwell.

"Like what?" asked Frank, cocking his head and batting his eyelids at Simon.

Harry chuckled. "Good answer, Frank. Tell him to mind his own business."

Blotwell sniffed and joined the crush of boys climbing the short flight of steps to the main entrance.

"Is Carstairs here?" enquired Frank.

Carstairs was Frank's best friend. Their relationship was based on a heady mixture of affection and argumentation.

"I think I saw him go inside," said Freddy.

"Which is where we ought to be," said Harry.

With a mixture of anticipation and apprehension, the three boys ascended the steps and entered the Great Hall. The summer term at Seekings School had begun.

Chapter Two

Illumination of the Text

A Little History of Seekings School by An Old Boy:

Seekings School for Boys is the fifth most prestigious academic establishment in Albion, after Oxford and Cambridge universities, Harrow School and Eton College, and is the youngest of the five by over one hundred years.

The Earl of Dorsetshire, later the Duke of Dorsetshire, was granted a charter by King Henry IX in 1663 to found a school on the site of a grand sixteenth-century manor house which had fallen on hard times. The school expanded gradually over the years and is presently a varied collection of houses, utilitarian buildings, woods and playing fields set in 200 acres behind a sturdy perimeter wall of local Portland stone. The red-brick manor, built in the style of Hampton Court Palace, survives as the Old School House, or 'osher' to the boys. In the centre of it is the Great Hall where the day-to-day assemblies are carried out and the non-religious ceremonies take place, such as graduation and prize-giving. It is surrounded by classrooms on two floors. The upper landing overlooking the Great Hall has a balustrade in the Spanish style.

The left wing is given over to the boarders of School House and has three floors, the uppermost reserved for fifth- and sixth-formers, including the School House captain and school captain. The right wing comprises a staffroom, rooms for administration, storage and a small medical facility. But its two main features are the school library and chapel, both enlarged and redecorated by the second Duke of Dorsetshire in the baroque style. The newly commissioned east window of the chapel, overlooking the altar, is of stained glass showing Christ blessing the children. Inscribed beneath the portrait is the school motto, taken directly from the Duke's coat of arms: *aut nunquam tentes, aut perfice.* Either do it perfectly or not at all.

Dr George Butler is the current headmaster, a doctor of divinity who graduated from Trinity College, Oxford, in 1794. As well as his headmasterly duties, he tutors the upper sixth in theology and mathematics. His wife, Sarah, is rarely seen as she is kept busy by four small children with another on the way. Under the Doctor are a staff of twelve masters and five assistant masters including his deputy, Mr Aubrey Topliss, who teaches alchemy and archery and who is also the school librarian.

In Mr Topliss's tower rooms he keeps his collection of wands, which has led the more romantically inclined to believe that he is also a conjuror, an offence under Albion law going back to the reign of Henry VIII. The bill in question, appropriately named the Bill against Conjuration and Witchcrafts and Sorcery and Enchantments, has long since fallen out of favour with the judiciary, but is still on the statute book.

All the masters bar one at Seekings wear black gowns and mortar boards to lessons. Mr Topliss is the exception, and he is the only one of the seventeen not to carry a cane. No one in recent times has ever seen him beat a boy. Others teachers, more violently inclined, brandish the rod like an extension of themselves.

At the beginning of Lenten term, 1826, there are two hundred and four boys at the school, of which one hundred and ninety-six are fee paying boarders. The remaining eight are from families in the locality who would not, or could not, afford the fifty guineas for lodgings on top of the ninety guineas per year for their son's education. These day boys are generally looked down upon, or ignored, by the boarders as poor relations, but there are exceptions, usually because an individual stands outside the run-of-the-mill. Two contemporary examples of this are Freddy Hall, who is a Newtonian scholar, and Harry East, who is a first-rate all-round athlete.

Seekings has seven class groups. Most boys start in the shell at the age of ten upwards, then move on to the lower remove, but only when they are deemed to have reached a high enough standard in their work. From there, they progress into the remove, upper remove and finally the fifth. Those who want to pursue higher education, if their parents are wealthy enough, can enter the sixth form. The fees in the upper sixth increase to one hundred guineas, the extra money paying for a pupil's candidature in university entrance exams. Naturally the preferred option is for one of the Oxbridge colleges, and the school has two places allocated in each.

There are five houses at Seekings. School House is the largest and is regarded as the most prestigious because it is situated in the main building. It is also the odd one out. The other four are named after Elizabethan adventurers: Drake, Raleigh, Hawkins and Frobisher. Drake is the smallest and was originally the estate steward's lodge. It has accommodation for up to thirty boarders and is also the home away from home for the day boys.

With few exceptions, shell boys live in their house dormitories, as do most of the lower remove. Every boarder eagerly anticipates having a study of their own. It is a rite of passage, part of growing up, though it is also something of a chimera, because each study is shared between two boys and the rooms themselves are small, sparsely furnished and a quarter don't even have a fireplace to keep out the winter chill. Only the upper sixth-formers have a study of their own, complete with fireplace, coal scuttle and toasting fork.

From the members of the upper sixth are chosen the five house captains and the captain of the school. They in turn appoint two prefects each from their ranks to oversee the younger boys. Dr Butler is a believer in self-regulation and allows these seniors to punish miscreants in a variety of ways, from lines for minor offences to a caning for serious abuses, though they are not allowed to use the rod on fifth- and sixth-formers. In fact, only Alfred Mayhew Cheeseman, the captain of School House, is a regular user of corporal punishment, and he prefers to birch offenders with a set of four hazel twigs he has fashioned himself. At the other extreme, the captain of Drake House, George Mark Fouracre refuses to use the cane at all. Instead miscreants can find themselves in the ring, boxing their way out of trouble, though for more serious breaches of school rules they are referred to the housemaster, Mr Tallow, who – despite his frailty – can still wield a painful rod.

Outside the school gates and over the coach road is the beach, leading down to the lagoon. This stretch of quiet water has a one-hundred-yard jetty, from which swimming competitions are held. Here the water is deep enough for diving, but the lagoon has an average depth of only four feet. This is also where the boys bathe, in all weathers, once a week at set times, usually overseen by the Reverend Croft, the school chaplain.

* * *

THE EXAMINER,
A Sunday Paper
19th March 1826
FOREIGN INTELLIGENCE
From our Correspondent in Constantinople

Such is the simmering hostility between Albion and Silesia that a simple nautical accident has become a full blown diplomatic incident with ambassadors called in from their respective embassies in London and Karlsbad.

When HMS *Leviathan* collided with a Silesian merchant vessel, the SS *Danzig*, sending her to the bottom of the

Bosphorus with all hands, it was due to bad navigation on the part of her master, said Captain Treggoran of the *Leviathan*.

A spokesman for Sultan Mahmud IV said that the petty rivalries of the northern states should not be fought out on the waterways of the Ottoman Empire. This was a clear reference to the SS *Tabor*'s unprovoked attack on HMS *Enterprize* last month when our ship was carrying the Earl of Chesterfield on a goodwill mission to the Black Sea resort of Sevastopol. Fortunately, in that incident the *Enterprize* only sustained minor damage to her fo'c'sle and was able to continue on her journey while the support ships HMS *Bounty* and HMS *Reliant* chased off the Silesian aggressor. Subsequently, consultation with the new tsar, Nicholas I, cemented a growing cordiality between Albion and the Russian Empire from which a Treaty of Alliance may be forged.

THE ROYAL EXAMINER

By a court correspondent

The reaction to Silesian provocations by our gracious sovereign King Henry and his Ministers has been moderation itself. Still, the augmentation of the Albion fleet will carry on with a heightened energy, while our fighting forces at home and abroad will be reinforced by reservists from the county regiments. Meanwhile, arrangements for a state visit by His Imperial Majesty, the Emperor and Autocrat of all the Russias, Nicholas I, are being made with alacrity. A new treaty between the two great powers would be a blow to the Silesian pretender's ambitions to the crown of Albion.

An official announcement on the forthcoming marriage of the king to the Right Honourable Anne Lennard, Countess of Sussex, is still expected within the month, but the wedding ceremony may be postponed until the New Year to accommodate the aforementioned state visit and the long delayed coronation.

The court circular notes that His Majesty and members of the Royal Family will be moving to Windsor Castle on 23rd

March for the duration of the Easter holiday.

THE POLITICAL EXAMINER
House of Commons, 17th March

The Committee of Ways and Means resolved that the Sovereign Grant (the sum of £14,000,000) would be raised by Exchequer Bills, for the service of the year commencing 1st April 1826. To offset the increase, an additional tax of two shillings per pound will be levied on tobacco leaf, bringing the total to eight shillings per pound, and the tax on an imported bottle of wine will be doubled to nine pence. This was agreed to, and a Bill ordered to be brought in by the Chancellor of the Exchequer.

The Prime Minister spoke about prognostications for the future health of heirs in consequence of the marriage of the King to the Countess of Sussex. He said he has been assured by the court physician Sir Richard Croft that there would be no deleterious effects on offspring due to the alleged familial relationship of the couple.

On a point of order the Rt Hon. Member for Dorsetshire North asked why any credence should be given to rabble-rousing Silesian sympathisers whose sole purpose was to denigrate this nation's Royal Family.

The Chancellor of the Exchequer rose to move a Vote of Thanks of the House to General Lord Viscount FitzHerbert, for the skill, decision, indefatigable exertions, and consummate judgment manifested by him in the recent siege of Heligoland, by which that important fortress has been wrested from the Silesian occupier over the space of eleven days.

Chapter Three

Freddy Gets Mad

Thirty-five shell boys sat silently in school room number four while Mr Hooke wrote in a spidery, but legible, hand on the blackboard. The first words, in slightly larger letters and underlined, were: *The Solar System*. At length he turned and, unsmiling, surveyed his class. For a moment, his eyes became unfocused, as if he was imagining being somewhere more appropriate for his talents rather than in a room full of ill-starred students in the wilds of Dorsetshire. He sighed and began to speak in a precise monotone.

"Today we shall discuss that great expanse that lies beyond our world, and look upwards and outwards to the planets that revolve around our star, which we call the sun. It was long thought that our own blessed plot was the centre of the universe, but Messrs Copernicus and Galileo Galilei showed us otherwise." He paused, then brought his cane down with a thwack on the centre desk at the front. Simon Blotwell, who had also been imagining himself somewhere more convivial than a natural philosophy lesson in number 4, nearly jumped out of his skin.

"Blotwell..." Hooke eyed the boy. "Blotwell, what planet lies between Venus and Mars, 31 million leagues from the sun?"

Simon Blotwell found direct questioning confusing at the best of times. His eyes went wide and his pupils danced around as if looking for inspiration among the dusty motes caught in the sunlight that streamed through the leaded lights of the high windows.

"Er…"

"No, Blotwell, 'erm' is not the answer. Would you like a clue?" Mr Hooke brought his head down and towards the boy like a serpent about to mesmerise its victim.

"Oh, yes please, sir," replied Blotwell. "That would be most helpful."

"You are what passes for living on it, boy…"

Simon knew that he should be able to process those few words, but the 'what passes for' and the gaunt face so near to his own completely flummoxed him. "Oh lord, sir, I'm afraid I'm in a bit of a tizz, just momentarily." He leaned far back in his chair to try to get as far away as possible from the scarecrow of a master, only to overbalance. The rear legs of his chair scraped alarmingly for several inches across the tiled floor. Blotwell's arms went into windmill mode and instinctively he moved his centre of balance forward. The chair stopped sliding and with a crash righted itself, jarring the boy's spine and knocking his teeth together. Silver stars twinkled before his eyes.

Mr Hooke rose up to his full height. "Blotwell, you are a boy of unparalleled stupidity. Sometimes I wonder if you aren't being duplicitous in your backwardness, but then I look at you and see your vacant expression and know that I really am dealing with a halfwit."

"Oh, it's true, sir," replied Blotwell weakly, looking at the master through the veil of stars. "Daddy says I'm as thick as two short planks."

Tittering, which had been nascent, poured forth from all corners of the classroom. It lasted only a few moments as the boys tried to stifle their natural tendency to see the funny side of things.

Mr Hooke, a man who never saw the funny side of things, at least not to the boys' knowledge, huffed. "Jennings, answer the question for the dolt."

John Jennings, a bright boy with gingery hair and a face full of freckles which during the summer months all but merged into one, sat immediately behind Blotwell and had almost been the recipient of a cracked skull.

"The Earth, sir."

"The Earth," repeated Mr Hooke. "The third of the eight known planets in our solar system." He scanned the class. "Now, can anyone in this benighted grouping name the eight in ascending order by circumference?" Many faces turned down to look with great interest at their chalkboards, or stare at the inkwells in the top right-hand corner of their desks.

Slowly, Freddy Hall raised his hand, his fingers scrunched into a loose fist. His hand hovered in the air for some time, while Mr Hooke looked anywhere but at him. At length, as his arm began to ache, the boy at the next desk, Gerald Gilmore, known as Gerry to his friends, whose brother Gus was in the lower sixth, spoke out.

"Hall has got his hand up, sir."

Since joining the school after Christmas, the majority of the shell were well aware that Freddy was one of the more gifted and capable boys, and most had worked out that Mr Hooke didn't like him, though the reason was known only to a few. This dislike, verging on pathological hatred, by a master for Freddy gave him considerable kudos with the fairer-minded boys, and most of the boys in the class were fair-minded.

"Gilmore, who asked you to speak?" snapped Mr Hooke.

"I thought it was my duty, sir," replied Gerry bravely.

"Your duty, boy, your duty!" Mr Hooke advanced down the aisle towards the errant pupil, his gown flowing out behind him. "Your duty is to speak when you're spoken to and not before, is that clear?"

"Yes, sir."

"Now, hold out your hand."

Gerry did as he was told, offering the right hand, palm upwards.

"The left, boy, the left, unless you're one of those Newtonian freaks, those spawn of Satan who write from the sinister side."

Gerry offered up his left hand without comment. It shook slightly as it waited for the blow to fall, which it did, wielded by an expert with the tip of the cane, causing a red welt to grow in the boy's soft flesh. The boy winced and clutched his hand but made no sound other than a short intake of breath.

Mr Hooke resumed his position at the front of the class but, while his back was turned, Freddy, who had long since retracted his hand, leaned across the aisle and mouthed 'sorry' at Gerry. The boy reciprocated with a shrug and a wan smile.

One hour and twenty minutes later, the double lesson was drawing to a close. Mr Hooke sat at his desk thumbing his way through some notes on the nature of light from the Royal Society, sent to him by an old and still loyal colleague. The sound of boys scratching chalk planets on their slate boards barely registered with him – that is, until the noise stopped abruptly.

"Why have you stopped working?" he asked, looking up, his temper rising, though more from the idiocies in the notes rather than anything the class had done.

No one dared to offer an explanation, though it was obvious from the noise outside that most classes had already been dismissed and the morning break had started.

"You will work until I tell you to stop, even if that is midnight on the 31st December in the year of tribulations. You are a very foolish and disobedient class. Your prep will be to draw all eight planetary spheres to a scale of 20,000 miles to the inch, one inside the other. You will then write 100 words of description on each one. This is to be delivered to me by 2 p.m. on Friday. Blotwell, for your lamentable performance earlier, you will do what I have set out in Latin, and if you fail to satisfy me, you will be given half a dozen strokes of the cane. Is that clear?"

Blotwell sagged in his seat. "Oh lor'," he whispered, and then in a louder squeak, "yes, sir."

"And you, Gilmore, for your egregious behaviour you will

do the same, only in Greek. And if you fail to satisfy me, you will get a dozen strokes of the cane on your bare buttocks. Is that clear?"

Freddy glanced to his right and saw tears welling in Gerry's eyes.

"Is that clear, boy?" thundered Mr Hooke.

Beside himself with anger, Freddy rose to his feet, pushing his chair back hard. A look of triumph stole over Mr Hooke's sallow features, as if this had been his intended outcome all along. A deathly hush fell upon the class; a confrontation of this nature could only end one way. Then the classroom door opened and Dr Butler entered. Immediately, in the courteous style they'd been taught, all the boys joined Freddy and stood up, while a startled expression passed momentarily over Mr Hooke's face, to be replaced by a forced smile as he too hoisted himself out of his master's chair.

The doctor stood for a moment taking in the scene, his eyes wandering benignly over his flock.

"Good morning boys," he said.

"Good morning sir," came the chorus of mixed voices.

The headmaster beheld his teacher. "Mr Hooke, I wonder if I might have a few minutes of your time?"

"Certainly, Headmaster." Mr Hooke gave a small bow, though behind his mask of civility was a barely hidden indignation at having been so interrupted.

"I thought by now these young scoundrels would be out in the autumn sunshine letting off steam," continued the doctor, unabashed. "Would you be so kind as to give an old hand like myself the honour of dismissing them?"

"Certainly, Headmaster."

Dr Butler turned slightly. "Now then, shell, let me see how well you can file out row by row, the back boy leading in good orderly Seekings tradition..."

The back boy in row one was Ralph Ballantyne, who needed a light, encouraging shove from Adam Wakefield, the next boy in line, to start the class exodus. From then on all went smoothly. Freddy was the third from last boy to leave. The headmaster followed him for some time with his eyes, but remained silent and motionless.

Once outside in the fresh air, Freddy flopped down on the grassy bank in front of the osher to let the last of his anger abate. Several of his classmates came up and gave him a pat of solidarity on his shoulder before haring away to play football or to spend a few pennies of their pocket money in the tuck shop.

"What are you doing, sitting there like a sack of old potatoes when there are games to be won?"

Freddy looked up at Harry's smiling face. "Nearly had the biggest bust-up ever with Hooke. I would probably have got expelled."

"Ah, it's time to talk to your Uncle H."

"I've got to make things right with Gilmore minor, too."

"Gussy's brother? What's he been up to?"

"Being a friend when I hardly know him."

"Well, my lad, we've only got ten minutes. This sounds as if it could take an hour."

"Scud, do you fancy one of Mrs Pattle's butter shortbread biscuits?"

"I do, but it's rather offset by having to pay extortionate prices to those horny-handed prefects in the tuck shop with their rancid fingernails."

Freddy drew a paper bag from inside his waistcoat. "Dad treated me."

Harry's face lit up and he dropped down onto the grass. "Your pa is a saintly man."

Freddy opened the bag and looked inside. "There's three. I think I'll give the third to Gilmore."

"Golly, he must have impressed you, and him just a little weed!"

"A little weed that's as big as I am," said Freddy.

Harry waved away the comment. "Come on, Federico, tell me the story while we partake of the widow's biscuits. I've got a double period of Latin declensions after break and need something beforehand to get my teeth into."

* * *

Simon Blotwell had made an appointment to see the chaplain, the Reverend Croft, during break and had entered the school chapel expecting to be welcomed with open arms. Instead, the building was deserted except for a lone figure sitting in one of the front pews. Uncertain of the identity of the sitter, but certain that it was not the Reverend Croft, Simon approached with caution. He was perfectly aware of his reputation and expected to meet hostility everywhere he went, even in church.

Though caution was his objective, try as he might, he couldn't stop the soles of his patent leather shoes clicking on the tiled floor. He paused halfway along the nave. The stained glass of Christ blessing the children in the east window threw multicoloured facets of light across the choir and he imagined himself one day wearing a cassock, hymnal in hand, singing his heart out to an enraptured congregation.

"So, you've arrived, Blotwell. I was beginning to think that by some miracle, God had locked you in the latrines to spare us all from your witterings."

Simon frowned, annoyed that his reverie had been cut short, doubly annoyed at the blasphemy, and trebly annoyed at the insulting tone of this strangely accented voice. As he drew closer, he at last recognised the short, stocky figure of Tom White, the captain of Raleigh House and the favourite to succeed Theo Oldham as school captain when he became a peer.

"I have an important appointment with the Reverend Croft."

"The chaplain asked me to tell you that he's been called away to see the doctor."

"But it's important," insisted Simon.

"It may be important to you, Blotwell, but I doubt that even registers on the chaplain's order of importance."

"Why are you speaking in that common, sing-songy way?" asked Simon, emboldened by the anger he felt at being snubbed.

"It's an accent," said Tom. "I'm from the Valleys in Briton. In any case, you have a sing-songy way of speaking too."

"I most certainly do not! Auntie Millicent says I speak in perfect standard Albion without inflection or accent."

"Well, I'm sorry to say, boyo, that your auntie is talking nonsense, because you've got an affected posh boys' accent, just like a lot of the other little twerps at this school."

Simon stamped his foot. "I have not!"

Tom laughed. "Blotwell, you're a misfit, just like me, and the sooner you realise it, the happier you'll be."

Simon wrinkled his nose, wanting to get his own back. "You've got an awful lot of spots on your forehead."

Tom ran a hand through his wavy black hair. "Thanks for reminding me. It's acne – a lot of boys in their teens get it."

"I won't," replied Blotwell. "Mummy says that my skin is as pure as porcelain."

"You wait and see."

"When will the Reverend Croft be back? I want to confess my sins."

"I don't believe the chaplain takes confession. He's neither Catholic nor high church."

"The Reverend McKellan, who is the vicar of Dunhambury, is low church, but he always hears my list of sins and absolves me."

"Then why don't you wait until the next time you're in Dunhambury?"

"I usually do, but I've got some extra-special sins that require immediate attention."

"You're quite an amusing fellow, underneath, aren't you, Blotwell?"

Simon was ready to stamp his foot again, but the bell

went and Tom rose to his feet. "Sorry, boyo, I've got to go. Net practice for the game on Thursday week."

Blotwell watched his muscular back recede up the nave and disappear out through the west door. "What a common person," he said to himself, "I would never choose him to be the next school captain."

Simon began to wonder what his next move should be. The first period after break was Greek grammar for the shell boys with Mr Ollerenshaw, the housemaster of Hawkins. But Blotwell had a mind to stay in the chapel and pray, which he considered to be more useful than Greek, and maybe in addition he would move into the choir stalls and imagine himself singing a delightful solo to the glory of God. Then, if the Reverend Croft should come along he would claim that White hadn't spoken to him and he had sat down to wait and had lost track of time. *Perfect!* he thought. The only problem was, he couldn't confess this lie to the chaplain, but would have to save it for the Reverend McKellan in Dunhambury.

* * *

Freddy lay on the grass in front of the osher, resting, his eyes closed against the bright sunshine while he waited anxiously for Harry. A large shadow passed in front of his eyelids which he took to be a fair weather cloud, though the sky had been completely clear.

"Hall!" a deep voice boomed above him.

Freddy jumped and opened his eyes, peering at the dark shape looming over him.

"What are you doing down there?" the voice boomed again.

Gus Gilmore squatted beside Freddy, who sat up and leaned back on his hands.

"Gilmore, what's the matter?" Freddy thought hard about how he might have offended the lower sixth-form pupil, who was renowned for his sporting prowess and muscular physique.

"I know seniors don't usually talk to you shell boys, but I just wanted to thank you for what you did for Gerry."

Freddy knotted his brow, his mind focused on the matter in hand: waiting for Scud. "But it was Gerry who tried to help me," he said.

"Did you not give my little brother a bag with a Pattle shortbread in it?"

"Yes, but..."

"And did you not include in the bag a perfect diagram of the eight planets of the solar system, one inside the other, at 20,000 miles to the inch, including Mercury at little more than a dot?"

"Actually, I used the French system – it's far easier. I got a rule from Monsieur Duillier with the metrics printed on it. It only took me five minutes between periods."

Gus grinned. "Gerry said you were a total swot, Hall, but also a decent fellow. Hooke hates your guts, doesn't he?"

"I think I'm in the middle of a feud between him and Mr Newton."

"Do you do sports?" asked Gilmore, switching to his favourite topic.

"Er, not really. I play a bit of football in the village sometimes."

"Don't mention that game here! It's rugger this and rugger that at Seekings. Do you swim?"

"Oh, yes. Everyone swims."

"Well, don't forget to enter your house swim team for the end-of-term gala. That'll up your prestige. Though you'll have to wear a costume with ladies present."

Freddy pulled a face. "I haven't got anything like that."

Gus patted him on the shoulder. "Where there's a will..." he said, standing up. "Are you going to the match on Thursday afternoon to cheer The Rest on? It's difficult for me to admit it, but with Cheeseman captaining School House, we'll need all the support we can get."

Freddy would have preferred to spend his time in the library, but attendance at the annual inter-house cricket match was deemed compulsory. "I expect so," he said.

Gus rose to his feet. "Good man. Now, I'd better be off before I get a terrible ribbing for talking to you."

Freddy smiled and blushed slightly at the attention he was receiving. "I'll put my name down for swimming," he promised rashly.

No sooner had Gilmore gone than Harry fell to earth beside him. "Well," he said, "you are honoured with a visit from Gus. You'd better watch out or you might become popular, and that would never do."

"Did you get it back?" asked Freddy, anxiety returning to cloud his face.

"Before I answer that, did you notice that slippery fiend Blotwell scampering forth with his right hand clasped tight to his blazer?"

"No." Freddy shook his head.

"How unobservant of you. He hot-footed it over to Raleigh as if he was being chased by Cerberus himself."

Freddy sat up and crossed his legs. "Up to no good, I'll be bound. Come on, Scud, did you get it back?"

A smile of triumph passed across Harry's lips. He took an exercise book from where it had been tucked in his trousers and threw it into Freddy's lap.

Freddy swallowed hard and took the book, his heart beating rapidly as he flicked through the pages, until he came to the last written page. "A+, Scud! A+, the villain! And you in the higher class."

"And what about that comment, Federico? *There has been a positive improvement in your work, keep it up.* How often does Hooke write compliments?"

"He wrote on one piece of my research that it was sloppy and that I'd never be a true man of science."

"It must be your spidery handwriting," sighed Harry. "Not as neat as my precise penmanship, and aren't I the expert copier?"

"Stop joshing me, Scud. I've got Tallow for another of his boring history lessons this afternoon. I could show him then."

"I've been thinking about that. It might be a bit impetuous to go direct to the old man – you know what he's like. Maybe we should speak to Fouracre first. He's an honourable fellow, by all accounts. Which is more than can be said for some other house captains I could mention…"

"All right. Let's go and see him now," said Freddy.

"But I haven't had my lunch yet," said Harry.

"Neither have I, but surely dinner can wait for five minutes."

In truth, Freddy's stomach was churning with a mixture of anxiety and anger, and he didn't feel like eating.

Harry chortled. "All right, Federico, you win. Like you always do."

"Don't talk such rot, Scud. You never do anything you don't want to."

They stood up and brushed themselves down before making a beeline for Drake House. At the door, Freddy unstrapped his satchel and took out his own exercise book.

* * *

Mark Fouracre was woken from a light doze by a tapping on his door. He yawned and rubbed his eyes, looking over at the clock on the wall. 1.45 p.m., meaning he'd been asleep for a little under an hour. Before that, he'd spent half the morning in the nets with Tom White, practising for the opening match of the season a week on Thursday. He was captain of The Rest and Tom, vice-captain.

"Come," he said, stifling another yawn.

"Fouracre…" began Freddy when he was barely through the door.

"Sit down, chaps, please, before you start. I've just been having forty winks and I'm not yet fully compos mentis."

The boys sat together on the Turkish divan placed for such occasions in front of Fouracre's deep leather armchair.

"Now, what's the matter with you two? I can see you're in a sweat, Hall."

"Take a look at the last essay in each of these exercise books and tell us what we should do," answered Freddy.

Fouracre did as he was bid, sometimes nodding to himself, sometimes raising his eyebrows at one of the boys, sometimes brushing back his curly brown hair. At length he handed the exercise books back. "You want to know what you should you do about this?" he asked.

"Yes," answered Harry.

"Nothing," came the reply. "Don't even think about it."

"But Fouracre…" began Freddy.

"It's deuced unfair!" interrupted Harry.

Mark looked carefully from Harry to Freddy. "Don't get upset, Hall, and I'll explain why 'nothing' is the best option. Then maybe we can find a way round this."

Freddy put his head in his hands, stifling a sob, and took some deep breaths.

"Are you ready?"

Freddy nodded, though his mouth was still turned down, his eyes watery.

"First, show this to a master, and the only thing he'll see is the fact that one of you copied work from the other. One or both of you will be sitting with sore backsides, or worse. Second, Mr Tallow and Mr Hooke are on the same wing of the Royalist Party – that is, they strongly support the monarchy of Henry XI over the Silesian Prince Christian. That makes them comrades in arms and a powerful force in the school. Third, and probably most important of all, no master is going to openly criticise the marking of another master in front of a boy. It's unheard of."

Fouracre paused to let his words sink in. Harry sighed and nodded, while Freddy's head drooped.

"I say, Fouracre's probably right, old chum," said Harry,

giving his friend's arm a squeeze, "though it's still beastly unfair on you."

"Hall, the only reason you might get kept down in the shell or even sacked is if you commit some major offence, and how likely is that? You're a Newtonian scholar, and rumour has it that Mr Newton will shortly get a knighthood – even though he supports the Parliamentarians and is lukewarm to the king. This school is like a microcosm of politics in the country and it is not going to stand by and let a protégé of the great man be thrown to the wolves because of an academic spat between him and Mr Hooke. It would be like taking sides with one political grouping over another, which would not do Seekings' reputation any good at all."

"But Mr Tallow said I would be kept down if my grades didn't improve, which they won't."

"You know, as captain of Drake, I go to the meetings with the doctor and the other house captains, don't you?"

The two boys nodded.

"Now, between you and me, not every decision the doctor makes is absolutely correct. For instance, in my opinion he gives us – that is, the prefects – too much power. But he is a fair-minded man on the whole, and is very much aware of your presence in this school, Freddy. We all are."

The last remark and the use of his first name made Freddy look up sharply.

Fouracre chuckled. "There, I've probably said too much already, and it's almost time for the afternoon bell."

"And we've missed lunch." Harry sighed.

"You can take an apple each from the dish," said Fouracre. "That should tide you over."

"Can you put me down for the swim team, please?" said Freddy.

Fouracre grinned, looking the boy up and down. "I hadn't taken you for the sporty type, Hall..."

"That's what I said," interrupted Harry.

"But with those square shoulders, you have got a

swimmer's build," Fouracre continued, "and the pleasure will be mine. You know it'll be breaststroke, don't you, not that splashy overarm thing we all do for fun?"

"I've got time to practise," replied Freddy.

"Good man! We start serious swimming for the event in May. What about you, East, do you want to take part?"

"I'm in the athletics."

"Of course you are, but it doesn't mean you can't swim as well. You could at least do the relay."

"All right, but only if Freddy is in the team as well."

This time Fouracre gave a hearty laugh. "Very well, you bounder, now go before you're late. The bell is about to ring in twenty seconds and I've got to get over to the doctor's theology class."

As they left the Drake house captain's room, Freddy counted down. Sure enough, as the twentieth second passed, Mr Topliss rang the bell for afternoon school.

Harry bit into his apple and chuckled. "So, you've decided to try and best me at swimming, have you? We'll see about that."

"I suppose you think you're the top dog when it comes to every sport," replied Freddy.

"Woof," said Harry. "In any case, it's true, isn't it? Just as you are top dog in academia."

"There's still no need to boast about it," said Freddy, his sense of humour once more in play.

"We'll have to do some surreptitious practice on your breaststroke and get that pigeon chest into shape before it's shown to the ladies."

Freddy blushed. "I haven't got a swimming costume."

"Never mind, you can swim buck naked like we usually do. I don't suppose the ladies will even notice."

"Shut up."

Harry laughed. "I say, Fouracre's mind is pretty sharp on school matters, isn't it?"

"Yes, and he's probably right. I hadn't thought about

masters closing ranks."

"It's a clique," said Harry. "But I don't think you need worry further about being kept down, if what he says is true about the doctor. Just don't expect Hooke or his allies to change."

"Who are his allies?" asked Freddy. "Besides Tallow, I mean."

"I'm not sure. I'm told that Mr King gets pretty snarky if you say anything against the monarchy, but you needn't worry about him because he only teaches the sixth form."

"Where does Mr Topliss stand on that?"

"Where he stands on anything – with his head in the clouds," said Harry dismissively.

"I think you underestimate him," replied Freddy.

"Oh so, now you're a fan of Mr T. as well as old Hawlings. You obviously have a taste for the weird."

"Double shut up."

Harry ruffled Freddy's hair. "So, what now, *mon ami*?"

"Half an hour of Latin with Mr Caulton-Harris, then an hour and a half of Tallow droning on."

"Will it be the wars with the Silesians?"

"I think we're doing Russia this week and next, but he is easily sidetracked onto his favourite subject, especially when prompted by that idiot Ballantyne."

"Lucky me, then, I've got your friend for alchemy. Lots of pops and bangs, especially if Foxy Talbot has anything to do with it."

Chapter Four

When Freddy Met Harry

Late April, 1825

Freddy kicked off his boots and socks, rolled up his sleeves and went down to the tideline to wash the sand from the piece of rock he was holding. The water lapped around his toes, feeling nicely cool in the heat of the afternoon. He stood up and took a small hand lens from the pocket of his knee-length breeches.

"I say, fellow, would you do me a favour?"

The voice took Freddy by surprise. For one thing, it came from along the strand and not the cliff path by which he had arrived an hour or so previously. For another, the possessor of the voice sounded posh, without the heavy Dorsetshire brogue he was used to. It was more like a much younger version of the Reverend Jeremy Smollett, the ancient vicar of All Souls, than your average Linburian.

He turned to find himself facing a boy of similar age and height to himself, busily tying a piece of white linen around his middle. Freddy noticed immediately that the stranger's otherwise naked body was muscular beyond the usual for someone of their age. He was also as brown as a berry, despite having blue eyes and fair hair which was close-cropped to his scalp. It made Freddy feel ashamed of his pasty-white scrawniness.

"Where did you spring from?" asked Freddy, tilting back his flat cap.

The boy put his hands on his hips and laughed. "You are a funny fellow. I don't suppose you have any idea of the time, do you? If you're not up to hours and minutes, an approximation would do."

Freddy frowned, not only because he was being laughed at, but also for the assumption that reading a timepiece was beyond him. Pointedly, he drew out his dad's fob watch by the chain attached to his scruffy waistcoat and looked at the dial. "It's twenty minutes to three," he said, giving the newcomer a stern appraisal.

"I say, you're a man of surprises," smiled the newcomer, "and you can put a body in his place with just a look. What's your name? I'm Harry, by the way. Harry East from Larkstone."

"Freddy, Freddy Hall from Linbury." He made a sweeping motion towards the top of the cliff, then pointed at the garment hanging off the boy's hips. "What do you call that?"

"It's a tunic – well, a half tunic, actually. All the boys in Ancient Greece wore them."

"But we're not in Ancient Greece."

"No, silly, but if you're running a marathon it does well to pretend. Keeps the chin up, so to speak. In any case, most of the way I was in the buff, just like Pheidippides would have been."

"You've run all the way from Larkstone?" exclaimed Freddy incredulously, ignoring the 'silly' and the 'Pheidippides', who he hadn't heard of. "That's twenty-five miles!"

"Well, I had to splash my way around the headlands," answered Harry. "Legend has it that Pheidippides ran the twenty-six miles from Marathon to Athens in something under three hours, but he was a trained courier. If your watch is correct, I've done the twenty-five in three and a half, which is… er…"

"Seven miles per hour," Freddy interjected. "That's impressive."

Harry beamed. "Why, thank you. A serious compliment from a serious fellow." He stepped forward. They were both now standing in the lapping tide. "What's that you've got there?"

Freddy blushed. "Oh, it's just a piece of old rock." He was about to throw it into the sea when Harry put out his hand to stop him.

"I was watching you examining it with your magnifier. It's an ammonite, isn't it?"

Freddy blinked. He hadn't met anyone else of his age who showed any interest in these rocks, except to use them as ammunition in fights.

"That's what Miss Antrobus, my teacher, calls them. There are hundreds scattered along the beach."

Harry gave his scalp a scratch. "I've been beachcombing this stretch of coast all my life, but I'd never noticed them until my tutor picked up one to show me. He said it was the remains of a long dead creature, but when I asked him to explain further, he went all *severus* on me and dropped it and the subject."

"That's strange," said Freddy, "because after I'd shown Miss Antrobus the ammonite, I collected several different types and brought them to school. She told me they were all fossils, but then said I shouldn't go meddling into things that God would disapprove of."

"That is a rum do. But I see her words have made absolutely no impression on you, which is what I'd expect." Harry smiled. "Have you drawn your own conclusions?"

Freddy spoke conspiratorially. "There are other, even stranger-shaped, rocks along here, some just hanging out of the cliff. They're like animals embedded in stone – but they're not like any animals I've seen living, not even like the pictures in nature books of elephants and tigers and such."

"So that's why you've got the little hammer and chisel on your belt. You are a deep fellow, Freddy, and I'd like to talk some more, but I suppose I ought to be making tracks." For the first time, Harry looked uncertain.

Disappointment welled up inside Freddy. "Do you really have to go?"

"If I don't get back by nightfall, Ma and Pa will probably

send out a search party."

"It seems a shame to come all this way, only to have to go straight back. You must be starving as well."

"It's true, I am rather famished. I've only had spring water, hardtack and a wizened apple since breakfast. But I don't see any alternative."

Freddy had a strong sense that this meeting was an important moment in his life. "If you wanted, you could stay with me tonight at the Sailor's Yarn Inn. My dad is the publican and the sub-postmaster, so we could send a message to Larkstone on the five o'clock coach." He blurted all this out, not knowing whether the offer would cause him trouble at home.

"I say, you are a very organised fellow. Are you sure your pa won't mind?"

Freddy shook his head with more certainty than he felt. He was usually so calm and collected, but this sudden excitement had left him in a daze. If he had been himself, he would be worrying that the food and accommodation wouldn't be up to the standard this posh boy was used to, which would leave him mortally embarrassed. As it was, he just felt profoundly happy. "Will you stay then?"

Harry nodded and grinned. "I'd be happy to. I say, we haven't shaken hands. I think chaps ought to shake hands when they meet, don't you? And please call me Scud. All my friends do."

Immediately, Freddy transferred the ammonite to his left hand and offered his right, which Harry grasped in a strong grip. "I'm so very happy to meet you, Freddy Hall."

"Likewise, Harry East. Scud, who runs like the wind."

* * *

"Dad, I've brought a visitor. I'd like him to stay over, if that's all right?"

Daniel Hall came bustling into the scullery from the bar where he had been trying to get the new-fangled pump to work. When his son had been born, he had expected him to grow into an outgoing extrovert, like himself. It's what a publican had to be. Instead he had on his hands a shy, sensitive introvert. It was a nagging concern to him – not that he said anything directly to Freddy about it.

Now, out of the blue, here was Freddy inviting a stranger to stay overnight.

"Well I never," he exclaimed, seeing Harry wearing nothing but his 'tunic'. "You're not from these parts, are you?"

"Larkstone," answered Harry with a smile, offering his hand. "Harry East, at your service, sir."

Daniel raised his eyebrows, gazed at his hand for a moment, then shook it vigorously. "Well, any friend of Freddy's is welcome here." Then he gave him a sideways look as his mind ticked over. "You wouldn't be related to Magistrate East of Larkstone, would you?"

"He's my pa."

"Well, I never," he exclaimed again, and cocked his head at his son.

"Are you sure you don't mind, Dad?" asked Freddy. "I met Scud on the beach. He ran all the way from Larkstone in three and a half hours, and we talked about ammonites and things..."

Daniel Hall may not have been an educated man, but he was finely attuned to his son's coded way of talking. So this new boy had given up his nickname and shown an interest in Freddy's pursuits, unlike the majority of village kids, who mostly yawned or laughed at him.

"Of course I don't mind," he said, adding with a twinkle in his eye, "the fact that Magistrate East has recently renewed my licence to sell alcoholic beverages in perpetuity, or at least during my lifetime, has nothing to do with it."

"Oh, Pa is good with his *in perpetuity*," said Harry. "It gets him off doing all kinds of work. Some people think he's a bit of a stickler, but Ma calls him the velvet fist in the iron glove."

"Dad, Scud needs to send a message home on the five o'clock. Just to let his folks know."

"Take him through to the backroom. I've got two other letters today: Miss Pattle's order to her supplier in Tadcaster and Mrs Snell writing to her sister in Sedgewick."

Harry scratched his head. "That wouldn't be the Mrs Snell who is always complaining to Pa about the smell from the pigsty or the farmer's dray going too fast past her window?"

"You've got it in one. She's a professional busybody, the only person who objected to the renewal of my licence owing to the 'drunken debauchery of those schoolboys from Seekings'. Even Miss Antrobus, who's temperance, didn't complain."

"That's my teacher," added Freddy.

"And Seekings is my school," said Harry, "or it will be this Michaelmas."

Freddy felt a pang of jealousy, but quickly subdued it. However, Daniel Hall didn't fail to notice and gave his son a sympathetic pat on the shoulder. "Now, I've got lots to do, two guests staying the night, and if I don't get this beer engine working we'll be the driest inn in Albion. That means the only person who'll be happy will be Mrs Snell. Oh – and of course Zebedee Tring, who will be laughing into his pint of scrumpy."

"Is Auntie Edie coming in to cook, then?" asked Freddy hopefully.

When the inn had guests, Edie Hingston, who was the wife of the village grocer, Sam, and also Daniel Hall's cousin, came in to cook for them all, and on most other evenings she would have a pot of some sort of stew for the regulars, as well as for her cousin and nephew. It worked out well, because the inn never went short of fruit and vegetables, even if sometimes they were the day's leftovers from the shop, and it gave Edie some much-needed pocket money for herself, as Sam was well known for his parsimony.

Daniel Hall chuckled. "Aye, that she is. So you and Master East needn't worry – you'll be fed well this night. She's doing lamb chops and a gooseberry tart, if I'm not mistaken. Meanwhile, you two get yourself some milk and shortbreads to tide you over."

* * *

Freddy took Harry across the recently cobbled Main Street onto the green, pausing by the pump and water trough to point out the village landmarks. Dominating the view was All Souls' Church and churchyard on their left, while across the way beyond the pond, where a duck was quacking over her new brood, there were five thatch and brick houses, four of which doubled for shops: the butcher, baker, grocer, and, largest of all, the dairy, which belonged to Eliza May and her daughter Clarrie.

They walked on towards a row of neat, well-maintained thatched cottages that stood at the opposite end of the green to the church.

"From left to right that's the Harvilles – Mr Harville is the carpenter; Miss Antrobus, my teacher; the Tree family, the village glaziers, and the big one with the roses growing round the door belongs to your friends, the Snells."

"Don't they do any work?" asked Harry.

"Complaining seems to be Mrs Snell's one occupation, and I hardly ever see Mr Snell."

"Perhaps she keeps him on a short leash."

They headed off down Big Barn Lane at the side of the Harvilles' then turned left onto a cart track which climbed past a row of five thatched cottages on one side and scrubby hedgerows on the other.

"Those are Farmer Stadden's labourers' cottages," said Freddy. "A bit less classy than the ones on the green."

"A lot less, by the look of them," remarked Harry. "Pa knows John Stadden. The richest man in the county, isn't he?"

"I don't know. Probably. He and his family have the box pew in the church." Freddy waved to a quartet of grubby children who were chasing a clutch of squawking hens across the open frontages which passed for gardens.

One of them, a girl aged about seven, stopped when she saw them. "Hello, Freddy," she squeaked. "Who's that boy?"

"This is Harry. He's from Larkstone."

She raised her eyebrows.

"What's your baby brother's name, Judy?" asked Freddy pointing at the smallest of the children who was doing his best to keep up with the rest by doing a half-walk, half crawl, whilst calling out to all and sundry in a language that only he could understand.

She smiled. "That's Lou."

"Loo?" said Freddy giving her a puzzled smile.

"Lou, he's naughty." Judy laughed.

"I bet he's no naughtier than you, chasing those birds," said Freddy. "They won't lay if you upset them."

"We're playing." Judy grinned, and scampered off.

They climbed on until they neared the brow of the hill. Harry stopped and looked back towards the village. The sunlit clock tower of All Souls rose out of the trees in the churchyard. It was ten to seven and Harry's tummy was rumbling. "When is supper?" he asked. "I'm looking forward to the lamb chop and even more to the gooseberry pie."

"The guests ordered theirs for seven forty-five, so that's when we get ours, or a bit after."

"Who are these tardy guests? I didn't see them."

"They were resting in their room. Two ladies from Eelmouth travelling alone."

"Unusual..."

"Dad told me that they're on their way to Larkstone to catch the ferry." He glanced at Harry to see if he had twigged.

"Are they nuns?"

Freddy grunted his approval. "Close. The daughter of one of them is taking the veil at Carisbrooke Priory and they're going to the ceremony."

Harry laughed. "No wonder your pa was keen to lend me one of your shirts and a pair of breeches in case they saw me in the flesh."

"When's your birthday, Scud?"

"I was thirteen on January 7th. You?"

"I'll be thirteen next month. June 11th."

"So, I'm senior! Hip hooray!"

When they came over the top of the rise, Freddy pointed across the field to his right, where on a knoll there stood a windmill, five storeys high with a fantail on the cap to guide the sails into the wind.

"A smock mill," said Harry knowledgeably. "So that's where you're taking me. Funny – you can't see it from the village even though it's on high ground."

"And you can't see it from the seaward side either as it's hidden by the cliffs."

A sign on the five-barred gate at the field entrance had the words *Tanner's Mill – No Trespassing* carved into the wood. Freddy held open the gate for Harry, then let it swing closed. They walked up the track towards a substantial thatched dwelling set in its own fenced garden appropriately named Windmill Cottage. A goat tethered on a long leash, outside the fence, eyed them suspiciously.

"That's Lucifer, or Lucy for short. She's a nanny."

"Does she butt?" asked Harry.

"Tickle her ears and she'll give you a lick," answered Freddy.

As they drew near, a short plump woman dressed in a white mop hat and long matching apron came out of the cottage and ambled down the path to the garden gate.

"Freddy, we haven't seen you for at least a week or two…"

"Five days," corrected Freddy. "I was here last Saturday."

"Seems longer."

"Auntie, this is Harry East from Larkstone. Scud, this is my Aunt Emily."

Harry held out his hand over the garden gate. "How do you do?"

Auntie Emily looked at it doubtfully. "Larkstone, is it? That's a long ways from here…"

"It's not that far," said Freddy.

"Far enough," said Emily firmly.

Harry withdrew his hand, unshaken, noticing a bewhiskered man in a checked suit and waistcoat approaching slowly down the path followed by an attentive Sussex spaniel, its woolly coat a rich golden brown. A clay pipe was grasped between the man's teeth and the smell of tobacco wafted towards them on the evening air.

Catching the scent, Emily turned. "Albert, Freddy's here and he's brought a boy from Larkstone."

As if on cue, the goat gave Harry's bottom a nudge, making him stumble forward.

The man took the pipe out of his mouth and pointed it at Harry. "She likes you."

She seems to be the only one, then, thought Harry.

"This is my Uncle Albert," said Freddy, "and that's Jasper the dog."

"Hello," said Harry, tentatively patting the goat, who was nuzzling the pocket of his breeches.

"You coming in for a bite to eat, Freddy?" asked Emily.

"No, Edie's cooking for us tonight and I just want to show Harry the inside of the mill."

Emily turned up her nose but made no comment.

Albert blew smoke through his nostrils. "You be careful up them ladders, then, and no roistering. I know what you young lads are like when you gets together."

"Don't worry, Uncle."

Freddy tapped Harry on the shoulder to signal they should move on, giving his aunt and uncle a smile. "See you later."

The two boys walked towards the windmill. Freddy took a key from his waistcoat pocket.

"Your aunt and uncle are a bit..." Harry couldn't think of a word that was both suitably descriptive and polite.

"Insular?" suggested Freddy, chuckling. "Wait till Auntie Emily hears from the village gossips that their nephew has made friends with the son of Magistrate East. She'll be wailing into her pinafore at the thought of not shaking your hand."

"I prefer people to be natural with me."

Freddy opened the door to the windmill. "Are you scared of heights?"

"Not especially – but I sometimes get the feeling that I ought to jump off when I'm on the edge of somewhere very sheer."

"Well, please don't jump off the ladders. They go straight up through the five floors and there's nothing to break your fall."

Although there had been no grinding for a day or two, the atmosphere was dusty and redolent with the floury smell of ground corn. Harry felt a sneeze coming on and pinched his nose.

"Don't worry, it's better up top," said Freddy.

They climbed quickly from the ground floor up to the meal floor where the flour was collected in troughs, through the stone floor where the grinding took place, then the bin floor into which the sacks of grain were lifted on a hoist and stored. Finally they reached the dust floor. Freddy swung himself off the ladder and stood waiting, a slight smile on his face. A few rungs behind, Harry pushed his head through the opening and looked round.

"Oh," he said, feeling somewhat let down. The room was empty except for the hoist winder and a large cast-iron cog attached to the drive shaft.

"Come on," said Freddy.

"Is this the end of the tour?" asked Harry, carefully stepping off the ladder.

Freddy tilted his head up to a hatch in the roof. "Not quite."

"You are a mysterious fellow, Federico. How are we getting up there?"

Freddy jigged the rope that hung from the hatch, then pulled it taut to stop the hatch from falling open too heavily.

Another rope uncoiled and fell into his hand. This was attached to the first rung of a ladder visible through the opening.

Harry found all this efficiency amusing and was grinning broadly when the ladder swung down gently.

Freddy clambered up, closely followed by his friend.

"Welcome to my den," said Freddy with shy pride.

"Oh, I say!" exclaimed Harry. "This is simply wizard!"

In the small space, behind the great vertical brake wheel, a modest room had been constructed, complete with home comforts. There was a makeshift desk, comprising a smooth plank of wood raised across two half-barrels, covered with a maroon velveteen cloth. On this lay an open notebook with a pen and ink stand, and a Davy safety lamp. Pushed beneath was a chair from the bar room of the Sailor's Yarn. To the side was a set of shelves on which were rows of books, their covers tattered and worn with use. There was even a little bed – a simple wooden frame strung with rope on which laid a straw mattress.

But the centrepiece of the space and what caught Harry's eye stood on another, full-sized barrel. A brightly polished brass telescope pointing towards a shuttered opening in the cap. It was supported on a pillar stand with three folding claw legs, made of the same polished metal.

"Wherever did you get this? It must be worth a fortune."

Harry's enthusiasm so pleased Freddy that for a few moments he couldn't speak, then it all came out in a rush. "Actually, it only cost two guineas, which *is* a fortune for us, but Dad knew I'd always wanted one. Astronomy is my number-one interest."

"What, even more than ammonites?"

Freddy laid his hand on the body of the telescope. "Oh yes."

"You are a strange but likeable fellow, Federico. And where did your pa pick up such a bargain?"

"When he was at a Licensed Victuallers' Association

meeting in Handley Cross, he saw this was on sale and splashed out. He'd just been made sub-postmaster then and also had some cash from my mum's dowry which he'd never spent."

Harry had not broached the question of why there was no Mrs Hall, and decided that now was not the time. "It must be worth ten times what he paid, at least."

"Well," said Freddy, "it was in a bit of a state when we got it. In fact, you couldn't see anything through it, not even the sun."

"So, is it fixed?"

"Yes. See the wooden box over there? That's what it came in, along with spare mirrors, two eyepieces and a sheet of handwritten instructions on how to look after it."

"Who wrote that?"

"It's signed *Mr James Short of Surry-Street in the Strand, London*. The same name that's engraved on the 'scope. He's dated it 5th March 1759 – it's over sixty years old."

Harry looked doubtful. "And you fixed it all by yourself?"

"Russ helped me. That's Russell Warren, the blacksmith's son. I got it the Christmas before last. Dad and I were really disappointed at first. He thought he'd wasted his money on a pig in a poke, but then I found the instructions and he suggested getting the blacksmith to help. So I went round to the forge on St Stephen's Day to see Russ. I knew he'd be interested, especially as there was free beer involved. I invited him back and he brought his fine tools and we took it apart. There were cobwebs inside, the focusing rod was seized and the mirrors were tarnished. They're made of speculum metal, which is an alloy of copper and tin."

"I thought that was bronze. My tutor, Monsieur Du Pain, goes on about the Bronze Age something rotten."

"It's just a different ratio. It took us days to polish them, even though Russ set up a lathe at the forge to speed things up. We used jewellers' rouge and a polisher made out of cooled pitch fashioned over the mirror, so it's the right shape. They came up really shiny."

"I don't know if I'd have the patience," admitted Harry, "or the nous."

"Would you like to look through it? It's still too light to see the stars and planets, but the moon's risen and it's a full one tonight."

"I thought you'd never ask!" exclaimed Harry. "I say, this is the best fun I've had in ages."

Between them, they removed the shutter. Freddy hand-cranked the windmill cap around until the narrow window was facing east. Over the trees in the distance a yellow moon had risen into the clear sky.

Using the sight, Freddy rotated and tilted the telescope on the stand until the lunar disc was centred, then he locked it off and stood back. "You'll have to focus using the brass screw."

Harry peered through the eyepiece and gently turned the thread. "This is amazing. I've never seen anything like it. I can see mountains and valleys. I thought the moon was just flat and dull."

"It's even better when the sun is shining obliquely," said Freddy, adjusting the azimuth for him slightly so that he was looking towards the south polar region.

"Has that great hole with the lines running from it got a name?"

"Tycho Crater," answered Freddy. "It's named after a famous astronomer."

"I say, do you think there are people on the moon, like us?"

"I don't think so, Scud, but maybe on Mars."

Harry looked round. "I'd love to come up here when it's dark. May I?"

That's what Freddy had hoped to hear, but he hid his delight by taking out his watch. "Of course you can. But we'd better get back. It's 7.30 and I'm starving."

They were just about to descend the ladders after putting everything back in place, when Harry sidled over to the desk and peered at the notebook. "What's all these sums and writing under these circles and squiggles?" he asked.

"Oh that. It's nothing," replied Freddy, defensively.

Harry pursed his lips in a show of disapproval. "Federico, tell your Uncle H what you're a-doing-of. I know already that you're a complete swot and a clever dick and I don't hold that against you. So, why hold it against me just because I have a brain the size of a pea? It doesn't mean I won't be interested."

"Sorry," said Freddy, "it's just…" He took a deep breath. "I've been watching the transit of Thanatos across the face of Jupiter and – well, I'm sure I saw the shadow of a moon on the planet."

"You mean on Jupiter?"

"No, on Thanatos. I watched it all night and made notes until it disappeared off the disc. Jupiter has four moons, which were discovered by Galileo, but I don't think anyone has observed a moon revolving around Thanatos. I did some rough calculations on its size and orbit."

"Then you must tell the world!" exclaimed Harry. "Don't keep it to yourself. Just think – you could have a moon named after you!"

"It doesn't work like that. And I don't know who to tell…"

"Federico, you are a chump. Hiding your light under a bushel is not going to make you rich and famous."

"I'm not sure I want to be rich and famous."

Harry gave Freddy a tight shoulder hug. "It's a good job I came upon you today, Federico. You may be the smartest boy in all of Dorsetshire, but you've got a lot to learn about the ways of the world, and I'm here to teach you. Now, come on, before that lamb chop is burnt to a cinder and the gooseberry pie has turned to charcoal."

Chapter Five

Cry Havoc!

Simon Blotwell walked peevishly along the corridor of School House and up the stairs to the second floor. It was lunchtime, and the thing that he resented above all was missing out on his food. The floorboards beneath his feet creaked as he made his way past the fifth- and sixth-year studies to the room at the end, where he knocked timidly on the door.

"Come in, you cretin," said a voice from within.

Blotwell opened the door and blinked into the fog of smoke that greeted him. Alfred Cheeseman was sitting in an armchair puffing on a meerschaum, appropriately dressed in a smoking jacket. Beside him, lounging in another wing chair, one leg over the arm, was his friend Donald Sanderson, captain of Frobisher House.

"Come here, you pansy," said Cheeseman, reaching down the side of his chair and drawing out a half-empty bottle of Glenlivet whisky. "Take this over to Raleigh and put it in White's desk in his study."

"Won't he be at luncheon?" asked Blotwell, feeling hunger pangs in his own stomach.

"Of course he will. That's the idea, you poltroon."

Simon took the bottle. "I don't like White – he laughed at me in church. He called me a misfit."

"The pot calling the kettle black," observed Sanderson.

Cheeseman handed Blotwell a small tumbler. "Pour some whisky into that and put it on the desk. And spill some round the study so it smells like a distillery."

"Isn't that a waste?" asked Blotwell.

"You are a sick-making toad with the intelligence of a gnat," said Sanderson.

Cheeseman reached for a large book on the side table and withdrew what looked like a series of bookmarks from the inside pages. "Lastly, you'll hide these handbills in places where they'll be found if anyone with half a brain searches."

"I don't know Raleigh House and I don't know which is his study," said Blotwell, knowing he was being led into some nasty business, but not knowing quite what.

"Idiot! What is my room number?"

"Er, number one."

"Well then!"

"What if someone catches me?" enquired Blotwell,

"Sneak, like you usually do, and if you're caught that's your lookout. Now, get along with you before I lose my temper." Cheeseman's gaze flitted over to the hazel twigs hanging by a strap on the door.

"If you beat me, I won't be able to accomplish the mission," said Simon, trembling slightly as he pushed the tumbler into a side pocket and the pamphlets down his trousers.

"Are you frightened of us, little girl?" sneered Sanderson. "You are a little girl, aren't you, Blotwell?"

Simon forced himself to smile. "Daddy says that if I was nicely made up and dressed in lace I'd make someone a perfect little mistress."

Cheeseman exchanged glances with his friend, then they roared with laughter.

"*Daddy* is definitely a man after my own heart," said the School House captain, almost choking on his pipe. "Now, get out of here, you dimwit."

"And I must leave too," said Sanderson, "otherwise I shall be late for the Briton. I have two beautiful crystal goblets and a matching decanter. Enough to entice any sot. I shall keep him talking at least until the bell goes."

"Excellent! And Pincher will be here shortly to sell his soul to me." Cheeseman smirked at his ally. "This has been a most productive day. On this form, I could easily become the youngest Prime Minister in Albion's history."

"It would be three steps up from the current occupant of Number 10," sneered Sanderson.

* * *

Blotwell tucked the bottle into his blazer and scuttled back along the corridor, the way he had come. When he had descended one flight of stairs, he glanced down through the banisters. His heart sank. Stalky and M'Turk were on their way up, deep in conversation. For a moment, Blotwell thought about rushing back up to the second floor, but then he would be in danger of bumping into Sanderson. He hesitated. A moment later, he heard M'Turk's Irish brogue.

"Well, if it isn't our favourite Tar Baby Blotwell," he drawled. "No question about it, he's in need of a tweak."

"What have you got there?" asked Stalky, his sharp eyes lighting on the bulge in Blotwell's jacket.

"It's a present," answered the beleaguered first year. "It's for White in Raleigh. I have to deliver it, or—"

"Buyin' presents for the druid now, are you? Is there any creeping you won't do, you gelatinous fag?"

Instead of keeping quiet, Simon opened his mouth. The words tumbled out. "No, not me. Cheeseman has bought the present and wants me to deliver it." He tried to move on, but Stalky stood tall in his way.

"And when did the Cheesemonger start buyin' presents for the likes of Thomas White? I smell a rat. Does you not, M'Turk?"

"I smell a rancid, red herring."

"No, it's not a rancid red herring, M'Turk. It's the truth," spluttered Blotwell.

"So, it's the truth you're telling now, is it? That'll be a

first," said M'Turk.

"Let's see it," ordered Stalky.

With a quivering hand, Simon slowly withdrew the bottle of Glenlivet.

"That's uncommon decent of Cheeseman to give his friend Tom a half-drunk bottle of the hard stuff," said M'Turk.

"Maybe we should sample a wee dram ourselves," suggested Stalky.

"Please let me go. I haven't had my lunch yet."

"It's beef pie and trifle, Blotwell," said Stalky, licking his lips.

"'Spect it's all gone," said M'Turk. "I had seconds..." He belched loudly.

How vulgar, thought Simon, though he felt like crying. "I love trifle," he moaned, "especially if it's strawberry with lots of cream and custard and jelly."

M'Turk beheld the unfortunate boy. "Since you eat like a pig, Blotwell, how is it you're as weedy as an overgrown garden?"

"Mummy says I'm too highly strung to have muscles like Daddy wants me to have."

"The cowardly wretch spends most of his time running away. That's why he's not a porker," observed Stalky, who folded his arms and tapped his right foot. "If you answer a question with *vérité*, we might let you go."

"Oh, thank you," said Blotwell.

"Where are you really taking the bottle?"

"I told you. It's for White. I'm supposed to put it in his desk with a glass and spill a little if I want, then hide handbills round his room. But I mustn't get caught."

Slowly, M'Turk and Stalky's heads turned until they were looking at each other. Simultaneously, they nodded and knowing smiles crossed their lips.

"That sleeveen Cheeseman has let slip the dogs of war."

"Show us them pamphlets, Bloater," demanded Stalky.

Simon withdrew one from his trousers and handed it

over.

"Oh lawks! Look at this, Turkey. Such a disgustin' item."

Stalky and M'Turk pored over the handbill.

"Shockin', ain't it?" said Stalky, his mind sifting through several nascent plans.

M'Turk sighed and looked at Blotwell. "And you such an innocent-lookin' lamb, Bloater face, carryin' around such offensive literature. Read some of them words, Stalky, as they is too ribald for my delicate sensibilities."

"*The king dog sniffs the Castlemaine bitch, though it is she who has him on a short lead.* Ooo, mon giddy tante, such talk is turnin' me immoral, Turk, and just look at that illustration."

"And Bloater paste is plantin' it on the Briton. 'Tis a rip of which Mephistopheles himself would be proud."

"But are we going to stand by and let the innocent druid fall victim to this ruse?" demanded Stalky, wagging an accusatory finger in the air.

M'Turk stood back in mock admiration of his friend's rhetorical pose. Now, Blotwell saw his chance to make a run for it and for once took it. He leapt through the gap between the older boys and clattered down the stairs, sweat trickling down his forehead and threatening to run into his eyes.

"Stay your hand, Turkey, dear," said Stalky, putting a restraining arm around his friend's shoulders. "Let the beastly blighter go, for this knowledge, I declare, is like nectar to my lips. A veritable feast on which we can dine for weeks and months. We are armed with the pamphlet and now must away to the Monkey Farm which is the Cheesemonger's study. Where is the gigger-eyed, beetle-browed beard, by the way?"

"He felt a *pome* coming on. That wench in the village has taken his fancy. He went to the beach to write it down and have a smoke."

"The scribbler!" cried Stalky. "The romantic fool. He doesn't deserve we men of action and resource. To horse, Turkey!"

***

Sneaking gave Simon Blotwell a purpose in life. Though he didn't realise it, the rush of adrenalin and the euphoric sense of completion it gave him were high points in his otherwise mediocre existence. The fact that nobody liked him at the school made it a much easier pastime than, say, doing schoolwork. He didn't mind if he was caught either. He could endure the pain of retaliation because he was so used to it.

He wouldn't steal or inform on someone for his own benefit. There was no point. He didn't want for anything materially and he was too indolent to go plotting and scheming for himself. It always had to be at the behest of another. So to be Alfred Cheeseman's vassal was the perfect solution. Even the fact that Cheeseman bullied him had an advantage, because Blotwell could simultaneously obey him without a guilty conscience and despise him. He also understood the type of person Cheeseman was: a combination of ruthless ambition and coldness, who ruled by instilling fear and inflicting pain, and who didn't mind who knew it. Whereas people who were kind-hearted and compassionate were a mystery to him. He felt that, deep down, their altruism must have a malign motive or, if not, they were somehow unworthy, like himself.

It had been easy to gain access to White's study. There was no one about on the first floor of Raleigh House and, better still, the door was unlocked.

The room was as spartan as his own and felt even less lived-in. A worn piece of carpet lay by the narrow bed, which was covered with uninviting, grey woollen blankets. A black leather armchair which had seen better decades stood in one corner, its sagging seat bolstered by an off-white cushion with a golden dragon embroidered on it. Beneath the small leaded window was a desk with a blotter and a candle in a holder, under which a rickety chair was placed. The drab walls were bare and, except for a row of school books on a shelf, there were no personal items on show. There was not even a fire in the grate to boil a kettle or make toast.

Suppressing a moment of pity for his fellow misfit, Simon put the bottle of whisky and glass on the desk and opened the centre drawer. Inside, there was a new, mass-produced fountain pen, a pencil and penknife, a wooden ruler, a set square and protractor, all in a cardboard tray.

In the smaller left-hand drawer, there was a book that looked like the Bible, but it was in a foreign language, and so Simon thought it might be the work of Satan. He took out one of the three remaining pamphlets from his trousers and slipped it into the book.

He looked round, noticing the biggest piece of furniture in the room for the first time: a wardrobe that almost reached the ceiling, with a large drawer in the base. As expected, this contained White's clothes, including a spare jacket on a hanger, into the inside pocket of which he slid another pamphlet. The last he tucked under White's pillow.

Blotwell went back to the desk and pulled open the right-hand drawer. Inside was a bundle of letters tied with a ribbon and a silver locket. He undid the ribbon and shuffled through the well-thumbed correspondence, but try as he might he couldn't decipher the writing. He thought it must be written in some sort of code, as in *The Black Sapper of Silesia*, a story in *The Boy's Leisure Hour Annual.* Consequently, in Blotwell's imagination, White became a spy for that infamous country and thus deserved whatever fate Cheeseman had in store for him.

Pleased with himself, Simon uncorked the bottle of spirits and poured a few drops into the glass, which he then splashed over the floor. He repeated the action over the armchair and carpet and threw an extra-large splash on the clothes in the wardrobe's drawer before putting the wet glass on the blotter, creating a damp ring. Finally, he corked the bottle and slid it into the right-hand drawer next to the letters.

His exit from Raleigh House was as easy as his entry.

* * *

A few minutes later, Blotwell sauntered along the corridor on the top floor of School House, feeling assured of a warm welcome in study number one after a job well done. The door was ajar, and as he approached he could hear voices from within. Naturally, he stopped to listen, and as he listened he grew more and more worried, for the voices belonged to Cheeseman, Stalky and M'Turk.

"Oh! He squealed all right, like the Gadarene swine possessed of demons, only he didn't run into the waters to be drowned, he ran straight down the sainted steps of School House and out into the sunny sunshine."

"What do you want, Corkran?"

"Want? We wants nothing. Only to be left in peace, perfect peace, eh Turkey?"

"The peace that passeth all understanding," confirmed M'Turk.

"You mean you want to be left to your own devices to smoke, drink and play the fool."

M'Turk nodded. "The perfect précis of our wants and needs."

"And if you'd be so kind," said Stalky, "Templeton-Smith, he of the sweaty palms and stinky feet, get rid."

"He is a disgustin' specimen," added M'Turk, shaking his head sadly.

"You want a study of your own, like a sixth-former?"

"*Nitimur in vetitum.*"

"And what if I don't agree?"

"One of them salty pamphlets that you gave the Gadarene has fallen into our hands, A.C. You don't mind us callin' you A.C., do you? Isn't that what that smarmy simpleton from Frobisher calls you? It will act as our insurance policy."

"I'll agree on one condition."

"We had thought that all the conditions was on our side, but carry on out of interest."

Cheeseman went back to the book on the table and withdrew one last pamphlet. "Give this to Tallow, and make sure White's name is on it."

"That's a jolly jape," said Stalky. "Can we agree to this, Mac-Turkey?"

"We could use the Beetle's brainpower at this point, as I am sore vexed by the question."

"I was going to get Blotwell to deliver it, but now he will be otherwise engaged," said Cheeseman.

"I almost feel pangs of sympathy for the beastly blighter," said M'Turk.

Outside study number one, Blotwell realised that he was due for another flogging. The fact that Cheeseman had been outmanoeuvred by the likes of Stalky & Co. would be a bitter pill for Cheeseman to swallow – and the repercussions would all fall on Blotwell. After spending a few moments in gloomy reflection, Simon put his ear to the door once more.

"But wait – while you two chatters away, I, Stalky, have formulated a plan so grandiloquent that it puts the Trojan horse of Odysseus to shame. And it will relieve us of any contact with the waxy Tallow candle."

"I don't want to know – just execute it with immediate effect," said Cheeseman.

"Come, M'Turk, let's away to Raleigh where the revered teapot Berty Wright resides."

"You're making me giddy with expectations, Stalky, though I am feeling a mite witless on account of not understanding…"

Blotwell ran for cover along the corridor, hoping his footsteps wouldn't give him away. It was clear that sneaking needed much quieter shoes, so he decided to write to his mother asking her to send him a pair of the new Petersburg slippers which he had seen in Clarks on Oxford Street.

Chapter Six

Another Delve into the Recent Past

Late May 1825

Beryl Antrobus, known to almost everyone in Linbury as Miss Antrobus, the school teacher, walked into the bar room of the Sailor's Yarn Inn. Silence fell, making the squeak of her heels on the floorboards seem exceptionally loud. The patrons who had come to quench their thirst after a hard morning's work looked at each other with a mixture of surprise and disapproval.

Daniel Hall put down the flagon he had been drying and blinked. "Miss Antrobus, this is a pleasure," he said doubtfully. "Can I get you a drink? We have small beer..."

"No, thank you." Beryl could not hide the mixture of suspicion and disapproval she felt about the place. It had been a long time since she had set foot in this drinking establishment, and to her refined nostrils the place reeked of stale ale and stale men. "Mr Hall, I'm here to talk about your son, Frederick."

Daniel's face clouded. "Oh dear, has he been up to no good?"

"No, he is generally a well-behaved boy, if a little stubborn and insistent."

"Ah! He gets that from his mother."

"God rest her soul," added Miss Antrobus piously. "As you know, Frederick will celebrate his thirteenth birthday in something under a fortnight and I want to talk to you about his education."

"Oh," answered Daniel, rather perplexed.

"Your son is a very bright boy. Some would say he's too bright for his own good. On the other hand, I would never say that. You cannot have too much education, but I have come to the point where I cannot teach him any more..."

"Oh," repeated Daniel, trying to understand. "But if he's a bright boy, why can't you teach him any more?"

"He has received a good elementary education from me, but *I* can do no more."

Daniel's mind ticked over. Miss Antrobus had been drumming 'the three Rs' into every boy and girl in the village for the last thirty years or more, including himself. She knew everything. Teaching was her vocation, her life. Surely she wouldn't be stymied by a scrap of a boy like Freddy.

It was the church that funded her work and allowed her to use All Souls' vestry not only on Sunday afternoons but most weekday mornings as well. In fact, Linbury had the best-educated populace for miles around.

"Are you saying that Freddy should finish school and start working here right away? He already does some evenings when we're busy, and weekends... except Sunday, of course," he added hastily.

A momentary look of exasperation crossed Miss Antrobus's plump face. "No, Mr Hall, I am not saying that. As a matter of fact, I don't believe children should work in establishments such as these. They'd be far better off on the land, growing and harvesting."

"Then what are you saying, Miss Antrobus?" replied Daniel, becoming exasperated himself. "You're going to have to spell it out for me, as I'm only the landlord of this den of vice."

There was a muted guffaw from one table, where old Zebedee Tring, the parish itinerant labourer, was downing his usual pint of scrumpy and being royally entertained by the goings-on at the bar.

Daniel gave him a sharp look. "And you can mind your own business, Zebedee Tring, and stop earwigging on other people's private conversations."

"Mr Hall," said Beryl patiently, wishing she had not vocalised her temperance thoughts, "you need to find a way to satiate his thirst for knowledge. Even before he found a soulmate in Master East, his constant questioning was getting me down. Now he is even more exuberant in class, almost to the point of insubordination. I have done my best, but I can no longer give him what he needs."

"But Miss Antrobus, I'm a widower who has to work for a living. That means getting up at six in the morning and working till ten at night. I don't know any teachers other than yourself and, even if I did, where would I find the money for such an endeavour? I get a few extra pence a week as village postmaster, but that just gets us by with a few little extras at birthdays and Christmas."

"I am quite aware of that, Mr Hall. It's a pity that, because of impecuniosity, your son is prevented from attending a school that would befit his talents, such as the one we have just down the road."

Daniel didn't know what 'impecuniosity' meant, but he understood the gist and looked at Miss Antrobus as if she had lost her mind. "Our Freddy at Seekings School? Don't make me laugh! The only way he could get over the front step there would be as a valet or boot boy to one of them posh lads, like his friend Harry."

"There are such things as scholarships, Mr Hall, and if you are so minded I can start the ball rolling, as they say in croquet."

The light finally dawned in Daniel Hall's mind. Amongst all the shilly-shallying, disapproval and obtuse language it finally became clear to him that Beryl Antrobus wanted to help his son, not hinder, or criticise, or give up on him, but she needed his permission. "Right! I see. At last I get your drift. Well, I'd better think hard about it. No, I don't need to think hard, or at all. Miss Antrobus, you do whatever you think's right by Freddy and you will have my gratitude. If I can help in any way, I shall. I told you, I want what's best for him, because he's my son, he's all I have in the world and I love him."

"That's all I need to hear for the moment, Mr Hall. I shall talk to your son after class tomorrow. I wish you a very good day."

Another silence fell as Miss Antrobus swept out of the Sailor's Yarn and into Main Street. Then a buzz of excited chatter started in the bar room. Ruffy Harris, the butcher, and Doughy Hood, the baker, who closed up their shops for an hour each day so they could have a natter in the pub, grinned at each other over their table by the window.

"Well, Daniel Hall, looks like you've made a conquest there," said Ruffy.

"That's right," agreed his drinking partner. "Play your cards right and you could have your feet under her table in no time."

There was a sprinkling of laughter from the other customers, but Daniel frowned. "You two can stop your blethering, as soon as you like."

"That *uman* needs taking down a peg or two," said Zebedee Tring in his rough voice. "Coming into a public house unaccompanied. I remember when she was just our Beryl, the daughter of the shepherd, Ted Antrobus."

"She's trying to help my lad," said Daniel.

Zebedee made a dismissive noise and took a large draught from his pint of scrumpy.

Sam Hingston, the grocer and Daniel's cousin-in-law, who always sat alone by the fireplace come summer or winter, spat into the hearth. "Looks like our Freddy is going places. Hobnobbing with the son of the magistrate and talk of scholarships and edumacation…"

"Why can't you all mind your own business?" said Daniel, wiping the same tankard vigorously for the fifth time.

"Best of luck to him, he's a good lad and he knows his onions," said Joe Warren, the blacksmith, eyeing the grocer. "Which is more than you do, Sam Hingston."

His son, Russ, who was sitting next to his dad, nodded and scanned the bar room for dissenters. Immediately, normal business resumed. No one was going to argue the toss with the Warrens, especially when father and son were in agreement.

* * *

Mid-July 1825

With a blow on the post horn, the morning mail coach rattled into the stable yard of the New Inn, Larkstone, and came to a halt. Freddy swung down from his seat behind the driver and stood to get his bearings. Three more passengers alighted from inside the coach as the postilion held the door open.

"Fifty minutes, ladies and gentlemen, before we depart," the driver said, dismounting as the ostler appeared from the stables.

"I trust we shall reach our destination on time?" questioned one of the passengers, who was wearing a frock coat and top hat.

"Of course we shall, sir," answered the driver, as if anything other was beyond the bounds of possibility. "We shall arrive at the Old White Lion in Walminster at 4 p.m. sharp." He caught Freddy's eye and winked.

Freddy smiled back and gave a small wave before walking under the archway of the inn and out onto the road. It was just after eleven o'clock on a fine, sunny morning. Ahead of him, a short but steep hill led down to the quayside. It was near deserted, as the mackerel boats had already put to sea. But a two-masted galiot was being unloaded of its cargo of tobacco while the ferry to the Isle of Wight, a converted lugger, was moored further down the quay, ready for its departure at noon.

Unlike his own compact village, Larkstone meandered along the coast for almost half a mile. The rows of fishermen's cottages, warehouses and shops gave way to thatched cottages and smallholdings, where busy hens clucked and pigs grunted.

Following the instructions on the map, Freddy stuck to the coach road until he reached the church of St Edmund, where the main Macadam road bore left, but his own way was straight on along Stour Lane. Here, between hedgerows and trees, he glimpsed several well-to-do manor houses set back off the road in their own acreages of wood and field.

At length, the lane ended at a high brick wall between which carved stone pillars, surmounted by spheres, supported a pair of tall wrought-iron gates. On the left pillar was a brass plate that read *Jersey House*.

Freddy paused to gather his thoughts. He was nervous about meeting new people at the best of times, never mind about meeting the family who lived here, who were far above his social status. Surely the tradesman's entrance would be more suitable for him?

A straight gravel driveway, wide enough for a carriage, led to the front of a red-brick mansion of symmetrical design. The drive was bordered by clipped box hedges. Beyond them was a mix of trees, flowers and vegetables planted in a harmonious display.

Freddy tried the gate, but found that it wouldn't shift. He scanned the notes accompanying Harry's map, but there was no mention of the gate being locked. He made a second attempt, giving the gate a good rattle, but again was denied entry. Hot and bothered, he looked skyward in exasperation. It was then that he noticed a bell attached to the crown of the furthest gatepost. A pull rope was attached. Annoyed with himself, he gave it a tug. The ring was surprisingly loud.

Freddy took off his cap and brushed back his hair, feeling beads of sweat on his brow. Shortly, a man with a hoe came panting up.

"What business do you have here?" he asked.

Freddy recognised bluster when he heard it. "I'm a friend of Harry's. I'm expected."

Clearly confused, the man didn't reply immediately. "All right, wait there, I'll have to see about this…" Off he went, the hoe slung over his shoulder, grumbling to himself about how he was never told anything.

Freddy watched him retreat, feeling slightly more relaxed.

The house had five sash windows in the upper storey and four bays in the lower, between which was a simple portico with two inset columns framing the doorway. Two chimney stacks with eight pots on each stood at opposite ends of the house.

Shortly the man with the hoe came back, huffing and puffing. He took a brass key from the top pocket of his jacket and unlocked the gate. "Come on in then, young sir…"

"Freddy," said Freddy. "My dad, Daniel Hall, is the landlord of the Sailor's Yarn Inn in Linbury."

"That right," said the man, more casually now. "You've come a long way then?"

"Harry can run that distance."

"Hmm. I've never been far from Larkstone m'self."

Just like my Aunt Emily, Freddy thought. *Stuck in his ways.*

"I expect you think I'm an old stick-in-the-mud," said the man, as if reading his mind. "Jethro's the name – Jethro Sowerbutts, head gardener. Though that's a grand title for not much, as I only have my boy to help me look after this lot."

"You keep it very well," observed Freddy. "I like the topiary."

The man snorted. "Topiary nonsense? That's my Arthur. Thinks he's clever. He wants to do a magpie. I ask you!"

When they reached the portico, the door opened. Harry stood grinning on the threshold. "Greetings, Federico, come in. You solved the mystery of how to gain entrance to Jersey House. Not everyone does…"

"I didn't realise it was a puzzle," said Freddy. "I thought you'd be there to meet me…"

His escort turned to go, but not before rolling his eyes.

"Bye, thank you," called Freddy.

The gardener glanced back, shook his head and wiped his

nose with his finger. "Topiary. Pah! My eye."

"Take no notice," said Harry. "Jethro's an old curmudgeon. Come in. We've got apple cake and tea, then I'll show you round the house. Then this afternoon we're bound for the beach."

Freddy took off his cap and stepped gingerly into the dark, narrow hallway.

"If you take your boots off, you can slide along the floorboards. Mary, our polisher, has been at it all morning."

"I can smell the beeswax," whispered Freddy, removing his boots but not sliding.

At the end of the hall they turned left into a much lighter and airier room with French doors that opened out onto a patio, beyond which was a knot garden.

Mrs East, a lady of some forty years, reclined on a chaise longue by the fireplace, dressed fashionably in a cream ankle-length dress and light blue bodice with ruffs at the shoulders. A matching bonnet with upturned brim was tied with a ribbon beneath her chin.

"Ma, this is Federico – Freddy Hall, the boy genius from Linbury."

Freddy tutted and went red, much to Harry's amusement.

Mrs East smiled and offered a gloved hand. Freddy almost bowed and kissed it, but quickly thought better and gave it a gentle shake.

"It's lovely to meet you, young man. Harry's been so looking forward to your visit. He's talked about little else since he arranged it with you."

Freddy knotted his brow and looked askance at Harry, wondering why someone so ordinary as himself should be so liked.

"It's nice to meet you too, Mrs East," he said quietly.

"I'm afraid my husband is on magisterial duties in Dunhambury with the squire today. But you should meet him tomorrow. I myself am going for a ride in the pony and trap, so you'll have free run of the house."

Freddy was about to make some suitably platitudinous

remark, but fortunately Harry made it unnecessary. "Thank the lord that's the intros over," he cried. "Now come along to the kitchen, Feds, and let's have some tea and cake."

* * *

Later that afternoon, the two boys lay side by side in a little sandy cove, protected on the landward side by a limestone cliff. A natural staircase led up to a gate which gave entrance to the back of Jersey House.

"A private beach all your own," said Freddy, covering himself with a towel so that only his feet and head were visible.

"You are a goose, Federico, swathing yourself in cloth like an Egyptian mummy."

"If I didn't, I'd be roast goose," answered Freddy. "It's all right for you – you go brown, but I just burn and go bright red."

Harry put his hands behind his head, exposing his recently grown expanse of armpit hair. "I love the sun," he said. "I think I shall go and live on a tropical island when I'm twenty."

"I shall be serving behind our dad's bar while you're roaming the seven seas."

"Stuff and nonsense," said Harry. "It's time we had our serious talk. The one you've been trying to steer me away from."

"I've not been trying to steer you away from anything. It's just that there's nothing to tell."

"That's a lot of rot. Has Mrs A. sent off your paper to Greenwich?"

"Yes, but it'll probably get lost in the post."

Harry laughed. "Federico, you are such a misery! Now, tell your Uncle H. what will happen next."

"I won't hear anything ever, or I'll get a 'thank you, but no thank you' letter from one of Mr Newton's acolytes."

"And when will you get this rejection letter?"

"The applications close on 1st September and the

scholarship is awarded on All Souls' Day."

"And you have to go up to London to receive it?"

"Yes, to the Greenwich Observatory... Harry East, you just tricked me!"

Harry's eyes followed a seagull which was rising effortlessly skyward. "No one will be more disappointed than me if you don't get it, Federico."

Freddy angled his head leftwards, feeling his heart aching in gratitude that he had found a soulmate in Harry East.

"If by some miracle I do get it, I'll be at Seekings for the Lent term."

Harry turned onto his side to face Freddy. "I know you'll get it. You've got to get it! You know I'll be in the remove while you're in the shell."

"Yes, age and influence," replied Freddy, without rancour.

"But," Harry continued, "with your brains you'll easily get into the same form as me by next summer."

"Hello, you two. Goin' for a swim, are you?"

The voice made Freddy jump.

Harry knelt and looked back towards the approaching figure. "Well, if it isn't that cheeky young pup, Arthur Sowerbutts."

"I'm only a year younger than you," said Arthur, his chubby features half-hidden under his peaked cap from which an untidy thatch of black hair stuck out in all directions.

"A year and a half, actually," said Harry, "which makes all the difference between being a young sprog and a man."

Arthur began to disrobe. "What's the water like today?"

"Warmish," answered Harry.

"I like your topiary," said Freddy.

Arthur's face fell. "Our dad keeps threatening to snip the central stems off."

"He won't," said Harry. "He's just trying to get a rise out of you."

"Succeeded then."

"I hear you want to clip a magpie?" said Freddy.

"A magpie, a hen and a gryphon," replied Arthur. "But box is so slow-growing, I'll probably be forty before I can do it."

"This is Freddy, by the way," said Harry.

"I know who he is. You's from Linbury, aren't you?"

Freddy nodded.

"Come on then," said Arthur and started off at a run towards the water.

"Shall we follow the pink bottom?" asked Harry.

"Why not?" replied Freddy.

Chapter Seven

Close the Wall Up with our Albion Dead

Mr Tallow was in an even fouler mood than usual, as well as being distracted. Even Ralph Ballantyne had been unable to penetrate the wall of bile and preoccupation.

"So, in reviewing last week's lesson, the history of Russia during the eighteenth century – er, yes, the eighteenth century – our attention was divided between the reign of Peter... That is, Peter the Great, with which the century began, and that of Catherine ... er, that is, the second Catherine of course, which reached near to its termination..."

The master's eyes were barely open and his mumbling drone could only just be heard at the back of schoolroom by the acutest ears, though few of the owners of these auditory exemplars were even bothering to listen. He paused, drew out a handkerchief and wiped the corners of his mouth where a viscous sputum had collected.

Freddy stifled a yawn and took a surreptitious look at his fob watch. Nearly three-quarters of an hour left of this purgatory before break, then prep at 4 p.m. At least when Tallow talked about the Silesian wars and the threat that craven country posed to Albion, his manner became a little animated.

The master shook out his handkerchief before returning it to his pocket, causing some of the boys to recoil in disgust. "I shall continue.." he said, his lower jaw working up and down. "This week we shall leave the stern despotism of Peter and concentrate on the voluptuous elegance of Catherine, who delighted in the splendid—"

A loud snore erupted from the centre of the classroom. Heads turned. The sniggers began, then giggling and finally laughter.

Simon Blotwell sprawled across his desk, head resting on his textbook, his hands hanging over the edge of the desk. His pen had come adrift from its inkwell and ink from the nib was dripping onto the floor.

"Silence!" roared Mr Tallow. His cane hit Simon's desktop just an inch short of his hair. "Blotwell!"

A bleary-eyed Blotwell lifted his head, a string of drool suspended from his bottom lip. "Yes, sir," came the feeble reply. "I wasn't asleep, just resting my head…"

"You liar, boy. You were snoring like a swine in a sty."

Simon looked puzzled. "But Henry says I never snore, sir."

"You are a deceitful disgrace to your father, Blotwell. Hold out both hands, palms up…"

Freddy noticed that there were already several red welts, some recent, some less so, across Blotwell's palms and fingers, and felt a pang of sympathy for the miserable boy. The blows fell, four in all. Simon grunted and let out a breath at each, then gingerly closed his hands and made to withdraw them, but Mr Tallow hadn't finished. "Turn them over, boy, fingers outstretched."

Freddy looked away. To be hit across the knuckles in addition to the palms was not a standard punishment.

John Jennings, who sat behind Blotwell, raised his hand. "Excuse me, sir…"

Mr Tallow glared at him. "Well, what is it, boy?"

"It was me, sir. I made the snoring noise…"

The master's mouth twitched, his face betraying a moment of uncertainty. Then the cane rapped across Blotwell's knuckles four times in quick succession. This time Simon whimpered in pain. "You see, Jennings, that is your punishment. To know you were responsible for someone else's misery." Tallow walked back to the blackboard and picked up a piece of chalk. "Take out your Millers and begin reading the chapter on the Northern System, 1721 to 1796. I shall write twelve questions on the board for you to copy. You will prepare the answers in the form of prep for our next meeting. And woe betide anyone who does not meet the required standard."

To emphasise the point, Mr Tallow raised his cane and brought it down sharply on his blotter, sending up a cloud of chalk dust.

* * *

"Why the long face, Federico, on this fine Tuesday afternoon?"

Harry had caught up with Freddy on their way to Drake House for refreshments.

"Blotwell got eight from Tallow. Two on each side of each hand for sleeping in class."

"The candle's a sadist when he wants to be, but how does that affect you?"

"It was partly Jennings' fault, because he made this snoring noise as a joke which alerted Tallow."

"How do you know it was Jennings?"

"He owned up."

"Well, that was…"

"Yes, I know, decent of him. That's what all his friends said as they crowded round him after the lesson. But he didn't get punished, and meanwhile Blotwell slunk off alone to lick his wounds."

"Federico, do you recollect what Fouracre said?"

"What?"

"Seekings is a microcosm of the outside world. Not everything that happens is going to be fair or just. In any case, if Blotwell wasn't such a bounder, he'd have friends commiserating with him."

"He never cries, you know. You'd expect him to cry like a girl when he's hurt, but he just takes it, as if he expects to be punished."

"I think you've got a serious case of the sympathies. Are you going to have cake with him tomorrow? Remember, he promised—"

"You want me to go and find that he was either lying or has completely forgotten, don't you?"

Harry chuckled. "Or both. Would you like a small wager on it? A bottle of ginger beer for the winner."

"All right, but I know there's a high probability that I'll be forking out."

"I wish I could be there, but home duties mean I have to leave on the one o'clock."

"What have you got on tomorrow afternoon?"

"Don't mention it. Ma is doing her good works. That is, taking round loaves of bread to the poor and needy of Larkstone, which means I have to drive the pony and trap and carry the baskets. Still, I shall now be able to daydream about the sharp taste of the Widow Pattle's ginger beer."

They entered Drake House and made for the refectory to take tea. Overseeing the distribution of the traditionally weak beverage was Lance Redwing of the upper remove – an appropriate position for someone who was an aspiring journalist and gossip.

"Two cups of your freshest dishwater please, Redwing," said Harry.

"Don't be so cheeky, East. Finest Assam this is."

"Yes, but one spoon to four pints of water doesn't really do it justice, does it?" said Freddy.

"Do you want tea, or not?"

"Oh go on then, and two macaroons, please."

"Where do you think you are, Lyon's Corner House?"

"What! No biscuits?" exclaimed Freddy.

"There's some hard tack on the end in that tin for cheeky shell boys. Take it or leave it."

"I'll leave it, thanks. I don't want a broken tooth."

"Please yourself."

"Anything in the *Acta Diurna* today, Redwing?" asked Harry.

"Don't try to be clever with me, East," sniffed Lance, then he smiled in a knowing sort of way.

"What?" asked Freddy. "You do know something."

"What's it worth?" asked Lance.

"Since we don't know what *it* is, we don't know how much *it's* worth, do we?"

"Oh all right, I'll tell you, but remember you heard it from me first." Lance leaned towards them and whispered, "White's been relieved of his post as house captain of Raleigh and has been sent down for the rest of this term, if not for good."

Harry blinked and stood back, staring at Lance, trying to decide if he was pulling their leg.

"Why?" asked Freddy.

"I was told, confidentially you understand, that strong drink was involved, namely a half-empty bottle of Scotch."

"But all the sixth-formers drink, most to excess, on Saturday nights," said Freddy, who remembered many such boisterous occasions in the Sailor's Yarn.

"Tom White had signed the doctor's pledge of abstinence."

"You mean he's temperance?" asked Freddy, thinking of Miss Antrobus. "But the doctor? I've seen him drink wine and beer."

"Not temperance, Hall, you nitwit. My source tells me that Thomas White had form – including D&D when he was just a lad. So, he was made to sign the pledge before being accepted as a pupil. Until today, he was seen as one of the doctor's greatest successes. Of course, it didn't do him any good when they found a stack of radical, not to say racy, pamphlets in his room. Pamphlets in support of Silesian domination!"

"Who is this source of yours, Redwing?" asked Harry.

Lance smiled indulgently. "That's for me to know and you to find out. Now go away and drink your tea. Little boys should be seen and not heard."

***

Harry took a sip of tea and grimaced. "Bad news," he said.

"What, the tea or Tom White?" said Freddy, stepping over a form and sitting down at the long table opposite his friend.

"There's nothing new about the so-called tea, but Cheeseman is one step nearer becoming school captain. Remember, he's not eighteen until Michaelmas, so we'll have to suffer under him for a whole school year."

"He might leave at Christmas."

"No chance. He'll be after one of the Oxbridge places in '27."

"Maybe it won't be so bad. I hear that Theo Oldham was a bit of a tartar when he was Frobisher house captain."

"Not true. Oldham has always been a hands-off captain in his lordly way. Good for ceremonials and able to smooth ruffled feathers, both masters and pupils, whereas with Cheeseman it will be a hands-on reign of terror."

"Like Silesian domination," suggested Freddy, blowing across his tea cup.

Harry smiled. "You may scoff... Hey, did you read that in the *Morning Chronicle* about the Silesians negotiating with Caledonia for a base on their border with Albion?"

"Where on the border?"

"Berwick."

Freddy nodded slowly. "That would put the cat among the pigeons."

"That would mean war," replied Harry, "With both Silesia and Caledonia."

"War, war, war," said Freddy. "Why can't everyone just calm down?"

"The Silesians won't rest until Christian is on the throne of Albion."

"Prince Christian – he's not much older than us, is he?"

"He's the same age as Cheeseman," said Harry, as if this

was somehow a judgement on his character.

"Come off it," said Freddy. "Not everyone born in 1808 is destined to become a mean brute."

"1808, that was a bad year..." said Harry airily.

"Our dad thinks that all this war talk is ramped up by newspapers, old buffers who are too old to be called up into the army and, not least, Lady C. herself."

Harry leaned forward and spoke quietly. "Ma calls her the whore of Babylon. She says that the Lady Castlemaine wants to rule Albion as if it was her own private brothel. She's said to have slept with every male in every palace from Buck House to Windsor, including the stable boys and their horses."

Freddy giggled. "I didn't know your mum was a radical. Does she talk to you in that way?"

"Oh no! It's between her and Pa and he tells her to shut up, especially when he knows I'm earwigging. She has some advanced ideas, I can tell you."

"I would never have guessed."

"Of course you wouldn't. She's the wife of the magistrate. And Federico, just keep that under your hat, will you?"

"My lips are sealed, though I'd like to hear her ideas."

"All you Dorset folk tend to the radical, don't you?"

"Compared to you stuffy, conventional Hampshire types, yes."

Harry's face fell. "Do you really think I'm stuffy and conventional?"

"You're the most honourable and gallant Scud, my best friend," said Freddy without hesitation.

"You are an old chump saying those things, Federico, and it's an awful lot for a chap to live up to." But Harry was smiling again.

"Do you think that King Henry will marry the Countess of Sussex, despite everything?"

"You mean having the same mother – in other words, Lady C.? Though you'll never see that in *The Times* or the *Chronicle*."

"And King Albrecht of Silesia sabre-rattling over it."

"Since anything King Albrecht says is honoured in the breach in this country, I would probably say that they will get married, though the Parliamentarians may not agree with the decision and the Church will have to turn somersaults to preside."

"I read that the Pope says the marriage would be unlawful and a sin against God."

"Yes, but the Pope is not head of the Church in this country, is he? Not to mention that he is from the Papal States and the Papal States are allied to Silesia."

"The Archbishop of Canterbury is a member of the aristocracy."

"So, a bit of a dilemma for him."

"If they do marry, do you think their children will have two heads?"

"Two heads, twenty-two toes and a forked tail, I shouldn't wonder," said Harry.

"Can I sit with you today?" chirruped Frank Kennedy, he of Clifftop Lighthouse.

"Why, Francis," said Freddy. "Why haven't you sneaked into Raleigh to be with your best friend?"

"Carstairs has a sore thwoat and has been confined to sick bay by Matwon. And don't call me Fwancis, Fweddy Hall. I'm Fwank."

Harry patted the form next to him and Frank climbed over and sat down. "Why are you so tiny, Frank?"

"And skinny," added Freddy.

"It's because I haven't gwoan up yet. But when I do, my dad says I shall be six feet tall." He held his arm up over his head, but even then it hardly measured much above five.

"I would say at least six feet," said Harry.

"I wish Wedwing would make us a nice cup of tea like they have in Waleigh."

"Who makes it in Raleigh?" asked Freddy.

"Wight – it's ever so nice."

"Tom White makes the tea?" exclaimed Harry. "I don't believe it."

"No, not Tom White, Berty Wight."

"Oh, you mean Berty Wright," corrected Harry.

"That's what I said."

"Why don't you ask him to come over to Drake to show Redwing how to do it?" suggested Freddy.

Frank shook his head. "That's a good idea, Fweddy, but unfortunately the other Waleigh boys would tweak me if I asked him to do that."

"Now then, Frank," said Harry, "Your ears are closer to the ground than ours, so what can you tell us that we don't know?"

"Well, when I went to see Carstairs, Matwon and the Weverend Cwoft were wowing something wotten."

"What were they rowing about?" asked Freddy.

"Bathing in the lagoon. Matwon said Carstairs got his sore thwoat through bathing for too long in the lagoon."

"And what did the Reverend Croft have to say about that, Frank?" asked Harry.

"Poppycock."

The house bell sounded, followed by the inevitable groans from the assembled pupils as they collected their belongings and made for the common room for prep.

Chapter Eight

Penny for the King..?

2nd November 1825

Though there were no legal restrictions on opening hours, Daniel Hall closed the Sailor's Yarn Inn from 2.30 p.m. until 6 p.m. to give himself a break and to prepare for the evening when there would be an inrush of regulars wanting a pint and maybe a bite to eat. In the winter months, a warm was just as important, especially if they'd been working outside.

In the bar room, Freddy placed a pot of Auntie Edie's mutton stew in the side oven to keep it simmering away for the evening, then set about banking up the fire. To keep his clothes clean, he was wearing one of Russell Warren's old leather aprons which the blacksmith's son had outgrown. When that job was complete he swung the blackened copper kettle back over the fire and commenced to stack the remaining logs on the wide hearth.

"Dad, we'll have to do something about the chicken coop. There's already a gap at the bottom of the door where the wood's rotting."

"I keep forgetting," said Daniel from behind the bar, where he was hanging up the regulars' tankards after giving them a rinse and a polish. "I'll have a word with Elias, next time I see him."

There was a bang on the outside door.

"We're closed," shouted Daniel.

Another louder bang rattled the door.

"Are they deaf?" he said.

"I'll see who it is," said Freddy, rubbing his hands on his leather apron. He unshot the two bolts, top and bottom and opened the latch.

"'Bout time," said Harry, who was carrying a wooden box out of which protruded several sticks.

Freddy's face lit up. "Scud, what are you doing here?"

"I come bearing gifts for the people of Linbury from the people of Larkstone."

"Is that box what I think it is?"

"I don't know what you think it is."

"Are you two going to stand there gassing while all the warm air is drawn out?" shouted Daniel. "Come in and shut the flaming door."

Freddy stood back to allow Harry to enter with his burden, which he placed on one of the tables.

"Good afternoon, Mr Hall," he called out, pulling off his gloves and throwing his coat and scarf over a chair.

"Don't give me that 'good afternoon', Harry East. What are you doing in Linbury at this hour on a Wednesday? It's nigh on dark."

"As you invited me to the Bonfire Night hog roast on Saturday, I thought I should return the favour and bring a little colour into your drab lives."

"What are you talking about?" asked Daniel.

Having secured the door, Freddy joined his friend at the table and surveyed the contents of the box. "I thought it was," he said. "Dad, Harry's brought us fireworks!"

"It was Ma's idea, actually, though Pa has a friend at Brock's so we got a good deal." Harry eyed his friend. "Any news?" he asked.

Freddy's face fell and he shook his head. "Nothing…"

"Well, what have you got there?" asked Daniel, coming over and peering into the box.

"Squibs, jumping jacks, rockets, Catherine wheels, Bronco matches, sparklers, Roman candles, plenty of bangers and…" – Harry delved into the box – "…this letter addressed to Master F.

Hall." Grinning hugely, he held it up in front of Freddy's face. "Special delivery from Greenwich, no less. I had to sign for it and pay the cost of the postage – one shilling!"

"You brute, East!"

"Don't 'you brute' me," said Harry. "Open it."

Freddy's heart thumped and his hands trembled as he broke the seal and opened the single sheet of parchment.

"Oh, my lord, I can't stand the suspense!" said Daniel, dabbing his brow with the dishcloth.

"Well?" exclaimed Harry.

Freddy focused on one word at a time and began to read.

Dear Master Hall,

It is my great pleasure to inform you that Mr Isaac Newton has seen fit to award you the Newtonian scholarship for the year 1825 for your excellent observations and computations on the transit of the moon of Thanatos...

"Scud, Dad, I've got it!"

"Then why are you crying, you ass?" said Harry, who was all but crying himself.

Daniel embraced Freddy. "My son, my clever son. Well, I never. Whatever next!"

Then Harry hugged Freddy, after which they held hands and swung each other round and round the bar room. "My friend, Federico, the genius..."

"Now come on, you two," said Daniel, at length, "shape up and tell me what the rest of that letter has to say."

Freddy wiped his eyes and nose on his handkerchief and took out the letter from his apron pocket.

Mr Newton will be pleased to receive you in his office at the Royal Observatory in Greenwich on Thursday 1st December at 3.30 p.m.

I have organised transport for you by personnel from the

Royal Naval Hospital. A post chaise will be at the Fox and Goose Coaching Inn, Bray, at 10.30 a.m. on the above date.

You may now arrange a placement at one of the educational establishments on the approved list. The endowment is worth £100 p.a. for a maximum of five years.

For all matters pertaining to your scholarship, please use this as your letter of authority.

I look forward to meeting you and remain yours very sincerely,

Nicolas Fatio de Duillier (Secretary)

Signed under the seal of Mr I. Newton, The Royal Observatory, Greenwich

Daniel mopped his brow again, his mind in a whirl. "That's Advent, that is, the first day of Advent. I shall arrange with Sam Weller at the Old White Lion in Walminster for you to stay overnight on the 30th. Then you can catch the Oxford coach to Bray. Oh! I'm all of a commotion. I shall have to sit down for two minutes. By Jiminy, I could do with a pot of china."

"I'll get us one," said Freddy, tucking the letter back into his apron pocket.

"Stay!" ordered Harry. "Let me oblige."

Shortly, all three were sitting at the closest table to the fire eating brandy snaps which Harry had brought for Saturday, but had decided now would be an appropriate time to share them.

"Has it brewed enough yet?" asked Daniel, staring impatiently at the teapot.

"I think so," said Harry. "Sorry, I couldn't find the cosy. Shall I be mother?"

"Aye," said Daniel. "Milk and two sugars for me, please."

"Same for me," said Freddy. "Milk and sugar first, my lad."

Harry shook his head. "You country folks."

"I must tell Miss Antrobus and Russ," said Freddy. "Without them I'd never have got it."

"You should parade round the village with a placard round your neck announcing your triumph," said Harry.

"Shut up," said Freddy.

"You make a good pot, Harry," said Daniel. "Not everyone has the knack."

"Dad means me. It's always tastes watery when I do it."

"I say, that cauldron of stew smelt rather good," said Harry. "Is it Aunt Edie's? I have to confess, I opened the oven door and took a peek."

"Well, it's certainly not our dad's," answered Freddy.

"Eh! None of your cheek," said Daniel.

"Does that mean you're stopping?" asked Freddy hopefully.

"Well, I did tell Ma this morning not to expect me home. Shall we let off a few bangers and a rocket to celebrate your bursary?"

"We could take them onto the green, near Mrs Snell's cottage."

"Now, now, you'll do no such thing. Mrs Snell may be a first-order busybody, but getting her riled is not going to help. I expect we'll get a torrent of complaints from her on Sunday after King James's Night."

Freddy leaned back in his chair with his mug of tea, feeling happy and relaxed. "Have you ever thought what might have happened if Guy Fawkes hadn't blown up the king and Parliament?"

"I doubt it would have made any difference to us here in Linbury." said Daniel. "In any case, it was over 200 years ago."

"I think your pa's right. Things carried on much as they had before. Henry succeeded, as he would have done anyway in time."

"Hmm, maybe..." said Freddy, not convinced.

"You've got more important things to think about than the Gunpowder Plot," said Daniel, "like getting a place at

Seekings School. When do you think would be the best time to see the headmaster, Harry?"

"I'll make some enquiries, and let you know."

* * *

5th November 1825

"Poor King James," said Freddy, watching the effigy with its paper crown being consumed by the bonfire. He was standing behind a trestle table near the churchyard wall at the edge of the village green doling out the traditional free (well-watered) beer from a barrel, while his dad was not fifty yards away serving proper pints in the bar of the Sailor's Yarn.

"Who is that girl?" Harry pointed through a crowd of senior Seekings boys to a young woman of some sixteen summers, her flaxen hair aglow in the firelight.

"Clarrie May. Her mum owns the dairy."

"May by name or May by nature?" asked Harry with a grin.

"Both, I think. Auntie Edie calls her a flighty piece of goods."

Their conversation was interrupted by a series of loud bangs. Clarrie screamed, and all but one of the Seekings boys fled to the four corners of the green.

"There's nothing like a jumping jack to keep the party moving," said Harry, "and look who's left to console the damsel in distress."

"Who is it?" asked Freddy.

"Beetle Kipling, one of the infamous Stalky & Co of the fifth."

"She doesn't seem too distressed to me," said Freddy.

"Not now that she's fallen into the arms of Mr Kipling. You can bet that his friends Corkran and M'Turk set the whole thing up for him."

Freddy was taken aback by the deviousness of it and wondered how he'd manage when he got to Seekings.

Russell Warren walked over with a pork sandwich, freshly carved from the hog roast. "I thought you could do with a bite, before the vultures from the school descend. There's a nice bit of crackling in there, too."

"Thanks, Russ," said Freddy, his mouth watering. "Is your dad keeping them off so far?"

"Just about."

"Am I one of the vultures?" asked Harry.

"If the cap fits," answered Russ.

"I'd offer you a drink, but you know what this weak stuff is like," said Freddy, munching on the sandwich. "Tastes good."

Russ smiled and they paused to look up as a series of rockets zoomed into the sky and burst into showers of green and red stars, to the approving oohs and aahs of the crowd.

"Salts of barium gives the green colour and strontium the red," said Freddy.

"Good to know," said Harry, sharing an amused glance with Russ, who started. "Uh, oh! Look who's coming over. I'll see you later..."

A tall, thin woman with thick black hair wearing a home-knitted, purple shawl wrapped tightly around her shoulders approached from the cottage at the far end of the green.

"Good evening, Mrs Snell," said Freddy. "Would you like a drink?"

The woman sniffed. "No, Frederick, I would not like a drink. I don't approve of thirteen-year-olds serving alcoholic beverages. And where was Russell Warren off to in such a hurry?"

"He had to get back to baste the hog, Mrs Snell."

"Are you enjoying the display?" asked Harry.

"It's a disgrace and an annual insult to our beloved Royal Family," said Mrs Snell. "Burning the king's image. It ought not to be allowed. And I hear you were partially responsible for this... this bacchanal! I'm surprised at you, Harry East, being the son of the magistrate."

"Actually, it was Pa who got the fireworks, all the way

from Brock's in London."

Mrs Snell drew in a deep breath then coughed as a trail of smoke wafted across from the bonfire. "I had hoped it would rain to dampen this orgy of over-indulgence. As it is, my living room is full of smuts."

"Freddy Hall?"

Freddy turned at the sound of his name. A stranger was standing in front of the table wearing a hooded smock, tied with a piece of old rope at the waist and laced haphazardly at the neck. Silhouetted against the bonfire, his face, deep inside the hood, seemed to shimmer for just a moment.

"Yes?" said Freddy.

"Hawlings," said the man. "From Seekings School. I have a letter from the headmaster."

"Oh!" said Freddy, taking the envelope. "Thank you."

"Don't mention it," said Mr Hawlings, stroking his stubbly chin. "I believe you are coming to us after Christmas."

"If I'm accepted," answered Freddy. "I think I know you from somewhere, don't I?"

Mr Hawlings chuckled. "I have occasionally supped a pint in your father's bar. Do you see those two young men over there, standing by the fire?"

"Er, yes."

"Keep an eye on the shorter one with the wavy black hair, will you?"

"I'll try," replied Freddy, "but..."

"Do your best," said Mr Hawlings, turning and walking away into the crowd.

"That was odd," said Freddy, almost to himself.

Harry made a disparaging noise. "Old Hawlings – you'd think he ran the show, but he's only the caretaker and general factotum at Seekings."

"Who was he talking about?" asked Freddy, no longer able to spot the young man with the wavy hair in the milling crowd.

"Search me," said Harry. "Take no notice. The old boy was

probably half-cut."

"And dressed like a tramp," sniffed Mrs Snell. "Harry East, come with me. I have a letter of complaint I want you to deliver to your father post-haste."

Chapter Nine

A Bucket and a Window

Roll call and prayers on the Wednesday morning was a sombre affair. Dr Butler, who usually gave the address, sat back, ashen-faced, while Mr King, the school housemaster, spoke to the assembly in the Great Hall.

"Yesterday, the headmaster was presented with certain facts about one of our pupils, one of our senior pupils, that caused him great distress. Most of you will know by now that the captain of Raleigh House, Thomas White, has been sent down for behaviour quite unacceptable for a scholar at Seekings School. That behaviour, which I shall not describe, was an affront to all loyal, right-thinking personages not only of our school but also of our great nation.

"It is true that Thomas White was not Albion born. His family moved across the border from Briton where the young White had garnered an unwholesome reputation in the Valleys for conduct that any Seekings boy would find thoroughly reprehensible.

"Despite his aberrant behaviour, and like any parent, his mother and father were intent on doing their the best for their son and getting him away from the bad influences in his life. They approached the headmaster five years ago with a plea to take on their son and bring him to manhood as an upright and decent citizen with a strong moral centre. Now we know that all the time and effort put in to nurturing this boy has been for nought. Thomas White betrayed the trust that the headmaster and the school placed in him, in the most foul and objectionable way."

Mr King surveyed the young faces standing silently in the Great Hall. He looked as if he was relishing the whole business.

"This morning, I can announce that the replacement for White is to be Jeremy Pincher, who will serve as the new captain of Raleigh House, at least until the end of term. Meanwhile, White's name will be expunged from all the school rolls. It will be as if he never existed, and you pupils must never bring up his name again."

Even before Mr King sat down, Dr Butler walked off the podium, his head bowed, leaving his deputy Mr Topliss to conduct the rest of the assembly.

***

After the last morning period, scripture with the Reverend Croft, Freddy skipped luncheon and spent an hour in the school library. Initially, his intention was to forget the events of the preceding twenty-four hours and find out more about the relationship between electricity and magnetism recently discovered by Hans Christian Ørsted, but soon he was reading the latest notices from the Astronomical Society of London.

"Well, well, if it isn't our very own Astronomer Royal, Mr Hall."

Freddy jumped, which amused Mr Topliss, who sat down opposite him.

"Deep in thought, are we, Hall, as usual?"

"I was just reading these notes from the ASL, sir. You keep the library very well stocked and up to date."

"Indeed I do, and for a very good reason. The library is meant for inquiring minds like yours, Hall, and if it was stocked with fusty old tomes it would only encourage fusty old minds. That is not to cast aspersions on anyone in particular." Mr Topliss smiled.

"I think the Society could do with a younger man in charge," said Freddy. "Nothing much seems to have happened since Sir William Herschel died."

"Ah, the discoverer of every schoolboy's favourite planet. Yes, a sad loss. Perhaps his son should take over, or even you, Hall."

Freddy smiled a modest smile. He liked Mr Topliss because he was easy to talk to and seemed genuinely interested. In addition, his alchemy lessons were always engaging and sometimes spectacular. The master had an air of mystery about him, not least because he did not wear a mortar-board, like many of his colleagues, but instead wore a brightly coloured pointed hat with yellow moons and stars on it, with a background that was sometimes red and at other times blue.

"When are you due to see Mr Newton again?" enquired Mr Topliss, putting his clasped hands on the table.

"I'm not entirely sure, sir. I asked Mr Duillier and he said meetings would be arranged to review progress, but I've heard nothing since."

"That could be because Mr Newton is leaving Greenwich. He has been offered a suite at Trinity House, near the Tower, by his friend Mr Pepys, and he is to become Warden of the Royal Mint."

"Is that the naval, Mr Pepys?"

"It is indeed, Hall. Mr Samuel Pepys is the Secretary of the Admiralty. How did you come to know him?"

"A friend of mine, Carl, at the Royal Naval Hospital School. His brother and sister work for Mr Pepys."

"Well, isn't it a small world? Have you heard of the railway, Hall?"

"I read an article in one of the newspapers that came bundled with the post. A steam engine on wheels, isn't it?"

"Correct, and it is mounted on iron rails, set side by side, and pulls several coaches. One of these marvellous inventions is about to be given a trial run in the north of our country. Mark my words, this is the coming thing. It will revolutionise travel for us all."

"You know an awful lot, sir."

"I keep my ear to the ground and my nose to the grindstone, and so should you, Mr Hall."

"Yes, sir. Can I ask you something?"

"Of course you can ask, my boy, but whether I answer or not depends on the question."

"What were those pamphlets about that were found in Tom White's room?"

Mr Topliss sat back and lifted his eyes towards the vaulted ceiling of the library, as if trying to form an answer that would satisfy curiosity without being indecorous. "Shall I just say that they were writings in support of Prince Christian's claim to the throne of Albion, with illustrations of the Lady Castlemaine and other members of the Royal Family in various states of undress."

A blush appeared on Freddy's cheeks while he took a few moments to digest this information. "She has a reputation, doesn't she, sir?"

Mr Topliss chuckled. "Indeed she has, Hall."

"Do you think there'll be a war with Silesia?"

"Not if I can help it," said Mr Topliss firmly. "Now, my turn to ask you a question. Why are you here and not dashing home on this free afternoon, or gallivanting with your friend, East?"

"I'm due to see someone in School House."

"Ah, I see! Then I'll say au revoir until tomorrow at noon, when I will see you for our alchemical lesson."

"I'll look forward to that, sir."

Mr Topliss rose quickly, gave a small bow and swept away into the depths of the library. Freddie took out his watch. 2 p.m. Time to make tracks and find out if he owed Scud a bottle of ginger beer.

* * *

Freddy walked through the Great Hall of the osher and into School House by a side door. As far as he could remember, this was the first time he had been in the left wing since his arrival and he scratched his head, wondering which way to go. Several boys muttered about interlopers and gave him scornful looks as they passed him in the corridor. Then John Jennings and his friend Darbishire happened along. Freddy sighed with relief.

"Hall, why are you standing about like a lost soul?" asked Jennings.

"And, more to the point, why are you in School House anyway?" added Darbishire.

"I'm looking for Blotwell," answered Freddy.

"Better you than me," said Darbishire. "That boy is a snake in the grass."

"Shut up, Darbi. What's he done now?"

"He owes me," answered Freddy.

"You know he's got a study, don't you?"

"They probably gave him a study to prevent him getting a good kicking in the dorm," said Darbishire, pummelling his palm with a fist.

"You can't kick someone with your fist," said Jennings, rolling his eyes.

"Which way are the studies?" Freddy interrupted, recognising that he'd be here for a long time if Jennings and Darbishire began to argue.

Jennings motioned with his arm. "Keep going along this corridor until you come to the stairs on your right. Blotwell should be somewhere on the first floor unless they've put him in the attic with Fox Talbot."

"They should take him up to the bell tower and throw him off the roof," suggested Darbishire.

"Darbi, don't be an ozard. He's never done anything to either of us."

"He keeps getting beaten by masters and threatened by boys," said Freddy.

"Yes, bad show," answered Jennings.

"No, good show," said Darbishire. "Hang, draw and quarter him, that's what I say."

Freddy left them disputing whether Blotwell should be summarily despatched or not, and soon found himself climbing the staircase, the steps worn down by generations of boys' feet. At the top, he was confronted by a long corridor of panelled wood and bare floorboards. Through the many doors that lined the left-hand side, some open, some not, he could hear the chatter of adolescent voices.

Each study had a number stencilled on the door in black paint. Freddy had just peered through the open doorway of study number ten to cries of 'I spy strangers' when a small boy rushed out of one of the studies further along, towards a door at the far end of the corridor marked *ATTIC*. Freddy didn't recognise him, though by his slight build and lack of height he should surely have been in the shell.

When he reached the open doorway, he found Simon Blotwell sitting, or rather drooping, on his bed.

"Blotwell!" called Freddy, noting that this was study number 15.

The boy slowly lifted his head. "Oh Freddy, I feel sick…"

"Would that be anything to do with the jam and cream around your mouth?"

Blotwell groaned and his deathly pallor became tinged with green.

Freddy entered the room and folded his arms. "You've eaten all the cake, haven't you?"

"Oh Freddy, I'm so ashamed…"

A spasm passed through Blotwell's body. "I can't wait any longer," he moaned, rising from the bed and tottering over to the window. He opened the casement, stuck out his head, and vomited.

Being a landlord's son, Freddy was used to this type of behaviour and knew what to do, though he didn't entirely escape a feeling of nausea himself.

"Was there anyone underneath that shower of sick?" he asked, filling a tumbler of water from the washstand.

"I didn't notice," replied Blotwell. "But Mr Hawlings may

have to give his bed of candytuft extra attention."

"Rinse your mouth and spit it out of the window, you ass," said Freddy, handing over the glass.

Meekly Blotwell did as he was told, then wiped his mouth on a spotted handkerchief which he withdrew from his trouser pocket. "I feel better now," he said, smiling, the colour already returning to his cheeks.

"I'm too late, aren't I?" said a deep voice behind Freddy. Freddy turned to see the little boy he had seen earlier, only now he could see that he was only small in stature.

"Hello. I'm Henry, Henry Perceval, at your service."

"Henry shares the study with me," said Blotwell, sitting on his bed again.

"Lucky him," replied Freddy.

"It's not so bad, actually," said Henry. "He's as quiet as a mouse usually and it's better than being in the dorm."

At this point, Freddy remembered his manners and turned to the boy, who was holding a wooden pail in one hand and a small blue medicine bottle in the other. "Sorry, I'm Freddy, Freddy Hall, pleased to meet you." He stuck out his hand.

Henry dropped the bucket with a clatter and clasped Freddy's much larger hand. "I know who you are and I know what you're thinking, because everyone thinks it. I'm just five feet."

"What year are you?"

"I'm fourteen and in the remove."

"What's in the bottle?" asked Freddy.

"Oh this is one of Fox Talbot's concoctions. Hydroxide of magnesium and some other ingredients. Foxy is a total hypochondriac if ever there was one. It's to calm Simon's stomach."

"I don't need it," said Blotwell, lightly bouncing up and down on the bed.

"You may do when I've finished with you," said Freddy. "Why did you stuff yourself with cake – my cake? I owe Scud a bottle of ginger beer too, because of you."

"I like ginger beer."

"You haven't answered my question."

"It wasn't my fault, Freddy. Those rough boys, Stalky & Co., threatened me with a good tweaking if I didn't give them half the cake."

"I don't see them."

Blotwell lowered his voice and spoke in a confidential manner. "They were on their way to a meeting with Cheeseman and said they'd be back when it was over."

"A meeting? I thought Stalky and Cheeseman were sworn enemies."

"Not any more, it seems," said Henry, going to sit on his own bed. "I passed them in the stairwell on their way up. Very jaunty, they were."

"Won't they be surprised when they come back and find the cake is missing?" said Blotwell, gleefully. "I shall tell them it was stolen."

Freddy shook his head. "Don't be ridiculous. They won't believe you and you'll end up getting a pasting."

Henry waved towards the chairs pushed under their desks, one on each side of the window. "Why don't you sit down, Freddy? We don't get many visitors."

Freddy was about to say that he ought to go when he noticed the row of books on a shelf above Blotwell's bed. They were books, but unlike any he had seen before, not least because of their brightly coloured spines.

He turned Blotwell's chair round and sat down. "What are those?" he asked, pointing up.

Simon smiled. "Oh Freddy, they're my very special books. When Mummy and I go up to town at Christmas, we always go to Hamleys toy shop in Regent Street first, then down to Lyon's Corner House in Coventry Street, where I have a French fancy, a bowl of jelly and a glass of lemonade, then we take a cab all the way to Whitechapel—"

"Blotwell, the books!"

"Yes, yes, I'm coming to that. We have an appointment at the Whitechapel Gallery and while Mummy is looking at the paintings, I go and choose my annuals for the year, the first of which Santa delivers on Christmas Eve…"

A silence followed, which was broken by Henry chortling at Freddy's obvious exasperation. "He's a caution, isn't he? Sometimes I think he doesn't belong in this world but comes from the moon or somewhere."

"You mean he's a lunatic," said Freddy, rising from his chair and taking down one of the books.

"Don't drop it," warned Henry. "It's worth an arm and a leg."

Freddy examined the cover, which was a full-colour illustration of a rocket ship travelling between worlds. "*Adventures in the Future*," he read out loud, then gulped when he saw the price. £20!

"Told you," said Henry.

"That's my second all-time favourite, after *My Beautiful Book of Fairy Tales*," said Blotwell.

Freddy dropped back into his chair and opened the book at a random page. On one side was a colour lithograph of the scene described in the text opposite.

"*On the topmost balcony of the pagoda, overlooking the great city of Xianyang, the Chinese emperor sat on his throne, to which was attached forty-seven rockets. He ordered each of forty-seven servants to light the fuses simultaneously. To which done, there was a terrible explosion, and in a billow of fire and smoke, the throne ascended into the air. The servants and the vast crowd in the courtyard below watched in awe as the throne carrying their emperor disappeared into the stratosphere.*"

"How do they do this printing, Blotwell? It's as good as a painting."

Simon blinked. "Freddy, I'm as thick as two short planks. You should know that."

"But did you see them print this?"

"They do it in a back room and all the books come out in a

cardboard box."

"Can I borrow it?" Freddy asked.

Henry sniggered.

"It's much too precious to be given out willy-nilly to any Tom, Dick or Harry," replied Blotwell. "I'm afraid the answer must be—"

A heavy knock on the open door interrupted them. "What's too precious, Blotwell, my lamb?" asked Stalky, crossing the threshold. "And what's a little grub from Drake doing in mighty School House?"

"Corkran, this is a private room, so please leave," said Henry.

Stalky took a further step into the room, closely followed by M'Turk and Beetle. M'Turk eyed the younger threesome. "All of them want a dashed good tweaking," he said.

"Anything is possible short of murder, now we have carte blanche thanks to our friendship with A.C.," added Beetle, rubbing his moustache with the side of his index finger.

"Methinks that murder may be the answer," said Stalky.

"What do you mean, carte blanche?" asked Freddy, putting the book down on the desk.

"It's French, pipsqueak, and pipsqueaks don't ask fifth-formers questions, Hall," said M'Turk.

"I'll ask, then," said Henry. "Come along, we're all agog."

"The petit Perceval speaks, and so Stalky & Co. submit," alliterated Beetle.

"Listen, Kipling, you're only half an inch taller than me. Though it's true, you are two foot wider."

"Tut, tut, tut." Stalky shook his head. "Now, you've done it, Tom Thumb..."

M'Turk gasped at the effrontery, but then his mind and stomach began to wander back towards the purpose of their visit. "What about the cake?" he hissed. "Let's not stray too far from the matter in hand."

"Capital thinking, Turkey," said Stalky. "Where the deuce is the cake, Blotwell?"

Simon opened his mouth, but nothing came out.

"It went out the window, if you must know," said Freddy. "Blotwell dropped it. He owed me a slice and was trying to hide it…"

"I expect you could salvage some of it, if you wanted to," said Henry.

At that moment, Mr King, the school housemaster, appeared in the doorway. "What is going on here?" he asked. "Six boys in one room and three of them fifth-form fools of the first order. Get ye gone, Corkran, and take the Turk and Gigadibs with you."

"Yes sir, we was just larkin'," said Stalky, as meekly as he could.

"When do you do anything else?"

Before they sloped off, Beetle managed to give Henry the evil eye, which also fell glancingly on Freddy.

Mr King shut the door on the retreating backs of Stalky & Co., causing the remaining three boys to wonder what was in store.

"You are Hall, are you not?"

Mr King taught classics to the sixth form and had no dealings with the lowly shell boys, except for those for whom he was housemaster.

"Yes, sir," replied Freddy.

"You are a day boy?" On uttering these words, Mr King's lip curled slightly.

"Yes, sir."

"Then what are you doing in School House on a Wednesday afternoon?"

"I came to borrow a book, sir," he lied, picking up *Adventures in the Future*.

Mr King's eyes narrowed, as he never trusted boys to tell the truth. However, in this instance the purpose of his visit lay elsewhere and he let the matter rest. "I had a visitor to my rooms not half an hour ago. A very perturbed Mr Crocker, who claims that he was sprayed with vomit from an upstairs window in School House."

Freddy let his eyes wander. He saw Blotwell had gone pale again and was fidgeting uncomfortably on the bed.

"My investigations revealed a quantity of some disgusting semi-solid material in Mr Hawlings' flower beds," continued Mr King, "suggesting that the aforementioned material came from this room, through that window." He pointed theatrically towards the casement, then eyed Blotwell. "Was it you, you insidious piece of fly-blown meat, you worthless, limp-wristed excuse for a Seekings boy?"

"Sorry, sir, it was me," Freddy lied again. "It must have been something I ate at lunch. When I got here, I just felt ill and had to get rid of it. I didn't realise that Mr Crocker or anyone else was underneath."

Henry scooped up the bucket. "It's true, sir. Freddy looked like death warmed up when he came in. I rushed out to get this but was too late."

"I see," said King. "You look remarkably well now, Hall."

Henry held up the blue bottle. "I got this cure from Fox Talbot, sir. It worked wonders."

"Two hundred lines, Hall, for impudence, on my desk by 2 p.m. sharp on Friday."

"Yes, sir. Any particular subject?"

"Exodus 16, manna from heaven, in Latin, if you please."

Mr King departed. Henry waited until he could no longer hear his footsteps before getting up and closing the door. "I say, Freddy, that was jolly decent of you. King would probably have given Simon a good lashing and lines. I don't think he likes him."

"I don't care," said Blotwell. "I've already got a thousand lines to do before the weekend and I'm not doing any of them."

"Well, time for me to get off home," said Freddy. "I've got this book to read."

"Freddy! I never said you could take my second all-time favourite book away with you."

"Fair's fair, Blots," said Henry. "He got you out of a sticky situation."

"Well, you must look after it and don't let those common Linbury people spill beer on it."

"All right, Simon," said Freddy, deliberately using his first name. "It'll be like a library service. I'll keep it for a week then swap it for another one."

Blotwell frowned and Freddy chuckled. "Do you think Mr King was trying to be funny when he gave me manna from heaven as a subject?"

"Most unlikely," replied Henry. "In my experience, King doesn't have a funny bone in his body."

Chapter Ten

Row, Row, Row your Boat...

1st December 1825

The Oxford-bound coach from Walminster had forded the River Thames at its shallowest point in the village of Bray, not 200 yards from the Fox and Goose. Even as the coach came to rest outside the inn, the ostlers were leading out two pairs of fresh horses.

Freddy was the only passenger to alight for the five-minute stopover. After collecting his worn carpet bag from the roof, he stole into the lounge bar to escape the penetrating cold of the frosty morning. There were several other people seated around the fireplace, leaving him no room to warm himself. They were waiting for the London-bound mail coach which was due at 11 a.m. It went as far as the Bell and Crown in Holborn, eight miles from his destination in Greenwich.

Freddy knelt on the window seat and wiped the condensation from one of the crown glass lights. Across the road, beyond the green and a swathe of rime-encrusted trees, the River Thames flowed at a steady pace towards London.

The landlord of the Fox and Goose came over to him. "You look lost, son," he said.

Freddy turned and sat properly on the seat, grasping his carpet bag tightly. "I'm waiting for a chaise to take me to Greenwich. It's due at 10.30." He looked over at the grandmother clock hanging above the mantle which showed 10.10. "Is that clock right?"

The landlord chuckled. "Right enough. That's Bray time, that is. But if you want the time in the metropolis you have to add fifteen minutes."

"That's confusing," said Freddy.

"I'd change it, but the regulars like things the way they are."

"My dad is the innkeeper of the Sailor's Yarn in Linbury so I know what you mean."

The sound of a coach turning in the road outside alerted Freddy.

"Dead on time," said the landlord with a smile, examining his pocket watch.

"Thank you," called Freddy, getting up and rushing towards the door.

The chaise was a two-horse, two-seater covered carriage driven by a postilion, a stern-looking young man of no more than eighteen years, dressed in red livery and tricorn hat.

"Get in," he said, waving away Freddy's attempt to show him the letter.

Freddy opened the door and, with his free hand, drew down the steps and clambered inside. No sooner had he reversed the process than the driver set off with a crack of his whip, depositing him heavily in his seat. Next to him, a pale, round-faced, sullen-looking boy of about his own age was slumped in the corner watching him with an uninterested expression. He was dressed in a gansey – a chunky black Aran knit jumper, dirty white bell-bottom trousers and a pork pie cap with *Royal Naval Hospital School* in gold lettering on the tally.

Freddy clutched his bag protectively to him, uncertain whether he should say something, but seeing that the boy was intent on ignoring him, he decided that silence was probably the best option. The coach gathered speed and seemed to be flying along, though in truth it was not doing more than ten miles an hour. At this pace, the forty miles from Bray to Greenwich, with stops to rest the horses and the traffic in the City, would take something over five hours to complete.

Freddy tried to relax but the hostile presence next to him

and the attitude of the postilion made him feel ill at ease. He closed his eyes and thought back to the day, a fortnight ago, when he had gone down to Seekings with his dad, who had been as nervous then as he was now. Daniel had rung the bell at the school gates several times before Mr Hawlings had appeared, a smile on his weather-beaten face.

"So, Mr and Master Hall, welcome to Seekings. Dr Butler is expecting you." He winked at Freddy. "I'll show you the way."

The headmaster was kind and attentive and even Daniel was put at his ease, helped by a pot of tea. The meeting lasted less than half an hour and the result never seemed in doubt.

"We should be happy to take your son on as a pupil from the beginning of the Lent term, Mr Hall. He will be the first Newtonian scholar we've had at the school and we are quite enthused by the prospect." Dr Butler stood up. "If you follow me, I shall introduce you to Mrs Anderson, the housekeeper of Drake House, where all our day boys are assigned. She will show you round the school and answer any questions you may have..."

The chaise hit a bump in the road. Freddy opened his eyes. He felt for his fob watch in his waistcoat pocket, then remembered he had left it at home on the advice of his dad who had warned him about highwaymen, though the days of Dick Turpin and his like were all but over.

Freddy fiddled with the handles of his bag and crossed and uncrossed his legs, beginning to feel bored as well as depressed. He opened the bag and saw the brown paper packet of oatmeal and gingerbread biscuits that Mrs Pattle had given him for the journey. His mouth watered and he took one out and bit into it. He glanced at the boy next to him and found him gazing at the packet.

"Would you like one?" asked Freddy in a whisper.

The boy blinked with surprise and looked at him. "Really?" he asked in a throaty voice.

Freddy offered the bag and the boy took one. "Coo, ta," he said, his sullen expression suddenly replaced by a large, toothy grin.

"I'm Freddy," said Freddy. "Freddy Hall from Linbury."

"Where's that, then?" asked the boy, a few crumbs spilling from his mouth.

"Dorsetshire," answered Freddy, offering the boy his bottle of Mrs Pattle's cherryade.

"That's near Portsmouth, ain't it?"

"That's next door in Hampshire."

The boy took a swig from the bottle and handed it back. "I shall be stationed at Portsmouth when I leave the school."

"What's your name?"

"Coo, strike me, I forgot to say. I'm Carl, Carl Birch, born in Limehouse." He swapped his biscuit into his left hand and stuck out his right. They shook. Carl's hand was rough and dry, but his grip was firm.

"I was told you was one of them stuck-up know-it-alls who wouldn't want to know me."

"Not really," answered Freddy. "You're at Greenwich?"

"Yeah, the Hospital School. There's loads of poor kids like me there, all naval orphans. My dad lost his life on the Barbary Coast in 1816, and my mum died when she was giving birth to my kid brother. So we was both looked after by Jane, my elder sister, till I got placed at the school and Wayneman went into service."

Freddy nodded. "My mum died of puerperal fever soon after having me, so my dad kind of took on both roles, though he can't cook to save his life." He handed the bottle to Carl, who took another drink.

"This is nice, thanks. Just think, we's wasted a whole hour when we could have been chatting like two mudlarks."

The chaise drew to a halt and the postilion appeared at the window. "Five minutes, if you want to relieve yourselves, but don't do it into the horse trough, or I'll skin you alive."

"You shouldn't talk to Freddy like that, posti," said Carl. "He's a guest of HM Royal Navy."

"Oh, Freddy is it, now?" sneered the postilion. "And you

telling everyone that you were going to cold-shoulder the snooty upstart and give him what for."

"Only cos I was misinformed."

"You cockney sparrows are all mouth and wind. Five minutes – that's all you've got before I leave, with or without you." The postilion withdrew to attend to the horses.

Carl nudged Freddy. "Take no notice of that one. He's only bein' like this cos he's been made up to petty officer and posted to the Tower for a week. Thinks he's the bee's knees."

The two boys dismounted onto the white road, bordered by a field ditch on one side and the overgrown bank of the Thames on the other. Up ahead there was a straggle of red-brick cottages and an inn, the Three Horseshoes.

"I'll be back in a jiff," said Carl with a grin. "Need to find a bush. That cherryade went straight through me." He scampered off down the bank while the postilion led the horses to the water trough at the side of the road, breaking the thin sheet of ice on the surface with the stock of his whip.

Freddy looked around. "Where are we?" he asked, breathing out a misty breath.

"Eton Wick," said the postilion without turning.

Freddy pointed across the field to where castellated rooftops were visible in the distance. "Is that the college?"

"I expect so," replied the postilion, who was now feeding a handful of oats to each of his horses.

"What's that?" Freddy asked, pointing in the opposite direction across the river to a row of buildings on the skyline.

The postilion ignored him.

Carl emerged from the bushes and ran up the bank. "That's Windsor Castle," he said. "They say that's where the Lady Castlemaine takes her pageboys for a bit of slap and tickle. Have you ever seen the Lady Castlemaine, Freddy?"

Freddy shook his head.

"I did once, at a pageant in Hyde Park. Dressed to the nines, she was, not young but a real beauty. I wouldn't say no to a bit of slap and tickle with her meself." Carl paused. "Only probably not today, on account of the frost which seems to have shrunk me lower orders." He grimaced. "I could hardly find it."

Freddy chortled at this, which made Carl laugh, and then they were both laughing fit to bust. "Lower orders!" spluttered Freddy, wiping his eyes, which made Carl laugh even more. Arms outstretched, they held on to each other's shoulders to stop themselves falling over.

"What a pair of nincompoops," said the postilion. "Get aboard. It's time to go."

It was another three hours before the spires of London became visible through a haze of smoke. The sun was already low in the southern sky and another hard frost seemed likely.

"This is the biggest city in the world," said Carl with pride. "A million and a half people live here. An' that's Hyde Park," he said, pointing through the left-hand window. "Where I saw the Lady Castlemaine."

Freddy smiled. "Are your lower orders ready for a bit of slap and tickle now, then?"

Carl giggled and gave Freddy a playful shove with his shoulder. "You're a right one, you are."

The chaise drew to a halt.

"Are we there already?" asked Freddy.

"Nah, we just stopped at the turnpike. This is Hyde Park Corner. Posti will show the orders and we'll be on our way. No fee for us."

The chaise moved off again along Piccadilly. At first London seemed very grand, almost awe-inspiring, with wide streets and vistas opening onto opulent buildings. The gentlemen wore top hats and greatcoats and many carried canes as they strolled along, while the ladies were decked out in velvety fabrics with matching shawls and fur muffs. But as they drove further east along Holborn and then down through Fleet Street to Ludgate, the roads became narrower and more congested. Tall buildings pressed in on both sides, their upper floors projecting out oppressively over the lower. A tide of grimy inhabitants pushed and jostled their way in the confined space.

"Don't like it, do you?" said Carl, not unkindly.

Freddy shook his head. "Too enclosed, too noisy, too many people."

Carl chuckled. "You country boys... Look, that's St Paul's."

Freddy gazed out, his eyes drawn up to the central Gothic spire of the huge cathedral.

"Some say it's on its last legs and will fall down in the next storm," remarked Carl.

Beyond St Paul's their pace slowed further and sometimes they stopped altogether as carts, coaches, hackney cabs, wagons and a ragged populace were funnelled relentlessly in both directions along the Whitechapel Road. The smell of smoke and horse dung filled the air. It was getting dark too – or so it seemed.

"That's where I was born," said Carl, this time pointing out of the right-hand window.

"Limehouse?"

"You remembered. Dingy place. Lots of Chinamen. They makes ropes for the Navy and repair ships in the docks."

They emerged from Limehouse onto a potholed track which took them due south past the West India Docks and down through the Isle of Dogs, following close by the Thames. The traffic had thinned to almost nothing and they seemed quite alone when they pulled up by a short pier.

"We've arrived," said Carl. "Now it's my turn to do some work."

The postilion opened the door of the chaise. "Hurry up, I haven't got all day."

"Back to the Tower is it, Petty Officer Posti?" replied Carl. "Hope they don't chop off your head. Not that it would make much difference, seeing as you keep your brains in your boots."

"Less of your cheek, Birch. I'll see you here tomorrow at first light – if you haven't drowned your friend by then."

Freddy wasn't sure what these exchanges were about

until Carl pointed to the rowing boat moored by the pier. "Your transport awaits."

"You're going to ferry me across the river?"

"Yeah. That's why I'm here."

Freddy looked out over the Thames. A cold wind blew in his face. The lights of the Royal Naval Hospital twinkled on the far bank – a very great distance away, or so it seemed to him. The postilion cracked his whip and the chaise moved off, leaving the two boys alone in the twilight. "The tide's just right," said Carl. "We'll be across before you know it. You can trust me, Freddy. Honest, I won't let you down."

Freddy smiled, but kept a nervous grip on his bag. "I do trust you, Carl. It's just that I've never been rowed across a river like this before."

"You get in the stern an' I'll look after you." Carl took the bag and stowed it under the seat, then unhitched the mooring line and pushed the boat away from the pier with an oar.

In the next ten minutes, Freddy learned why Carl had such broad shoulders, as the boy sculled easily across the Thames at a diagonal, reaching the south bank right in front of the Naval School gates.

"That was brilliant," said Freddy carefully stepping out onto the bank.

Carl grinned his big toothy grin and jumped out holding the mooring rope, which he hooked onto a bollard. "Right, let's get you fixed up."

They passed through the iron gates of the RNHS with a nod to the sentries and made their way across a wide courtyard where a huge cannon stood in front of a fully rigged, three-masted sloop-of-war.

"Is that a real ship?" asked Freddy.

"That's our training vessel, *Fame*. The only difference between it and a real ship is that it don't float."

"Have you been right to the top?"

"We scramble up like monkeys to unfurl the sails. Some boys do it barefoot, they say it gives them a better grip on the ropes, but I prefer me boots." Carl pointed to a building on the summit of a hill behind the school. "See them lighted windows? That's the observatory where you're headed."

"Where is everyone?" asked Freddy.

"Working or learning," replied Carl. "School goes on till four. Then after a break we has our skivvying duties."

"Have you ever met Mr Newton?"

"Nah, but I seen him a few times at the parades with his friend Mr Pepys. Mr Pepys is a bigwig in the Navy, though he's only a civilian. My sister and brother are in his service. Jane likes him, but Wayneman thinks he's too strict. But then, he's just a little kid."

They passed through the door of a square two-storey building into a black-and-white tiled lobby where a quartet of sailor boys were mopping the floor. A pair of symmetrical staircases led to a balcony where three men dressed in dark naval suits were deep in conversation.

"The tall one with the beard is Commodore Hughes, the headmaster," whispered Carl. "He teaches us navigation, nautical astronomy, chart-making and mechanical drawing."

As if he'd heard, the headmaster turned and looked down over the balustrade. Immediately, Carl removed his cap and held it in front of his chest.

"It seems your mission has been a success, Birch?"

"Yes sir. This is Freddy Hall, Mr Newton's guest."

The headmaster walked slowly down the stairs, followed by his retinue. When he reached the bottom, he nodded. "Master Hall, I read your piece on the Thanatos moon. An excellent piece for one so young."

"Thank you, sir," said Freddy, following Carl's lead.

"You intend to make Seekings School your place of education. Mr Newton will no doubt have words about that."

"It's just down the road from my village, sir, which means I don't need to board."

"I understand. Has Birch done his duty by you, Master Hall?"

"More than his duty, sir."

Freddy glanced at Carl and was surprised to see a blush of pride on his face.

"Very good," said Commodore Hughes, continuing to scrutinise the newcomer while addressing his student. "Birch, your section is on kitchen duty this watch. Once you have reported in you can join your crew mates peeling potatoes."

"Excuse me, sir," said Freddy, going red himself. "Would it be possible for Carl to accompany me to the observatory?"

Almost hidden under his beard, a small smile crossed Commodore Hughes' face. "Did you know you were going to be berthed with us tonight?"

"No, sir, I wasn't sure what was going to happen after the meeting."

"Normally, it would be the duty of one of the senior boys to mentor you through your time here, because newcomers often find the school overwhelming at first. But in this case I think it would be appropriate for Birch to have that honour. What say you, Birch?"

"I'd be very pleased to do that, sir."

"Then report to the Chief and tell him I have given permission. And obtain a lantern from the stores. Castle Hill is steep and unpredictable at night."

The two boys glanced at each other, hardly able to contain their smiles.

"I hadn't realised you were a blondy," whispered Freddy when they were safely out of earshot of the officers.

"It's my curse." Carl grinned, smoothing down his thatch of almost white hair before replacing his cap. "'Towhead' is one of the more complimentary names I gets called."

When they entered his office, the Chief Petty Officer was studying a chart, rocking back and forth on his heels with his back to them.

"Workin' on your sea legs, Chief?" asked Carl, nudging Freddy.

The tall man turned, displaying a luxuriant moustache

which had been pomaded to sharp points at each end.

"Aren't you and your fellow miscreants on spud duty, Birch?"

"The 'eadmaster has given me special permission to *h*escort Mister 'All to the *H*observatory, Chief." Carl smiled.

"If you're lying to me, Birch, I shall have you swabbing the deck of the *Fame* on middle watch with a toothbrush in the altogether."

"It's the God's honest truth."

"And what have you done today to deserve such an accolade?"

"Done my duty, Chief, as always."

The petty officer turned his attention to Freddy. "You realise you've got yourself tethered to one of the cheekiest young whelps this side of the Spanish Main?"

"He's been very kind and looked after me the whole journey."

The Chief narrowed his eyes. "So he didn't pretend to have a fit in the middle of the Thames and start rocking the boat so that you were scared out of your wits?"

Freddy shook his head. "Carl is an officer and a gentleman."

The Chief narrowed his eyes still further and shook his head. "It strikes me that if you two were in the service together, there'd never be a moment's peace for anyone."

"And the headmaster says I can requisition a lantern from the stores," added Carl brightly.

"Is there no end to your brass neck, Birch? Wait while I write out the form in triplicate, otherwise Mr Pepys will want to know the reason why."

Chapter Eleven

A Grave Situation

Alfred Mayhew Cheeseman took the meerschaum out of his mouth for a moment. "Why are you a worm, Blotwell?" he asked, settling both feet on Simon's back.

Donald Sanderson laughed and added another coal to the fire. "You have to admit, A.C., he does make a very good pouffe."

Cheeseman raised and lowered his legs several times, making Simon groan. "Not springy enough, are you, worm?"

Simon closed his eyes and didn't answer, hoping the two house captains would get bored soon and let him go. He had been roused by Sanderson at 6.45 a.m. and taken in his pyjamas to Cheeseman's study on the top floor. Now, it was 7.15, breakfast time, and he was hungry.

"Why is that plebeian day boy hanging about with you, Blotwell? It seems rather perverse, you being a minor member of the aristocracy."

"I think it's my books he likes, and my cakes," murmured Simon.

"Ah, yes, he's one of those swot types, isn't he? Too clever by half. He needs cutting down to size." Cheeseman pressed his boot heels into the small of Simon's back. "The next time you get a cake, worm, you will bring it to me. A plebeian day boy should not be eating aristocratic cake, should he?"

"No, Cheeseman, though he didn't actually eat any of it..."

The School House captain lifted his legs and kicked out at Simon, sending him sprawling across the floor. "Get up, you vermiform slug, and unwrap that painting by the bookcase. And be careful – it cost my father one hundred and twenty guineas."

The picture that Alfred Mayhew Cheeseman was referring to was wrapped in an oilskin cloth, two feet tall by one and a half feet wide. Blotwell undid the string and let the wrapping fall away to reveal a head and shoulders portrait of twenty-one-year-old King Henry XI dressed prematurely in the coronation Robe Royal.

"You weren't brought here to admire it, worm," said Sanderson. "Hang it over the fireplace."

"I can't reach," said Simon.

"Use the stool, you fool," said Cheeseman.

"You're a poet, A.C.," said Sanderson, sniggering.

Simon pushed the three-legged stool near to the open fire. "Shall I take the old one down first?" he asked, looking up at the Italian landscape which was barely visible through layers of grime.

The two older boys regarded one another. "You snivelling, brainless, walking corpse," said Sanderson.

Simon stood on the stool and reached out across the hearth, but he was not close enough to get a grip on the painting. "I'm too far away," he said.

"Then put the stool nearer, dolt."

"But it's hot and I shall burn my feet and pyjama bottoms and Mummy will be cross when Mrs Perkins the housekeeper tells her that my pyjamas are singed."

Cheeseman fetched his birch, which was hanging on the door. "Mummy is not going to be half as cross as I am if you don't get on with it." He flexed the bundle of hazel sticks.

Blotwell pushed the stool nearer the fire and stood on it. He had to have several goes before the old painting came free of its hook, by which time the heat had penetrated through the cloth of his pyjamas to his shins. He swayed and stepped backwards off the stool, barely managing to keep upright.

"If you damage the new painting, Blotwell, you will be flogged to within an inch of your life," said Cheeseman.

Simon took the portrait. "Daddy was invited to Windsor

to pay court to King Henry," he said, stalling for time as his legs and toes still felt hot, "but Mummy didn't go as she had a fit of the vapours..."

"You'll have a fit of the vapours if you aren't on that stool in two seconds flat," said Sanderson.

By some miracle, the cord went over the hook at the first attempt. Blotwell breathed a sigh of relief and half-turned.

"It's not straight, imbecile. Straighten it," said Cheeseman, disappointed at the lack of effort needed.

The two house captains sat in their chairs and proceeded to direct Simon, vying with each other over each minute adjustment.

"Just a quarter of an inch down on the left, worm..."

"Now, a tenth of an inch on the right."

"No, you fool, that's too much!"

They enjoyed their sport until Blotwell let out a scream and fell backwards off the stool, his pyjama bottoms smoking and his feet a livid red.

"Do you think it's straight now?" asked Sanderson, cocking his head first this way then that.

Cheeseman sniggered and blew a smoke ring. "It'll do. Get up, worm, make Sanderson and me some buttered toast, two slices each, and if there is one-tenth of an inch of charcoal on it, we shall both give you a good flogging."

Simon whimpered and rose unsteadily to his feet. Sweat was running off his brow and his legs and toes felt as if they were on fire.

"He never did answer your question, A.C."

"No, he didn't, did he? What a disobedient, disagreeable worm you are, Blotwell."

* * *

The door of study number fifteen opened. Henry Perceval looked up from reading last Sunday's edition of the *Examiner* to see Simon Blotwell, still in his pyjamas, totter into the room and fall face-down onto his bed.

"Where have you been and whatever's the matter? You're as white as a sheet."

Simon stared at him through watery eyes, but said nothing.

Henry stood up and immediately saw what the matter was. Blotwell had been flogged so hard on the buttocks that his pyjamas bottoms had frayed, there were red welts across his skin and the tattered fabric was stippled with blood.

"Oh, I say! This is outrageous. They've gone too far this time. Was it Cheeseman and that Frobisher toady Sanderson?"

Blotwell said nothing, but buried his face in the pillow.

"I shall take you to Matron. You need to have those wounds attended to, and what's that smell of burning?"

"I'm not going," groaned Blotwell. "I'm a worm, I have no spine." He looked up with an unusual expression of defiance. "I burnt their toast... on purpose."

* * *

Freddy opened the louvred shutters of his bedroom window and looked out onto an overcast day. The air smelt of rain and it was cooler than of late. He frowned. Thursday was bathing day for Drake and Raleigh House, when they would all be marched down to the lagoon by the Reverend Croft to wash. Freddy deemed this unnecessary because bathing on Sunday nights in the old tin bath was a ritual for himself and his dad. Still, he consoled himself, he would be able to practise his breast stroke for the gala.

"Freddy! It's time you were downstairs. Your porridge is ready."

"Coming!" No sooner was the word out of his mouth than he blinked, for across the road in the churchyard, a head had popped up above one of the coffin-shaped tombs. He watched as Clarrie May stretched, brushed off her dress, straightened her hair then bent with her hands on her hips and a smile on her face. Freddy's mouth dropped open. Beetle Kipling emerged and, half-hidden behind the tomb, proceeded to pull up his trousers. The couple embraced and kissed and continued to kiss...

"Freddy!" called Daniel.

"Coming!" he shouted, his voice inadvertently carrying over Linbury so that both heads in the churchyard turned towards him. A flurry of activity followed. Freddy blushed and reached for the shutter handles to pull them closed. Clarrie disengaged from her clinch and fled for the lychgate while Beetle, still buttoning his jacket, dashed after her.

Daniel placed a bowl of porridge and a mug of tea in front of his son. "What's the matter with you this morning, Freddy Hall? You look as if you've lost a shilling and found sixpence."

"Nothing," said Freddy. "Just a funny dream."

"You're at that age for funny dreams," observed his dad. "Take no notice of them."

Freddy wasn't sure what his dad was alluding to, so said nothing.

"I've put a towel in your bag," said Daniel. "Don't stay in that water too long either, or you'll catch a chill."

"We won't be too long as we're bathing at the end of the morning this week. It's the inter-house cricket match this afternoon and a lot of bigwigs will be there."

"We've got two guests staying at the inn tonight, from Handley Cross. The Honourable James Brydges and his wife, the Honourable Mrs Constance Brydges. They mentioned the school in their letter."

Freddy smiled. "They sound posh. Better get the best room ready and have Auntie Edie come round to do over the snug."

"Oh my Lord! I think you're right. She's already on call to do the cooking."

"Dad, do you know where I can get a swimming costume?"

"What do you need one of them for? They only hold you

back."

"For the school gala. There'll be ladies present."

Daniel smiled. "I see. Well, I'll see what I can do, but I can't promise anything. Maybe I can speak to one of our ladies to see if they can knit something."

"Thanks, Dad."

***

The mail coach from Larkstone was approaching fast down the hill when Freddy arrived at the school gates.

"Get Master East to look after the mail, will you?" called Mr Hawlings, holding out the keys through the metal bars. "There's a matter that needs my urgent attention."

This was getting quite a regular occurrence: Freddy would be in charge of locking the gates at 8.55 when Mr Topliss rang the bell, and Harry would have to deliver the mail to Miss Chawner, the school secretary, in her office.

Freddy took the keys from the caretaker, who made off down the drive. The coach pulled up, the postilion blowing a note on his post horn to make Freddy jump, preoccupied as he was. Harry clambered down from the seat behind the coachman, who handed him the Seekings mailbag.

"I'm afraid there's no cakes for the greedy boys today," he said.

"Pity," replied Harry and gave a wave as the coach started off westward towards Linbury.

"We're in charge again today, Scud," said Freddy.

"Is the old man..." Harry made a tippling gesture.

"I don't think so. I've got some interesting news..."

"That's funny, so have I."

"Who goes first?"

"Is yours news good or bad?"

"Neither, really. It's just interesting."

"In that case," said Harry, "you go first, because mine will need some clear thought."

Freddy related what he had seen in the churchyard earlier on. "I don't want to split on them, but they were practically doing it in public."

Harry nodded. "If the school finds out, Beetle will be sacked, there's no doubt about that."

"If Mrs Snell was watching through her telescope from the other end of the Green, it'll be all round the houses by noon and Clarrie will become the village whore and there'll be a letter to the doctor."

"Has Mrs S. got a telescope?"

"I was speaking figuratively," replied Freddy.

Harry clapped him on the back. "Well, Federico, my figurative friend, here's my news. Yesterday evening, when the coach pulled into the New Inn, who should I see reeling across the stable yard but Thomas White, late of Seekings School."

"What was he doing?"

"As I said, reeling. Blind drunk, stewed, three sheets to the wind. He was holding an empty bottle of mother's ruin and smelt like a brewer's yard."

"Poor chap. Did you say anything?"

"He came up to me, looked me up and down as if he couldn't quite remember who I was, then put his hands on my shoulders. 'I didn't,' he said."

"I didn't what?" asked Freddy.

"Search me. I tried to unhand him, but he only gripped me tighter and started to cry. It was a bad show, Federico. Talk about embarrassing. Then two of the ostlers from the inn got him by the scruff of the neck and threw him out onto the road, where he proceeded to vomit most of the mother's ruin he had consumed into the gutter."

"Where does he live?"

"Not a clue."

"Maybe we should tell Fouracre. They are friends, after all."

"Were, more like. Who'd want to be friends with a pie-eyed has-been?"

The bell began to toll and at that moment Frank Kennedy came into view, trotting down the path from Clifftop House with his satchel on his back. Harry nudged Freddy, who sniggered. They both entered the school grounds and Freddy made a great play of locking the gates.

Frank ran the last fifty yards and stood on the other side, pink-cheeked and breathless.

"You're too late," said Freddy.

"Oh, Fweddy, don't be like that," chirruped Frank. "Please let me in."

"You know the rules..."

"Mum forgot to bwush my hair and I had to stand in the garden while she did it. She says I can't go to school looking like a scarecwow. That's why I'm late."

"That's no excuse for tardiness, Francis."

"Don't call me Fwancis, Fweddy Hall, I'm Fwank."

"And he's so cute, Federico," crooned Harry. "Can't you make an exception in this case?"

"I am not cute, Hawwy East. My dad says I'm a man's man."

"But you're still a very cute man's man," said Harry. "Go on, Federico..."

Freddy huffed and puffed for a few moments, as if the decision to open up was of major importance. "Oh, all right!" he said finally. "Just this once, mind." He turned the key and swung open the gate. Frank trotted in, grinning and batting his eyelids at them.

"Now then, you cheeky young sprout," said Harry, "Would you like Federico and me to arm-swing you down the drive?"

"Oh, all wight," replied Frank, his grin widening and his eyelids batting some more. "Just this once, mind."

* * *

Mark Fouracre paced his study, scowling as he perused the team sheet for the match that afternoon. Tom White's departure had left him a man short and so far he had been unable to find a replacement to satisfactorily fill the void. It was strange how so many potential players had other obligations to occupy their time. Even Michael Stevenson, the captain of Hawkins House, had cried off, though a broken collar bone incurred during a rugby scrum was one of the better excuses. In addition, having to put up with the untrustworthy, not to say mediocre, talent of Donald Sanderson as vice-captain made the probable humiliation of The Rest by School House all but certain.

He glanced out of the window. A light shower earlier in the morning had given him some hope that the match might be abandoned, but now the clouds had receded and there were patches of blue sky.

A knock at the door did not improve his mood. He huffed as he opened it to indicate his displeasure.

"Fouracre, could I speak to you for a minute?"

"Look, I'm rather busy at the moment, Hall, so if you wouldn't mind coming back later, preferably tomorrow…"

"It's about Tom White," said Freddy.

Fouracre paused, sighed and relented, holding the door open. "Sit down, why don't you?" His hair still wet from the morning's bathing, Freddy sat on the divan and explained about Harry's encounter while Fouracre paced the room, only half-listening and eventually interrupting. "Look, Hall, what has this got to do with me?"

Freddy stopped short. "You're his friend—"

"No, Hall, I am not his friend! Tom White was a loner who had colleagues and acquaintances like me. As far as I know, he didn't make and didn't want any friends."

"But he needs help," said Freddy.

"I need help!" said Fouracre. "I need help to find an all-rounder who is perhaps half as good as Tom White, but who doesn't go around getting drunk and giving away pamphlets containing naked illustrations of the Lady Castlemaine plus inflammatory, treasonous messages about the Royal Family in general!"

"Oh," said Freddy.

"Yes, oh," replied Fouracre. "Now if that's all..."

"Maybe Scud could play for you?"

Fouracre sighed, trying to be patient, but failing. "East is in the lower remove. The teams consist of fifth-formers and above."

"Shall I ask him?"

Mark Fouracre closed his eyes and forced himself to calm down. It occurred to him that Harry East would probably be no worse than any of the other prospects he'd got in mind and it would save him a few more hours of stress.

"All right, Hall. Send him up if he wants to play. Thank you."

Freddy rose from the divan. "Don't mention it."

* * *

Four hours later, Mark Fouracre stood at square leg, hands on hips, wishing the ground would swallow him up. It was as bad as he'd feared. Of course, the whole school was present and not just the school either. Dr Butler had invited the governors, old boys and local dignitaries to watch the annual event. A marquee had been erected for their comfort and he hoped most of them were inside eating scones, sipping tea or quaffing fruit punch.

School House were 256 for eight wickets. If they got to 270, it would be a record score, beating the 269 made by a former eleven in 1799. Cheeseman was on ninety-three and his current batting partner, Sam Meredith, a lower sixth-former, who was a useful spin bowler, was on six.

There had been five dropped catches, including two by Sanderson, who had fumbled an easy one from Cheeseman when he was on twenty-seven, and fourteen no-balls which had contributed fifty-two of the runs, including two sixes. It was a depressing liturgy, made worse by the fact that Gus

Gilmore, who had taken four of the School House wickets for a mere forty-six runs, had been carried off the field after being in a collision with Cheeseman, who had 'accidentally' managed to strike him on the head with his bat.

Fouracre was certain that Cheeseman would declare as soon as the team reached 270 – and, more importantly, he had reached his century. Then there would be a ten-minute break before The Rest had their innings. Without White and Gilmore, it was a grim prospect, and this clouded his mind so that he heard the next delivery hitting the bat rather than saw it. The ball went straight through his legs to a mass groan from the spectators, and he turned to watch helplessly as it ran on and bounced over the boundary rope before the outfielder could stop it. Cheeseman chuckled. He was now on ninety-seven.

"Over," called the Reverend Croft who was umpiring, along with Mr Williams, the music master.

"Sorry," said Mark apologetically to his teammates as they crossed to their fielding positions. He threw the ball to Jack Marriott, a ginger-haired boy in the lower sixth who was a medium fast, if somewhat erratic, bowler. "See what you can do, Jack."

Sam Meredith tapped the ground with his bat, waiting for the opposition to get to their positions.

Marriott came in with four steps. The ball bounced once and the bails went flying. A cheer went up, quickly stifled as Mr Williams called, "No ball" with his usual precise diction and whispered, "Front foot."

Meredith smiled and raised his eyebrows at Marriott, who shook his head. There wasn't much luck going for The Rest today. There were still six balls of the over remaining and School House were now on 261 for eight.

This time Marriott took three steps. His front foot landed correctly, the ball bounced once in the middle of the pitch and was rising again as Meredith went forward. The ball hit the bat two-thirds of the way up and came straight back to the bowler, who caught it cleanly. Mr Williams raised his finger. Sam Meredith was out.

"Idiot," mouthed Cheeseman, who would now have to rely on Allan Quartermain not to get out before he could receive again. He gazed over to where his father was standing, a glass of punch in his hand, talking to Mr King, hoping his triumph would be appreciated.

Quartermain, an upper sixth-former who was on course for a place at Oxford, was short and wiry with a dark beard. He had been chosen for the team because of his fast and accurate bowling, not because of his batting skills, which were those of a proficient tail-ender.

"Middle and leg," he said, holding the bat sideways in front of the wicket. Mr Williams gestured for him to move the bat an inch towards the middle stump then nodded his approval.

Marriott ran up and bowled a full toss. Quartermain connected, sweeping the ball up over the bowler's head, over the heads of the fielders and over the boundary for six. A cheer rose from the spectators. Quartermain took off his cap to acknowledge the applause and to register his surprise. Mark Fouracre sighed inwardly.

Quartermain flashed at the next ball and missed. In turn, the ball missed the off stump by only a couple of inches. Cheeseman gestured at his partner to concentrate. With just three more balls of this over remaining, the glory of a century and school sporting history would soon be his.

Jack Marriott bowled what he hoped was going to be a Yorker, with the intention that the ball would land at the batsman's feet, but it turned out to be a good length, and Quartermain managed to turn it and send it towards mid-wicket.

"Two!" he called, annoying Cheeseman, who only wanted to run one.

Two hundred and sixty-nine for nine, equalling the record score.

"How many left?" asked Marriott, who had lost count.

"Two," said Mr Williams, feeling the remaining pebbles in his left pocket.

Cheeseman glared down the wicket at his partner, who was mature enough to take no notice.

Marriott took a short run and bowled a bouncer. Quartermain swung at the ball and the bat connected powerfully but not cleanly. It travelled in an arc over Donald Sanderson at mid-on, heading for long-on where there was no fielder. Mark Fouracre watched with a mixture of disbelief and misery: he had let his side down once again by not placing a man there. It seemed certain that the ball would hit the ground and travel for a few more yards over the boundary for four. Cheeseman was smiling again. He and Quartermain didn't even bother to run.

But no one had reckoned on Harry 'Scud' East racing like the wind in a fifty-yard dash from long-off where he had been positioned by Fouracre to keep him out of the way. Now the ball was coming down fast. Harry threw himself the last few yards and felt his hands close around the ball. Keeping a tight grip, he hit the ground hard, scraping the skin from his knees and elbows, even through his whites. But he held on to the ball. A roar went up from the crowd as he stood up and raised the ball above his head. Mr Williams gave Quartermain out. School House's inning was over.

No one would remember Cheeseman's ninety-seven. No one would remember that The Rest lost the game by five wickets. Instead, they would remember the miraculous running catch by young Harry East from the lower remove. Alfred Mayhew Cheeseman threw down his bat and vowed revenge on those responsible.

His teammates crowded round to congratulate Harry, especially Jack Marriott, who could now claim two wickets in one over. Mark Fouracre shook Harry's hand. Then, like a good sportsman, Allan Quartermain came up and shook his hand too.

Looking on from the crowd, Freddy Hall beamed with delight as if he had made the catch himself.

Chapter Twelve

Greenwich Mean Time

1st December 1825. Late afternoon.

"Welcome to Flamsteed House, Master Hall. I am Mr Newton's secretary, Nicolas Fatio de Duillier."

They shook hands. Monsieur Duillier was twenty-five years old, much younger than Freddy had expected. The building too was not as he expected. It was smaller, not much bigger than the Sailor's Yarn. The interior was uncluttered and elegant with large windows, even in the living quarters.

"How do you do," said Freddy. "This is Carl Birch from the school. I hope you don't mind him being here too – he's looking after me during my stay."

Carl doffed his cap and Monsieur Duillier nodded. "A pleasure, Master Birch. It is not often that we get to know individuals from the Hospital School. Come, both of you. I have a little refreshment for you. Mr Newton is in the Octagon Room and will see you shortly."

They sat together on dining chairs upholstered in red velvet around a small eight-sided table.

Monsieur Duillier poured tea out of a silver teapot. "All the decorative items that would normally be circular are eight-sided in the observatory. A small conceit of our architect. Help yourself to cream and sugar, and do try these biscuits and tell me what you think. They are called Mailänderli, and they remind me of home."

"Where is your home, Monsieur Duillier?" asked Freddy.

"I am from the Republic of Geneva, though you may know it better as part of Switzerland."

"Nice biscuits," said Carl – almost the first words he had spoken.

"Hmm, lemony," said Freddy.

"Ah yes – butter, sugar, flour, eggs and lemon. My mother used to bake them at Christmas-time. A family favourite. I'm afraid my poor efforts do not compare with hers."

"We could bake these in the school kitchen for Christmas," said Carl.

"Then I shall give you the recipe, Master Birch, and you must bring along a sample to see how they compare to mine."

A bell rang. Monsieur Duillier looked up at the chronometer on the wall and then at Freddy. "Five minutes late. Not bad for Mr Newton. Now, Master Hall, a word of advice. The great man can seem rather short – some have even called him rude – but it is just his way. He is of a melancholy disposition and choleric by nature, so do not be offended. Knock and enter while Master Birch and I get to know each other a little better."

Freddy had half-hoped that Carl could go with him, but it was not to be. He steeled himself and entered the Octagon Room as instructed. The first thing he noticed was Mr Newton himself, standing at a cloth-covered table bathed in the light from a brazier which stood on a stone slab. Whether this was there to merely provide heat and light or had some other purpose, was not clear. Mr Newton had the fingers of his right hand immersed in a crucible while in his left he held a pen poised above a notebook. He was a little taller than Freddy. His brown hair hung down to his shoulders and was streaked with grey.

Freddy glanced around the plainly furnished room. It was indeed octagonal, with a very high ceiling. Numerous clocks and chronometers hung on or stood against the walls and, combined to make a discordant noise. A sextant was positioned at one window and a long thin telescope looked out of the one opposite.

"Hall, come over here into the light where I can see you."

Freddy advanced to the table. There, he could see that the open pages of the notebook were filled with diagrams and small, neat handwriting.

Newton turned to face him. "You know of the transmutation of light into its primary colours?"

"Yes, sir – red, green and blue."

"And the complementary colours?"

"Cyan, yellow and magenta."

"Do you believe that metals can be transmuted in the same way as light?"

"I have never heard it done, sir."

"Don't try to be clever with me, Hall. Just answer the question."

"I don't believe that a metal can be transmuted into another metal, no."

"Then you are a fool. One day we shall be able to take the atoms from one metal and twist and turn them into another." He withdrew his fingers from the crucible and shook drops of mercury onto the cloth. "At my suggestion, your moon has been named Erebus by the Astronomical Society. Do you approve?"

"Yes, sir, it's very appropriate. Perhaps the next one could be called Nyx."

"So you think more moons revolve around Thanatos?"

"Most worlds have more than one."

"You were using one of Short's telescopes?"

"Yes sir, from 1759. The speculum mirrors needed polishing."

"I expect they did. Be certain to watch the lunar eclipse next year on 21st May. It promises to be of particular interest."

"I've already made a note of it in my diary, sir."

Mr Newton almost smiled. "Did you know that Duillier is a master of lens grinding?"

"No sir, but he seems a very nice gentleman."

"Meaning, I don't?"

"No, sir, I never meant that!"

"Mean what you say and say what you mean, Hall. You are going to this school in the wilderness, is that true?"

"It's in Dorsetshire, sir, near my home. Not really a wilderness."

"It is in the wilderness of scientific thought. You will be under the tutelage of that fraud, Hooke. That liar, cheat and abomination! A believer in the divine right of kings!"

"I haven't met Mr Hooke yet."

"Then you are lucky. Do you believe that King Henry has the ear of God, that he is above the law?"

"No sir, he is a man like you and I."

"They want me to become a lackey of theirs, you know. It would serve me well, but I have a mind not to be."

"Lackey is not a position to be taken lightly."

Mr Newton made a noise that might have been a chuckle. "You may go now, Mr Hall. I shall call you again to review your progress. I do not accept failure."

"I shall do my best for both of us, sir."

"See you do, and keep your sights raised above petty politics. One feat that I am unable to accomplish."

Both Monsieur Duillier and Carl laughed when Freddy emerged from the Octagon and blew a sigh of relief.

"Come, Master Hall, a cup of tea will restore your equilibrium."

Freddy sat at the table and drank two more cups of tea and ate three Mailänderli.

"Master Birch was telling me that you didn't speak to each other for the first hour of your journey to Greenwich."

Freddy looked at Carl and grinned. "That seems like a long time ago now, though it was only a few hours."

"In my experience, many friendships have difficult births," said Monsieur Duillier with a smile. "Now, since Mr Newton is not a raging sea at this moment, it seems you have made a good enough impression. Therefore I can inform you that an account will be opened for you at Coutts & Co. on the Strand and the sum of £100 will be deposited there each 1st January for the next five years. Seekings School will have a standing order on the amount, but any excess is yours to do with as you see fit. Coutts will send you a chequebook and an annual statement."

"I can barely believe this is happening to me," said Freddy. "Thank you, Monsieur Duillier, and of course Mr Newton as well."

"Coo!" murmured Carl. "One hundred quid..."

"Of which 90% or more will be spent on school fees," responded Monsieur Duillier.

"I wonder how much it is to keep me at the RNHS. About tuppence, I shouldn't wonder."

"You do yourself and the school an injustice, Master Birch. There have been many large charitable donations to keep the Hospital afloat, including an annual amount from the Navy. Now, Master Hall, I have a little gift for you that Mr Newton and I thought apropos to your studies."

Monsieur Duillier rose and went over to an escritoire. "There you are," he said on his return.

Freddy pulled out a double-hinged strip of metal from its cloth envelope. "Oh! Why, thank you, sir," he said. "It's perfect."

"What is it?" asked Carl.

"It's a rule," said Freddy, opening it out. "Look, it has the French system on one side and the Albion system on the other."

"Why do we need two systems?"

"We don't," answered Freddy, "and the French system is more logical. It is based on ten, not twelve. This length is one metre, or three feet three inches, approximately."

"The pride of nations can stifle scientific progress," commented Monsieur Duillier. "Now, it is almost time for us to part ways. But first I have something to give you, Master Birch."

* * *

Freddy and Carl walked down the hill towards the school, the light from their lantern illuminating the grass, which was covered in a layer of frost. The sky was obscured by cloud which intensified the darkness and a light mist hung in the air.

"Coo, I'm ready for me tea," said Carl. "We should make it back just in time."

"What a day I've had," said Freddy.

"You'll remember it for the rest of your life."

"I shall, without a doubt," he said, gripping his bag tightly and thinking of the rule he had been given.

"What was Mr Newton like, Freddy?"

"Fierce."

"I don't suppose he knows much about kids, being a bachelor and all that."

"He didn't give any quarter, that's for sure."

"When I seen 'im on the parade ground with Mr Pepys, I noticed that he can't keep still. He's always fidgeting and jiggling."

"Are you going to make those biscuits from the recipe Monsieur Duillier gave you?"

"If the boys like them when I pass around the samples he gave me, yes."

"I think they will."

Conversation lapsed as the buildings of the Royal Hospital School loomed out of the darkness. Carl led Freddy along the colonnade to the east wing of the school.

"It's very quiet," whispered Freddy.

"It won't be," said Carl with a grin.

They passed along several short corridors and through a series of double doors until Carl pushed open a final door, where they were met with a wall of warmth and noise. Row upon row of boys in sailor suits sat on forms eight abreast at long trestle tables, either side of a central aisle which seemed to stretch away to infinity. Carl doffed his hat and beckoned Freddy to follow.

The great room with its symmetrical lines and clerestory

windows looked like a cathedral to the boy from Linbury, though the nearest he had come to a real cathedral was the school chapel on his visit to Seekings.

As Carl walked confidently down the aisle he was met by good-natured jeers from all sides. At intervals older men in naval uniforms, positioned to supervise the pupils, nodded as he passed. Nervous and overawed, Freddy followed close behind, noticing that four adjacent tables, two on each side of the aisle, were empty, meaning that sixty-four boys were absent, though places were set out for them with bowl, tumbler, knife, fork and spoon and a jug of milk.

"Here we are," said Carl at last, having walked almost two-thirds the length of the dining hall. "My section. Hutch up, boys, make room for two."

Fifteen expectant faces turned towards Freddy, who felt his cheeks reddening. Carl pushed his way onto the bench, making room for Freddy on the end. "Don't worry, you'll get a bowl and some cutlery."

"Who's this, then?" asked one of the boys.

"This is Freddy Hall from Dorsetshire. That's not far from Portsmouth. He's just been up to the observatory to see Mr Newton and I went with him."

"Skiving off your kitchen duties," said another boy.

Carl smirked. "Shut up, Charlie."

Freddy nudged Carl and murmured, "Aren't you going to introduce them?"

"Oops, manners..." Carl pointed to each boy in turn and rattled off their names so quickly that Freddy still wasn't certain who was who.

"Why are there four empty tables?" he asked, pointing down the aisle.

"You'll see in a minute," answered Carl.

"What part of Dorsetshire are you from?"

Freddy looked diagonally across the table. "Are you... Pete?"

The boy smiled at him and nodded. "Pete Walker. I used to

live in Thieves' Wood – do you know it?"

"It's just up the road from Linbury, where I live."

"We used to go shopping either in Linbury or in the market town of Dunhambury." For a few moments, Pete's face stilled, as if he were revisiting those times in his mind's eye.

A bell rang and the cavernous room went silent. An officer walked up the aisle to the mid-point, looked around to see that everyone was paying attention, and bowed his head. All the boys bowed their heads too and some put their hands together.

The officer's voice carried from one end of the refectory to the other. "For what we are about to receive, may the Lord make us truly thankful."

There was a moment's silence then the boys picked up their spoons and drummed them on the tables in a ritualistic fashion, accompanied by whoops, laughter and general chatter. Suddenly, the sixty-four missing boys appeared through the double doors, pushing thirty-two trolleys loaded with large pans and a stack of bread.

On the double they came down the aisle, spacing themselves out equally then serving out the food. Each table got a plate of watercress and a loaf of bread. One boy from each table began to saw the bread into eight equal pieces.

"Are you Freddy?" asked their server. When Freddy nodded, the boy picked up a bowl from the lower shelf of the trolley and set it and a spoon before him. "Chef's special," he said with a smile.

"Thank you," said Freddy, touched by how friendly everyone was.

The other boys hooted good-naturedly at him. "Special treatment," said Charlie. But the food Freddy got was exactly the same as everyone else: haddock hotpot – layers of haddock, potatoes, carrots and onions in a rich fish stock thickened with flour and butter.

Carl handed him the plate of watercress. "Got iron in it," he said.

Freddy took a handful and put it in the stew. "I didn't

expect the food to be so nice," he said.

"That's cos we grows it and cooks it," said a boy named John Fairbrother.

"Except the fish," said Pete. "That comes from the market."

"They are really quick at serving," said Freddy.

"If they weren't, by the time they'd finished their food would be cold," said Carl.

The hotpot was followed by steamed apple dumplings. Freddy poured some of his milk over his and half of the boys noticed and followed suit. After the meal was over, a second group of sixty-four boys began to clear away while the rest made themselves comfortable, leaning against one another and dozing.

"Have you ever slept in a hammock, Freddy?" asked Carl.

"Never."

"Well, tonight's the night. It's one of the ways they make us think we're on board ship."

"Do we sleep in the *Fame*?"

"You guessed it."

"Will I fall out?"

The other boys who were not half-asleep laughed.

"Not with me there you won't."

"Unless we tip him out," said Charlie.

Carl beat his fist into his palm at Charlie.

One of the officers came along and handed John a letter. "Your lucky day, Fairbrother," he said.

Freddy looked round to see that other envelopes were being distributed, though it was a small percentage compared to the number of boys present. John opened the letter with trembling fingers and scanned quickly through it.

"Go on – tell us what it says," said a chorus of voices.

"All right," said John.

Every boy at the table was now paying attention, craning towards the letter.

"It's from my sister in Westford.

My dearest John,

I hope you are keeping well and that you are doing your studies to the satisfaction of the school.

I have some good news to impart to you being that I am expecting, and that William and I are overjoyed at the prospect. We don't mind if it's a little boy or a little girl, though I think Wm would treasure a son. If it is a little boy we thought to name him John, after you, my beloved brother..."

John sniffed and paused to wipe his eyes and nose on his sleeve.

"Go on, John, you're doing good," said Charlie quietly.

"By the Grace of God, the child is due on Ash Wednesday next year, so we are hoping it will be born in time for pancakes (jest). You will be invited to the christening, of course, and we shall send you the fare to Westford, so you needn't worry.

It is a little early, but Wm and I would like to wish you and all your friends in Greenwich a very Happy Christmas – and just to tell you, there may be a little gift on its way.

Your ever loving sister,

Ellen Lacey"

* * *

Freddy felt the gentle rocking of the boat and snuffled contentedly in his sleep. A cool breeze blew on his face but the rest of him was warm and comfortable. From far away, he heard laughter. He smiled. The laughter grew louder and he opened one eye.

Carl looked down on him, surrounded by the smiling faces of his friends.

"You was well away there, Freddy."

"He's a natural in a hammock," said John.

"Were you rocking me?" asked Freddy.

"Like a baby in a cradle."

"What time is it?"

"Past reveille, so hurry up or we'll miss the tide an', more important, miss breakfast."

Ten minutes later they filed into the refectory where they joined a long line to be served toast and dripping with a spoon of greengage preserve and an enamelled mug of tea.

After breakfast, Freddy said goodbye to the boys and he and Carl walked out of the Hospital grounds, past *Fame* and onto the jetty where the rowing boat was moored. More confident in the morning light, Freddy stepped in and stowed his bag. Carl pointed across the river to where the chaise was already waiting.

"Better get a move on, or posti will give me hell," he said.

The journey across was as uneventful as the trip the night before, though Freddy realised how busy the river was. Merchantmen, tugs, traders and barges, some in full sail, crossed their path. It seemed to him that a lot more skill than just rowing was required to navigate it.

"Was there this much traffic last night?"

Carl laughed as he pulled on the oars. "Nearly, but fortunately you didn't notice."

When they reached the north bank, Freddy stepped out of the boat and onto the jetty, nodding at the postilion, who ignored him. He turned to Carl, expecting him to be by his side, but he was still in the boat. Suddenly Freddy realised and felt a tug on his heart. "I thought you'd be coming back with me."

Carl shook his head. "Wish I could, but I done my duty and that's that."

Freddy was lost for words for a few moments, then he blurted, "Can I write to you, Carl?"

The sailor boy looked at him. "You really want to write to me?"

Freddy nodded.

Carl stepped onto the jetty, keeping hold of the mooring line, and gave Freddy a hug. Then they shook hands. "You're a good shipmate, Freddy Hall. You know, I'm not good with a pen meself, but me and the boys love getting letters."

"Then I'll write," promised Freddy, "and don't bother about writing back, or if you do just sign your name."

Carl chuckled. "That's about all I can manage."

"Are you two lovebirds going to bill and coo at each other all day?" said the postilion.

"Oh posti," said Carl, "did you get out of bed on the wrong side today? Oh no, of course not, cos you gets out on the wrong side of the bed *every* day."

"Less of your cheek, Birch. I've been ordered to take this one all the way back to Walminster. Which I can tell you severely brasses me off."

Carl sniggered. "Another feather in your cap, Freddy – brassing off posti. Ta-ta, mate, have a good journey and watch out for them highwaymen."

As the chaise pulled away, Freddy looked back out of the window and waved at Carl who grinned and raised his cap high over his head in a farewell salute.

Chapter Thirteen

Deliver Us from Evil

Simon Blotwell was snoozing on one of the two beds in the school infirmary when he was disturbed by a door banging.

Botheration! he said to himself. *How inconsiderate, and it's only just getting light.*

He was lying on his stomach, still uncomfortable despite the calendula poultice Matron had applied to his bottom. Still, it had relieved most of the sting and soreness of the birch and enabled him to get a good night's sleep. The door banged again and this time there were voices – raised voices. Simon lifted his head to listen.

"Matron, I am a very busy man and don't take kindly to being summoned, especially at this hour of the morning."

Blotwell recognised the speaker but couldn't yet put a name to him.

"I didn't summon you. I merely asked the deputy headmaster if he minded me requesting that you attend one of your boys, who has suffered a grievous injury at the hands of what I can only describe as a sadist."

"Matron, I know English isn't your first language, but please be careful what you say. And please tell your girl to leave. I don't want our conversation broadcast to the whole of Dorsetshire."

"Betty, would you mind going down to the store cupboard and fetching some clean bed linen?"

"Yes, ma'am."

Betty Golightly is a common working girl with very cold

fingers, mused Blotwell, moving onto his left side so that he might better hear the exchange.

"If you think I'm exaggerating, you can follow me to the ward and examine the patient for yourself."

Oh! I hope not, thought Blotwell. *Having my body inspected by persons or persons unknown is not something to be encouraged.*

"I don't think that will be necessary. It is your job to look after the malingerers – I mean, patients – and set them on their feet again."

"So they can be brutally mistreated once more."

Blotwell smiled. *She's laying it on a bit thick.*

"I don't think I like your tone, Matron. I'm the school housemaster, not a nanny. If they can't stay on the straight and narrow, the boys must learn self-discipline through being disciplined. Seekings School is not some namby-pamby institution for delicate girls. Albion needs men and leaders of men, and that is what this school provides."

I doubt Matron will get much change out of Mr King.

"I trust you will at least reprimand these young men for their disgusting behaviour?"

"Which young men?"

"Alfred Cheeseman and Donald Sanderson."

"I shall do no such thing. Sanderson isn't in my house and Cheeseman is going to be elected school captain. A post he most richly deserves, especially now that treacherous drunk has been expelled."

"If he is appointed, it will be a travesty, Mr King."

"No, Matron, it will be in the best interest of Seekings given that his father, Gerald Cheeseman, is the MP for Dorsetshire North. He's a staunch Royalist and a strong advocate for this school."

"Dorsetshire North – isn't that one of your rotten boroughs with two MPs and ten voters?"

"I shall treat that with contempt it deserves."

"And what of Blotwell, the boy he so mercilessly thrashed?"

"Hah! Now you have put your finger on it, Matron. Blotwell is a sneak, a liar, a nancy boy who will walk the primrose path. His father has stated categorically that he needs strong discipline to keep him in check and has given the school a free hand in delivering that discipline."

"Perhaps if his father could see the injuries..."

Blotwell sighed. *No, no, he'd be only too happy to congratulate Cheeseman and give you a good telling-off.*

"Matron, why have you taken the word of this fabricator, who would betray Jesus Christ for half the amount Judas was paid?"

That's not true. I love Jesus – just ask the Reverend McKellan.

"Blotwell was not the one to report your house captain, Mr King."

"Then who did report him?"

"I don't think I shall divulge that."

It was Henry. For some reason he was angrier than I was.

"Matron, some people in this school think you're a Silesian sympathiser. There are those that actually think you are a Silesian. Even your name is very Silesian, Mrs Amfortas..."

Amfortas? No wonder she talks strangely – like that treacherous drunk, Tom White.

"I am from the kingdom of Bavaria, and have a Bavarian name."

"Ah yes, the kingdom ruled by the mad king allied to Silesia."

"Bavaria has a non-aggression pact with Silesia, that is all."

"You sow discord among masters and pupils like confetti, Matron..."

"This is nonsense, Mr King, and you know it. I shall have to speak to the headmaster if you do not do something about the outrageous behaviour of those two sadists."

"The doctor is not inclined to listen to hysterical tittle-tattle, Matron, and even if he were, it would be foolish in these troubled times. We are beset by threats from our enemies at home and abroad, and so punishing two patriotic young men of Albion, especially after they were deceived by the traitorous White, would be tantamount to a dereliction of duty on his part."

"You are losing your reason, Mr King."

"And you, Mrs Amfortas, are very likely to lose your job. I wish you a very good day!"

The outer door of the infirmary slammed shut. A minute or so later, Matron entered the ward where Simon lay feigning sleep. She drew the curtains to let in the morning light and turned to her patient, who opened a bleary eye.

"How are you feeling today, Blotwell?"

Simon noticed that, except for a nervous tremor in her hands, Matron was largely unruffled by her confrontation. "Oh, a little better, Matron, thank you. But I am much too poorly to attend lessons..."

"Would you like breakfast?"

He smiled wanly at her. "Oh, yes please. I think I could manage two slices of toast spread with butter and orange marmalade, and perhaps a milky cup of hot chocolate..."

"I shall see what I can do."

Blotwell decided that he quite liked Matron, even though she was a Bavarian.

***

When Freddy opened the shutters of his bedroom that Friday morning, there was, thankfully, no sign of Beetle or Clarrie in the churchyard, though he did catch sight of Clarrie's mother delivering milk to Doughy and Maisie Hood's cottage on the other side of the green. He leaned out and looked to his left down Main Street where Mrs Pattle was, as ever, sweeping the frontage of her shop.

"You'll fall out of there one of these days, Freddy Hall," she called.

He waved and smiled at her then ducked back inside.

After folding back his blankets to allow the bed to air, he shook off his nightshirt and dressed quickly, then sat down at his desk to write a letter to Carl about the cricket match yesterday.

Fifteen minutes later his dad called him down to breakfast, where tea and a poached egg on toast were waiting. Freddy handed over the sealed envelope.

"You'll bankrupt me with all these letters you keep sending that lad, who never sends a reply."

"I got one," replied Freddy.

"Yes, a month ago, and it was all of three lines long."

"I like telling him my news."

Daniel smiled at his son. "I know you do, lad, and I expect he likes to hear it too."

"Have our guests gone?"

His dad shook his head. "They've decided to stay another night, to view the seashore, according to Mrs Brydges. I've a mind that they might be interested in your old rocks."

"Fossils," corrected Freddy. "Are we getting Auntie Edie again then?"

"She's already in the scullery washing up after last night, then she's doing eggs and bacon for their breakfast. And for dinner..." Daniel nodded and smiled, "we could be treated to a couple of roast pullets with all the trimmings."

Freddy's eyes lit up.

**

Mr S.G. Dearman, known as S.G. to boys and masters alike, was the teacher of mathematics at Seekings School and had been for some considerable time. His lessons had an eccentricity that some found endearing, while others found infuriating. For instance, boys were encouraged to correct S.G. when he made an intentional – or sometimes unintentional – error and the pupil with the most corrections at the end of the lesson was rewarded with a chewy caramel.

It very much depended on Freddy's mood whether he found the master endearing or infuriating, but because he had a naturally even-tempered disposition he generally sided with the former.

"Today," boomed Mr Dearman, "we shall concentrate on the triangle. Not the delightful, feminine ping-ping of a musical triangle, but the robustly masculine triangle of Pythagoras. As everyone knows, Pythagoras is an Egyptian boat-builder who lives on a barge on the River Severn…"

Among several others, Gerry Gilmore languidly raised his hand.

"Do you have a point to make, G.G., my good friend?" enquired S.G.

"He was a Greek philosopher, sir, with the emphasis on *was*."

"I do believe you're right. I don't know what came over me."

Gerry and Freddy exchanged smiles while their master wrote on the board *Gilmore 1*, then proceeded to draw a triangle which he tapped with his short cane. "Pythagoras stated that the square on the hypotenuse is equal to the sum of the squares on the other two sides…"

Freddy looked round the class. Seeing that no one else had bothered to put up their hand, raised his.

"Do you have something to say, Maestro Hall?"

"It has to be a right-angle triangle, sir."

"Well, aren't you the clever one? No wonder Mr Newton was so impressed." Mr Dearman wrote *Hall 1* on the board, having made the same comment in every lesson since Freddy had arrived at the school.

Twenty-five minutes later, the blackboard was covered with a mixture of boys' names and the proof of Pythagoras' theorem.

Mr Dearman surveyed his class with a kindly beneficence then wrote *QED* along the bottom with such a flourish that it splintered his stick of chalk. "*Quad ergo demonstrandum*," he said triumphantly, not seeming to notice the crunch beneath his feet as he pulverised the errant pieces of chalk.

Adam Wakefield raised his hand for the first time in the lesson. "Excuse me, sir, shouldn't that be *Quad erat demonstrandum*, that which was to be proved?"

"I'm so glad you're awake, Wakefield," said S.G., apparently not noticing the sighs at another oft-repeated comment.

His stub of chalk was poised to write *Wakefield 1* when he paused, having noticed the large, but unusually silent, figure of James Carstairs at the back of the room. "Why, J.C., you have returned from your sojourn in sick bay."

"Yes, sir," Carstairs replied in a doleful voice.

"Then why the long face? I thought you'd be full of the joys of spring. Or are you still sick?"

"Sick of someone," came the reply.

At this Freddy turned in his seat. Next to Carstairs, the diminutive figure of Frank Kennedy sat in a huddle, his face as crestfallen as his friend, his chin almost touching his chest.

"Looks like Large and Little have had a bust-up," whispered Gerry Gilmore.

Freddy nodded and at that moment the bell rang for the end of the period.

"You may go," boomed Mr Dearman. "Prep, in case you haven't guessed, is committing to memory the gracious Greek's theorem. A caramel for you, Jennings, with a score of five." S.G. tossed the sweet towards the boy. "And one for your school housemate, Blotwell, J.J. Do tell him to get well soon. I so miss his indolence." Jennings caught the second sweet and nodded.

Three-quarters of an hour later, after a period of Latin grammar spent with Mr Caulton-Harris in school room number three, the shell contingent filed out of the osher to enjoy fifteen minutes' relaxation in the sunshine along with the other 170 or so boys at Seekings.

"Why are you wandering instead of lying on the grass?"

asked Harry, who had spotted Freddy marching along the path between school and Frobisher House.

"I was looking for Frank."

"Why?"

"Because he's fallen out with Carstairs."

"Isn't that the way of small children?" asked Harry. "And why should you be bothered?"

"Something's not right, Scud. I can feel it."

"You know, Federico, if I look ahead five years, I can see you as school captain with the weight of every pupil's woes on your shoulders."

"The much more likely scenario is that Harry East will be school captain, because of his athletic prowess and his all-round decency," replied Freddy flatly.

"All right, I give in. Let's go and find the little termite."

They found Frank sitting against a retaining wall in the shadow of Raleigh House, his knees pulled up and his head lolling.

"What's the matter, Francis?" asked Freddy, sitting to one side of him while Harry sat on the other.

When he made no attempt to correct them, they knew that something was up. "Come on, Frank," coaxed Harry. "You've fallen out with Carstairs, or more likely he's fallen out with you."

"He doesn't like me any more."

"Why is that?"

Frank spoke in a whisper. "Because I got White the sack."

"I doubt it," said Harry.

"How did you manage that?" asked Freddy.

"I gave the naked lady picture to Mr Tallow and now Waleigh have got Jewemy Pincher who is as useless as a dead fwog in a jam sandwich and lets all the bullies wun wild."

Freddy and Harry exchanged bemused glances over Frank's head.

"We're not quite understanding you, Frank. Where did the naked lady picture come from?"

"Wight gave it to me to give to Mr Tallow. He said I should tell Mr Tallow the twuth, if he asked where I got it."

"Tom White gave you a picture of a naked lady to give to Mr Tallow and wanted you to tell him who you got it from?" said Freddy.

"It's not making much sense to me," said Harry.

"Yes, only it was Bert Wight not Tom White."

"You mean Berty Wright, your tea-maker, gave you the picture of a naked lady and told you to tell Mr Tallow that Tom White gave it to you?"

"No, that wasn't the twuth. He told me to tell the twuth – that Wight gave it to me."

"I think I'm beginning to see a chink of light," said Freddy.

"Wright, White, light? If you can shine a bit of it this way, I'd be grateful," said Harry.

"What did Mr Tallow do when you showed him the picture?" asked Freddy.

"He went wed in the face, then asked me where I got it. I told him the twuth and said Wight gave it to me and then he got angwy and stormed out of Dwake."

"Did he say anything after he got angry?"

"He said 'I knew that Bwiton was the enemy within'."

Freddy looked at Harry. "What's going on here, Scud?"

Harry raised his eyebrows. "You're asking me? I got lost about ten minutes ago."

"We've got to talk to Wright," said Freddy.

"He's a fifth-former. He won't speak to a shell boy or even me."

The large and formidable figure, for a boy just turned eleven, of James Carstairs hove into view around the corner of Raleigh House. He walked purposefully up to his erstwhile friend.

"Are you as miserable as I am?"

Frank nodded and looked up at him. "I didn't mean to get White the sack, Carstairs. I'm sowwy that you've now got Jewemy Pincher, who is as useless as a dead fwog in a jam sandwich."

Carstairs sniggered. "He looks like a dead frog too."

Frank giggled. "Oh, Carstairs! That's not a vewy nice thing to say."

"I think I'll forgive you, like the Bible wants us to," Carstairs said, offering his hand. "It's better than feeling sad."

Frank took his hand and was pulled to his feet as if he weighed little more than a farthing. "Forgive us our twespassers, as we forgive them that twespass against us..." he said, all smiles again.

"I've got something to tell you, but it's a secret," whispered Carstairs.

"Ooo, I like secwets, and I pwomise I won't tell..."

The two youngsters walked off, chatting to each other, oblivious of the two older boys they'd left behind.

"Well, there we are, glad we could help, thank you..." said Harry. "Now what?"

* * *

Freddy entered the snug room of the Sailor's Yarn dressed in a clean white apron with his hair brushed and his nails scrubbed. "Good evening sir, madam, would you care for some wine with your dinner?"

The Right Honourable Mr James Brydges was a heavily built man with a double chin which wobbled when he spoke. "Do you have the grape, or the rustic variety?"

At the latest meeting of the Licensed Victuallers' Association at the Bell Inn, Tadcaster, his dad had been given two complimentary bottles, a claret from Bordeaux and a sherry from Cádiz, which Freddy duly described. "We also have the elderberry from our own country."

Mr Brydges frowned. "What do you think, my dear? Will it have turned to vinegar?"

Constance Brydges gave a bird-like laugh. She was wearing a large bonnet tied with a ribbon around her chin, which made her already quite small head appear even smaller. "A little sherry wine, perhaps…"

"Very good," said Mr Brydges and nodded his approval at Freddy.

The bottle was already waiting on a side table. With the skill of an innkeeper's son, he uncorked it and poured a little into a glass goblet for Mr Brydges to taste. Mr Brydges gulped it down, made an approving noise and indicated that both he and his wife would like their goblets filled to the brim.

"Leave the bottle," he commanded.

Fifteen minutes later, Freddy entered the snug again, this time with a tray laden with a roast pullet on a platter surrounded by a selection of spring vegetables, roasted new potatoes and a dish of sage and onion stuffing. He noted that the bottle of sherry had already been consumed down to the dregs.

Freddy set the meal in the centre of the table on the spotless linen tablecloth and placed a warmed plate in front of each of his guests.

"Honest country fayre." Mr Brydges smiled and broke a leg off the pullet.

"Would you cut me a small slice from the…" Mrs Brydges paused, loosening her bonnet. Her cheeks had gone pink. "…Breast," she whispered. "I'm not sure I can manage any more."

Freddy had started to back away towards the door when Mr Brydges eyed him quizzically. "Have I not seen you somewhere before, young man?"

"You may have seen me at school, sir," replied Freddy.

Mr Brydges stabbed a piece of carrot with his knife and put it in his mouth. "You mean Seekings?"

"Yes."

"Do you work there, perhaps, during the day?"

"As a pupil, yes."

Both Mr and Mrs Brydges swallowed what they were eating and turned their heads to him, their expressions a mixture of confusion and incredulity.

"And your father is the village innkeeper?"

Freddy smiled and nodded.

"Are you a charity case?" asked Mrs Brydges, glancing at her husband as if she had never heard such an absurd story.

Freddy blushed. "No ma'am. I'm a Newtonian scholar."

They gazed at Freddy then at each other. Their jaws had dropped. "These are strange times, indeed," said Mr Brydges, taking a large mouthful of sherry wine and waving his hand to dismiss the Newtonian scholar.

Freddy gave a small bow and went out into the main bar, feeling a sense of relief. Then he noticed that the room was unusually quiet. Even Zebedee Tring was not grousing about anything. Instead, all the regulars were staring towards the hearth where his dad sat, in the flickering firelight, talking in a firm but low voice, probably because he didn't want Mr and Mrs Brydges to hear, to a figure partially hidden in his shadow.

"Now then, lad, it's time you were on your way. You shouldn't be here in your condition."

"Don't talk to me like that, old man. All I asked for was a drink…"

"You've already had more than enough," said Daniel, raising his voice just a little.

It was Freddy's turn for his mouth to drop open, for he had recognised the voice. He strode up behind his dad. "It's Tom White from the school," he whispered. "You know, the one I was talking about."

Daniel glanced round at his son, then back at Tom, who was unrecognisable as a pupil from Seekings. His face was streaked with grime; he had no coat; what had once been a white shirt was torn and covered with foul-smelling vomit; and his dusty trousers were ripped at the knees, his shoes scuffed.

"Oh, my life," said Daniel, turning to face his son. "What are we going to do with him?"

Freddy looked over his dad's shoulder at Tom. He was

so startled that his body convulsed as if struck by a jolt of electricity. In his mind's eye, he no longer saw the pathetic drunken figure in front of the bar fire, but the young man with neat, dark wavy hair standing before the bonfire on King James's Night, six months ago. He heard Mr Hawlings' voice. *Do you see those two young men over there? Keep an eye on the shorter one for me, will you?*

"Whatever's the matter, son? You look as if you've seen a ghost."

Freddy spoke quietly. "I think I should take him upstairs. I'll look after him."

Daniel nodded towards the door of the snug. "What if.."

"I'll put him in my room."

"If you're sure, son, you know him."

In truth, Freddy didn't know him, except in passing and by reputation. But now, not only Mr Hawlings' words but also his own words to Mark Fouracre came back to him. *He needs help.*

"Come on, Tom, you're coming with me," he said, taking him by the arm.

"I know you," slurred Tom. "You're one of the little twerps from Seekings, aren't you?"

"Yes, come on."

"Are you taking me for a drink?"

"That's right."

Freddy wasn't sure what he would have done if Tom had refused. They might have been the same height, but the sixth-former was far more powerfully built.

Chapter Fourteen

Poster Boy

A light tap on the door woke Freddy from a doze. He got up from the floor by the window where he had been lying on his quilt, and went to answer.

"Are you all right, son?" asked Daniel. "It's time you were getting ready for school."

Freddy nodded sleepily and opened the door wide.

"Phew," said his dad, taking a few steps inside. "I take it that the whiff is not you."

Freddy laughed quietly. "I got his shoes and socks off, put an old horse blanket on the bed and wrapped him in it. He's probably wet himself, otherwise he's as was. As far as I know, he hasn't woken since he collapsed there last night."

Daniel regarded the heap critically. Tom was lying face-up on the iron bedstead, snoring softly. His eyes, nose and feet were the only visible parts of his body and all of them were grimy and dirty. "You've done a good job, lad, but I'll look after him for now. School comes first."

"You won't send him away before I get back, will you?"

"Don't worry – it's a an innkeeper's job to mind the drunk and disorderly. The first thing I'm going to do is open those shutters."

"What happens if he tries to escape?"

Daniel chuckled. "He's not a prisoner. But I reckon if he's been on a three-day binge, then he's not going to wake up in a hurry, and when he does, it'll be with a sore head."

"Are Mr and Mrs Brydges still here?"

"They're due to leave on the nine o'clock."

"Did they enjoy last night's meal?"

"Well, judging by the pile of pullet bones, the empty dishes, the empty sherry and claret bottles and their cheerful state when they retired, I would say yes."

"Snooty couple," said Freddy.

"Yes, but that's our bread and butter, son, whereas Zebedee and his ilk are the bread and scrape. Now, you go and eat your porridge and boiled egg, then get dressed for school."

* * *

Freddy arrived at the school gates some five minutes later than usual, expecting to have an awkward and evasive talk with Mr Hawlings about Tom White. Instead the school caretaker was already deep in conversation with the diminutive figure of Frank Kennedy.

"Good morning, Mr Hawlings, good morning, Francis."

"Don't call me Fwancis, Fweddy Hall. I'm Fwank."

Mr Hawlings tipped his hood back, exposing thick salt-and-pepper hair. "Are you two ever going to agree on a name?"

"It's fun, isn't it Frank?"

"Fweddy and Hawwy are my fwends," said Frank.

"And what about Master Carstairs?" questioned Mr Hawlings.

"Carstairs is my best fwend," confirmed Frank. "We share secwets."

Mr Hawlings turned. "And do you share secrets, Freddy Hall?"

Freddy blushed and was stumped for words. The caretaker chuckled. "No? Good! These are dangerous times to be sharing secrets, except with your very best friends. Remember that a secret written down is easily read by prying eyes."

Frank covered his ears and squeezed his eyes shut as the mail coach arrived with a blast on the post horn. Harry vaulted down from the passenger seat behind the driver and stood by

Freddy, a frown on his face.

"Some specials today, Mr Hawlings," said the coachman, "and there's even one for Clifftop Lighthouse."

"Ooo, goody," said Frank. "My mum says corwespondence helps gwease the wheels."

"He hasn't seen what it is yet," whispered Harry.

The driver gave Mr Hawlings a sheaf of letters and three pieces of rolled-up parchment tied with ribbon.

"There's a lady and gentleman to pick up in Linbury," said Freddy, not wanting the Brydges to miss their connection. The driver nodded and the coach pulled away.

"What do you want me to do with yours, young Frank?" asked Mr Hawlings.

"Can I see?"

The caretaker handed one of the rolls to the boy, who smiled excitedly. "I've not had one of these before. Can I unwap it?"

"It's yours – you do with it as you see fit."

Frank undid the ribbon, his hands shaking with anticipation, but when he unfurled the parchment, his face fell and he went pale. "I don't want it," he said and dropped it on the ground.

"Maybe you should take a look, Freddy Hall," said Mr Hawlings.

Freddy scooped up the roll and opened it out.

£20 REWARD!
WANTED

FOR THE MOST HORRIBLE CRIME OF SEDITION!
THOMAS WHITE, A NATIVE OF BRITON
whose apprehension is desired for the distribution of inflammatory and obscene material relating to libels against the Royal Family.

WOODCUT AND DESCRIPTION

Aged 17 years and five months, 5ft 6in tall, black hair and blue/grey eyes. Gentlemanly appearance and address, except for a coarse British accent. A late pupil of Seekings School for Boys, Dorsetshire.

The reward will be paid by the Court of Marshalsea, Southwark, to any person that gives information leading to the arrest of this individual.

Signed this 14th day of April, 1826.
George Christopher East (Magistrate)

* * *

"Blotwell, my friend..."

Simon sat up straight. Only one person had visited him in the infirmary so far, Henry Perceval, who had brought him a book to read. He certainly hadn't expected anyone else, least of all Alfred Mayhew Cheeseman.

"Are you nice and comfortable, Blotwell?"

"Yes, thank you."

"I see Matron has provided you with three pillows. I only have two on my bed. And is that the shell of a boiled egg and toast crumbs on that tray? I didn't have time for breakfast this morning. And what is this with all the pretty pictures on the cover?"

Simon began to gabble, which he often did when he was nervous. "It's my fourth favourite book, Cheeseman, *The Rabbit Companion*. My favourite book is *My Beautiful Book of Fairy Tales*, followed by *Adventures in the Future*, which that common boy from Linbury borrowed, and then *The Illustrated Silver Treasury of Bible Stories for Boys*. My fifth favourite book is *The Boys' Leisure Hour Annual*, especially the amusing story of —"

"Shut your mouth, Blotwell. I'm thinking." Cheeseman sat down on the bedside chair and picked up *The Rabbit Companion* with one hand while scratching his upper lip with the other. "These are very expensive books, aren't they?"

"Yes, they are. That one cost twenty guineas because it has twenty-five full-colour lithographs. Mummy bought it for me the Christmas before last, because she knows how much I love rabbits."

"And that plebeian boy has borrowed one, has he?"

"He tricked me into lending it to him and Henry backed him up."

Cheeseman dropped the book back on the bed. "Ah, yes. Perceval, another one who needs to be taught a lesson. Well, Blotwell, you're living the life of Riley here, aren't you? Perhaps giving you a good flogging was the wrong thing to do, as you seem to be enjoying yourself far too much."

Simon had the jitters. From the beginning, he was fully

aware that this false bonhomie was leading somewhere he wouldn't like. He was now merely waiting for Cheeseman to strike.

"Where is Matron?" he asked, hoping she might be his saviour.

"Matron is otherwise engaged. An interview with the headmaster and governors. Her last, I shouldn't wonder. Yes, there's just you, me and, beyond the door, that silly child Betty Somebody –"

"Golightly," offered Simon.

"Don't interrupt! It seems I have a way with young ladies. I've arranged an assignation with her tonight in the school chapel at the altar, if you know what I mean?"

Although Simon wasn't certain what an assignation was, nor its connection to the altar, he thought – correctly – that it was bound to be both scandalous and blasphemous. "What if the Reverend Croft comes by?"

"The Reverend Croft will, as usual, be snoring his head off in the glebe house, having quaffed a quart or so of porter beer."

"Why did you come to visit me, Cheeseman?" asked Simon, wanting an end to the unbearable tension he felt.

"You mean nothing to me, Blotwell. You know that, don't you?"

"Yes, Cheeseman."

"I feel the same for you that I do for the spider I find in my room when I'm pulling its legs off."

"Spiders are our friends," said Simon weakly. Surely Cheeseman wasn't going to pull his legs off?

"Why did I come to visit you? Is that what you want to know?"

"I think so..."

The School House captain rose from the chair and put his hands around Blotwell's throat. "You know I'd like to kill you, don't you? It would be so easy. You don't have to speak because I can see the answer in your eyes." Cheeseman tightened his grip and pressed on Simon's windpipe with his thumbs. "Do you remember the day you blabbed my plan for Tom White to those mindless morons in the fifth and allowed them a moment of victory over me? I surprised you by not punishing you for that, didn't I? Well, their moment of victory will shortly be up and you are going to help in their downfall. But if you should ever breathe a word about our little subterfuge with the whisky and pamphlets to anyone else, I shall throttle you, like they do deserters from the army. Do you understand?" His hands tightened again. Simon, red in the face and gasping for air, nodded vigorously.

"Good! Have a pleasant day, Blotwell."

When Betty's giggles had subsided and the outside door had closed with a click, Simon relaxed back into the pillows. Despite a sore throat, he felt that somehow he'd got off lightly. He was unsure why Cheeseman had made an issue out of sneaking into White's room and planting the drink and papers. It was over, in the past, and except for making it part of his confession to the Reverend McKellan, he had put it to the back of his mind. In any case, who would believe the inveterate liar, even if he was telling the truth?

* * *

As Freddy walked out of the osher for break at eleven o'clock, he felt a tug on his sleeve and looked round.

"Fweddy," said Frank Kennedy in a tremulous voice. "You won't tell on me, will you, for getting White into twouble?"

Freddy stopped and turned to face him. "Of course I won't, Frank, but I'm going to speak to Berty Wright. He was the one who put you up to it."

"Carstairs has pwomised not to tell on me as well, even though he was angwy with me for getting Jewemy Pincher the job." The small boy blinked up at Freddy with watery eyes.

"Frank, you're ten and I'm almost fourteen. There's a world of difference."

"I'm eleven in July..."

"Good, can I come to your birthday party? Are you having a cake?"

Frank giggled. "I'm going to invite you and Hawwy and Carstairs."

"Thanks. Now, off you go and play, and don't worry, Francis," said Freddy.

"All wight, and I'll let you call me Fwancis, Fweddy Hall – just this once, mind."

Freddy watched Frank skip down the steps and into the throng of boys on the grass, pleased that at least one person's cares had been alleviated. He sighed and rubbed his tired eyes, then felt a hand on his back.

"You're carrying a big weight on those shoulders, Federico, but you know you can share it with your Uncle Harry."

"Scud, listen, I don't want to put you in a position where you have to choose between me and your family."

"Ah! Time for a serious talk," said Harry. "Come on, let's walk."

They meandered along the path around School House, between Mr Hawlings' flower beds and on towards Drake House.

"What do you think about Tom White?" asked Freddy.

"I knew it! You've been going on about this for days and I guess that poster was the final straw."

"Do you think it's true what they're saying about him?"

"I don't know, Federico, but it's not our problem, is it?"

"It is my problem, Scud."

Harry stopped and pulled Freddy to a halt. "Look, if it is your problem then it's my problem too."

Freddy looked Harry straight in the eyes. "He's at my house. Asleep in my bedroom."

It took several moments for Harry to assimilate this before he threw up his arms and laughed. "Oh Federico! You are an extraordinary fellow. And you think you can't trust your best chum with that information?"

"I just did, didn't I?"

"It took you long enough."

"I don't know what to do."

"Have you spoken to him?"

"He was drunk."

"Lord, the sot!"

"I think my dad will be having kittens, especially if he's seen that poster."

"It's a good job it's Saturday and Scud is here to help. I'll tell you one thing, Federico, he can't stay at the inn. They've sent for the militia from Oakleigh."

"How do you know that?"

The bell sounded for the end of break and automatically they turned to walk back towards school.

"I have a little anecdote to tell you, but it will have to be at lunch now. Somewhere private."

"The library."

"All right, but food first."

"Food's always first with you."

"You can't think on an empty stomach – at least I can't."

"Thanks, Scud."

Harry clapped him on the shoulders. "You are the biggest chump, Federico, as well as being the brightest."

Chapter Fifteen

Bull's-eye

After lunch, the two boys climbed the stairs to the library where, in the furthest recess, sitting at an oak table, Harry began his story. "Pa told Ma and me this over dinner last night. He had spent two days in Dunhambury at a series of meetings of magistrates and other officials involved in policing the county. On the Friday morning they were all summoned to the Old Market House for a special address by Squire Blotwell – yes, Simon Blotwell's old man. High Sheriff and Lord Lieutenant of Dorsetshire, MP for West Dorsetshire and – well, the list goes on. I asked Pa what he was like. Six feet tall, ramrod-straight back, square jaw, broad shoulders, baritone voice, clipped moustache, ruddy complexion, thick greying hair, immaculately turned out in a red tunic with gold buttons and epaulettes, navy-blue trousers and black shoes you could see your face in.

"Pa then asked me to describe our Blotwell – you know, five foot two, scrawny shoulders, pigeon-chested, slightly stooped, pinched face, thin mousey hair, sing-song voice, wears clothes that are too big for him. We had a laugh about that. I know Ma wanted to make a comment about the wife sowing her wild oats, but didn't because I was there.

"The squire sat on a podium behind a table on which the Albion flag was draped. He was flanked by all of our Members of Parliament, including the MP for Dorset North, who's none other than Alfred Cheeseman's father, though most of his estate is around Yardlow in Wiltshire. They all had on their most serious faces and Pa and his colleagues wondered what was in store for them.

"Squire Blotwell stood up and stated that he had received a petition from Seekings School signed by several masters, alleging that Dorsetshire in general and Seekings in particular had become a hotbed of anti-Royalist sympathisers who were fomenting an insurrection in support of the Silesian pretender. It was then that Tom White's name came up, and the literature that had been discovered in his room. The petition described his behaviour as abhorrent and outrageous and demanded that he be hunted down and brought to justice, so an example could be made of him.

"Knowing something of the school, Pa tended to take all this with a pinch of salt, but soon found himself in a tiny minority. The squire held up the poster you saw this morning. Since he's the magistrate for this area, Pa was told in no uncertain terms to put his name to it, which he duly did.

"And that's not all. Squire Blotwell announced to the meeting that, as Lord Lieutenant of the County, he was ordering the garrison in Oakleigh to send a detachment of special militia to root out the plotters and seditionists and arrest all those involved. They would then be arraigned not to the assize court here but to the Marshalsea, in London. There, what do you think to that?"

"Frightening," said Freddy. "Verging on the hysterical. Do you know who signed the petition?"

"No, but I can guess the first three names: Tallow, Hooke and King."

"I wish school was over for the day so I could get back home. Dad will be going frantic."

"At least it's an early finish on Saturday. I'm coming with you, of course. Don't want to miss any of the fun."

"It's no joke, Scud. I don't know what I'm going to do. How could I have got myself involved in this?"

"Because you're Federico Hall, insurrectionist and first-order plotter."

"Scud..." Freddy frowned at his friend's flippant attitude.

"Don't worry. I can be as serious as they come when the time is right."

"If Tom White is really a Silesian sympathiser..."

"You mean as well as a drunk?"

Freddy looked down the aisle between the bookshelves to where Mr Topliss was busily engaged in cataloguing some new arrivals. "I wish I could ask him what to do."

Harry looked round. "Old Topper, you mean? Good for pops and bangs, but I doubt he's into politics. Head in the clouds and all that."

Freddy took out his watch. "We've got fifteen minutes. Let's go and talk to Berty Wright in Raleigh."

"I've told you once, a fifth-former isn't going to cooperate with a shell boy."

"We'll see," said Freddy. "Just back me up."

They nodded to Mr Topliss on their way out and he watched them go with his head on one side and a small smile on his face.

Five minutes later on the threshold of Raleigh House, they bumped into Gus Gilmore, who was hanging onto the door's architrave doing pull-ups.

"Is this a deputation?" he asked. "Are you offering Drake's unconditional surrender in all sporting events to save yourselves the humiliation of ignominious defeat?"

"No," said Harry, "we've come to demand your unconditional surrender in all academic competitions because of our secret weapon, Federico Hall."

Gus chuckled. "So now we've got that out of the way. What do you want?"

"Berty Wright," said Freddy.

"Oh, you can have him with pleasure... No, on second thoughts we'll keep him. He makes the best tea in the school."

"So we've been told," said Harry. "Do you know where he is?"

Gus pointed to a group of trees a hundred yards away to his right. "I think you'll probably find him and the other lumbering giant in that copse, but watch out for the darts."

In a glade of dappled sunlight in the centre of the copse, surrounded by a tangle of undergrowth, they found Berty White and his friend Rufus Cleave throwing crossbow bolts at an archery target hanging from a tree. Both fifth-form boys were heavyweights, a solid mass of fat and muscle in equal proportions.

"This is private property," said Rufus, zinging a bolt across the glade which hit the target just inside the yellow, then dropped out. "Sissy boys from the shell and lower remove aren't welcome."

"Can I talk to you for a minute, Wright?" asked Freddy. "It's important."

"You'll probably be interested in what he's got to say," said Harry.

"I doubt that," said Bert, looking uncertain.

"It's about tricking Frank Kennedy," said Freddy.

A blush appeared on Bert Wright's face. "It wasn't my idea."

"Why are you talking to these two, Berty?" asked Rufus. "They're nobodies from nowhere."

"You tricked Frank and you've made serious trouble for Tom White," said Freddy.

"I have not!"

"They've called out the militia to look for White and anyone else involved in the plot," said Harry.

"What plot?" said Rufus, staying his hand at the last moment. "What are you talking about?"

"Haven't you seen the poster, Cleave?" asked Harry.

Rufus looked hard at his friend. "What's going on, Berty? Why are you acting guilty?"

"I'm not acting guilty! I've done nothing."

"You look guilty to me," said Harry.

"Shut up, East," said Berty.

"Just tell us who put you up to it, Wright," said Freddy, "and we won't say anything to the militia men when they come to school."

Bert Wright blanched. "They won't come here, will they?"

"Of course they will," said Harry. "My pa is the magistrate and he told me they'd be here next week."

"Look, it was supposed to be a bit of fun. It was Stalky's idea to trick old Tallow, because Kennedy can't pronounce his *rs*. I didn't think Tallow would go berserk over it."

"Stalky?" said Freddy. "You let Corkran talk you into joining one of their schemes?"

"I thought it was funny at the time, and he gave me a stick of liquorice."

"You silly ass, Berty," said Rufus. "Getting involved with those three archfiends."

"Thanks," said Freddy. "We'll let you get on with your game now."

***

On Saturdays the school day finished after house roll call at 3.45 p.m. Then the boarders either stayed in their houses, retiring to their dormitory or study, or went out to play games or find a place for a quiet smoke – or to get up to the type of mischief that boys of that age have always done.

The day boys went home.

Frank Kennedy turned and fluttered his hand at them before starting the climb up the steep path to Clifftop House.

"I think he's going to invite us to his birthday party in July," said Freddy, walking quickly away from the school up the New Coach Road towards Linbury.

"That might be interesting. I've never been in a lighthouse before," said Harry, looking back over his shoulder towards the promontory where the domed lantern room was visible above a screen of trees.

"I don't think they actually live in the lighthouse," said Freddy, quickening his pace still further.

"If you don't slow down, you'll be out of breath in a

minute and you'll have to rest."

"Rubbish," replied Freddy who was imagining a posse of soldiers already at the Sailor's Yarn, dragging his dad and Tom out to face an angry mob led by Mrs Snell.

They soon passed the village boundary stone and entered Main Street where all was quiet, except for Zebedee Tring who was clipping the shrubbery which had started to advance through the railings on top of the churchyard wall.

"Afternoon, Zeb," said Harry.

"Don't you be so cheeky, Harry East, it's Mr Tring to you. You folks from that school think yourselves so high and mighty, then look at you..." Zebedee pointed with his shears to the church noticeboard, where a copy of the wanted poster had been given pride of place.

It wasn't quite as bad as the posse of soldiers, but it was enough to make Freddy recoil.

"And to think that rogue was in your father's inn last night," continued Zebedee. "I hope they catch 'im quick. I shan't rest easy in my bed till he's safely in chains."

"I don't think he's going to attack anyone in their bed," said Freddy.

"Don't you be so sure. If he's all fired up with the drink, anything could happen."

The two boys walked on towards the Sailor's Yarn, stopping briefly to peruse the wanted poster.

"Where does the old blighter live?" asked Harry in a quiet voice.

"Do you mean Tom or Zebedee Tring?" whispered Freddy.

"Guess."

"If you carry on up past the windmill, you eventually get to Alum Chine. There are steps down and he has a cottage – or, rather, shack – just above the beach. I've never been in it."

The front door of the inn was locked so they went round the back to the scullery where Daniel Hall was visible through the window, busy washing clothes in a large dolly tub. On a clothesline, two sheets were already flapping in the breeze.

Freddy tapped on the window, which made his dad jump.

The back door opened and Daniel looked out. "Is it just you two?" he said.

"Were you expecting anyone else?" asked Freddy.

"Of course not. You're home early."

"He was in a hurry," said Harry.

"Come on in, then. The kettle's on."

They entered the scullery which was hot and muggy and smelt of lye soap. His dad pressed down forcefully several times with the dolly stick on the blankets in the tub, splashing himself in the process.

"Are you all right, Dad?"

Daniel gave a tired smile and dried his hands. "I've been worse, lad, but those posters knocked me back a bit. I don't know whether the coachman suspected anything, but he gave me a funny look when I saw what they were. I put one out on the noticeboard to show willing, but the other is still in the back room."

Freddy took off his jacket and rolled up his sleeves. "What about the regulars? Have they said anything? Zebedee Tring had a go at us when we went by."

"There was a lot of talk, but no one passed any remarks. Still, I was in a bit of a tizz and closed up early, much to your Uncle Sam's disgust. At least it gave me time to get the chores out of the way, but I'll have to open at six tonight."

They went through to the bar room. While Daniel made the tea, Freddy fetched the biscuit barrel from the store cupboard, then they sat at a table.

"Where is he?" asked Harry.

"Lying down in one of the guest rooms with the shutters closed. I managed to get him into the bath, but he's been like a bull with a sore head."

"How's my bedroom?"

"I've sponged your mattress as best I could. I think it'll be dry by tonight. Your floor has had a good brush and I strewed some mace over it in case he was verminous. I had to burn his clothes – they weren't fit to wash. And as for his shoes … one of the soles was missing and the other had all but come away from the upper."

"That accounts for the state of his feet," said Freddy.

"You've done a lot more for him than I would," said Harry.

"He's just a lad to me," said Daniel, "but I'd be lying if I said I was happy about him being here."

Harry related the story of his pa's meeting with the squire in Dunhambury. By the end, Daniel was even less happy.

"I know he can't stay here, Dad, but there's been some funny business going on at school about this, and I don't just mean masters putting the cat among the pigeons."

"Well, you know him better than me."

"I'm not sure we do," said Harry.

Freddy gave his friend a look. "We'd better go up and see him."

***

Armed with a mug of tea, Freddy knocked and entered the second guest room at the back of the inn, followed by Harry who had the poster under his arm.

In the semi-darkness, Tom White lay face-up on the bed, dressed in a pair of Daniel's ankle-length drawers but nothing else. Though clearly awake, he didn't seem to notice their entrance until Freddy bent over him. Then his face, which was drawn, with black circles under his eyes, registered surprise. "What are you doing here?"

"I live here."

Tom moved his head left and right. "Where am I?"

"Linbury, at the Sailor's Yarn. You've been here since last night."

"Who was that man with the bath tub who washed my back?"

"That's my dad – he's good at washing backs. Drink this tea."

Tom sat up, then groaned and held his head. "I don't understand any of this."

Harry made a contemptuous noise. "I think I'll let some light in here." He went over to the window and opened the shutters. The back of the inn was bounded by a hurdle fence and looked out over fields and hedgerows. In the middle distance was the Stadden farmhouse, a large thatched country house with barn and stables attached. Beyond was a long line of trees, broken only by the encroachment of the New Coach Road, indicating the south-eastern edge of Thieves' Wood.

Tom shielded his eyes from the light, but Harry was having none of it. "Take a look at this, White," he said, unfurling the poster and holding it before him. "Not a bad likeness, is it? A bit young-looking, perhaps."

Tom's hands trembled as he took hold of the paper and read the contents. A tear formed in his right eye and ran down his cheek, then another fell from the left. He sobbed. "It's not true."

"Feeling sorry for yourself won't help, and neither will getting blind drunk and being thrown out of the New Inn in Larkstone then coming here and wetting Federico's bed."

"Harry, leave off a bit," said Freddy. "Tom, put the poster down and drink your tea. It's getting cold."

"You are a ninny sometimes, Federico. I'm going downstairs to help your pa hang out the washing. You stay – you're better with the tea and sympathy…"

Harry marched out and pulled the door closed so that it rattled on its hinges.

"He doesn't like me," said Tom, rubbing the patch of dark hair in the middle of his chest.

Freddy sat on the bed. "You accosted him in Larkstone – I think it left its mark."

"I don't remember."

"What do you remember?"

"I need a drink, Hall, a proper drink."

"You're not getting a drink, Tom, not while you're here.

I'm a publican's son and I know what it's all about. And don't call me Hall; we're not at school now. I'm Freddy."

"How old are you?"

"Nearly fourteen."

"Please..."

"No, concentrate on telling me everything you remember about getting into this mess."

Chapter Sixteen

Tom White Remembers

"Donald Sanderson had asked me to go over to Frobisher during the dinner hour to talk about the cricket on the Thursday. I missed lunch but then had to wait outside for ten minutes before he came. When I was in his study, I was taken aback because the first thing he did was take out a decanter of whisky and ask me if I wanted a snort. He said it was a present from his father, a single malt from a new Caledonian distillery. I told him I didn't think I ought to, but he was insistent and poured one for me and another for himself.

"I was itching to try it. Seeing him obviously enjoying his, I eventually gave in. We chinked our glasses and we drank. As far as discussing cricket was concerned, neither of us said anything of any consequence. He offered to refill my glass several times, but I refused, which took an awful lot of willpower.

"When the bell went, we said our goodbyes and I wandered back to Raleigh to collect my books, feeling relaxed. I heard a commotion when I was climbing the stairs, but thought nothing of it until I reached the top, where a gaggle of boys were chattering excitedly. I pushed my way through them and saw the doctor outside my study. Then Tallow emerged, holding some papers which he handed to the head. He was obviously agitated. I walked up and asked them what the matter was. I saw the look on Dr Butler's face as he smelt my whisky breath.

"The next thing I knew, I was in the school office being

asked where I had come by these handbills and who else was involved. Tallow held one between his finger and thumb and accused me of mocking and vilifying the king and consorting with Albion's enemies. Even though they were supposed to be mine, they were reluctant to show me the handbills, but I could see what they were about and I told them I'd never set eyes on them before.

"By this time, Mr King had joined the other masters. He held up a whisky bottle and asked whether I had set eyes on that before. Dr Butler had gone pale – I could see the anger and disappointment in his eyes. He said that I had disgraced the school, disgraced him, and most of all disgraced myself. I tried again to tell him that I was innocent, but I knew I was done for. King scoffed that my breath stank of innocence and Tallow said that he hoped being a Briton wouldn't save my neck from the gallows, so the doctor told him quietly that using such hyperbole was not appropriate.

"I was given the choice of being locked in a room until my parents arrived to collect me or leaving the school on the next coach. I chose to leave, knowing that my parents would never come for me if they found out the circumstances.

"Old Hawlings carried my case as he escorted me off the school grounds. He asked me why I had been such a fool to start drinking again after five years of abstinence. I was shocked that he knew my business, so I scowled at him. He chuckled and said I was going to learn a hard lesson but that it might be worth it in the end."

"Hmm," said Freddy, non-committally.

"I don't understand what I've done wrong. I thought if I kept my head down and worked hard, I would be able to finish my studies at Seekings and go on to university. I want to study law, but I suppose that's out of the question now, and my parents will disown me when they find out what's happened."

"Where's your case?" asked Freddy.

"My case? I don't know. Does it matter? I got off the coach at Larkstone and went into the inn there, and that's all I remember."

"Because you got blind drunk."

"Don't rub it in, Hall."

"There's a party of militia men coming this way. They'll be looking for you and your accomplices, as well as going round asking questions."

"Accomplices? I haven't got any accomplices."

"You can't stay here."

Tom hoisted himself off the bed, then stopped and looked down at himself, as if realising for the first time that he only wore a pair of underdrawers. "I've got no clothes."

"No, you've got nothing. No clothes, no money, no shoes, nothing."

Tom put his head in his hands. "Perhaps I should give myself up. That would probably be best for everyone."

"Not for you it wouldn't and, if you're telling the truth, not for the school either."

"Don't you believe me?"

"I don't know why you'd bother to lie to me. Why make up a story when there's only the two of us in this room?"

"That doesn't answer the question."

"I know it doesn't. Actually, I do believe you. Mr Hawlings believes you. He asked me to help you in a roundabout way."

Tom looked across at Freddy. "Old Hawlings? I don't see what he's got to do with this. That's a very odd thing to say."

"Take it from me, Mr Hawlings is a wise man, though I seem to be the only one who notices."

"I don't understand what you're talking about, and how would giving myself up affect the school? They were only too pleased to see the back of me."

"It's obvious, isn't it? If you're telling the truth, there are people there who planned to discredit you! If you give yourself up, they'll have won hands down, and who knows what other schemes they've got up their sleeves."

"Hall... Freddy, I really do need a drink. If you let me have a drink I'll cope much better."

"In your dreams."

Tom knelt on the bed and wrung his hands. "Please, Freddy, you don't know what it's like…"

"Are you trying to prove to me that Harry was right about you?"

The guest room door opened and Harry East entered. "Did I hear my name mentioned?"

Freddy looked hard at him. "It's so obvious that you were eavesdropping."

"It's true. I confess. Each time I went back into the scullery to fetch another blanket to put on the line, your pa would harangue me about the effects the demon drink has on people and how I shouldn't be hasty in my judgement. So, I thought, to save myself another tongue-lashing, I'd come back up here and see what's to be done."

"We need a plan," said Freddy. "Are you stopping overnight?"

"Of course I'm stopping. I've already written the folks a little billet-doux for the five o'clock coach. *Dear Ma and Pa, I won't be home this weekend as I am helping a desperate criminal to escape justice. I remain your obedient and ever loving son, HE.*"

"Ha ha," said Freddy.

* * *

On Sunday, the bells of All Souls parish church rang out from nine o'clock announcing the morning service at ten. Come rain or shine, health or infirmity, everyone was expected to attend. It was a social as much as a religious gathering.

Freddy, in his Seekings School uniform, hair neatly parted on the left, sat with his dad in their regular place, the third pew from the back on the left-hand side. In the same row were Uncle Albert and Auntie Emily, Aunt Edie and her husband Sam Hingston. Regular placements were important, because it was easier to spot an absentee, to whom remarks would inevitably be directed on the Monday. It might even result in the cold shoulder if it happened more than twice in a row. Miss Antrobus played the organ, which was situated near the choir stalls. She liked to sway while she played, and she was particularly fond of the new melodies by Mr Handel who, though Silesian by birth, had become a naturalised subject of Albion.

Freddy watched Farmer Stadden, his wife and several children, including their eldest Gavin, walk self-importantly up the aisle to their box pew at the front on the right, which they rented for £10 per annum. Then his focus drifted to the left-hand side where Mrs Snell and her husband were usually seated, but had not yet arrived. Anxiously, he looked back to the door where the two ushers, Joseph and Russell Warren, were on duty.

"What's the matter with you today, Freddy?" whispered his Aunt Emily. "You're a right fidget, and your dad's not much better."

"Sorry," he murmured.

There was a click of heels, an audible sniff, and the tall figure of Mrs Snell wearing a wide-brimmed yellow hat decorated with lilac flowers marched down the aisle with her husband, who was not quite so tall, one pace behind.

"How does she keep that thing on board?" whispered Daniel to his son.

"Pins and needles," chuckled Freddy in a quiet voice, much relieved.

"Ssh!" scolded Aunt Emily.

The bells fell silent and the church clock began to toll the tenth hour. On the last stroke, Russell Warren closed the west door, while Miss Antrobus began to play 'The Arrival of the Queen of Sheba', which some parishioners would most certainly have disapproved of, had they known the title.

Now two events occurred. The first was the appearance of the Reverend Jeremy Smollett, wearing a greying lace surplice over a black cassock. He hobbled into the church from the vestry. Approaching his eightieth year, he was the oldest

Linburian and had been the vicar of All Souls for fifty-three years. His escorts were twins Andrew and Michael Mason, two of the choirboys, there to ensure he made it safely up the three steps to the pulpit. On a Sunday, with scrubbed faces and whiter than white vestments, these two twelve-year-old tearaways became little angels for the day. On other days, their favourite pastime was to throw stones from the clifftop onto anyone on the beach below. In this way, they had raised Freddy's ire on several occasions, resulting once in Michael getting a black eye and running home in tears. After this, and some parental involvement, a truce had been called which has held to this day.

The second event, which was much less noticeable, was the fleeting appearance of Harry East's face pressed against the outside of the lancet window on the north side of the church in line with the third pew from the back. Freddy nodded, then the face withdrew. As if on cue, the congregation rose and began to sing 'All People that on Earth do Dwell', lustily accompanied on the organ by Miss Antrobus.

An hour and a half later, to another breezy tune, this time from Mr Handel's *Water Music*, the congregation filed out of the south door. With a cursory nod to the Reverend Smollett, who was sitting on a stool in the porch with his elderly wife, waiting to be told how inspiring his sermon had been, Freddy walked rapidly down the path to the lychgate, turned sharp right onto the green and ran across Main Street to the door of the Sailor's Yarn.

Harry East slouched in a comfortable bar chair, a mug of tea in front of him.

"Well?" said Freddy.

"Well, what?"

"Don't be an ass, Scud."

"Oh, are you talking about Harry's daring mission to hide the dangerous agent provocateur Thomas White from the Albion militia?"

"Scud!"

"Assignment complete. Agent White is ensconced on the fifth floor of your uncle's windmill. As far as I could tell, we were observed by a rabbit, a crow and two magpies. It's two for joy, isn't it?"

Freddy sat down. "What sort of mood was he in?"

Harry folded his arms and looked up at the ceiling, his head cocked. "On the whole, given that he was running in a pair of your pa's old shoes and wearing a frilly smock over his underdrawers, not too bad. He even asked me to thank you and your pa for what you'd done."

"That's good…"

"Hmm, though my feeling is that he would have swapped it all for a quart of strong porter."

Daniel arrived, smoothing down the cow lick across his forehead that he had created with Rowland's Macassar oil. "Everything gone according to plan?"

The boys nodded.

"Right then, shape up. It's roast beef and Yorkshire pudding at your Aunt Emily's."

"Frabjous!" said Freddy.

"I don't suppose I'm invited," said Harry gloomily.

"Of course you're invited – we wouldn't go if you weren't."

"But she doesn't approve of me. I'm from Larkstone."

"Of course she approves of you, now she knows you're the magistrate's son."

Chapter Seventeen

A Stitch in Time

The mood at Seekings School on Monday was subdued. Masters and pupils studiously followed the routines and rituals with the intention that normality should be resumed as quickly as possible. But by now, almost everyone was aware that an investigation into subversive activity loomed over the school.

One sacrifice to this new mood of uncertainty and antagonism was Mrs Amfortas, Matron, who left the school that morning, suitcase in hand. Not even Mr Hawlings was there to see her off. She endured a lonely walk up the drive, seen only by a few, including Simon Blotwell, who watched from the infirmary window with a tinge of regret and a total lack of comprehension.

Less than ten minutes after her departure Betty Golightly, now nominally in charge, came into the ward and told Blotwell to sling his hook, as there was nothing wrong with him. As his few days of peace and quiet ended, his tinge of regret became a full-blown anger.

Simon slouched down the stairs from the infirmary on the lookout for someone he could direct his ire at. As he crossed the hall, coming towards him was none other than the diminutive form of Frank Kennedy.

"Hello Blots, are you feeling better?" chirped Frank.

The effrontery of this upstart from the lighthouse stopped Simon in his tracks. He wanted to both knock him to the ground and insult him, but two things prevented him from doing either of these things. The first was remembering who

Frank's friends were and the second was, the boy was batting his eyelids at him as if he was actually interested in his health.

"No, I'm not feeling better. I am in fact very poorly. Matron has been sacked and that common piece of baggage Betty Golightly has been put in charge."

"Oh dear," said Frank, holding up his finger, which was covered in blood. "I was sharpening my pencil. Will she be able to fix this?"

"I very much doubt it. The slattern told me to sling my hook!"

"That's not vewy nice."

"No it's not," said Simon, now feeling thoroughly sorry for himself rather than angry, "and I've decided to write a strong letter of protest to my Auntie Millicent."

Frank's eyes went wide. "I wish I could wite stwong letters of pwotest."

Simon wasn't sure whether Frank was being sarcastic or not, but decided to give him the benefit of the doubt. "I don't think I'm quite well enough to attend lessons yet," he said, drooping even more than usual to emphasise the point.

Frank smiled sweetly. "But it's your favouwite upstairs in number thwee. Mr Campbell-Bannerman, and he's weading *Fwankenstein* in Fwench."

Simon was taken aback by Frank's knowledge. "How do you know Mr Campbell-Bannerman's lessons are my favourites, little boy?"

"Because he talks to you about your wabbits, *vos lapins*. Carstairs says you and Mr Campbell-Bannerman are both eccentwics, and Blots, I'm not going to be a little boy for much longer. My dad says I'm going to gwow and gwow." Frank stood on tiptoe and stretched his arms up as high as they would go.

And he calls me an eccentric, thought Simon, as the two boys went their separate ways. The door to school room number three had three decorative arrow slits, the middle one of which Simon peered through. The lesson was in progress. Mr Campbell-Bannerman was emoting with his right hand while reading a passage from the 1821 translation of Mary Shelley's novella, *Frankenstein, ou le Prométhée moderne.*

Modern languages was a relatively new subject for Seekings School and C.B., as Mr Campbell-Bannerman was known to all, was the pioneer teacher employed for that specific purpose. He was first and foremost a fluent Silesian speaker, but since that language was now out of favour he had to make do with teaching French, in which he was less proficient. Nevertheless, like his colleague Mr Dearman, he was relatively well liked by the boys, the paramount reason for this being the xylophone on wheels which he kept by the side of his desk. If he was pleased with the way a lesson had gone or was in a particularly good mood, he would regale his class with spirited renditions of the popular tunes of the day. A favourite of the moment was an arrangement of the final movement of Mr Ludwig van Beethoven's piano concerto number four. The boys would clap or drum their desks in time with the percussive notes, which always ended with a huge flourish and a bow, followed by a generous round of applause and shouts of 'Huzzah!'

Simon was torn between entering the classroom or spending an idle day in his study. He was still ruminating on this when he was suddenly flattened against the door and punched in the kidneys. This was followed by laughter as Jeremy Pincher and Donald Sanderson strolled away along the corridor.

As he climbed the School House stairs, Simon groaned and stretched to try to ease the pain in his back. His mind had been made up for him. He would spend the rest of the day lying on his bed in study number 15.

*　*　*

All Souls' clock was chiming the hour of six when Freddy arrived back in Linbury. As he walked up Main Street, he spied a man in a navy-blue military uniform lounging against the wall of Pattle's shop, puffing out clouds of smoke from a clay pipe. A musket was slung carelessly over his soldier.

When Freddy drew closer still, another similarly dressed man came out of the shop with a stoneware demijohn and handed it to his comrade, who uncorked it and took a swig. They nodded and smiled at each other, taking turns to drink from the flagon, each time wiping their lips on the back of their hand.

As he passed them, Freddy turned his head to look into the shop. There was no sign of Mrs Pattle.

"What's so interesting, sunshine?" asked the soldier with the pipe.

Freddy had a mind to ignore the question and move on, but the other soldier had seen him. "Come over here," he said, nudging the other with his elbow. "And tell us what you're about."

Freddy took a few steps towards them, thinking he could probably outrun them if necessary.

"Where's Mrs Pattle?"

"We're guarding the shop for the old witch," said the second soldier, upending the demijohn arm and taking a large mouthful, some of which spilled down his chin and onto his uniform.

"Eh! Careful," said the soldier with the pipe. "Save some for me."

"Plenty more inside." He winked at Freddy. "Spoils of war, you know."

Freddy noted that the soldier's shako plate bore the insignia *HR* surrounded by the embossed lettering *Honi soit qui mal y pense*. "We're not at war," he said.

"Of course we're at war!" said the soldier with the pipe. "Subversives, Silesian sympathisers, those who would strip the crown from the head of the rightful monarch and place it on a foreign princeling."

"You have to declare a war," stated Freddy.

"Well, aren't you the clever one?"

"I think he must go to that fancy school down the road. You know, the one we're due to visit tomorrow."

"Can I go now?" asked Freddy.

"Of course you can go. It's a free country, isn't it?" Both the soldiers laughed and continued to drink from the flagon.

On the village green, a small crowd of children had gathered to stare at a temporary military encampment consisting of five two-man tents set around a campfire over which a kettle boiled. Nearby, a four-wheeled wagon with a cage on top stood, ready to transport prisoners, and a dozen horses were tethered to makeshift hitching posts. Three soldiers sat on logs around the fire making small talk, oblivious of their audience.

When Freddy entered the Sailor's Yarn he had expected to see a few of the regulars already there but the room was deserted, except for his dad, standing behind the bar, who motioned for him to come nearer.

"There are a pair of army officers in the snug. Major Foster and Captain Maunday. They're intent on interviewing everyone in the village," he said quietly.

"What, even the kids?"

"Especially the kids. They've taken rooms for the next three nights so they're not going away fast."

"There were two soldiers outside Mrs Pattle's shop, but no sign of her. They'd stolen one of her brews."

"She's in there with them," said Daniel. "Everything is at sixes and sevens today. You must be very careful, son."

After getting changed in his room, Freddy came down to find Mrs Pattle sitting at a table with his dad. Though she tried to smile at him, there were tears in her eyes.

"Mrs Pattle, what's the matter?" he blurted out.

She shook her head at him, again trying to smile.

He looked through the open door of the snug where the two military officers were sitting side by side at the dining table, busily writing notes.

One of them glanced up. "You, boy, come here."

Freddy looked over at his dad, who gave him a stern nod.

"I said come here," the officer repeated.

Freddy walked into the snug, feeling a hot resentment.

"Close the door and sit down," said the elder of the two, a man in his forties with greying hair and sideburns.

"Who are you?" asked Freddy.

"We are soldiers of the king, sonny," said the younger one.

"No, I mean why are you here?"

"It's not your place to ask us questions."

The older man touched the younger one's arm, signalling him to desist.

"I am Major Foster of the King's Regiment of Light Dragoons and this is Captain Maunday. And you must be the son of the landlord of this establishment, Frederick Hall, a pupil at Seekings School?"

Freddy sat down. "Yes, I am."

"Then you should know why we are here," said the major.

"I'd understand it if you were at the school, but why come to the village?"

"Have you seen the poster relating to Thomas White?" asked the captain, ignoring the question.

"Yes, I have."

"Do you have information that might lead us to the arrest of this individual?"

"No," lied Freddy.

"Were you acquainted with this person at school?" asked the major.

"Only by sight. He was in the upper sixth and I'm in the shell. There isn't a lot of vertical communication."

"Did you see any of the traitorous literature that White was distributing?"

"No."

"Do you know of any illicit print shops either in the village or at school?"

"No."

"Have you heard talk of a rebellious or insurrectionist nature?"

"No, I haven't."

"Nothing, not even a casual word?"

"Nothing," replied Freddy.

"Then you must have cloth ears," said Captain Maunday.

"No, I just don't listen to tittle-tattle."

The major sat back in his chair and twiddled his thumbs. "So you have heard some tittle-tattle. Perhaps you can tell us who these tittle-tattlers are?"

Freddy felt as if he was being led into a trap. "No, what I mean is I don't listen to gossip."

Captain Maunday handed a page of notes to the major, who nodded and beheld Freddy.

"You are the Newtonian scholar, are you not? The boy who discovered the moon?"

"That's right."

"Where is your telescope?"

There was an urgent rap on the door, which Freddy hoped had disguised his startled reaction.

"Come," said Major Foster.

A soldier entered and saluted. "Sir, we've found the press. It was in the cellar..."

"We shall be over shortly to see for ourselves," interrupted the major. "Dismissed."

The soldier stood to attention and saluted again, then left.

"Answer the question, boy," said the Captain.

"What question?"

"Where is your telescope? It's a simple question and requires a simple answer."

"It's at my Uncle Albert's," replied Freddy.

The captain consulted his notes. "Is that Albert Tanner, the miller?"

"Yes, it is."

"And why do you keep it there?"

"Because it's darker."

"When were you there last?"

"Sunday, for dinner."

"Have we interviewed the miller?" asked the major.

"No sir, we haven't been up that way yet."

Major Foster regarded Freddy. "What sort of mill is it?"

"Wind," answered Freddy, folding his arms to mask his accelerating heartbeat.

"And you were there yesterday?"

"Yes, but not in the mill. We had dinner in the house."

The major turned to the captain. "Have a couple of the men give this place a thorough going-over."

"Yes, sir."

"Very well," said the major, standing up and addressing Freddy. "We shall continue this discussion tomorrow when we are at Seekings. Meanwhile, keep your eyes and ears open."

"Your soldiers are stealing," said Freddy, wanting to delay them for as long as possible. "If that's what you mean by keeping my eyes and ears open?"

"Explain yourself," said the captain sharply.

"They were stealing drink from Mrs Pattle's shop."

"They're allowed to forage," said the major, dismissing the charge. "Now, Captain, let's go and see about this printing press. Unusual in a village this size, wouldn't you say?"

"Definitely, sir, most suspicious and almost certainly unlicensed."

* * *

Freddy found his dad seated by the fire in the back room, as it was known, between the bar and the scullery, reading an old copy of the *Observer* Sunday newspaper.

"How did it go, son? You survived."

Freddy slumped into the chair opposite. "They knew about the telescope. They're sending a couple of men up to the windmill to look round."

"Oh my! I hope that lad has his eyes and ears open."

"Do you think I should go up to there and try to warn him?"

Daniel sat up. "Not on your life! If you go and get discovered, not only you but Albert and Emily will cop it."

"I hadn't thought of that," said Freddy.

"If the boy's got his head screwed on correctly, he'll be all right."

"The major said they'd be at the school tomorrow."

"I don't know why they had to come to the village at all. No one in Linbury – no one in the whole of Dorsetshire is going to start a revolution, are they? This is a bad business all round – bad for trade, bad for everyone. Mrs P. was really upset."

"You mean about the soldiers stealing stuff from her shop? The major called it foraging."

"She didn't mention anything about stealing. No, about what she let slip to that sharp-nosed captain."

"What did she let slip?"

"The printing ink she orders for the Snells."

"Mrs Snell isn't exactly my idea of a subversive. She was ready to arrest Harry on King James's Night for insulting the monarchy."

"Sometimes those who shout loudest have the most to hide."

"Did they interview you, Dad?"

"They did, but I'm just a simple country innkeeper, aren't I? Yes sir, no sir, three bags full sir."

Freddy smiled for the first time that evening. "Are those two officers paying for their board?"

"They've given me one guinea for the three nights."

"Each?"

"No."

Freddy frowned. "Do you think our regulars will be in later?"

"They've got two options," said Daniel, rising from his chair. "and in case they make the right one, I'd better get the tea ready. It's a meat and potato pie, one of Doughy's, so it should be all right. Now, off you go for half an hour and see how the land lies. But don't go near your uncle's, hear?"

When Freddy went out into the late evening sunshine, he saw that almost half the village had gathered on the far side of the green in front of the Snells' cottage. Two soldiers were guarding the gate to the small front garden. There was little noise or movement from the crowd, merely an uneasy curiosity.

Freddy wandered over, noticing the familiar broad shoulders of the blacksmith's son. "What's going on, Russ?" he asked, coming up beside him.

"I don't know what to make of it, Freddy. They say they've found an unlicensed printing press in the Snells' cellar."

"But everyone knows the Snells print the village flyers and the parish newsletter, near enough for free, and if they had to pay a licence fee, we'd all be worse off."

"People are talking…"

"Talking through their back of beyonds," said Freddy.

Russ chuckled. "Fancy you defending Mrs Snell."

"This is just like one of those witch hunts they used to do a hundred years ago."

"If this is a witch hunt, they'd definitely have to arrest Mrs Snell," said Russ.

Freddy laughed. "Good one, Russ. Are you and your dad coming in later?"

"Should be. Don't want those army people listening into our conversations, though."

Chapter Eighteen

The Slings and Arrows of Outrageous Fortune

Simon Blotwell sat bouncing up and down on his bed in study number 15. It was an unconscious action, because he was actually concentrating on reading the story of Rapunzel from his all-time favourite piece of literature, *My Beautiful Book of Fairy Tales.* Since being banished from the infirmary, he had successfully kept up his lethargic lifestyle by the simple expedient of not returning to the classroom. For this he had Donald Sanderson and Jeremy Pincher to thank: their assault had forced him to take the indolent path.

While recovering from the painful punch to his kidney which one of the house captains had inflicted on his person, it had occurred to him, rightly, that Betty Golightly, Matron's successor, would be unable to complete the discharge docket required by the school office, and therefore his absence would go unnoticed.

The only activity he had seriously engaged in since that episode was to write a strongly worded letter to Auntie Millicent concerning the unfair dismissal of Matron and the vulgar commonality of the girl who had replaced her, especially her antics in the school chapel, though, of course, he made no mention of the person with whom the antics were performed.

'Rapunzel, Rapunzel, let down your hair...' Simon wondered what it would be like to have hair as long as Rapunzel. He concluded that it would be much too heavy and impossible to keep clean, but that it would make him slightly less ordinary. 'Homely' was the least worst description of him that sympathetic family members could come up with. Others less charitable said he was the runt of the family and he should have been rolled on at birth.

His musings were interrupted by the arrival of his study mate, Henry Perceval.

"Are you still here, you lazy dog?"

"I've been reading Rapunzel. I think she and I are opposites."

"Why?"

"She wanted to escape from the tower, while I would be quite content to stay there."

"You'd soon get bored."

"Henry, is it lunch time yet? My tummy is empty."

"It's break time."

"Oh, botheration! I don't suppose you've got a biscuit on you, have you? If I'm seen I shall have to go back to lessons, and it's Greek followed by Latin."

Henry offered him one of the two biscuits he'd bought at the tuck shop. Simon seized it greedily. "I'm surprised you haven't been called yet."

"Archer, Atkins, Ballantyne, Bishop then me," said Blotwell through a mouthful of crumbs. "Though if they think I'm still in the infirmary, I might not be called at all."

"I wouldn't get your hopes up. You weren't in assembly this morning when the doctor introduced Major Foster. A man who means business, if ever I saw one. The remove are being done tomorrow and I'm not looking forward to it, even though I've got nothing to hide."

"What should I tell them, Henry?"

"Well, you could tell the truth for once in your life."

Simon put *My Beautiful Book of Fairy Tales* beside him on the bed. "I couldn't do that."

"Why not? Just like me, you've got nothing to hide. You aren't a Silesian sympathiser and you hardly knew White."

"I didn't like him. He called me a misfit."

Henry chuckled. "You are a misfit, Simon, you silly ass."

"He pronounces 'Auntie' as 'Anti' which is very common."

"He's a Briton. They all speak like that."

"I wouldn't like to live there, then."

"So, are you going to tell the truth and shame the devil?"

"Cheeseman would kill me."

"Cheeseman? What's he got to do with it?"

"He said he'd kill me if I told anyone what happened."

Henry sat down on his bed opposite Simon. "What are you talking about?"

"I can't tell you either, because Cheeseman would kill me then probably kill you as well."

Henry leaned forward, his hands clasped between his legs. "Simon, you're worrying me. What are you saying?"

"I would probably have made a full confession to the Reverend McKellan when I got back to Dunhambury. I might even have confessed to the Reverend Croft but he's not interested and drinks a lot of porter."

"What are you feeling guilty about?"

"I'm a very great sinner, Henry, and unless I'm able to offload my sins I know I shall go straight to Hell."

"I don't believe that, Simon."

"I told Stalky & Co. what I was going to do, otherwise they would have tweaked me. But that was before White was expelled and before the poster came out. I'd almost forgotten about it when Cheeseman came to the infirmary, but he pressed his thumbs into my windpipe and threatened to throttle me."

"What have you done, Simon?"

"Cheeseman gave me the drink and the pamphlets and I planted them in White's study." Blotwell took out his handkerchief and blew his nose. "There, I've told you now. That means we're both going to die."

A knock at the door made them both jump. Ralph Ballantyne stuck his head into the study and smirked in triumph. "I knew you'd bunked off, Blotwell. They want you in school room number one, stat! I hope they give you a good grilling. Then you're going to get extra prep from Ollerenshaw and, if you miss Latin, from Caulton-Harris as well."

"But Bishop is before me," said Simon.

"He's in there now. I volunteered to find you. Ha ha!" With that, Ballantyne made off down the corridor still chuckling to himself.

"Oh, botheration!" said Blotwell, standing up and stamping his foot.

"Tell them the truth, Simon, please," said Henry.

* * *

At 12.45 p.m. Mr Caulton-Harris dismissed his Latin class with the dreaded line, 'You will translate *The Story of Cadmus* from Ovid Book III for prep, and if you think you can get away with copying Mr Addison's version you are very much mistaken.'

Freddy hung back from his shell classmates as they bounded down the stairs from school room number three to the ground floor. His slower than usual progress was down to the desire to find out what was going on in school room number one, where Major Foster and Captain Maunday had made their base.

At the bottom of the stairs he turned 90 degrees through the double doors into the corridor, where all was quiet except for a lone figure sitting on a bench outside the classroom.

"Blotwell, what are you doing here?"

"Waiting."

"Who's in there at the moment?"

"I don't know. Freddy. When are you returning my second most favourite book, *Adventures in the Future?*"

"I'll bring it up to your study tomorrow afternoon," replied Freddy absently, putting his ear to the door. There was no sound. "Are you sure there's anyone in there? It's awfully quiet."

Simon sighed. "I've been sitting here for a long time and

I'm getting very hungry."

Tentatively, Freddy turned the handle and opened the door a fraction, then he pushed it wide open. The classroom was deserted, with merely a lone chair set before the master's desk to indicate that interrogations had taken place.

"There's no one in here, Blotwell."

"Oh goody, in that case I'm going to get some lunch."

"Where are they?"

Simon shook his head, smiling broadly, relief spread across his face.

"Has anyone gone in or out since you got here?"

"Not that I noticed, Freddy."

A voice echoed down the corridor. "Blotwell!"

"Oh Lord!"

Mr Caulton-Harris walked up to the two boys, but his eyes were fixed on Simon. "You are a lazy, good-for-nothing shirker, Blotwell. You will translate Ovid Book III, *The Story of Cadmus* and *The Transformation of Actaeon into a Stag* for prep which will be completed by Friday. Is that clear?"

"Yes, sir," said Simon, his smile now a distant memory.

"Excuse me, Mr Caulton-Harris. Do you know where the two officers are who were doing the interviews?" asked Freddy.

"I do not, and the sooner they are out of this school and on their way back to Oakleigh, the better." The master turned on his heel and strode off.

While Simon headed for the School House refectory, Freddy made his way to the osher's main entrance. It was raining, which dampened his enthusiasm for further investigations of the soldiers' whereabouts. Instead, he ran over to Drake House where he found Harry waiting for him.

"Have you been interviewed?"

"No, I went to have a look and found Blotwell sitting outside in the corridor."

"Blotwell? You mean they're still doing the Bs?"

"I mean, there was no one else there. The classroom was empty."

"Is that good or bad?" asked Harry.

"I don't know, but it feels wrong."

"Come on, let's get something to eat."

In Drake House, Mrs Edith Palmerston and her daughter Ellen presided over the preparation and serving out of the food. They stood behind two folding tables, one with the main meal, the preserve of the cheerful Mrs Palmerston, and the second with the pudding and drink, usually milk, the domain of her daughter.

The two boys joined the queue behind Frank Kennedy and his friend, Carstairs.

"I spy strangers," said Harry.

Frank looked round. "Hawwy East, Carstairs is my guest."

"That right? What's the matter with the food in Raleigh today?"

Carstairs turned. "It's gone to the dogs since Pincher took over. Today it's potato soup and a herring followed by tapioca pudding. Yuk!"

"Fwog spawn," said Frank disgustedly.

"I like tapioca pudding," said Freddy. "Mrs May makes it in the dairy in Linbury. It's chewy and creamy and sometimes she'll put a dollop of preserve on it."

"It's watery lumps in Raleigh," said Carstairs, grimacing.

"Veal and ham pie, luvvies?" asked Mrs Palmerston. "Onion sauce and peas?"

"Yes pease," said Frank and he and Carstairs giggled.

"Tut, tut, tut, the children of today," said Harry. "Surely we weren't like that at their age?"

After collecting his main course, Harry moved on to the pudding table where Ellen was standing over a large earthenware dish of stewed rhubarb.

"Hmm, this should keep me regular," he said, grinning and waggling his eyebrows.

Ellen's cheeks went slightly pink but her expression didn't change.

"A bowl for me and a large one for my irregular friend."

"Shut up, Scud," said Freddy.

* * *

A fine drizzle coming off the sea made the walk back up to Linbury a miserable affair for Freddy that afternoon. As he approached the village boundary marker, a double line of soldiers came into view riding out of Main Street. In their midst was the prison wagon pulled by two horses.

Freddy stood back to let them pass. At the head of the column were Major Foster and Captain Maunday. They rode past without acknowledging his presence. Two more riders followed then the prison wagon came by, rattling on its metal rims. Peering out through the bars was Tom White, wearing only a loincloth. With him, bewildered and unresponsive, propped against the back wall of the wagon was Mr Snell.

Freddy saw the look of hopelessness on Tom's face. Their eyes met for a brief moment before the wagon rolled on down the incline. Freddy stood, as if transfixed, as the rear guard of horsemen passed by. Then the last soldier broke ranks. He came at Freddy and punched him in the face, knocking him backwards so that he lost his balance and fell to the ground.

The soldier re-joined the line and the troop carried on as if nothing had happened.

Freddy picked himself up and wiped the blood from his nose. He felt like crying but instead turned resolutely towards Linbury and home.

* * *

"Oh my, whatever next?" said Daniel, setting a bowl of warm water on the table next to his son, who sat in front of the fire, draped in a blanket.

"How did it happen?" asked Freddy, his voice nasal.

"I should be asking you that question. They chased him into the churchyard. That's where they cornered him, as naked as the day he was born." Daniel carefully wiped Freddy's face and nose with a cloth, then began to dry his hair gently with a towel.

"But if they were searching the windmill, why didn't he hide on the beach or somewhere until they'd gone?"

"I don't know, lad. Maybe he just panicked, like Mrs Snell. She was beside herself. I've never seen her like that before. She was practically clawing at the wagon. The soldiers were laughing at her, the poor woman, until Miss Antrobus came over and took her away."

"I hate them," said Freddy.

Russell Warren put his head round the door. "Afternoon, Mr Hall. I came to see how Freddy is. I saw him from the shop. Looked like the walking wounded."

"Come in, Russ," said Freddy. "I'm all right. One of the soldiers gave me a bang on the nose as he was riding by."

"Why?"

"I'm guessing he was the one I reported for stealing from Mrs Pattle's shop."

"Park yourself on a chair, lad," said Daniel. "I'll make us all a pot of tea."

Russ pulled up a chair opposite Freddy. "I'm certainly glad they're gone, and I hope they don't come back."

"Will you come up to the mill with me, Russ? I want to see what's been going on."

"Do you think them soldiers might have damaged the telescope?"

Freddy nodded. "I wouldn't put anything past them."

"Now then," said Daniel, "I don't want you gallivanting around when you've just been punched. You might have concussion."

"I'm all right, Dad, honestly."

Russell rubbed his bristly chin. "Folks is sayin' that they found Silesian propaganda at the Snells'."

"Folks is sayin'!" said Daniel. "Blether, blather. Name anyone who has any proof."

"Why would they take Mr Snell away if he was innocent?"

"I don't know, but I am of the opinion that a body is innocent until he is found guilty in a court of law. Not by soldiers riding roughshod over people's lives."

"That's my dad." Freddy smiled.

* * *

Later, after tea and bacon sandwiches, Freddy and Russell meandered up the track towards Tanner's Mill, sidestepping the puddles. Water still dripped from the overhanging boughs, though the rain had stopped and a little late evening sunshine glimmered through the high cloud, bathing the countryside in a pinkish glow.

"Your dad's a good man, isn't he?" said Russ.

"Is that a statement or a question?" asked Freddy with a smile.

"You take after him."

"I don't know about that."

"I do."

Freddy gave Russell a sideways look, but the blacksmith's son was staring straight ahead.

"I saw your friend Harry and that boy on Sunday coming out of the Yarn and darting over the green. I wondered who it was at first, until I remembered the poster."

Freddy was stopped in his tracks. "Russ..."

"There's no need to worry. I'm not going to let on. That's why I like being an usher at the church, so I can get out and have a smoke while the Reverend is droning on..."

"Sorry to put you in that position."

"Them soldiers never got to the Ws anyways so I didn't have to lie to them." Russ looked bashfully at his friend. "You can trust me, Freddy Hall. I won't let you down."

"Oh God, Russ, I do trust you!"

"That boy from Briton. What's he like?"

"To be honest, I didn't know him that well. He was a house

captain at the school and I think he was generally well thought of. I was told that he preferred to keep his own company and that when he lived in Briton he got into some bad ways, including heavy drinking."

"Why were you helping him, then?"

"That's the oddest part. I was asked to, in a roundabout sort of way, even before he got into trouble."

"Oh, now you're confusing me."

"It is confusing and I don't really understand it myself."

"But now they're taking him to that prison in London along with Mr Snell."

"The Marshalsea. Dad says it's a debtors' prison, but it's also where the Royal Navy houses its prisoners and the king keeps the seditionists there who aren't important enough to lock up in the Tower." Freddy twitched his nose, which was sorer than he liked to admit.

As they neared the top of the rise, the windmill came into view, its sails revolving slowly, the fantail pointing north-east.

"Looks like your uncle has been milling today," said Russ, swinging the gate open.

"I doubt it," said Freddy. "I don't think there's anything to mill at the moment."

They passed the cottage where Lucy the goat was tethered and walked down the rutted track towards the windmill. The door was open. Inside they found the miller one floor up inspecting the flour troughs, while Jasper was lying at the foot of the ladder.

"You were right, Russ," murmured Freddy who then called out. "Hello, Uncle Albert, have you been grinding?"

The miller's head appeared in the hatch above them. "Just a few leftover bags, makin' sure them pesky soldiers did no damage. I thought you might be along, young Freddy, for an inspection."

"Evening, Mr Tanner," said Russ.

"Russell Warren as well. You've brought the heavy gang with you."

"Have you been up to the cap?" asked Freddy.

"No, that's your territory these days. I only go up there if I have to, what with my leg an' all."

"Did the soldiers search the mill?"

"Four of them there were, on horseback. They frightened your Auntie Emily. Two of them went through the cottage without so much as a by-your-leave, while the other two came down here. The door was unlocked, but no sooner had they come inside than that boy was charging back down the track towards the gate. Don't know where he was hid. Stark naked he was, but running like greased lightning. The soldiers tore after him and one even fired his musket, but the lad was way too fast. They got on their horses and rode off after him down the road. Left the gate open. Jasper was barking and poor Lucy took fright and was bleating for all she was worth."

"They caught him in the churchyard," said Russ. "Put him in the cage along with Mr Snell."

"Bad business. Are they still camped in the village?" asked Albert.

"No, they rode out this afternoon. One of them punched Freddy."

Albert looked closely at his nephew. "I thought your face was a mite puffy, lad. Why in the world would one of His Majesty's troops do that?"

"I think it was because I'd reported him for stealing from Pattle's shop."

"Well, I never. Ruffians. Good riddance to the lot of them. Disturbing our peace."

Freddy and Russ climbed through the mill floors to the top where they found the den neat and tidy.

"He's even left Dad's old drawers and smock nicely folded on the bed," said Freddy.

"It's a while since I've been up here," said Russ, who had to stoop around the perimeter of the cap to avoid bumping his head.

"I don't get so much time now that I'm at school, but

if you wanted to come up here and have a look through the telescope, you're always welcome."

Russell nodded and bent to look through the sight on top of the telescope barrel. "Oh, I can't see anything."

Freddy walked over and had a look for himself. "You're right. It's blocked." He unscrewed the front lens and peered inside the narrow bore. Then with finger and thumb he reached inside and pulled out a rolled-up sheet of paper.

Russell stood behind him as he unfolded it, revealing a letter written in a neat hand.

My dear Freddy,

By the time you read this, I shall either be dead or on my way to the Marshalsea. What lies before me, I do not know.

Thank you for your patience and understanding during my time of troubles. Please thank your father for his kindness, and that rascal Harry East for showing his true character when a chap is in need.

Now that I am to be the subject of a hue and cry, I couldn't let you or your family become party to my misdeeds, whatever they may be. I shall therefore make myself known to the officers of the law and confess to my 'crimes'.

It is for the best. I have no relatives to turn to and nowhere else to go.

Please forgive my cowardice.

Your sincere friend,

Thomas White

Chapter Nineteen

Burn!

"Fweddy Hall, why are you sad this morning?"

Freddy sighed and smiled at Frank. "I've got a lot on my mind at the moment."

The two boys were standing outside the gates of Seekings School, which were locked. There was no sign of Mr Hawlings and it was almost quarter to nine.

"It's music first perwiod," said Frank. "I like Mr Williams, even though he's a bit spiderwy."

"Did you know his first name's Francis?"

"Is it weally Fwancis or is it Fwank?"

"It's really Francis, though I have heard people call him Frank."

"My dad says I should learn the twumpet or the twombone, but they're too loud for me, Fweddy."

"Everyone says I'm tone deaf, but I don't think I am."

Mr Hawlings appeared at the gates with a bunch of keys. "Had to go back and get them," he said breathlessly. "Getting forgetful in my old age."

"How old *are* you, Mr Hawlings?" asked Frank, knotting his brow.

"Well now, there's a question. I'm your age, times the age of the oldest magpie in the school grounds, plus your age."

"That's vewy old," said Frank, raising his black eyebrows.

Freddy went up to the gate. "I've got a letter to show you, Mr Hawlings."

The caretaker stepped backwards. "Now, what have I told you about writings, Mr Hall?"

"But..."

"No buts." Mr Hawlings looked at Frank. "Who do you share secrets with, Master Kennedy?"

"Carstairs."

"There, does that answer your question, Freddy Hall? And here comes the mail coach, just in time. Now, do you want me to give you a piece of advice?"

Freddy nodded.

"Take a Lucifer to that writing."

Frank had already covered his ears and shut his eyes when the post horn sounded.

"Just this one today, Mr Hawlings," shouted the coachman, throwing down a parcel wrapped in brown paper. With surprising agility, the old caretaker caught it easily.

Hardly had Harry scrambled down from the passenger seat than the driver cracked his whip and the mail coach set off for Linbury.

"He was in a huwwy today," said Frank.

Mr Hawlings held the gate open for them. "Needs must when the devil drives. He's late, so hurry along before you're late as well."

As if in response, the school bell tolled out its five-minute warning.

* * *

At break, Freddy sat on the steps outside the entrance to the osher, waiting for Harry to appear. He had not slept well the night before and the double period of music had only added to his lethargy. So much so that he was finding it difficult to stay awake. Freddy was among the pretenders in music lessons: that is, when they were asked to sing, he had to mime the words while the rest warbled away.

"Now, what's this sack of straw doing on the steps?"

Freddy yawned. "It's been waiting for you."

"Oh, it speaks. The very first talking sack of straw."

Freddy picked himself up. "Scud, let's go somewhere quiet."

Harry leaned against the trunk of a beech tree standing singly between Drake House and the playing fields. "That was a waste of time, then," he said, handing back the letter written by Tom White. "All that subterfuge on Sunday."

"He gave himself up so none of us would get into trouble, and now he's on his way to prison in London."

"Federico, we can't do anything about it, so you'll have to stop worrying. I know you – like a dog with a bone, you won't let go. What if he is a Silesian agitator or even a spy?"

"What would a spy be doing at Seekings? What happened to the Declaration of Rights? Why was Mr Snell arrested, even if he did print those pamphlets?"

"Did he print them?"

"I don't know, and neither does anyone else in Linbury."

"I would like to have seen one. Especially one with the Lady Castlemaine…"

"Scud, you are a ridiculous ass."

Harry chuckled. "I know, but at least I made you smile."

"Mr Hawlings says I should burn this letter."

"Hooray, old Hawlings has said something that makes sense for once. Burn it and forget it!" Harry laughed. "You looked so glum. I bet you were tossing and turning in bed last night, thinking about poor Thomas White."

"There's something not right here. I wish you could understand that."

"Come on, old fellow. I'll treat you to a exorbitantly priced pick-me-up at the tuck shop."

**

Three-quarters of an hour on the Third Punic War and the sacking of Carthage followed by another three-quarters of an hour on St Paul's Epistle to the Galatians did nothing to raise Freddy's spirits. If anything, he felt more worn out and useless.

"Luncheon," said Harry.

"Not hungry," said Freddy.

"Come on, I bet Mrs W. or sweet Ellen will have something to tempt you."

They headed for the Drake House refectory and joined the queue. When it was their turn, Harry had a plateful of Irish stew while Freddy could only manage a bowl of lemon flummery and a glass of water.

They joined Frank and Carstairs at one of the long tables. They were deep in conversation concerning their plans for the afternoon.

"The best of three games of chess," said Carstairs, who was using a spoon on his Irish Stew and peas rather than a knife and fork.

"All wight," replied Frank.

"Then one hour of butterfly hunting in Coneycop Spinney."

"All wight."

"Then half an hour paddling followed by half an hour beachcombing around the lagoon, then you go home."

"All wight."

"Do you always decide what you're going to do on Wednesday afternoons, Carstairs?" asked Harry.

"We take it in turns," the big eleven-year-old replied.

"So, what do you do when it's your turn, Frank?"

"It depends on the season, Hawwy East, but usually I choose the best of thwee games of chess, butterfly hunting in Coneycop Spinney, paddling in the lagoon followed by beachcombing, then I go home."

Harry nodded. "I guess great minds think alike."

Frank tried to ease a forkful of peas into his mouth, but several wouldn't cooperate and landed in his lap. "Oh dear," he said.

Carstairs tutted and waved his spoon at Frank. "I eat my peas with honey, I've done it all my life. It makes the peas taste funny, but it keeps them on the knife..."

Both boys roared with laughter. "Oh, Carstairs, you are funny," said Frank.

"My Auntie Annie taught me that one." Carstairs beamed.

"That is so silly," said Harry, smiling despite himself.

"I've got a bit of business in School House," said Freddy, pushing away his half-eaten bowl of flummery. "I'll see you tomorrow."

On the spur of the moment, he had decided to go up to study number fifteen ostensibly to return Blotwell's book, but really to find out which was Beetle Kipling's room, for they were due a conversation. He wasn't yet certain whether he was going to 'borrow' another of Simon's books; that would depend on whether or not he was too tired to argue the point.

After knocking several times with no answer, Freddy stuck his head round the door. Blotwell was lying prone on his bed, his head buried in *My Beautiful Book of Fairy Tales*.

"Simon, why didn't you answer the door?"

Blotwell looked up. "No one knocks for me."

Freddy entered the study and closed the door. "I just did. Where's Henry?"

"Probably up in the attic with Fox Talbot. I say, Freddy, have you read 'The Tinderbox'? It has a dog with eyes as big as teacups and another—"

"Is that the one where the soldier cuts off the witch's head?"

"Yes, it is, but that is not a very nice part."

"I've brought back *Adventures in the Future*. It was interesting, especially the story on electromagnetic telegraphy."

Simon swung himself off the bed and began a close inspection of the book.

"It's all there," said Freddy. "And the only common Linbury person to touch it was me."

"It seems undamaged."

"Can I borrow another one?"

"Freddy, you put me in a very difficult position."

"Really, and what position is that?"

"The position of having to say no." Simon bent and adjusted his new pair of Clarks Petersburg slippers which he had received that day.

"If you say yes, you don't have to put yourself in a difficult position," said Freddy, eyeing the rack of books and picking one out. "This one looks interesting."

"Which one?"

"It's called *Johnny the Jungle Boy: Friend to All the Animals.*"

Simon looked up. "Oh that's just a penny dreadful for common working boys."

"A penny dreadful? Fully illustrated in colour, price £15. I don't know many common working boys who could afford that. I certainly couldn't. It's been well thumbed as well."

"Oh, all right, you can borrow that one. It's not important."

"Thank you, Simon. What's it about?"

"Er, a coarse farm boy called Johnny runs away to sea after his family is slaughtered by brigands. He serves as a cabin boy on board a Royal Navy ship called the *Frigate Fancy,* but is foully treated by the first mate, Femur Fawcett."

"Femur?"

"Yes, Freddy. Then during a raging storm the *Frigate Fancy* flounders and all hands are lost except Johnny and Femur, who are washed up on a tropical island…"

"Sounds good, but don't tell me any more, or it'll spoil the story." Freddy put the book in his satchel. "How many lines have you got to do so far this week, Simon?"

"Oh, I don't know. I lose count."

"Do you ever do your lines?"

"No, it's too much trouble." Simon yawned, which made Freddy realise how tired he was.

"What number is Beetle Kipling's study?"

"I'm not sure. It's down the corridor somewhere."

"Can you be a little more precise?"

Simon climbed back onto his bed. "Not really. Go left at

the door marked *ATTIC*."

Freddy hadn't appreciated that the corridor on the first floor of School House continued at ninety degrees to itself. He paused to look down the much shorter passageway to a flight of stairs at the end. By his elbow, someone had hung a sign on the wall: *Senior Fifth-Formers Only.* He moved on. There were only five doors to choose from. The first two were open, but it was the third one that caught his attention, for even outside there was a strong smell of pipe tobacco. He knocked.

M'Turk answered, holding a half-bent Dublin pipe in his right hand. He gazed around and over Freddy's shoulder, then looked back into the room at a dark shape sitting in an armchair, visible through a cloud of pungent smoke. "Well, shiver me timbers, Beetle dear, there be no one here, by the powers." He began to shut the door, but Freddy stuck his foot out.

"I want to speak to Kipling."

M'Turk sucked in a hot mouthful of Mrs Pattle's famous shag tobacco smoke and blew it out at Freddy. "You is a persistent little monkey, ain't you?"

Freddy held his breath for a few seconds before replying. "It won't take long."

"Confound the fellow and let him pass, Turkey," said a voice from within.

Once inside, Freddy felt his eyes watering. Even though the bar room of the Sailor's Yarn was often smoky, it was not as concentrated as this.

"Why don't you open the window?" he said.

"What, and let this delicious aroma leak out?" said Beetle. "What do you want, Hall? And make it snappy. You already look as if you're blubbin', which is not a pretty sight."

"Where did Stalky get that handbill that he passed on to Berty Wright to fool Frank Kennedy into giving it to Tallow?"

"Are me lugs out of order?" said Beetle, putting his left index finger in his ear and wriggling it. "Has my brain gone dead? I can't keep up with all that namin' an' shamin'."

"You know what I'm talking about."

"I don't answer for the Great Man. He lives next door."

"Whatever you three do, you always do it together."

"Well, it turns out I was AWOL for this jape."

M'Turk waved his pipe in Freddy's face. "Why are you asking the third-hand Beetle and not the first-hand Stalky?"

"He knows why."

"Oh, horrid Hall," said Beetle. "You have the gummy cheek to come in here all high and mighty and then resort to blackmail?"

"Only because you won't tell me otherwise."

"And what if I don't tell you? What of Clarrie May when you broadcast your giddy filth?"

"I'm not understandin' this biznai one bit," said M'Turk. "Why are you conversin' with a shell lack, as if it was normal?"

"Just give me a name and I'll go," said Freddy, who was swaying with the effects of tiredness and tobacco.

"I'm only tellin' you cos it turned out more immoral than it should, and I wasn't consulted."

Freddy nodded.

"Ask that rotting carcass Blotwell. He's in it up to his beastly neck."

"Blotwell?"

"*Fermez la porte* on your putrescent way out and never darken these doors again," said Beetle.

Once outside in the passage, Freddy took some deep breaths before moving away from the door, which had been slammed shut behind him. As he turned right into the familiar corridor the attic door opened and Henry Perceval almost bumped into him.

"You smell of smoke," said Henry.

"I'm feeling a bit light-headed," said Freddy. "And I've got to talk to Simon."

They walked together down the corridor. "I'm afraid we've had a disagreement and we aren't speaking. Sad, really, isn't it?" said Henry.

"What did you disagree about?"

"Duty and honour."

"I think I know which side Blotwell falls on."

They reached number 15 and entered. Simon was still lying on his bed engrossed in 'The Tinderbox'. Henry sat on his own bed while Freddy took a chair, both viewing the recumbent figure with a critical eye.

After a moment or two, Simon raised his head. "I can't concentrate while you're both staring at me, and I've just got to the very interesting part where the dog with eyes as big as teacups marks all the doors in the town with a chalk cross."

"It's good that you can't concentrate," said Freddy. "Put the book down and listen."

"Are you going to lecture me on sin and redemption, like Mr Perceval?"

"No, but I've got some questions and I'd like you to tell the truth."

Simon put a leather bookmark with an embossed image of a rabbit into the page he was reading, closed the book, knelt on the bed, put the book carefully back on the shelf, swung himself round and sat down on the edge of the bed. "Daddy says I'm a congenital liar with no more morals than a stoat in a sack."

"Why don't you prove him wrong then?" asked Henry – the first words he'd spoken to Simon in twenty-four hours.

"Because I'm an abject coward as well."

Freddy leaned forward and spoke quietly. "Beetle Kipling says you know about the handbill that Berty Wright gave to Frank Kennedy to show Mr Tallow."

"I had nothing to do with that," said Blotwell, his eyes flitting up to the ceiling.

"You knew about it, though?"

"Only in passing."

"Beetle says you're in it up to your neck."

"Is this about Tom White?" enquired Henry.

Freddy turned his attention to the older boy. "Yes, it is."

"Tell him, Simon, or I will."

"Do you want Freddy to die as well?"

"The truth will out and it's time it did," said Henry. "Never mind who's going to die."

"What's this about?" asked Freddy.

"Go on, Simon, tell him what you told me."

Blotwell smiled and folded his arms loosely over his chest. "Cheeseman gave me the pamphlets and the bottle of whisky and I planted them in White's study."

There was a rushing sound in Freddy's ears. He had to shake his head to dispel it. "This isn't some kind of joke, is it? You do know that Tom White was taken prisoner and is on his way to the Marshalsea jail, don't you? You do know that he's going to confess to these crimes he didn't commit to spare us any trouble."

"Oh, I say!" said Henry. "Now you have to report that brute Cheeseman, Simon."

"I shall do no such thing," replied Blotwell. "White is very common and probably a spy as well."

There was a slight noise outside the door. Henry looked up, momentarily distracted, then fixed his eyes back on Simon. "You're talking nonsense. If you don't do something, I shall. This episode has gone on far too long."

"So, this was all a conspiracy to get Cheeseman the school captaincy, and in doing so Tom White's life has been ruined?" said Freddy.

"Cheeseman will become school captain and I shall be his slave, otherwise he will kill me," said Blotwell. "But that doesn't matter, so long as White doesn't go to jail."

"Shut up, Simon," said Henry. "How do you know about all this, Freddy? You must have some inside knowledge."

"Tom White came to Linbury and we hid him from the soldiers."

Henry's eyes went wide. "Why?"

"Because I was asked to. I can't say any more than that."

"But if you hid him, why did he get caught?"

"He gave himself up." Freddy took the letter out of his satchel and handed it to Henry.

"How did you come by this?"

"It was rolled up and hidden in my telescope."

"Let me see," said Blotwell.

"Only if you agree to go with me to see Dr Butler," said Freddy. "Because that's what we've got to do."

Simon stood up, stamped his foot and snatched the letter. Then the door opened. Donald Sanderson entered and snatched the letter from Simon. "Thank you. I'm sure A.C. will be very happy to receive this." He laughed, turned on his heel and was away down the corridor before they could react. Henry went to the door and looked out, but Sanderson had already disappeared from sight.

Freddy held his head in despair. "I was told to burn it, but I didn't listen. What a fool I am!"

"That's that," said Blotwell. "Either we'll all be dead or in jail. All because of that common Briton who called me a misfit."

Freddy swayed as he stood up. "I'm going up to get that letter back from Cheeseman."

"He'll laugh in your face," said Henry.

"If Mr Tallow gets hold of it, you'll be a dead duck," said Simon, gleefully. "Which is why we should let sleeping dogs lie."

"I can't do that."

"Freddy," said Henry, "the letter implicates not only you but also your father and Harry East."

"I know. I don't seem able to concentrate."

"I think you ought to go home, old chap. You're looking quite ill."

Freddy wiped his nose. "I do feel hot and bothered."

"Right! Come on, I shall escort you up to Linbury. I don't want you falling by the wayside."

Simon smiled. "And I can get back to my book and pretend all this never happened."

Chapter Twenty

A House Divided

Thursday 25th May 1826
 To: Harry East,
 Jersey House,
 Larkstone,
 Dorsetshire.

Dear Scud,

I've made a complete hash of things and now I'm home in bed recovering from the measles. Cheeseman has got hold of the letter that Tom White wrote, which means we could all be in trouble. Mr Hawlings kept telling me to destroy it, but I just kept putting it off. What an idiot I am! Knowing Cheeseman, he'll use it to blackmail me into not reporting his scheme to discredit Tom. What do you think I should do?

If you're still friends with me, I'd like you to come to my birthday party at 2 p.m. on the 11th June.

Your best friend,

Freddy

PS Burn this letter!

* * *

Saturday 27th May 1826
 To: Mr F. Hall,
 The Sailor's Yarn Inn,
 Linbury,

Dorsetshire.

Dear Mr Hall,

Because of your behaviour over that letter, I have no alternative but to end our friendship forthwith.
I should be obliged if you would cease all communication with me as of now.
Yours,
H. East

PTO

Dear old Federico,

If you believed that, you are the biggest blockhead this side of the Albion Channel. Of course I'm coming to your birthday party. Even if you didn't invite me, I'd still come.

As to that letter, Henry told me what happened, and I say let it go hang. Do the right thing and report Cheeseman – that is, when we get back, as the school is under quarantine until the 19th!

See, there are some good things about measles. Ma told me I had them when I was seven, but I can't remember a thing about it. Anyway, I hope you're over the worst now. Stop mooning and worrying and enjoy the rest.

Your best, best friend ever,

Scud

P.S. I've booked the pony and trap and will stop by the school at 1.30 on the 11th to pick up our little friend.

PPS. Your letter has gone up in smoke.

* * *

Tuesday 30th May 1826

To: Carl Birch,
c/o Royal Naval Hospital School,
Greenwich.

My dear friend Carl,

I've had the measles, spots all over everywhere. I'm still at home and the school is under quarantine. Almost eighty boys are affected. The day boys have been told to stay away until the 19th June. That means there'll be only three weeks of school left before we break up for the summer holidays!

Apart from me, no one in the village has been affected as far as I know. Harry and Russ are all right – they both had it when they were little. For a time, I couldn't stand the light and had to have the shutters closed, but I'm over the worst now.

There's a lot I'd like to tell you about what's been happening in the village and at school over the past few weeks. It's not good news, and I think that's what made me more sickly than I should have been.

It's my birthday on the 11th, and I was hoping you might be able to get permission to visit me. Please try. Get the coach up here on the Friday before and stay for as long as you're allowed. It's only fair that I pay for your travel out of Mr Newton's bursary.

Everyone is looking forward to meeting you, most of all me. Let me know.

Yr affectionate friend,

Freddy

PS Say hello to everyone from your spotty chum(p).

* * *

Friday 2nd June 1826
To: Frank Kennedy,
Clifftop Lighthouse,

Between Linbury and Larkstone,
Dorsetshire.

Dear Francis,

I'm having a party for my fourteenth birthday on Sunday 11th June and you're invited. (I'm expecting a reciprocal invitation from you in July.) If you want to come, and to save your little legs, Harry will be waiting at the school gates at 1.30 p.m. (school time) in his pony and trap.

Your friend,

Freddy

* * *

Saturday 3rd June 1826

To: Freddy Hall,
The Sailor's Yarn Inn,
Linbury,
Dorsetshire.

Dear Freddy,
Commodore Hughes has said it'll do everyone good to get me out of their hair for a bit. So, the trip's on. I can't wait! All my crew mates are jealous that I'm getting a pass by way of holiday leave. But I've got to be back on the 14th.

It's been frantic here, but more of that when I see you.

Someone must love me a lot, 'cos they've got posti to drive me all the way to Bray. And is he in a fit about it? I'll be able to catch the coach from there, which will save you a few bob.

I had measles when I was a nipper. Can't remember much about it except I was in a dark room too. Maybe for the same reason as you.

See you late Friday,

Your old china,
Carl (John helped me to write this)

PS Everyone – me, John, Pete, Charlie and everyone else – says hello and hopes you're better.

* * *

Monday 5th June 1826
Clifftop Lighthouse,
Clifftop,
nr Linbury,
Dorsetshire

Dear Freddy,
Thank you for the invitation.
Mum says I can go to your party, but I'd like Carstairs to be invited as well. If I don't hear from you, I shall take it as read.
Your friend,
Frank

PS My name's not Francis, Freddy Hall. I'm FRANK.

* * *

9th June 1826

"You're like a cat on hot bricks," said Daniel. "Have you made up your friend's room?"

"Yes, it's all ready."

"Then why don't you go outside and run around a bit until the coach gets here?"

"What if he's not on it, though?"

"You'll wear yourself out worrying like that. You've only just got over the measles. Now go on – get some fresh air inside you and take the mail sack, not that there's much in it today."

"And don't you go spreadin' those spots around," said Zebedee Tring, who was sitting in his customary place with his customary pint of scrumpy, listening in to other people's conversations with his customary nosiness.

"Take no notice of that old duffer, lad, you're well past that time," said Sam Hingston from the fireside in an unusual show of family solidarity.

Once outside, Freddy looked at his watch. It was 6.15 p.m., ten minutes before the westbound coach was due to stop in Linbury, from where it would go on to its overnight halt at the Red Lion in Dunhambury. Wending his way up the street was Elias Harville the journeyman carpenter, leading his old horse with his tools piled into a two wheeled cart behind.

"Your dad got any odd jobs for me, young Freddy? I'm a bit short next week."

"Worth an ask," said Freddy. "The chicken coop door is rotting and we're worried that a fox might get in. There's a broken bar chair and the shutters in the big bedroom aren't closing properly."

"In that case, I'll have a word and maybe stop for a pint."

"The mail coach is due any minute, so I'd watch your horse."

"I'll put her on the green. She'll be all right grazing there."

Elias led the old mare across Main Street to the water trough and tied her to the pump on a long rope attached to her head collar. As he was about to re-cross the street, the post horn sounded and the coach hove into view. The carpenter steadied himself at the edge of the green, unwilling to sally forth. Freddy stepped back, looking up at the church clock. It was twenty-four minutes past six.

Even before the coach had stopped, the passenger behind the coachman was on his feet and waving. It was Carl. Freddy jumped in the air and waved back. The coach halted. Carl practically threw himself off the coach and into Freddy's arms, almost knocking him over. They gave each other a good hug before standing back to look at each other. Carl was in his familiar gansey and bell-bottoms, his cap stuck firmly to his head.

"Oi, you two," said the coachman, "there's a little matter of payment."

Freddy put his hand in his pocket, where he had two golden guineas. "How much?"

The driver sniffed. "The fare from Bray to Dunhambury for an outside passenger is two guineas, but we're not at Dunhambury yet. Your dad gets a discount for being the Linbury postmaster and there's another discount for this cheeky young man keeping us amused on the journey. Shall we say ten and six?"

Freddy smiled at the coachman and handed over one of the guineas and the mail sack. "Thank you. Take a shilling for yourself and one for posti."

"Very generous, sir," said the coachman with a grin. "And here's your mail and eight and six change. Now, the lady's luggage, which the cheeky young sailor boy can take along with his kit bag."

Carl smirked, shouldered his bag and took the small suitcase from the driver. "You and posti be careful with those blunderbusses of yours. They can be dangerous in untrained hands."

Freddy was about to ask about the 'lady's luggage' when a voice came from inside the coach. "Frederick, would you be so kind as to open the door and let down the steps?"

"Mrs Snell?" said Freddy in surprise, doing as he was bid.

The tall, dark-haired woman descended onto the street. She looked tired and, for the smartest dresser in Linbury, almost dishevelled. Freddy noticed dark circles around her eyes and some grey hairs among the black. He closed up the coach and banged on the door, signalling that all was ready for the off.

"See you anon," said the driver and the postilion gave another blast on his horn. The coach pulled away, leaving the three standing outside the inn. Across the street, Freddy noticed Elias look disdainfully at Mrs Snell then spit into the road before turning away to untie his horse.

"Would you like me to carry your case, Mrs Snell?" he asked.

"Thank you, Frederick, but I can manage from here."

"Have you been to see Mr Snell?" asked Freddy tentatively.

Mrs Snell did her best to control herself. "Yes. It's a dreadful place."

"Sorry. I didn't mean to upset you."

"That's all right. It's good of you to ask."

"How is he?"

"Oh, bearing up, I suppose. Putting on a brave face. I took him some food and some tobacco to barter, but I didn't have enough money to pay the full amount of board to the marshal, so I shall have to go back very shortly. It's a most unsanitary and depressing place, Frederick."

"You didn't happen to come across Tom White, the boy who was taken away with Mr Snell?"

Mrs Snell shook her head. "There are those who can pay and there are those who can't. If you can pay, then life is bearable. If you can't, then.."

"I see," said Freddy.

Mrs Snell took her case and walked slowly away towards her cottage on the far side of the green.

"What was all that about?" asked Carl. "Why did that man spit like that?"

Freddy forced himself back to cheerfulness. "I'll answer all your questions when we've fixed you up. Dinner's on: lamb chops with new potatoes and mint sauce and a rhubarb and gooseberry pie for afters."

"Lovely grub. I'm starved," said Carl, "and you need building up after your illness. You're a bit pasty-faced."

"Thanks – that's made me feel a whole lot better."

Carl slung his arm over Freddy's shoulder and squeezed. "My pal," he said. "We'll soon have you to rights."

***

As it was a special occasion, Freddy and Carl had their dinner in the snug, while Daniel had his on top of the bar while still serving customers. Elias Harville sat with Zebedee Tring and grumbled about Mrs Snell, saying she should be run out of the village. This was overheard by Ruffy Harris and Doughy Hood, who growled their agreement. Several others put in their twopenn'orth as well, pretending that they'd always thought there was something fishy about the Snells.

Daniel shook his head, despairing sometimes of his fellow Linburians, but said nothing. Instead, he took a couple of small beers into the snug for his son and their guest.

"Coo, Mr Hall, I thought there was excitement a-plenty in the Navy, but Freddy's been telling me about all the goings-on in the village and at 'is school."

"What we need now is a period of calm. A village like ours is best in a state of tranquillity."

From their first meeting, Daniel had regarded Carl as something of a Jack the lad and thus not entirely trustworthy. He feared that the boy might take advantage of his son, or hurt his feelings. Freddy was clearly much taken by him. However, he decided to keep his reservations to himself unless circumstances changed because, he reasoned, he might be wrong and in any case Freddy must learn by his own mistakes.

"Dad, Carl says they're building new ships in the dockyards and doing extra drills. He thinks they're preparing for war with Silesia."

Carl nodded. "They've laid down three in Chatham – the *Royal Henry* and the *Neptune* have one hundred and twenty guns and the *Foudroyant* is an eighty-gunner. There's one being built at Woolwich, the *Lady Castlemaine*." Carl raised his almost invisible eyebrows at Freddy. "I'd like to go aboard her."

Freddy giggled. "Lower orders permitting."

They both laughed uproariously, while Daniel gave them

a sideways look. "We shouldn't be rushing into war with anyone," he said.

"I could be called up before I'm fifteen to serve, maybe even as a midshipman," said Carl, more seriously. "Well, I can but hope."

"I hope not," said Freddy.

"Right, you two, when you've finished your drinks, time to do some work. Feed the chickens, wash the dishes, then get ready for bed."

"Mr Hall, you've done me proud with me own room and all that," said Carl. "But I'm a bit used to company of a night..."

Freddy responded immediately. "We've got a truckle bed we can move into my room. It won't take a minute between us and it's quite comfortable. Is that all right, Dad?"

"Very well," said Daniel, "but no gassing till the early hours. There are your Saturday chores, and you don't want to be tired out before you get things ready for the party on Sunday."

* * *

In the twilight, Freddy looked over the side of his bed to where Carl was lying stiffly under a linen blanket on a feather and down mattress beneath which was the rope straw truckle.

"What's the matter?" asked Freddy.

Even in the poor light, he could see the blush on Carl's pale skin.

"Don't laugh."

"I won't."

"It's the dark. It gives me the shivers. Always has. Even when I had the measles, Jane or Wayneman had to stay in the room."

"Shall I light a candle?"

"If you don't mind."

Freddy struck a Lucifer match and lit the candle on his bedside table. Immediately, Carl relaxed and snuggled down into his bed. "Thanks," he said, smiling sleepily. "You won't tell anyone about that, will you?"

"Of course not."

"That older boy you were talking about to Mrs Snell. He's really in the Marshalsea?"

"Yes – is it anywhere near you?"

"'Bout five miles upstream in Southwark."

"Do you know it at all?"

"I don't want to worry you, Freddy, but it's a grim sort of a place and quite terrifyin' for a young 'un, 'specially one used to gentlemanly ways. And if 'e's got no money, life is going to be hard – very hard. As like as not, he'll have to sell himself if he's going to come out the other side."

"What do you mean?"

"I mean, he'll have to do 'favours' for older, richer men."

"Oh," said Freddy, still not fully understanding. "I hope you don't have to go to war, Carl."

"That's what they train us for."

"But so soon. How will I write to you if you're on board ship?"

"If it happens, I'll let you know where I'm posted. There is mail, but it can take a long time to find its way. Do you want us to try to find out about that boy in the Marshalsea?"

"Would you?"

"I will, but what's most likely to get returns is money."

"I can give you a cheque on Coutts for £5. That's all I can afford. In fact, it's all I've got."

"Lord! I've never had that amount of money in me life. He must be something special to you."

"Actually, I hardly know him. But I said I'd help him, and that's what I'm doing."

"I've never met anyone quite like you, Freddy," said Carl, shifting his position. "What's that book on your bedside? It looks different to them others."

Freddy held up *Johnny the Jungle Boy* with its colourful cover. "It's an adventure story. I borrowed it from a boy at school. Blotwell, the sneaky one I was telling you about."

"So, he's your mate is 'e?"

"I wouldn't say that. He's completely self-centred and causes more trouble than he's worth."

"But 'e lets you borrow his books."

"That's a fair point."

"Read some to me, Freddy, so I can drop off before the candle goes out and I start shivering in me socks."

"Have you still got your socks on?"

"No, I took them off. I gave myself a thorough wash, in the other room, so you wouldn't be ashamed of me."

Freddy looked over the side of the bed. "I would never be ashamed of you, Carl. Do you want me to start from the beginning?"

"Where else?" said Carl with a snigger.

Freddy began in a high falsetto.

"Oh Lor' ha' mercy, brigands!" cried Mrs Davenport, holding her pinafore in front of her mouth. "Brigands at the garden gate and they're waving the death's-head flag!"

Mr Davenport handed his son Johnny a pair of flintlock pistols. "Defend your mother's honour," he said. "This is the Black Hand Gang, for sure. The meanest, vilest set of cut-throats in the south-west."

"Yes, sir," said twelve-year-old Johnny, a handsome lad with curly red hair and perfect teeth.

Mr Davenport took down his matchlock musket from the wall where it had hung for many a long year.

"How many are there, Mother?" asked Johnny.

His mother peeped out of the tiny window of their cottage. "I count ten coming up the path with lanterns and torches and weapons..."

There was a hammering at the door and a cruel voice spoke. "Open up, ye dogs! Hand over your valuables and we'll spare your lives."

"That's Red Rupert!" whispered Mr Davenport urgently. "He's

wanted for killing at least a score of men and carrying off their women and children to be sold into slavery."

"Please leave us alone, we're just a poor family," called Mrs Davenport, her voice breaking with the strain.

There was ominous laughter from outside the door. "Poor family be damned!" shouted Red Rupert. "We know you've got jewels a-plenty."

"Mother, quick, get the box of valuables from the dresser and put it under the floorboards," ordered Mr Davenport. "Get ready, Johnny."

"Yes, Father."

"Break the door down, lads!" barked the leader of the cut-throats.

The door was battered five times before the bolts gave. Three men with sabres led the charge inside. Johnny and Mr Davenport stood shoulder to shoulder behind their kitchen table.

"Say when, Father," said Johnny.

"Fire!" ordered Mr Davenport.

Johnny shot one of the brigands between the eyes, as he had been taught. The brigand dropped dead. Mr Davenport raised his musket and – horror! The charge exploded in his face, sending him reeling back against the wall. Red Rupert laughed as he strode inside. Johnny took aim again, but the powder was damp and the pistol clicked.

"Run, Johnny!" cried his mother, going to her husband's side. "Out the back. Head for the hills. There's no saving us or our jewels!"

Johnny threw the pistol at Red Rupert, who batted it away with his huge fist. "Where's the gems, woman?" he said, grabbing her by the arm and pulling her away from her stricken husband.

"I'll never tell 'e!" she cried. "Do your worst!"

"Hand me a cutlass, Dirty Don," bellowed Red Rupert. "I'll show her who's boss."

The last thing Johnny saw before he fled was the sabre flashing through the air, cutting off his father's head with a clean swipe. His mother screamed blue murder. Blood spurted out of the *corpse like a fountain, spattering the walls and windows and even the ceiling while Red Rupert howled like a wolf as he and his men bathed in the glorious shower of crimson gore...*

A long, low laugh came from below. "It don't really say that, do it?"

Freddy couldn't hold back his own laughter any longer. "I thought I'd make it a bit more colourful."

Carl rocked in his bed, his shoulders shaking with mirth. "You're supposed to be sending me off to sleep, not giving me the fits."

"Sorry," whispered Freddy with the utmost insincerity, which set them both off again.

Chapter Twenty-One

Let Them Eat Cake

It was a fine late spring day in Linbury. Daniel Hall leaned against the door jamb of the Sailor's Yarn watching his son, who was waiting anxiously for his guests to arrive. Carl was standing with him by the village pump. It was ten to two by All Souls' clock. The more devout parishioners were filing in for the afternoon service, casting glances at the boards set out on the green for a game of rounders. Behind Daniel, the bar room was decked out in bunting, while a pile of food – egg and watercress sandwiches, jam tarts, mince pies, wedges of cheese with slivers of apple, a ham hock and pickles from Ruffy Harris the butcher, a selection of Mrs Pattle's biscuits, and two trifles made with wild strawberries and cream from May's Dairy – lay in the cool of the cellar covered with tea cloths, along with four jugs of lemonade made with real lemons. A two-tier sponge birthday cake with fourteen candles, coated in marzipan and blue-and-white royal icing, was to be brought over from Doughy Hood's shop at five minutes to four o'clock. The baker had agreed to do the transport himself, not least because his two fifteen-year-old twins Charles and Georgina were invited to the party.

Daniel sighed as the nagging uncomfortable feeling surfaced once again: he did not share Freddy's regard for Carl. He didn't dislike the boy, but he thought his son could do better, much better. Harry was an example of that. If he was being unkind, he would have described Carl as an urchin or even a guttersnipe. He was a sallow-looking boy, his hair coarse and his skin rough. His features were stolid like his body. The fact that he was barely literate and numerate, but possessed a street wisdom greater than Freddy yet an intelligence far below, baffled him even more. Above all, Daniel had seen too many lads like Carl pretending to be as nice as pie while their motives were anything but.

The clock struck two. Russell Warren and his younger sister Charlotte – known to everyone as Lottie – joined Freddy and Carl on the green. Shortly after, more young Linburians walked up to add their birthday greetings and join in the games: Freddy's cousin, Dorothea Hingston, also aged fourteen; Sarah and Anthony Harris, Ruffy's progeny; Charles and Georgina Hood from the bakery, Molly and Dick Pitt, the shoemaker's children from Big Barn Lane; and the Harville four: Constance, Rosemary, Rachel and young Stanley. Some twenty-five young people from the village gathered to wish Freddy a happy birthday, but there was no sign of his school friends.

"When are we going to start?" piped Stanley as the clock shuffled on to ten past the hour.

Freddy's anxiety was alleviated at last as the pony and trap came into view around the side of the churchyard. Harry was standing up, showing off his driving prowess. He waved to the crowd as all heads turned his way, and there was some excited chatter, especially from the older girls.

Freddy went forward with Carl to greet his friends, then stopped short when he noticed among them the unlovely form of Simon Blotwell.

"Federico, look who I've brought!" Harry laughed. He jumped down from the trap and tied up the pony. "Happy birthday, old chum. Sorry we're late, but Carstairs had difficulty getting over the wall."

"I did not!"

"Scud, meet Carl Birch. Carl, this is Harry East, known as Scud because he can run like the wind."

Harry beamed as the two boys shook hands. "I hear you can row like the wind, and I'm not surprised with those shoulders."

"Good to meet you," said Carl. He was half a head shorter than Harry and if anything slightly broader.

Henry Perceval climbed down from the trap and went to greet Freddy. "I know you didn't invite me, but it's been a hellish few weeks being cooped up at school."

Freddy shook his hand. "How are you, Henry? I would have invited you but I thought you'd be in quarantine."

"Officially, yes, but everyone's been over it for days. I'm afraid there were a couple of fatalities, though – Daniels and Carruthers, both from Hawkins."

"Oh," said Freddy. "Did you know either of them?"

"Only by sight. Once they'd turfed out you day boys, Drake House was turned into a sanatorium for the most ill. Mrs Palmerston and her daughter have done most of the nursing while that girl Betty from the infirmary has been looking after the recuperators – not too well, I understand."

"What about Cheeseman?"

"The same. No worse. He's turned himself into a military martinet, complete with the uniform of a Royal Navy Lieutenant, would you believe? It's all show, of course. Every morning we have to get up early, ready to be standing to attention in front of the osher at seven fifty-five. We then get drilled for an hour and have to parade before the flag and a portrait of the king, marching in time to a drum beat. If we aren't there on time or if our steps aren't up to scratch, we get demerits. More than three demerits in a week and we get beaten. The masters either ignore it or wholeheartedly approve. Next week Frobisher and Raleigh will be joining us. I expect Cheeseman has given the orders to his toadies Sanderson and Pincher."

"Why don't you all refuse?"

Henry's chuckle was humourless. "Because a good third of the house actually like doing it. With anti-Silesian feeling running high and the promise of uniforms and even muskets, it seems that some find the call to arms irresistible. It's horrible, Freddy. By the end of a parade, they're all chanting 'death to traitors' and 'death to Prince Christian'. Cheeseman calls him the great pretender, working up the easily led, the gullible and those of unsound mind, like a master manipulator."

"What does the doctor think?"

Henry shook his head. "Heaven knows. We hardly see him any more. That whole business with Tom White seems to have hit him for six. Anyway, Freddy, please don't let's dwell on that any more. This is your day."

"So you and Blotters are on speaking terms again, are you?"

"Well, he's speaking to me, but I can hardly get a word in edgeways."

Freddy looked beyond Henry to where Frank Kennedy was standing smiling at Carl.

"Good afternoon, Francis. I'm glad you made it."

"Many happy weturns, Fweddy Hall, and don't call me Fwancis..."

"I'm Fwank!" mimicked Carstairs, who stepped up and pumped Freddy's hand for all it was worth. "Thanks for inviting me and it wasn't me who was a pain, it was him..." He pointed to Blotwell, whose nose was twitching with a very superior air.

"Hello, Simon," said Freddy. "I see you invited yourself."

"Is there a cake? Mrs Strout always bakes a most delicious chocolate cake with cream and Morello cherries for my birthday."

"Do you scoff it all by yourself?" asked Freddy.

"Auntie Millicent makes me share it with the servants and their common children."

Carl came to stand by Freddy. "They want to start the games," he whispered.

Freddy nodded. "Simon Blotwell, this is my friend Carl Birch from the Royal Hospital School, Greenwich. Carl, Simon is the squire's son."

Blotwell looked Carl up and down as though he had just come from cleaning the drains. "Daddy says I shouldn't talk to sailors, just in case."

"Just in case of what?" asked Carl.

"I don't know, mummy shushed him, which was very unusual, because normally she won't say boo to a goose."

"Are you weally a sailor?" asked Frank, walking over and looking up at Carl admiringly. "My dad is the lighthouse keeper." He pointed vaguely in the direction of Clifftop. "He wears a uniform too, but I pwefer yours."

Uncertain where this interest was leading, Carl decided to ignore it as best he could and looked over to where the party goers were getting restive.

"When I've gwoad a bit, I'll be the captain of a ship and we'll sail past Clifftop at night and I'll say to the cwew, 'That's my dad's light that is pwotecting us from the weefs beneath.'"

"Only in your dweams, shwimp," replied Carl, leaving Frank standing while he went to join the crowd.

On the periphery of the green, the twins Andrew and Michael Mason, Freddy's old adversaries were watching with their friend, Matthew Peters from Berry Hill Lane.

"Look at those three lost souls, over there," said Harry. "Do you think they want to join the fun?"

"They used to throw stones at me," said Freddy, "then pretend to be nice choir boys on Sundays."

Harry chuckled. "Did you call them double yolks and ginge?"

"No," answered Freddy. "In any case Matt Peters never joined in. The twins live in the Glebe Cottages and used to stand on the clifftop and lob bricks at anyone on the beach, including me."

"Nice. So how did you put a stop to it?"

"I gave Michael a black eye and when the parents came round to complain, dad gave them a piece of his mind."

"Another triumph for the Halls," said Harry. "Shall I be your go-between, and tell them they're invited?"

"I suppose so. It all happened a long time ago."

The first game was rounders, for which they split into three teams of ten with two teams fielding at a time. Freddy, Carl and Harry were the captains, while Henry volunteered to be the umpire for all the games that afternoon. The girls vied with each other to be on Harry's team, which led to bickering, but in the end he chose Georgina Hood to be his deputy.

At first, Blotwell refused to play any games, because a member of the aristocracy didn't mix with the hoi-polloi – until Freddy told him there'd be no cake unless he did. He said the same to Carstairs who asked, guiltily, if it was all right to play games on the Sabbath.

By accident or design, after two innings, Freddy's team won by twelve rounders to Harry's ten and Carl's seven.

The next game was high cockalorum which all but one of the girls, Lottie, said was unladylike and beneath their dignity. Simon also protested that it was a vulgar game for rough boys, but his reservations were overcome once again by the promise of cake. Two teams were formed with Carl and Harry as captains. Wisely, Carl's first and second choice were Russell Warren and his sister, Lottie, while Harry rather unwisely chose Frank and Stanley.

Henry tossed a coin. Carl won, and chose to form the first horse, quickly organising his team, as he had learned to do at Greenwich. Russell was the foundation, bracing his back against one of the pillars of the church wall, while Carl, after handing his hat to Henry, hooked his hands around the blacksmith's waist and ground his head into the older boy's abdomen. The next boy held Carl around the thighs and pushed his head into his rump. This continued boy after boy, until only Lottie remained to bring up the rear.

Now, each member of Harry's team had to vault as far as he could onto the back of the 'horse' without his feet touching the ground. If the rider was able to remain seated for more than a couple of seconds, he would cry out 'cockalorum!' and gain one mark. Carl's team took advantage of their lightweight opponents by bucking them off at every opportunity. This happened to Frank, who manoeuvred himself all the way along thirteen backs until he reached Carl.

"Gee-up, horsey!" he ordered, digging his heels in as if he was riding point-to-point. Frank was about to shout 'cockalorum!' when the older boy reared sideways and threw him off with such force that he landed several feet away in the dirt by the church wall.

"Tough luck, shwimp," said Carl. "You should have said it sooner."

Shakily, Frank picked himself up, holding his left arm to his chest. Then he charged at Carl and battered him in the ribs. "I hate you!" he cried. "You're a howwid boy. I'm never going to speak to you again."

Frank trotted away to find commiseration among the rest of his team, while Russell looked down at the back of Carl's head. "You made a friend there then. Did it hurt?"

"Not as much as when he kicked his heels into me before I threw him off."

"I thought I felt you wince. Good job he wasn't wearing spurs."

When it was their turn, Harry's team were penalised a total of six marks for collapsing three times in a heap on the ground with Carl's heavy mob on top of them. Ironic cheers and laughter were aimed at those beneath by the audience of girls who sat on the church wall pointing and swinging their legs. Though unwilling to participate themselves, they were not above gossiping about the merits or demerits of each of the boys who took part. In the end, Carl and Russell's team was the clear winner, not least because they had both remained steadfastly on their feet during their turns as the horse.

The final game was hare and hounds. Freddy and Carl were the first hares, each with a sackful of shredded newspaper. They set off with a three-minute head start, leaving the paper trail 'scent' in their wake. The only rule was that they had to stay within the village boundary. The hounds followed, yelping and barking. As there was little wind, the trails weren't difficult to follow at first. Harry easily caught up with Carl, who had to hand his sack over and make his way back to the green. Freddy hid behind the milk churns at May's Dairy but couldn't resist jumping out at Frank and Carstairs, who screamed in fright.

"We caught you," said Carstairs, when his heart was beating normally again.

"All right," said Freddy, giving up his sack. "It was worth it seeing your faces. I expect Carl's back on the green by now too."

"I hate him, he's a howwid boy," said Frank.

"Stop going on about him, will you?" said Carstairs.

"What's this about?" asked Freddy.

"Crybaby Kennedy is upset because the sailor called him a shrimp and accidentally tossed him into the wall."

"He hurt my arm and it wasn't an accident," said Frank, pulling up his sleeve to reveal a bruise.

"Carl did that?"

"It was in the game," said Carstairs, exasperated. "He wasn't the only one to get a cut or a bruise."

"He did it on purpose to hurt me, and I don't like being called a shwimp. I could be a sailor when I'm gwoad up, if I want." Frank lifted his head defiantly and clasped his hands behind his back. "My dad says I can be anything I like as long as I work hard at school and mind my Ps and Qs."

"Well, for a start, making cow eyes at him wasn't minding your Ps and Qs. You do it to everyone you meet, and some people find it disconcerting. If you continue to do it when you're older, you'll get a reputation," added Carstairs loftily.

"What reputation?" asked Frank.

"I'm not rightly sure."

"Why say it, then?"

"I'm not rightly sure," replied Carstairs, deadpan. They both giggled.

The sound of barking hounds alerted Freddy. "You two hares better get going, otherwise you'll be for the pot."

"Come on," said Carstairs, "and stop sulking like a baby."

The two made off, squabbling as usual, while a pack of baying hounds appeared around the side of the dairy.

Freddy walked back to the green where the majority of the girls, after fruitlessly chasing after Harry, had formed a skipping group. Simon Blotwell sat primly on the edge of the water trough, leaning against the spout of the pump.

"Why aren't you chasing the hares, Simon?"

"Freddy, I don't enjoy pointless pursuits. When are we going to eat?"

"Soon."

"I hear there's a trifle. I love trifle."

"No hogging the trifle," said Freddy.

"That coarse sailor boy is in a mood. One of the girls took him to task for being a bully, then she linked arms with East and off they went to feed the ducks." Simon pointed across the green to the pond where Harry was showing Georgina Hood how far he could throw a piece of stale bread.

Freddy looked around for Carl and saw him sitting hunched up on the church wall. "I'll see you in a bit, Simon, and I'll be watching you to make certain you only get one dish of trifle."

"Don't worry, Freddy. Mummy says I have to be on my best behaviour when I'm around the commonalty."

Freddy sighed and went to join Carl on the wall. "What's up?"

"I'm all right, just feeling the heat."

"Is that the heat generated by Georgina Hood?"

Carl adjusted his cap. "Oh, you heard... Coo, Freddy, these country girls have got tongues on them like any Limehouse scold. Made me blush with what she came out with."

Freddy chuckled. "She seems to have taken to Harry, though."

"Yeah, I suppose that makes it worse cos she's quite handsome, ain't she?"

"Do I detect a bit of the green-eyed monster?"

Carl hunched a bit more. "'Spect so."

"What did you do to cause the put-down?"

"Got told off for throwing that little kid off me back."

"Frank?"

"Yes. He hates me too. Maybe I shouldn't have thrown him off quite so hard, but the little blighter did kick me in the ribs and tell me to gee-up."

"Ah!" said Freddy. "Now I understand. Would you like Frank to be your friend for life?"

"I think I'd prefer Georgina. The little guy reminds me too much of my pesky brother."

"Yes, but one step at a time…"

* * *

The clock struck four, and within five minutes everyone was back, assembled on the green. Freddy stood on a box in front of the crowd while Daniel stood proudly by, amazed how much his shy son had come on in the last year.

"Before we have tea, there is one more race to decide the overall winner of the afternoon. They will take home this prize cup," announced Freddy, holding up one of his dad's old pewter tankards which had been hastily polished to a sheen for the occasion. "Come forward, Harry East and Georgina Hood, who won the rounders." Loud cheers. "Russell Warren and Carl Birch, who won the cockalorum." Muted cheers. "And Frank Kennedy and Carstairs, who won the hare and hounds." Surprised cheers.

"Me and Dad have drawn lots. The three pairs will be Harry and Carstairs, Georgina and Russell, and Frank and Carl. This is a piggyback race, though actually it's a piggy-shoulders race because one member of the team has to sit on the shoulders of the other. The race is from the lychgate to the other end of the green and back."

"But," said Harry, slightly piqued, "aren't we at a disadvantage?"

Freddy shook his head. "No, because each team has to swap round at the halfway point."

Now, Harry and Carstairs were smiling broadly, Georgina and Russell were looking uncertain and Frank was looking up at Carl in horror.

"Don't worry, we'll win easily, like Harry said," whispered Carl.

"But I'm not wery stwong," replied Frank, forgetting that he had vowed never going to speak to Carl again.

"You'll manage."

They lined up at the lychgate. Russell, Harry and Carl knelt and their partners climbed on board. Meanwhile, the other party guests assembled along the course to cheer on the contestants, joined by half the adult population of Linbury, among them, now the service had finished, some of the churchgoers, dressed in their Sunday best.

"Hold on tight," said Carl. "I'll explain the plan as we go along."

"All wight," replied Frank, still worried by the thought of the impossible task that lay ahead of him, whatever the plan might be.

"On your marks," said Freddy.

The contenders stood up. Harry swayed under the weight of Carstairs.

"Get set..."

Harry swayed some more.

"Go!"

Carl ran, but Russell, carrying the relatively light Georgina, ran faster. Harry lumbered along, unused to having such a handicap, but he managed to keep a reasonable pace and was only a few yards behind Carl and Frank when they reached the far end of the green. Meanwhile, Russell, way out in front, had already changed over. Georgina was no slouch, but carrying the blacksmith's son was a burden too far. The pair collapsed almost immediately on the return journey.

"This is going to be too easy," said Carstairs confidently.

Harry laughed and pointed at Carl and Frank. "Well, what are you two waiting for?"

"We are westing before the big push," said Frank, more confident now that he was party to the plan.

Carstairs chuckled and knelt down to allow Harry to climb on his shoulders. "We'll see you also-rans in the middle of next week."

Eleven-year-old Carstairs lifted Harry like a trooper and began a manful, if tottering, progress up the green towards the finishing line.

"Right, you know what we're about, don't you?" said Carl, throwing his cap on the ground then stripping off his gansey.

Frank held up his arms so the jumper could be slid down over him. Carl picked up his cap and plonked it on the head of the small figure who had otherwise disappeared inside the navy-blue fabric.

"Right, climb aboard, shipmate."

"I can't weach," said Frank, shaking his hands so that the sweater arms flapped in time.

The older boy lifted him easily, turning and settling him on his bare shoulders before standing up. "Keep tight hold of my cap, Carl," said Carl.

"All wight, Fwank, I'm weady," replied Frank.

They overtook Russell and Georgina after a few strides and were level with Harry and Carstairs just as the latter staggered to a halt and collapsed.

"Hey, what are you two up to?" cried Carstairs, looking up from where his chin was buried in the grass. "Look, East, what a couple of cheats."

"No, we aren't. I'm Carl," said Frank in the gruffest, deepest voice he could muster, which was neither very gruff nor very deep.

"And I'm Fwank," called Carl in a rough approximation of a squeaky pre-adolescent voice.

To cheers from the adults and bemusement from the young people, Frank and Carl reached the finishing line before their opponents had even got to the middle of the green on the return journey.

Minutes later, the three pairs of contestants were standing before Freddy on his box.

"And I declare that the ingenious winners of the 1826 Freddy Hall piggy-shoulders race to be... Frank Kennedy and Carl Birch! Please come forward and accept your prize."

Everyone clapped and cheered, except for Carstairs, who booed until Harry elbowed him into silence.

"And now," said Freddy to even greater cheers, "it's tea time!"

There was a rush towards the door of the Sailor's Yarn, where the food had been laid out on several tables by Daniel and Edie. Standing in pride of place was Doughy Hood's cake, which had fifteen candles (the fifteenth was for good luck in the coming year) in two circles on the top tier.

Harry sidled up to Freddy. "I suppose that little escapade on the green was all your idea?" he whispered.

"I don't know what you mean," replied Freddy.

Harry chuckled and slapped his friend on the back. "My friend, the peacemaker."

When the guests had eaten and drunk their fill and Simon Blotwell was smiling, having had two bowls of trifle, as evidenced by the strawberry jelly and cream around his mouth, everyone gathered round for the cutting of the cake. But first Daniel lit all the candles then turned to say a few words.

"My son Freddy is fourteen years old today and no man could be as proud as I am, not only because he's more intelligent than his old dad..."

"And prettier," came a voice to a ripple of laughter.

"Thank you Doughy, yes and prettier," continued Daniel, "but because he's a decent honourable sort of boy, who knows right from wrong, works hard, has made some good and loyal friends, and always does his best..."

"Hear, hear," murmured Harry.

"So, while Freddy blows out the candles..."

"And makes a wish," said Aunt Edie.

"And makes a wish," continued Daniel, "I ask you all to join me in a chorus of 'For He's a Jolly Good Fellow'."

"Oh, Dad!" said Freddy, going scarlet.

The song was sung and the cake was sliced. A line of Linburians, young and old, formed to receive a piece and wish Freddy a happy birthday before they wended their way home. Shortly only Daniel, Carl, Russell, Freddy's school friends and one raggedy child were left in the bar room. The late arrival was Judy Barnes from the labourers' cottages.

"You should have come earlier," said Freddy.

Big eyes looked up at him from a dirty face. "We was playing," she whispered.

Freddy fetched a small wicker basket and filled it with some of the remaining food. Then he put four slices of cake in it as well. "Share this with your brothers and sisters, and don't drop it on your way home."

Judy grinned. "Thank you, Freddy. Happy birthday..."

The girl skipped off on grimy, stick-like legs, almost colliding with a tall dark figure who was standing in the doorway of the inn.

"Oh, my sainted aunt," murmured Russell, backing away. "Look what the wind's blown in."

"Oh lord!" muttered Daniel. "And everything was going so well."

There was a click of heels as the figure approached across the wooden floor of the bar.

"Mrs Snell," said Daniel, putting on a brave smile. "To what do we owe the pleasure?"

"Don't worry, Mr Hall, I haven't come to complain about the noise on the green or the fact that Sunday is a supposed to be a day of rest." She sniffed and turned to Freddy, holding out a rectangular parcel covered in brown paper and tied with string. "Many happy returns of the day, Frederick."

"Oh! Mrs Snell." Freddy blushed. "Er, thank you. What is

it? I wasn't expecting…"

Harry elbowed Freddy. "Stop waffling and undo it."

Inside the wrapper was a framed watercolour painting of the Sailor's Yarn with good likenesses of Freddy and Daniel standing outside, waiting for the Royal Mail coach, which could be seen coming up Main Street.

Freddy gazed at Mrs Snell as if seeing her for the first time. "This is so good, thank you. Look, Dad…"

"Well, I never. Whatever next!" said Daniel. "That would look a treat hanging over the bar."

"I could do that," said Russell. "A bent nail and a hammer and it'll be up in no time."

"That's real smart, ain't it?" said Carl and they all nodded.

"Would you like a slice of birthday cake, Mrs Snell?" asked Freddy.

"That's very kind of you, Frederick. My little kettle is on the boil at home, and a piece of cake would go well with a cup of tea."

Mrs Snell collected her slice and wrapped it in a spotless white handkerchief, then with a click of her heels she was on her way back to her cottage.

"That was a surprise," said Russell.

"I like Mrs Smell," said Frank to stifled giggles, especially from Carstairs.

Carl nudged him. "You mind your manners, *Francis*."

"Right, boys," said Daniel. "I know some of you may have little gifts for my son, so if you'd all like to retire to the back room, I can open up the bar to some paying customers. Oh, but wait…" He reached under the bar. "This is for you, Freddy. Your Auntie Emily produced these. I don't know what to make of them myself. It's a costume for your swimming gala." He held the garment up by his fingertips.

"You'll look really smart in those, Federico," said Harry, "not to say unique."

"Shut up," mouthed Freddy.

The costume was a cut-down pair of red-and-white

striped linen underdrawers, now knee-length with elasticated legs and a drawstring to tie around the waist.

"Coo," said Carl, feeling the texture. "They've been dipped in wax."

"Don't forget to thank your auntie," said Daniel. "She's invited you and Carl for dinner on Tuesday night, by the way."

"Excellent," said Freddy, perking up at that news.

The boys filed into the back room, where a jug of small beer and a plate of biscuits was waiting for them on the table. Some of the bar chairs had been moved too, to accommodate them.

"I didn't know any of you had bought me presents," said Freddy.

"Oh, we haven't," said Harry nonchalantly. "It was a joke." He went over to the armchair and from behind it pulled out his wooden box, previously used for fireworks. "But some of us put a few things in here which we hope you like."

"Happy birthday, Freddy," they chorused, clapping and whistling.

"Well, go on, dip in," said Harry.

The first present was in a brown paper bag. Freddy reached in and withdrew a sailor's cap with the tally *RHS GREENWICH*.

"Carl?" said Freddy.

The sailor grinned. "Me and the boys clubbed together and the Chief gave permission. You are now an honorary member of the Royal Hospital School."

Freddy felt his eyes watering. "This is really special." He put the cap on his head and wiped his eyes. "Thank you."

Everyone cheered except Frank, who began to jump up and down and make hooting sounds.

"Will you keep still and stop making those silly noises?" said Carstairs. "You're acting like one of those monkeys in the Tower menagerie."

"I want one," murmured Frank.

"I want doesn't get," said Carstairs.

"Carl, is it all right if I let Frank wear this just for this evening?" asked Freddy.

"Well, as long as it's just for this evening. You have to earn a cap like that."

Freddy put the cap on Frank who beamed, though his ears had to be tucked inside to make it a tight fit. "I'm going to be a sailor when I gwow up and I'm going to work hard till I have muscles like my fwends Carl and Wussell."

"Cupboard love," said Carstairs.

Freddy delved into the box again and withdrew a weighty tome with a plain wine-coloured cover. His look of puzzlement turned into an almighty grin when he opened it to the title page.

"Scud, this is just what I wanted, thank you." Freddy turned the book round for everyone to see. "It's the *Nautical Almanac and Astronomical Ephemeris* for 1829. That's four years' worth of data on the movements of the planets and their moons."

"It's all beyond my comprehension," said Harry.

"That's what you've put in the inscription," laughed Freddy. "*To Federico, hope this means more to you than it does to me. Your chum forever, Harry.*"

The next present in the box was a large rolled-up piece of parchment tied with a blue ribbon emblazoned with the Trinity House coat of arms. "Now, I wonder who this can be from?" said Freddy, carefully undoing the ribbon and spreading the parchment across the table. Everyone gathered round to look. It was a coastal chart of the whole of Albion showing the sea lanes and the location of every lighthouse in the kingdom, each marked by a blue crown with its name printed by the side.

"This is from me and Carstairs," said Frank.

"Carstairs and I, if you don't mind," said Carstairs. "Though I feel much credit goes to Mrs Kennedy for her cartographic skill, while Frank did the crowns with his printing set and I did the copperplate writing."

"It's amazing – I shall hang it on my wall," said Freddy, "and you'll have to thank your mum from me, won't you, Frank?"

"All wight."

"What if it falls into the hands of Silesian spies?" asked Blotwell.

"You mean like Tom White?" answered Freddy.

"He's being ridiculous as usual," said Henry.

"You didn't bring a present, did you?" said Blotwell, pointing at his roommate.

"Neither did you," said Henry, blushing.

"I don't expect presents," said Freddy. "You all being here is enough."

Simon's face acquired a sanctimonious smile. "Actually, I've decided to let you keep that book you borrowed."

Freddy thought for a moment. "You mean *Johnny the Jungle Boy: Friend to All the Animals*?"

"Yes, it's only for common working boys anyway."

"Charming, isn't he?" said Harry.

"That's a real good story, that is," said Carl, "'Specially the way Freddy tells it with all the voices."

Simon looked down his nose at Carl. "What are you talking about, all the voices?"

"Each character has his or her own voice the way Freddy tells it, and he makes embellishments to make me laugh."

Simon snorted haughtily. "I would never try to imitate the coarse voices of the peasantry."

"Just a minute," said Henry. "Are you saying that you have actually read this book out loud, this book which is only for common working boys?"

A blush appeared on Simon's face and his eyes darted this way and that, as if he had revealed a guilty secret.

"Yes, come on, Blots, tell us more about your oratorical skills," said Harry.

"I don't discuss Bruton Manor business with outsiders," said Simon, his nose back in the air.

"I think there's more to Simon Blotwell than meets the eye," said Carstairs.

"What do you know? You're only ten," snapped Simon.

"Eleven," corrected Frank, "and Carstairs has his head scwewed on the wight way,"

From the bottom of the box, Freddy drew out the smallest gift, wrapped in a piece of chamois. It was a slip joint knife, the handle engraved with his name and along its length a three-inch rule measured in tenths of an inch.

"I know you made this, Russ. It's so skilful."

The blacksmith smiled.

"It must have taken you ages," said Harry, as Freddy opened the blade and showed it around for everyone to admire.

"The spring loading was the most difficult. I had to follow the instructions in a book."

Even Simon was impressed. "I shall speak to Mummy and Auntie Millicent to see if we can't offer you some work," he said. "Sharpening things, or something..."

Russell chuckled.

"Such social graces," said Henry.

Freddy went over to Russ to shake his hand but the blacksmith gave him a bear hug. "You're a good friend, Freddy. There's no one else quite like you in this village."

"Well, I suppose I should be getting some of these baby boys back to Seekings. It must be getting past their bedtime," said Harry.

"Hawwy East, it's nowhere near our bedtime. It's still light outside and I thought we could have a game of cwicket."

Carstairs nodded. "We promised old Mr Hawlings we'd be back by nine, so we've got almost two hours left."

"That reminds me," said Henry. "I have got something for you, Freddy, only it's not from me. I almost forgot. Mr Hawlings made me promise to deliver it to you without fail. Sorry, it's got crumpled, though it doesn't seem to be much of anything." Henry handed Freddy a creased half-sheet of newspaper which had been folded twice and glued together around the edges. "He said you would know what to do with it this time."

"The man is bats, I'm sure of it," said Harry.

Because it was from Mr Hawlings, Freddy peeled the newspaper apart rather more carefully than he otherwise would have done. Out dropped another folded sheet of paper. Puzzled, he picked it up and opened it out. He gasped, then his face broke into an incredulous smile. "It's the letter," he said, holding it up. "Tom White's letter, which Sanderson snatched off me."

"Oh, I say!" said Henry.

"Well, I never," said Harry, in imitation of Daniel. "How did the old duffer get hold of that?"

"O frabjous day! Callooh! Callay!" shouted Freddy, dancing round. "Thanks, Henry. This has been the best birthday ever!"

Chapter Twenty-Two

Ready, Aim, Fire!

Tuesday, 13th June

A lone blackbird was singing its evening song in a nearby treetop when Freddy and Carl left the Tanner's cottage to spend the twilight hours in the cap of the windmill. At the garden gate, Freddy turned to wave to his uncle and aunt, while Carl lifted his cap and gave a small bow.

"That was a slap-up meal, that was, Freddy," said Carl, patting his stomach. "If I stayed in Linbury much longer, I'd become as fat as one of Monsieur Montgolfier's balloons."

"You mean full of hot air," answered Freddy with a chuckle.

"Eh! Smart alec."

"Actually, I wish you could stay longer. Like forever..."

"But duty calls, Freddy, just like you'll be going back to school next week."

"I suppose so, and at least I've got one less thing on my mind now."

"Did it feel good burning that letter?"

"I should have heeded Mr Hawlings' warning in the first place," said Freddy.

"He sounds a rum old cove, that one."

"Mr Hawlings is a wise man, whatever Harry and the others say."

Freddy took the key from his waistcoat pocket and opened the windmill's door. "You made a good impression on Auntie Emily. She doesn't usually approve of anyone who comes from further afield than... er, well, Linbury actually. Even Scud got a hard time when they first met."

Once inside the dusty room Carl twitched his nose as if he was about to sneeze. "I don't think your dad likes me very much."

Freddy was shocked. "Of course he does. What makes you say that?"

Carl looked down at the floor and shrugged. "He's always on guard with me and sometimes he seems to be watching me, like he's waiting for me to do something wrong. I don't know, maybe it's me imagining things..."

The two boys looked at each other. It was their most uncomfortable moment since their first meeting.

"I don't know what to say," said Freddy. "I haven't noticed anything."

"It don't matter. I'll be gone tomorrow."

"But it does matter. I want you to feel welcome. I want you to come again."

"And I will come again, if you invite me and I can get leave. It's been really topping, Freddy. I've had the time of my life, understand? Now, come on, let's not dwell on that any more. You've got a lot to show me and I should have kept my big gob shut."

"No, I'm glad you told me. People are always saying that I notice the obscure and overlook the obvious."

"You mean like them fishy things you was showing me this afternoon."

"Ammonites."

"I still don't get it. How can a fish turn into rock? It's like someone has carved it out like a statue."

"Except it's inside the rock. Experts think they're very old – very, very old."

"You mean before the flood?"

"I mean millions of years old."

Carl looked up at his friend to see if he was being serious, then he shook his head and chuckled. "You're a right one you are Freddy. I don't know why your head isn't spinning with all them thoughts going on inside it."

Carl didn't need any instructions on how to climb the ladders to the top of the mill. Once inside the little room Freddy had made for himself, he sat on the bed and took off his boots, wriggling his toes inside his socks.

"Coo, that's better. Me poor old plates of meat got all hot and bothered."

"I told you not to take off your boots and socks when we were tramping along the beach. Your feet are not used to the shingle."

"Maybe I should start going barefoot at Greenwich, like a lot of the boys do."

They took down the shutter and Freddy hand-cranked the cap until the window was facing north. "It's a first-quarter moon tonight, so we should get a good view of the terminator – that's where the sun's light is cut off." He adjusted the telescope then stood aside to let Carl have a look.

"Use the brass wheel to focus..."

"I've used a telescope at the school, but never bothered to turn it skyward," said Carl. "Coo, it's big. Why is it called a quarter moon when it's half visible?"

"Because when the disc is half lit, it's a quarter through its cycle."

"This is a smart piece of equipment you got here, Freddy. Oh, it's going cloudy."

"Cloudy?" said Freddy sceptically, as earlier in the evening the sky had been completely clear. He looked up through the shutter, then walked quickly forward and stuck his head out of the window. "That's not cloud, it's smoke," he said, "and it's coming from the village. We'd best get back. They'll need our help."

Below, he could see his aunt and uncle standing in their garden watching the thick pall rising above the trees to the north-west.

Carl grabbed his boots and slid down the ladder to the

bin floor. Then he did the same through the remaining four storeys, reaching the ground floor so far in front of Freddy that he had time to stuff his feet into his boots and tie the laces.

Outside, they could see a glow in the sky over the village. Freddy's heart thumped, imagining the Sailor's Yarn ablaze.

"You be careful!" cried Aunt Emily as the boys ran down the track from the windmill and out through the five-barred gate.

"There's never been a fire in Linbury that I can remember," panted Freddy.

They passed the labourers' cottages, sprinting hard down the slope. A rightwards turn into the lane and they could see flames roiling into the sky and smell the acrid, strangely rancid smelling smoke.

"It's the Snells' cottage," said Freddy, partially relieved but also shocked by what had happened

Even before they ran onto the green they could hear people shouting to one another. "Come on, you lads!" called Joseph Warren, the blacksmith, when they came into view. "We need more strong ones in this chain."

Buckets were being passed hand to hand from the water trough across the hundred yards or so to the Snells' front door where Elias Harville and Duncan Tree, the glazier's son, were trying to douse the flames. But already the fire had spread across the thatched roof, smoke was billowing out through the bedroom shutters, and downstairs flames were shooting through the broken windows.

Joseph and Russell Warren were taking it in turns to operate the pump, trying to keep the trough full. Freddy and Carl joined the chain midway between Daniel Hall and Doughy Hood.

"Where's Mrs Snell, Dad?" asked Freddy.

"She's all right. Miss Antrobus has taken her in."

"How did it start?"

Daniel handed him a bucket, the water sloshing over the side. They could feel the heat even from that distance. "Heaven knows. The first I knew was when your Auntie Edie came rushing into the Yarn."

A second chain was formed as more people came to help, meaning that the Warrens had to pump even harder to keep the trough topped up. During one of his brief rests, Joseph came over and tapped Carl on the shoulder. "You're a big strong lad and used to being aloft. We need someone to help Duncan keep the flames from spreading to their house. Ruffy and Sam have gone for a ladder. I think the Snells' house is done for."

Carl nodded and ran towards the fire. The thatched roof of the Trees' cottage had begun to smoke, and it was clear that a spark could ignite it at any moment.

Shortly the ladder arrived and was propped against the overhang. Carl climbed up and began to douse the thatch with water from the two lines of villagers, who were now concentrating on saving Arthur and Joyce Tree's cottage.

After fifteen minutes, his arms aching, Carl was relieved by twenty-year-old Duncan Tree. No sooner had they made the swap than the Snells' thatch collapsed in on itself, sending up a gout of flame and smoke into the night sky. Sparks fell on the Trees' roof but the reed was now sufficiently wet for the sparks to be extinguished as soon as they landed.

After another hour, the smouldering ruin of the Snells' house was once again being sluiced with water to dampen the remaining fires. All four walls leaned inwards, the upper floor had collapsed into the lower, and most of the roof joists had burnt away. Of the contents, there was little or nothing that was salvageable.

Covered in smuts and smelling of smoke, Carl, Freddy and his dad returned to the Sailor's Yarn to find Zebedee Tring sitting in his usual place, an empty tankard before him.

Daniel stood over the itinerant labourer, his arms folded. "Why weren't you out there helping with the rest of the village?"

"Why should I help that uman?" said Zebedee. "She's a traitor to king and country."

Freddy flicked Carl's arm and nodded for him to follow. "Dad, we're going for a wash."

"I need me bed," said Carl sleepily, flexing his arms.

"And then we're going to bed," said Freddy.

Daniel lifted his arm in acknowledgement. "As soon as I've got rid of this miserable wretch, I'll be joining you. We all need a good night's sleep after this carry-on."

* * *

Despite a fresh breeze from the east, the smell of charred wood and cinders hung heavily in the air over Linbury that Wednesday morning. All Souls clock struck ten. Moments later, the mail coach from Dunhambury pulled up outside the Sailor's Yarn. Daniel stepped forward to shake Carl's hand. "Goodbye, son, you did sterling work last night. Take care and have a good journey home."

"Thank you, sir," replied Carl. "I've had a really ripping time."

Daniel handed the mail bag up to the coachman and received one in return.

"I see you've had a bit of excitement in the village," said the driver – the same one as on Carl's inward journey.

"Excitement we could do without," said Daniel.

Freddy and Carl shook hands then hugged each other as they said their farewells.

"I'll do my best to get that money to the Marshalsea, but it may take some time," said Carl in a quiet voice.

"Just don't get into any trouble on my account."

Carl chuckled. "Trouble, me? That's my middle name. Ta-ta, Freddy. Keep well and keep writing, please."

"I shall, and you must come again in the summer holidays."

"If I'm not aboard a man o' war, I'll see what I can do. Coo, an' you'll be able to read me another instalment from that book."

Carl handed his bag to the coachman then clambered up onto the passenger seat.

"Outside seat to Bray. That'll be ten and six, young sir."

"All right, keep your powder dry," said Carl, handing over a half-guinea piece. "And if you and posti can promise me a smooth ride, there's an extra shilling each at the end."

"It'll be as smooth as silk. We wouldn't want to get your delicate *derrière* sore now, would we?"

"Right, then. Is posti going to give us a toot on his tin whistle before we sets off?"

The coach pulled away to the sound of an extra-loud blast on the post horn. Freddy raised his honorary Navy cap in salute and held it aloft until he could no longer see his friend's cap being waved in return.

At a loose end and feeling deflated, Freddy wandered over the green to the burnt-out shell of the Snells' cottage. From the gate, he could see, through the black and broken window frames, small wreaths of smoke eddying upwards from the pile of ash and timber.

"Morning, Freddy." The voice belonged to Duncan Tree from next door, who had come to stand by his garden gate. "Thanks for your help last night. That sailor friend of yours proved really useful too."

"Do you know how it started, Duncan?"

The glazier's son shook his head. "No. We were finishing supper when Mrs Snell came hammering on our back door. When we got outside the roof was already alight and there was smoke everywhere. Dad tried to get in but he was driven back by the heat. The flames had taken a real hold inside by then."

"So it started in more than one place?"

"Now I come to think of it, you're right. That's a mystery, isn't it?"

"Is Mrs Snell staying with Miss Antrobus?"

"I believe so. I haven't seen them since last night."

Curiosity overcame Freddy's reticence. After he had said goodbye to Duncan, he went up to the door of Miss Antrobus's cottage and knocked. Only then did he remember that she would be teaching in the church vestry. He turned to leave, but the door opened. The pale, exhausted figure of Mrs Snell appeared in the doorway, still dressed in her night attire.

"Why, Frederick..."

Freddy blushed. "I'm sorry, Mrs Snell, I didn't mean to disturb you, I forgot that Miss Antrobus would be teaching this morning."

"Is there anything I can help you with?"

Freddy didn't want to bring up the subject he was most interested in, and his blush deepened as he hesitated on the doorstep.

"You want to ask about the fire, don't you?" said Mrs Snell. "It's perfectly all right. I'm not such a delicate little flower as all that. Come in. It'll be a relief to talk to someone instead of turning everything over and over in my own mind."

Mrs Snell showed him into the front parlour where a kettle, standing on a small range set in the hearth, was emitting a gentle jet of steam. Freddy couldn't remember ever being in Miss Antrobus's cottage, but it was everything he had expected it to be: neat and homely with comfortable furniture and shelves crammed with books.

"Sit down, Frederick, let us not stand on ceremony. Take one of the armchairs. You will share a pot of tea with me, won't you?"

"Thank you."

Mrs Snell warmed the teapot and added three spoons of tea, then poured on the boiling water from the kettle. "We'll let it brew," she said, placing a knitted tea cosy over the pot. "Tea is the great comforter, don't you think? Do you take milk?"

"Please."

Mrs Snell poured milk from a porcelain jug decorated with a floral design into two matching teacups. "Help yourself to sugar."

Freddy added two level teaspoons of sugar to his cup, which Mrs Snell then filled through a tea strainer.

The two of them sat back in their chairs, both trying to relax. Mrs Snell sighed. "Go on then, Frederick. Ask away and don't be shy."

Freddy took a sip of tea. "Do you know how the fire started?"

"I was upstairs in the front bedroom getting ready to retire when I heard someone moving about downstairs. In the past our doors were never locked but, given my present circumstances, I had bolted the front and back doors."

"So someone had forced their way in. Have you any idea who it was?"

"No, and I can tell you that it was an unnerving experience. I decided discretion was the better part of valour and locked my bedroom door to prevent them accosting me, if that was their intention. I looked out of the window but there was no one on the green, and the only light I could see was from your inn."

"When did you realise a fire had been started?"

"By the smell, Frederick. Smoke and a fishy smell like whale oil."

"You think they used oil to set light to the house?"

"When I fled the building, I looked up to the roof. I could see there were torches burning in the thatch."

"Did you manage to save anything?"

Mrs Snell sighed and shook her head. "Sadly, nothing but what I was wearing. We have a little money coming in each month but most of that goes on renting accommodation at that awful place where my husband is incarcerated. I am, to all intents and purposes, destitute. If it hadn't been for the kindness of Miss Antrobus last night, I shudder to think what might have become of me."

"I know people in the village have been talking, but I can't believe anyone in their right mind would actually do such a thing."

"But someone obviously did, Frederick, right mind or otherwise. I received a threatening letter not so many days ago too, but took no notice."

"What did it say?"

"Just what you'd expect. *You're not wanted here. Get out now or suffer the consequences. Death is too good for traitors.*"

Freddy finished his tea and put the cup back on the saucer. "I know it's soon after the event, but have you made any plans?"

"I shall do what I should have done when the talk and the threats started. My sister lives in Sedgewick and I shall write to her and throw myself on her mercy."

"But you still own the land your cottage was built on, don't you?"

"Unfortunately not. The house we bought from John Stadden, but the land is still his. It's on a ninety-nine-year lease, for which we pay a peppercorn rent."

"I've not heard of that before."

"In that case, you'll probably be surprised how much of Linbury is owned by the Stadden family."

"Would you mind if I had a look round the cottage? If I find anything, I'll let you have it."

"Oh, go ahead. I have no feelings for the place any more."

Freddy bid Mrs Snell farewell and walked the few yards to the ruins of the cottage that had once been the pride of Linbury. As he opened the gate, out of the corner of his eye he spied movement inside the burnt-out building. He cocked his head and waited. Moments later, Zebedee Tring appeared framed in the square that had once been the front parlour window.

Freddy moved quietly up the path to what had been the front door, but which was now just a hole in the wall. Zebedee was digging through the smouldering rubble with a spade.

"What are you doing here, Mr Tring?" asked Freddy in a loud voice, making the village labourer jump.

It only took a moment for him to recover. "Mind your own business, Freddy Hall. Why are you sneaking up on your elders and betters like that?"

"Whatever you find here belongs to Mrs Snell," said Freddy, getting angry.

"That uman should have been tarred and feathered and cast out of the village."

"You are a stupid, ignorant old man with about as much intelligence as one of the ducks on the village pond."

"You cheeky young varmint. I shall have words with your father about you."

"Do that!" Freddy turned on his heel and stalked off down the garden path and across the green. His temper cooled quickly, however, and once he was back home, he went in search of his dad.

Daniel was upstairs making up the bed in the best guest room, but the starched sheets were being uncooperative. "Give us a hand here, Freddy. We've got guests coming on the four o'clock – a clergyman and his wife, all the way from Cambridge, no less."

Together they made short work of the job, finishing by laying a white knitted counterpane over the bed.

"There now! All fresh and clean. Floor swept, furniture polished, new candles."

"What about a jug of water for the washbowl?"

"We'll give them warm water when they come. Could you run over to Pattle's and get some of that fancy Pear's soap? We want to make a good impression."

"Dad, I just called Zebedee Tring a stupid, ignorant old man."

Daniel chuckled. "Well, he's all of those things, but you shouldn't lose your temper with him. He's a harmless old fool who gets little enjoyment out of life."

"He was digging around in the ashes of the Snells' cottage. I told him anything he found belonged to Mrs Snell."

"I thought that was where you'd been. I can smell the smoke on you."

"I spoke to Mrs Snell. The fire was started deliberately. I want to find out who did it."

"Now then, the last thing you want to do is go around accusing anyone. I know what you're like once you get the bit between your teeth. Like a bull in a china shop."

"She's leaving, so all those people who wanted her out of the village have got their wish."

"Freddy, it's all blether, blather, pub talk. Last evening we had a bar full of regulars so none of them could have started it, even if they had the gumption, which few of them have."

"Was everyone here?"

"Well, the vicar wasn't and nor was Miss Antrobus..." Daniel waited for a reaction from his son.

"Dad, be serious!"

Daniel chuckled. "At least I got a smile out of you. I knew you were glum after your friend left."

Immediately Freddy reverted to his previous serious state. "I gave Carl a Coutts cheque for £5 to pay for Tom White's board."

Father and son looked at each other for a few moments.

"It's your money, son," said Daniel quietly.

"Do you like Carl?" asked Freddy, their eyes still locked on each other.

His dad paused before replying. "Not as much as you do."

"He said you didn't like him."

"I don't dislike him, Freddy, it's just that I think you can do better. In fact, you have done better in Harry and that nicely spoken boy, Henry."

Freddy felt as if a hand was clutching at his heart. "He's just as good as Harry and Henry – in fact, better in some ways because he hasn't had their advantages."

"I understand how you feel about him, son, and make no mistake, while he is your friend, he's as welcome here as anyone, and if I made him feel unwelcome that was very wrong of me."

Freddy nodded. "I suppose you can't help the way you feel, just as I can't."

"You have a wise head on your shoulders, son, but

it's still young and impressionable and may be due for disappointments."

"Carl will not let me down."

Daniel put his hand on his son's shoulder. "Shall we go down and have a cuppa?"

"I had one with Mrs Snell," said Freddy with a smile. "Miss Antrobus's house is really nice."

"Ah! Hobnobbing, were you? But can you manage another?"

"Yes, they were very small cups. Who is this clergyman you were talking about?"

"He signed himself as the Reverend John S. Henslow, and he and his wife are staying for five nights."

"Does Auntie Edie know?"

"I was hoping you would go across and tell her."

"I shall, and I'll get the soap too. I wonder what they're going to be doing in Linbury for five days?"

"A good question. Maybe you'll get the chance to ask."

Chapter Twenty-Three

Hard Lessons

It was with mixed feelings that Freddy walked to school on the 19th June. He was pleased that he would be seeing his friends again, pleased that he was free to proceed with reporting Cheeseman to the headmaster, but anxious about the trouble it was likely to stir up.

That it was pouring with rain with low cloud over Clifftop Lighthouse did nothing to keep his spirits buoyant. It was only when he reached the school gates that he had the first laugh of the morning. Mr Hawlings was chatting to Frank Kennedy, who was buried in a yellow oilskin jacket which came down to his ankles and a matching wide-brimmed sou'wester that covered his head and hid the top half of his face.

"Is that you in there, Francis?" he asked.

"No, it isn't, Fweddy Hall, it's Fwank."

"And how are you on this wet and windy day, Master Hall?" asked the old caretaker.

"I'm fine. Thank you for my birthday present, Mr Hawlings," answered Freddy.

"And did you make short work of it this time?"

"It went on the fire in the bar room."

"I hope you have a fire in your belly for this coming week."

The mail coach arrived on time, despite the weather. Harry got down more carefully than usual to avoid slipping. Like Freddy, he was wearing a waxed cotton rain cape and hood.

"Morning, Federico," he said blowing water off the end of his nose. "And what is this little yellow mushroom doing here?"

"Hawwy East, I am not a mushwoom."

"Sorry, I meant toadstool."

Mr Hawlings swapped mail bags with the coachman, who drove away without the usual fanfare from the postilion.

"I think he's got water in it," explained Harry.

Mr Hawlings opened the gates and the three friends walked down the drive. Through the trees they could see row upon row of boys in front of the osher parading this way and that, getting wetter and wetter, for they wore neither overcoats nor hats.

As they drew nearer, their eyes were drawn inexorably to a figure in blue frock coat with a gold epaulette on the right shoulder, white lapels, gold buttons and a matching cocked hat. It was Lieutenant Alfred Mayhew Cheeseman RN. He stood beneath the archivolt of the main entrance, completely dry. Below him, on the steps, sheltering under umbrellas held by a pair of soaked shell boys, stood his two subs, Donald Sanderson and Jeremy Pincher. They too wore blue uniforms with gold buttons, but without epaulettes or white lapels, and were taking it in turns to shout orders to their bedraggled ratings.

The five-minute bell sounded. Cheeseman gestured with the white gloves he was holding. "Dismiss them, Sanderson. Pincher, make a record of the slackers and defaulters." Having given the order, he marched away and disappeared inside the school building.

Freddy, Harry and Frank hung their coats on hooks in the corridor before going into the Great Hall. Assembly began with roll call like any other Monday morning at Seekings School, except that neither Mr Topliss nor Dr Butler was present. Instead Mr King deputised the proceedings. The rest of the masters sat on the dais in neat, self-satisfied rows while the pupils stood in not-so-neat rows in the main body of the hall, the majority dripping water onto the floor and not a few steaming following their exertions on the parade ground.

After the hymn – sung to the accompaniment of a

fortepiano played by Mr Williams – 'When I Survey the Wondrous Cross', and the Lord's Prayer, Mr King came forward to the lectern. "There will be a joint meeting of Hawkins and Drake houses here in the hall at 1.30 p.m. today. Attendance is compulsory. That is all the announcements. House captains, take your charges away in a quiet, orderly fashion and make sure they get to their first class in a dry state." Mr King collected his notes and swept out, followed by the masters in their black gowns and mortar boards, like so many crows following the plough.

Harry and Freddy frowned at each other. No mention of their time away from school; no mention of the measles or its victims. No mention of the militarisation being carried out at Seekings. Instead their free time would be eaten up by a house meeting.

"I'll see you at break," murmured Freddy.

Harry nodded.

* * *

"I'm not changing my mind."

Henry Perceval paused in the vigorous towelling of his hair to look at Blotwell.

"You've got to."

"Freddy Hall is a no-account village boy and not worth my time."

Simon Blotwell lay on his bed in study number fifteen completely dry, having gained one demerit for non-attendance at the morning's drill. He opened *The Rabbit Companion* and pretended to be engrossed.

"You're scared," said Henry, pulling a clean shirt over his head.

"I shall make a full confession to the Reverend McKellan next time I'm in Dunhambury, but until that time I shall remain silent."

Henry sat down on his bed, removed his socks and

proceeded to dry his feet. "You're scared."

"Sticks and stones…"

"Why don't you do the right thing for a change?"

"I'd love to have one of these new Dutch black-and-whites, Henry."

"Don't change the subject."

The bell rang for class.

Simon put his book back on the shelf. "I wish Mr Hooke would talk about something interesting for a change. All he does is ramble on about the stars or springs or longitude. The only animals he ever talks about are those hideous creatures you can see in a drop of water."

"Spirogyra is my favourite," said Henry.

"That's just green weed."

"So, you do take notice."

"Are you going to class in bare feet?"

"No, I'm waiting for them to be completely dry before I put my socks on. Otherwise I might get the itch."

"I suppose you'll be out parading in the rain again tomorrow?"

"If you did the decent thing, Cheeseman would be finished and no one would have to muster."

"I'm an abject coward."

"Just because someone calls you an abject coward doesn't mean you have to act like one."

"Daddy says I'm an abject coward who should have been strangled at birth."

Henry picked a pair of off-white woollen socks from his trunk and pulled them on. "He has a point, I suppose."

**

Before going to Mr Hooke's class, Freddy made his way down an ill-lit corridor, lined with ancient wood panelling and paintings of similarly grim looking ladies, into the heart of the administration wing. A faintly musty smell hung in the air, which grew stronger as he progressed. The school secretary's door was right at the end. Freddy knocked and entered.

A single window illuminated the desk behind which Miss Chawner, the school secretary, sat examining a pile of paperwork. "Yes?" she said with a hint of irritation at the intrusion.

"I'd like to see Dr Butler, if I may."

Miss Chawner, who had been at Seekings since the turn of the century and felt she knew all about boys, peered up at him. "The doctor is at a meeting of governors today and won't be back until four o'clock." She returned her gaze to the papers, as if that was the end of the matter.

"Four o'clock or sometime after would be fine."

This time the school secretary looked up sharply, though her iron-grey hair seemed not to move at all.

"The doctor will no doubt be tired after his meeting and will need to rest."

"Dr Butler says that his door is always open to pupils," countered Freddy.

Miss Chawner narrowed her eyes. "You're Hall, aren't you, the day boy from Linbury?"

"That's right. It's important that I speak to Dr Butler and I think he'll be interested in what I have to say."

"Perhaps you could tell me and I could pass it on."

"It's confidential," answered Freddy, knowing he was being forestalled and feeling his temper begin to rise.

Fortunately, no confrontation was necessary because Miss Chawner was now satisfied that she had exerted enough pressure to deter a frivolous request to see the headmaster. "Very well," she said, opening a drawer from which she withdrew a leather-bound diary with a reverence that might have been more appropriately reserved for a religious or philosophical work.

Freddy noticed that the bookmarked page she turned to was otherwise empty, but said nothing.

The school secretary dipped her pen nib into a silver

inkwell and scratched a line near the bottom of the page. "Four-fifteen in the school chapel."

"In the chapel?" repeated Freddy, disconcerted.

"That's what I said."

"Oh right, thank you." He turned to go.

"One moment, Master Hall," said Miss Chawner.

He turned back. The secretary gazed steadily at him. "Do not distress the good doctor."

Freddy kept his expression neutral and slowly nodded his head.

* * *

"A rum do," said Harry after Freddy had described his meeting with Miss Chawner. "You're getting quite brave in your old age, bearding the battle-axe in her den."

Freddy chuckled. "I didn't feel brave, just wound up."

They climbed to the first floor of School House and walked along the corridor to study number fifteen. The door was open. Henry and Simon sat opposite each other on their beds, silently attempting to stare each other out. As soon as Freddy and Harry entered, Simon lay down and closed his eyes.

"We're seeing the head at four-fifteen today in the chapel," said Freddy.

Henry directed his gaze to his recumbent study mate. "That one is still refusing to participate."

"I've decided to join the choir instead," said Blotwell, smiling up at the ceiling.

"What's that got to do with anything?" asked Freddy.

Simon chuckled. "Choir practice is three days a week for half an hour starting at eight-fifteen."

"You are a craven, lily-livered malingerer," said Harry.

"Yes," said Blotwell. "And it won't be too long before I shall be spending two lovely long weeks malingering with Auntie Millicent at Bruton Manor."

"What a perfect world you live in," said Henry.

"If you don't come with us, we shall still tell the doctor what you told us," said Freddy.

"Good," said Blotwell, "but if anyone asks me I shall deny everything."

"I'll frogmarch him there," said Harry, "and make him confess."

Henry shook his head. "That probably wouldn't do our cause much good – *vi coactus* and all that."

"Dr Butler will believe us anyway, I'm sure of it," said Freddy.

* * *

As 1.30 approached, the members of Drake and Hawkins houses began to assemble in the hall. The house captains, Mark Fouracre and Michael Stevenson, took a roll call of pupils as they filed in grumbling quietly about the intrusion into their free time.

Frank Kennedy stood between Harry and Freddy in the middle of the ruck. "I can't see," he whispered.

"There's nothing to see," responded Freddy.

The doors closed behind them, meaning that the roll call was complete. Fouracre and Stevenson made their way to the dais where they sat, expressionless, looking out at the assembly.

Shortly, the housemasters appeared, climbing the steps onto the dais. Mr Ravenshaw sat beside his house captain while Mr Tallow came to stand at the lectern.

"Be quiet," he growled, silencing the remaining grumblers. "You may be aware that this country faces an unprecedented threat from the Continent. Our way of life, our very existence is being challenged by the Silesian war machine. King Henry has let it be known that he expects his subjects to be prepared for hostilities. Therefore, it is beholden on us here at Seekings, masters and pupils alike, to lead by example, to show the lower classes that we are ready to face the foe and to serve our sovereign with unquestioning loyalty.

"As of tomorrow, Drake and Hawkins houses will join the other houses for an hour's drill, commencing at 7.55. You will be under the command of Lieutenant Cheeseman of the Seekings School Naval Cadets and his drill instructors Pincher and Sanderson. Breakfast will begin half an hour earlier at 7.15 and will finish at 7.45. Day boys will be expected to attend like any other pupil. God save the King!"

The two housemasters left the hall to a deathly silence. Fouracre and Stevenson stood and came to stand at the front of the dais. Then a babbling began which grew in intensity until Fouracre clapped his hands and shouted for quiet. "If you have questions, ask them now."

"I can't see," said Frank.

"Shut up," hissed Freddy.

"When do we get to gunnery practice?" asked Adam Wakefield.

"In your case, hopefully never," answered Stevenson.

"Are we actually at war?" asked George Bishop.

"No," said Fouracre. "Are there any sensible questions?"

Harry put up his hand. "I have one question. How am I expected—"

"I don't know," interrupted the Drake house captain. "You'll have to ask the lieutenant."

The sarcasm in his voice didn't go unnoticed.

"Fouracre, what will you be doing while we are all drilling?" asked Derek Mortimer, a bespectacled lower sixth-former and Drake House boarder.

"I shall be watching you all from my study window, while dining on coffee and bacon and eggs, of course, Mortimer."

"I like bacon and eggs with fried bread," whispered Frank.

"Hmm!" said Freddy, who put up his hand. "Will you beat us if we get three demerits, Fouracre?"

"Probably not. One hundred lines of Cicero. *Cedant arma togae concedat laurea laudi.*"

Michael Stevenson stepped forward. "*Si vis pacem, para*

bellum. As far as Hawkins House is concerned, that will be our motto. We may disapprove of the methods being employed, but the defence of the realm is our duty, as Mr Tallow stated. Unlike the non-boarders in Drake, there is no excuse for any member of my house not to be present at drill practice tomorrow morning. I shall be there, doing my bit for king and country."

* * *

Henry Perceval waved from the entrance of the osher as Freddy and Harry approached, still wearing their cricketing whites. It was five past four. The rain had cleared long ago and in the sunshine the greenery looked fresh.

"Are you sure you're allowed in the chapel dressed like that?" said Henry.

"We did leave our bats in the changing room," said Freddy.

"I think we come across as two rather smart gentlemen," said Harry.

"And why are you looking as if you've not done any sport this afternoon?" asked Freddy.

"I did go swimming earlier, but archery was cancelled," replied Henry.

"Why?"

"Old Topliss has locked himself in his tower, according to the school gossips."

"Don't believe it," said Freddy.

"Would you believe that Simon is getting a very special visitor on Wednesday who will be bringing him presents and a cake?"

"Not the famous Auntie Millicent?" enquired Freddy.

"The same, so he says."

"It could be another of his fantasies," said Harry.

"Well, he did get a letter which he wouldn't show me because it was private and strictly confidential, according to him."

"He doesn't deserve presents or cake, or visitors for that matter," said Harry.

The boys crossed the hall to the west door of the chapel and quietly entered the nave. Dr Butler was sitting with the Reverend Croft in the choir stalls, deep in conversation. Occasionally one or other of them would glance up at the ceiling and frown.

The three boys reached the transept before either master noticed them.

The Reverend Croft rose from his seat. "Ah! Your petitioner has arrived, or should I say petitioners. I shall make myself scarce."

"No, no, sit," said Dr Butler, grasping his colleague lightly by the wrist and pulling him back down. "I'm sure the boys won't mind. Come, the three of you, take a seat opposite us."

Freddy looked down to the flagstone floor where a bucket a quarter-full of water was surrounded by a wet patch. "Is the roof leaking, sir?" he asked.

"I'm afraid it is. Providence has not been kind to us today," said the doctor. "I fear the cost of repair may mean that the bucket remains there for the foreseeable future."

"I would prefer to blame the rain and those scoundrels who skimped on the flashing, rather than the Good Lord," said the Reverend.

The three made themselves as comfortable as possible on the hard wooden forms of the choir stall.

"So what have you got to tell me?" asked the headmaster.

Compared to when he had first seen him only six months ago, Freddy noticed how old Dr Butler looked today. He sat stooped and careworn, worry lines etched deep in his forehead. A pang of guilt stole up on him for the extra burden he was about to lay upon the man.

"It's about Tom White," said Freddy, nervousness making his mouth dry.

"Go on," said the doctor, a flicker of bitterness crossing his face.

"The pamphlets and the bottle of spirits you found in his room – they were planted there, by... someone."

There was no discernible reaction from either man, though their gaze became just that bit more intense.

Henry took up the story. "What Freddy... I mean, Hall, may not be going to say is that Simon Blotwell confessed to me that he had put those things in White's room on the instruction of Alfred Cheeseman."

"It was meant to discredit Tom," continued Freddy, "so that Cheeseman would become a foregone conclusion for school captain."

The Reverend Croft half-turned his head to look at his colleague, while the doctor remained quite still, except for a slight tremor of his hands, which he hid in his lap.

"You cannot rely on Blotwell's word," he said at last.

"Under normal circumstances, that's true," said Henry, "but in this case he was telling the truth. There are others involved too, though most unwittingly."

"Thomas White confessed to his crimes," said the Reverend.

"That was to stop those who had helped him from getting into trouble," said Harry.

The doctor looked at him sharply. "Do not say more on that subject."

Harry blushed at the rebuke and bowed his head.

"If Blotwell has a hand in this, why isn't he here?" asked the Reverend.

"Because he thinks of no one but himself," said Harry, recovering his poise.

"Blotwell says that when he was in the infirmary, Cheeseman came in and threatened to kill him," said Henry.

"He hates Cheeseman, yet he's in thrall to him," said Freddy.

The doctor took a deep breath. "Who will believe any of you when Cheeseman denies all knowledge and Blotwell won't talk about it?"

"You will, sir," said Freddy.

Dr Butler closed his eyes and chuckled humourlessly. "Oh, Hall, if you only knew the half."

The three boys exchanged mystified glances.

The Reverend Croft cleared his throat, as if he were about to start a sermon. "I think we've all said enough for now. Doubtless we shall want to return to this subject at a later date. Meanwhile, you have given us plenty to think about and we thank you for bringing the matter to our attention." He put his right palm under the elbow of the doctor to encourage him to stand.

"But…" began Freddy.

The Reverend Croft held up his left hand to silence him, while his right guided the headmaster out of the choir stalls. "As I say, we have all said enough, and Dr Butler and I have other business to attend to."

The two masters walked away up the nave, leaving the boys rooted to their seats. It was some time before Henry broke the silence. "I am flabbergasted," he said. "That can't be the end of it, surely?"

Freddy gave his head several shakes, as if to wake himself up. "All that effort for nothing. They didn't even seem surprised, never mind shocked."

Harry stood up. "And meanwhile Tom White is in jail, Cheeseman gets away with anything short of murder and is ruling the roost…"

"And the masters are as much in thrall to him as Blotwell is," added Freddy.

Chapter Twenty-Four
Blotwell's Triumph

A cluster of pupils had gathered around an elegant, four-wheeled carriage parked outside the osher, making observations on its possible top speed, style and lineage. Freddy and Harry, on their way to Drake House for lunch, gave it a cursory glance.

"A vintage model," said Harry.

"Much like the groom," said Freddy, noticing the liveried figure asleep inside.

"How's your mood after two days?"

"I'll get over it, eventually. I'm just… disappointed."

"That's adults for you. Nothing but shades of grey."

"I shall never go to one of his parades. I'd rather be beaten black and blue."

They entered Drake House. Harry collected his meal and went across the refectory to sit opposite Frank Kennedy and Carstairs.

"Where's Fweddy Hall?" asked Frank.

"Call of nature," answered Harry.

Carstairs sighed. "I wrestle with the fact that human beings are full of imperfections, yet we are made in the image of God."

"Eleven-year-olds shouldn't have to worry about questions like that," said Harry.

"It's my lot," said Carstairs, "if I'm going to be a man of the cloth."

"When he becomes a man, Carstairs is going to be a clot," said Frank, getting a nudge and a giggle from his best friend.

Freddy came over with his tray. "Steak and kidney pudding and jam roly-poly and custard," he said. "My two favourites all in one day, and it's Wednesday afternoon to boot!"

"He's cheered up at last," said Harry, "and all it took was a pair of Palmerston specials."

"We call jam roly-poly dead man's leg," said Carstairs, narrowing his eyes to slits.

"Why?" asked Frank, not altogether sure he wanted to know.

The big eleven-year-old licked his lips and leered at his friend. "Because the whole pud is like a sawn-off leg, the colour of necrotic skin, and inside is the blood-red jam!"

"You're being silly, Carstairs," said Frank, giving his bowl of dead man's leg a worried look. "And it's my turn to choose, isn't it?"

"No, I don't think so. You had your turn right before you had to spend forty days in the wilderness."

"But if we do it by the number of weeks..."

"No, that's not fair."

"Instead of arguing, why don't you toss a coin for it?" suggested Harry.

"Here you are," said Freddy, "a shiny new 1826 penny."

"Ooo, let me see..." said Frank, craning forwards.

"Where did you get that from?" asked Harry.

"We had guests, a vicar and his wife, and they gave me a tuppenny tip every evening for five nights. I've got ten of them."

"Gosh!" said Carstairs. "Impressive."

"Who'll call?" asked Freddy.

"I will," said Frank. "Tails."

Freddy spun the coin, caught it and turned it over onto the back of his hand. "Heads. Carstairs wins."

"Oh..." said Frank, his face crumpling.

"Right!" said Carstairs. "Hold on to your hats. Here are my choices. First, best of three games of chess."

"All wight," said Frank reluctantly.

"Second, butterfly hunting in Coneycop Spinney."

"All wight."

"Er, let me guess the third one," said Harry. "Half an hour paddling in the lagoon, half an hour beachcombing, then Frank goes home."

Carstairs looked at Harry in amazement. "How did you guess what I was going to say?"

"It's a special talent I have..."

"Yes, for stating the obvious," added Freddy.

* * *

Simon stretched as far as he could out of the window in study number fifteen, but could only see the back right-hand wheel of the carriage parked outside the osher's main entrance.

"You're making an exhibition of yourself," said Henry, who was sitting at his desk attempting to translate 'The Death of Hercules' from the ninth book of Ovid's *Metamorphoses*. "*Iamque valens et in omne latus diffusa sonabat, securosque artus contemptoremque petebat flamma suum...* Now the roaring fire... no, flames spread on every side..."

"There's bound to be a cake. Do you think I might get a new book, Henry?"

"Will you shut up? With a great crackling sound..."

"I wonder what they're talking about. Auntie Millicent is so regal, I expect the doctor is quite taken with her."

"His limbs unconcerned and defiant... No, that can't be right. Simon Blotwell, will you calm down. You're like a febrile squirrel."

"I'm over-excited, aren't I?"

"For heaven's sake, why don't you go down and join them?"

"Oh no, that would be unseemly."

Henry tossed his pen onto his desk. "Right, I can't stand any more of this. I'm going to get some lunch before it's all gone."

However, as he stood up, the study door opened. Donald Sanderson and Jeremy Pincher stood on the threshold, dressed in their drill uniforms.

"Don't you knock?" Henry growled.

"Shut your mouth, Perceval," retorted Sanderson. "Get moving, Blotwell. Lieutenant Cheeseman wants to have a word with you."

Blotwell simpered. "I'm afraid I'm otherwise engaged at the moment. My very important guest has arrived at the school."

"Do you want to come like a good little boy, or do we have to drag you out by the hair?" said Pincher.

"Well, put like that, I shall accompany you. What does Cheeseman want of me?"

"Cheeseman wants very little of you. It's a matter of the demerits you've earned. Three in three days."

"I'm joining the school choir," said Simon.

"I don't think that excuse will wash with the lieutenant," said Sanderson.

"What satisfaction do two seventeen-year-olds get out of bullying a single inept twelve-year-old?" asked Henry.

"The same as we'd get bullying a bumptious cockney like you, my diminutive friend," answered Pincher.

"I am not a cockney and I'm certainly not your friend, Pincher," said Henry. "I was born in the village of Hampstead, a long way from St Mary-le-Bow."

"Ignore that pile of tripe," said Sanderson. "We've got what we came for."

Simon scuttled along between the pair of house captains until they reached Cheeseman's study, where he was pushed so hard through the open door that he stumbled and fell to his knees before the blue-uniformed figure.

"I'm pleased you decided to humble yourself before me. It

makes me feel almost benevolent towards you."

"I say, Cheeseman, I can't stay. I have a very important guest awaiting me."

"Is that the old biddy in the worn-out carriage?" enquired Cheeseman, catching sight of himself in the mirror and liking what he saw.

"Auntie Millicent is not an old biddy, she's a lady, and her carriage is an antique Berline from Brandenburg."

Cheeseman slapped Blotwell across the face.

Simon whimpered. "Why did you do that?"

"Because you contradicted me, you effeminate pansy."

Blotwell wiped tears away and attempted to stand.

"Stay where you are unless you want another one," said Cheeseman. "Pincher, close the door. Sanderson, hold him by the scruff of the neck."

"I'll come to drill tomorrow, I promise," said Simon, fearing another beating.

Cheeseman held Blotwell by his fringe and pulled his head back. "Those two day boys, Hall and East, have been meddling in my affairs for too long. Not only that, but they've been criticising the morning drills which they have both failed to attend. They and your radical study mate need to be taught a lesson."

Simon wondered how much the School House captain knew about his confession to Henry and the subsequent meeting between Freddy, Harry and the doctor. "I never told anyone about what we did after you threatened to kill me," he lied.

"What do you know about the letter that Sanderson took off you in your study? The one that Hall showed you? The one that White wrote to Hall? The one that has gone missing from this room?"

Simon remembered the almost ritualistic burning of the letter at the Sailor's Yarn, but decided his best course of action was to lie again. He doubted if Cheeseman would believe that Mr Hawlings had taken it. "Nothing! I hardly got a chance to read it."

"Did you steal it from me, Blotwell?"

"No, Cheeseman! I swear on the Holy Bible that I didn't."

"I think I believe you, but that begs the question of who *did* take it from this room? The door is locked when I'm not here. The window is three storeys high."

"Maybe they sent that common little lighthouse boy down the chimney or up the drainpipe," said Blotwell, desperate to appease the senior officer of the Seekings Naval Cadets.

"Who?" said Cheeseman, ignoring the absurdity of the comment.

"He means Kennedy, one of the other day boys, A.C.," said Pincher. "He's a big friend of Carstairs in my house and they're as thick as thieves with Hall and East. He lives in Clifftop Lighthouse across the way."

"Interesting. Was he on parade this morning?"

"No – he'll follow whatever Hall and East do."

"And Fouracre will not punish them for missing drill either. In fact, he'll probably be on their side," said Sanderson.

"Fouracre is another thorn in my flesh. Maybe it's time for me to show him who's boss. Fetch Kennedy – bring him here now. It's time we had some decent sport. I'm getting tired of this mangy lickspittle." He raised his hand to Blotwell, who shrank away.

"What if he's gone home?" asked Sanderson.

"He won't have," said Pincher. "He and Carstairs spend their Wednesday afternoons together."

"Well then, get a move on," said Cheeseman.

Sanderson and Pincher left the study, leaving Blotwell alone and still on his knees with the captain of School House.

"May I go now, Cheeseman? I'm expecting my special guest at any time."

"You'll go when I tell you to and not before."

Simon worried that if they found Frank, he might divulge what happened to the letter at the Sailor's Yarn. "Yes,

Cheeseman. I don't think the common lighthouse boy climbed the drainpipe or dropped down the chimney."

"Who cares what you think? I shall mould him into being my vassal, just like you are." He sat down in his armchair. "Make yourself into a pouffe, Blotwell."

Simon went down on his hands and knees and Cheeseman put his feet up on his back.

Some five minutes passed before the door opened to reveal a frightened Frank Kennedy standing between the two house captains. "We found him playing chess with the fat buffoon," said Sanderson. He held Frank by the back of his Eton coat and pushed him in front of Cheeseman.

"Well, what have we here? The runt of the litter. No wonder I've never noticed it before."

"I am not a wunt, Cheeseman. My dad says that when I gwow up—"

"Shut up and listen to me, runt. You are going to be my eyes and ears as far as East and Hall are concerned. You will report daily on everything they say and do. Is that clear?"

"No, Cheeseman. Fweddy and Hawwy are my fwends…"

The School House captain stood up, grabbed Frank by the throat and pushed him backwards until he was against the wall. "You're not likely to ever *gwow up*, runt, unless you do as I say."

Frank's fear and shock communicated themselves to Cheeseman, who bared his teeth in a broad satisfied smile. "Another sissified crybaby girly-boy. Are you listening, Blotwell?"

Simon shook his head. "No, he's not like me."

Sanderson put his boot against Blotwell's side and sent him sprawling backwards. "Don't contradict your master."

Cheeseman found that his hand could almost encompass Frank Kennedy's small neck. He squeezed, wondering if he could get his middle finger and thumb to meet around the back. "You are going to do as you're told, aren't you, runt?"

Frank's normally pale face went red, his eyes watered and

he tried to retch. He grabbed Cheeseman's wrist with both hands and kicked out, catching him on the shin.

"Why, you chitty-faced little devil!" cried Cheeseman. "You two hold him over the stool. I will beat him until his backside runs red."

* * *

Freddy and Harry walked up the drive towards the school gates. It was almost time for Mr Hawlings to unlock them to allow the day boys home and the boarders freedom to roam. A small crowd had gathered, mostly carrying towels for an afternoon of swimming and sunbathing.

Freddy looked back at the clock. "Unusual. Almost 1.30 and no sign of Mr Hawlings."

Harry made a tippling motion with his hand.

They joined the throng, which was getting restive. One boy held on to the gates and shook them. "Come on, you old booby!" he shouted, as if this would make the caretaker magically appear.

Harry and Freddy, on the periphery of the crowd, turned as a distant voice hailed them. "Well, there's a sight you don't often see," said Harry.

Carstairs was lumbering up the drive, waving at them, his face puce with exertion.

"Something's the matter," said Freddy.

They ran the short distance to where Carstairs was bent double, his breathing coming in gasps. "Glad I've caught you... They took Kennedy... upset the chessboard and trod on the pieces..."

"Who?" asked Harry,

"Pincher... and Sanderson."

"Where are they taking him?"

"They didn't say... but ... must be... Cheeseman's orders."

Freddy glanced at Harry. "Find Fouracre, Carstairs, tell him what's happened."

"All right..."

"If they hurt him..." said Harry.

"Let's go," said Freddy.

They ran, Freddy almost as fast as Harry, passing Mr Hawlings at the main entrance. Their feet clattered on the stairs. School House pupils pressed themselves against the wall to avoid a collision. By the time they reached the corridor on the second floor, Freddy was flagging. "Go on, I'll catch up..." he panted. They could hear Frank's screams coming from study number one.

Harry hurtled down the corridor and flung open the study door. Frank was bent double over the stool, his trousers round his ankles. Pincher and Sanderson were each holding one of his arms, their free hands pressed into the small of his back. Cheeseman raised his arm to strike another blow with his hazel rod.

"You brute!" shouted Harry. Using his momentum, he collided with the older, bigger boy. They toppled over. The birch went flying. So surprised were Cheeseman's accomplices that they let go of Frank. Then Freddy arrived. He seized the birch from where it had fallen and started to beat Pincher and Sanderson. "Run, Frank!" he said, but the small boy turned and threw himself at Cheeseman, pummelling him with his fists. Though it had very little effect, it allowed Harry time to position himself and punch his foe on the jaw.

Cheeseman rose like a wounded animal. He lunged at Harry, at the same time trying to shake off Frank, who was holding on to his coat collar and kicking him. Harry took up a boxing stance, moving this way and that, his fists up, but Cheeseman caught him with a punch to the face which made him see stars.

Freddy kept flailing the birch, attempting to keep the two house captains occupied, but they had recovered their wits. Sanderson circled around him and grabbed him by the arms.

"Now then, village boy," said Pincher, balling his hand into a fist. But his partner let out a shriek and let go of Freddy, who ducked the blow.

"The beastly pansy stabbed me!" cried Sanderson, holding the back of his neck, where blood was running through his fingers. Freddy half-turned to see Blotwell, looking very surprised, holding a green pen with the gold nib pointing up in the air.

"What is the meaning of this?" boomed a voice, loud and familiar. "Desist immediately!"

Mr King marched into the study, his gown billowing behind him. Close on his heels were the headmaster and the Reverend Croft. All six boys stopped and stood, as if frozen to the spot.

Then Sanderson cried out, offering up his bloody palm. "Blotwell stabbed me, sir!"

"Be quiet, boy!" roared Mr King, striding up to the School House captain. "Alfred Mayhew Cheeseman, get out of that uniform, pack your bags and leave this school immediately! As for the rest of you, this brawling will not be tolerated. What are two upper-sixth captains from foreign houses doing in here anyway, fighting with boys from the shell, if you please?"

"And from the lower remove, sir," murmured Harry, holding his left cheek.

"What are you saying, Mr King?" questioned Cheeseman, as if he was the wounded party. "That I should leave the school because I was doing my duty by way of these disobedient and incorrigible little horrors?"

The headmaster stepped forward. "No, Cheeseman, you are being expelled because of your egregious behaviour in the school chapel. Behaviour which I cannot bring myself to describe in front of these innocent boys from the lower school. Do I make myself clear?"

"And on the altar," said the Reverend in an outraged whisper.

Understanding broke slowly over Cheeseman's face. "I paid that slut to keep her mouth shut. What has she been saying?"

"I shall not discuss the matter with you. You've brought shame upon the school. Mr Hawlings will be here directly to escort you off the premises. Your trunk will be sent on later, along with a letter to your father. You can take the coach to Handley Cross or walk, whichever you prefer."

"I will slit that stinking whore's throat," vowed Cheeseman. "My father will not tolerate this outrage. We shall revenge ourselves on all of you!"

Frank Kennedy buttoned his trousers and rubbed his sore bottom. "You are a howwid boy, Cheeseman."

Mark Fouracre appeared in the doorway with Carstairs, still huffing and puffing, by his side.

"Ah! Fouracre," said Dr Butler. "Would you please take your charges away to Drake House so we can start to put this unedifying business behind us. Sanderson and Pincher, I have numerous questions for you, and if you don't have the answers I require you may suffer the same fate as your erstwhile colleague. You will report to me in my office tomorrow at 7 a.m., and as of this moment you can consider yourselves stripped of your house captaincies."

"But what about drill, sir?" asked Sanderson, almost in tears.

"Drills and parades are cancelled... permanently. This school is here to educate and broaden the mind and body, not to create a lot of rude mechanicals."

"What about me, sir?" asked Blotwell who, realising he was still holding the pen in his hand, quickly hid it behind his back.

"Lady Bruton is waiting for you in your study. I believe she is being entertained at this moment to tea and biscuits by Mr Perceval."

* * *

Seated in his armchair, Mark Fouracre looked at the four boys gathered around him. One was holding a cold compress over his left eye, another was sitting on a cushion, a third was relaxing on the divan drinking a cup of coffee, while the fourth was peering out of the open window towards the osher.

"The villain is leaving now. Old Hawlings has made him carry his own case." Carstairs turned to them. "The reign of terror has ended."

"Thwee howwid boys," said Frank, fidgeting uncomfortably on his cushion.

"And you've got Blotwell to thank for their removal," said Fouracre with a smile.

"Oh, please!" said Harry, removing the compress for a moment.

"Talk of the devil," said Carstairs. "There he is walking down the path with a lady."

Freddy put his cup on the side table and went to the window. "So that's Auntie Millicent, is it?"

"What's she like?" asked Harry.

"I'm not sure. Tall, elegant. She has her back to us and is carrying a parasol."

A few minutes later there was a knock on the study door.

"Come!" called Fouracre.

The door opened and Mr Hawlings stood there, the hood of his kaftan around his shoulders and his salt-and-pepper hair framing his bewhiskered face.

Mark Fouracre looked at him in surprise. "Mr Hawlings, what can we do for you?"

"I thought one or two of you gentlemen might like to go with me to Master Cheeseman's study to see what we can see."

Although the words were directed at everyone, the old caretaker's gaze was firmly fixed on Freddy.

"I'll pass," said Harry.

"Carstairs and I are going paddling shortly," said Frank, who wanted to get back to a normal Wednesday afternoon.

"I'll go," said Freddy.

"There, you have your volunteer, Mr Hawlings," said Fouracre.

The two exited Drake House and walked along the path towards the osher.

"Do you see what a mess all of those feet have made tramping up and down on my lawn with their military marches?" said Mr Hawlings.

Freddy looked at the worn, compressed stretch of grass. "Now you come to mention it…"

The old caretaker chuckled.

They entered School House and climbed the stairs to the second floor. All was quiet as they passed along the corridor to the end study.

"What do you think we'll find?" asked Freddy, sure that Mr Hawlings had expectations.

"Who knows?" came the reply. "But I suggest you keep your wits about you."

Once inside, it seemed to Freddy that Mr Hawlings was merely making a perfunctory search and leaving him to find anything of significance, if there was anything of significance to find. He moved from the wardrobe, which was empty, to the desk, ignoring the Bible on top. The first two drawers he tried were bare except for a pencil stub and a piece of string. In the third was an untidy pile of papers made up of receipts and invoices for multifarious items. He sat down in the chair and began to sort through them.

"Ah, here's a bill for a bottle of Glenlivet whisky – unpaid, as far as I can see."

Mr Hawlings made an uninterested noise and sat down on the lid of Cheeseman's trunk.

"Isn't there anything in that chest?" asked Freddy.

"Only clothes, a cricket bat and a spare birch."

"He wasn't a bad cricketer, was he?" said Freddy. "Here's a receipt for tobacco." He passed over several more. "Oh, and here's the bill for the naval lieutenant's uniform from Meyer and Mortimer, 36 Conduit Street, Mayfair, London. Twenty-six guineas. I don't think it's been paid either."

Mr Hawlings sniffed. "Nothing else?"

Freddy frowned, rifling through the rest. "No, I don't..." He stopped short. A small, flimsy piece of paper had caught his eye headed: *John Turner, Grocer, Wine and Spirit Merchant, Yardlow, Wiltshire.*

"Mr Hawlings!"

"Well, what have you got?"

"It's a receipt for a quart of whale oil and three brace of torches." Freddy stared at the old caretaker, dumbfounded. "It was Cheeseman who set fire to Mrs Snell's cottage."

Slowly, Mr Hawlings nodded. "So, there you are. Another mystery solved, another crime uncovered. I dare say, nothing will come of it."

* * *

Simon Blotwell stood on the steps of the osher, waving farewell to Auntie Millicent with his right hand while holding a new book in his left. A self-satisfied smile wreathed his face as he proceeded indoors and up the stairs to his study, where Henry had just finished translating *The Death of Hercules* and was resting on his bed.

"Good news," said Simon loudly, for once sitting at his desk.

Henry opened an eye and looked over at his study mate. "I know. Cheeseman out, Sanderson and Pincher demoted..."

"No, not that." Simon's face lit up. "Matron has been reappointed as Matron and that common country girl has been given her marching orders."

"Oh," said Henry, somewhat underwhelmed by the news. "What have you got there?"

"It's my new book. The Reverend McKellan sent it. He told Auntie Millicent that it would be sure to uplift my soul."

"Well, that's certainly something that needs uplifting. What's it called?"

"*Eric, or Little-by-Little.* It's about a schoolboy who starts out good and gets progressively worse."

"And that's uplifting, is it?"

"I don't know, Henry. It's got a lot of words in it and not too many pictures."

"No cake, then?"

Simon's face fell a little, then brightened again. "No, but Auntie Millicent will be coming back for the end-of-term gala and she'll be sure to bring something then."

Chapter Twenty-Five

In the Swim

As soon as Harry touched the jetty, Freddy dived over his head into the lagoon to enthusiastic cheers from his fellow members of Drake House and polite applause from the guests assembled on the beach in their Windsor chairs. The second of the swimmers in the 4 × 200 yards relay, Freddy was up against four opponents from the other houses, including Gus Gilmore, the captain designate of Raleigh House, and the strongest swimmer in the school.

It was the last race of the annual sports gala, and it was the day before Seekings broke up for the summer holidays. A day blessed with fine weather, with a gentle southerly breeze to take the edge off the heat.

"Your friend's costume is very striking."

Simon Blotwell was sitting between Auntie Millicent and Matron.

"I'm not sure if I would exactly call him my friend, Matron," said Simon. "He is, after all, only a common village boy."

"Don't be ridiculous, Simon," said Lady Bruton.

Lady Bruton, Auntie Millicent, had been something of a surprise to those at Seekings School who had got to know Simon Blotwell. They had expected an elderly dowager duchess dressed in layers of extravagant silk with a bustle and a huge bonnet decorated with ostrich feathers. What they got was a plain-speaking woman in her mid-thirties, auburn-haired and slim, wearing a long, flowing cotton print dress with a high waistline and carrying a pink parasol. Until her return, with Simon, to Bruton Manor on the Monday, she was staying at Seekings as a guest of the headmaster.

"Mrs Amfortas, what happened to that girl – Betsy. Was that her name?"

"Betty Golightly," said Simon.

Matron leaned across Blotwell and spoke confidentially, as if he wasn't there. "The nuns have her on the Isle of Wight."

Lady Bruton frowned. "Alfred Cheeseman ought to have been horse-whipped from here to kingdom come. The trouble is, his father is no different. I know, I have had dealings with the man."

Grizelda Amfortas nodded. "Like father, like son. It can be a blessing or a curse."

"It's a blessing to have you back, Matron," said Simon unctuously, as if he'd personally organised her re-employment.

A small boy came up, smiling and batting his eyelids at them. In his hand was a sheaf of envelopes. "This is for you, Simon Blotwell. Tomowwow is my eleventh birthday and you are invited to my party because you stabbed that howwid boy in the neck. I shall be back shortly to collect your weply."

Frank Kennedy trotted off to distribute more invitations.

Simon glanced at the hand-printed card. "I'm not sure I shall be able to go. His father is the lighthouse keeper."

"I hear they are making ice cream for the party," said Matron. "Apparently there's an ice house in the cliff constructed when Seekings was still a manor."

"Ice cream..." murmured Blotwell, his eyes going wide.

Lady Bruton smiled. "Have you decided to accept the invitation after all, Simon?"

There was a ripple of applause around them and shouts of 'huzzah!' from the jetty. Drake House had won the relay and were overall winners of the swimming competition. Freddy had just about held his own against Gus Gilmore, thanks in no small part to his unique red-and-white striped, waxed linen bathing costume. All the other swimmers were dressed uniformly in dull coloured woollen suits that soon became heavy with water and dragged their wearers down.

Gus came over, dripping, to shake Freddy's hand. "Not just a brain, then," he said.

"You still beat me," said Freddy.

"Only by a touch."

"All the ladies are swooning over his bare chest," said Mark Fouracre, who was now tipped to become school captain next term.

Freddie went red and covered himself with his arms.

Harry East, who was still nursing the remains of a black eye, clapped him on the shoulder. "Federico, my man, let's go and get changed, then duck into the marquee for some refreshment."

It took them no time at all to dry off and put on their uniforms in the small tent provided, from where they headed to the bright green-and-yellow marquee set in the small area of no-man's land between the beach and the road.

Edith and Ellen Palmerston were serving a variety of drinks, including a summer fruit punch made with the latest London fashion, Pimm's No. 1.

"Hmm, not bad," said Harry, taking a sip.

"Now, don't drink too much of that lest you become tiddly, Master East," warned Mrs Palmerston.

Harry took a larger mouthful and winked at Ellen, who remained studiously expressionless.

Freddy gazed round the marquee. "Have you seen my dad, Scud?"

"Not for a while. Last time I saw him, he was jawing with old Hawlings, probably about us."

"More likely talking about Cheeseman and his gang setting fire to the Snells' cottage."

"You'll be surprised to learn that Pa has had no luck in trying to get the authorities interested in that receipt."

"Yes, very surprised, given the fact that Squire Blotwell and Cheeseman's dad are friends and they probably encouraged him to take the law into his own hands anyway."

"Federico, you and your conspiracy theories."

"You'll see…" said Freddy.

Harry chuckled. "Did Mrs Snell get off all right?"

"Yes, most of the village chipped in to pay her fare, especially after the Reverend Smollett's sermon on 'Love thy neighbour as yourself'."

"What about the cottage?"

"Farmer Stadden wants to start the demolition as soon as possible. They say he's hired a London architect to design a new cottage."

Their conversation ceased as Dr Butler came over, a purposeful look in his eye. Following the incident with Cheeseman, the headmaster had recovered much of his former zest and looked an altogether new man.

"Good afternoon, sir," said Freddy.

"Good afternoon, gentlemen, and may I congratulate you both on your athletic performances today? The school has a duty to build healthy bodies as well as healthy minds, and we seemed to have succeeded with the pair of you."

"Thank you, sir," said Harry, who had easily won all the races he had entered during the morning's track and field events.

"Hall, your father wished me to tell you that he has gone back to Linbury to see to the mail and to open up the inn."

"I was wondering," said Freddy.

"Principally, though, we were discussing your eventful first year at Seekings and the progress you've made."

Freddy's face fell. "Oh, I see, sir."

"From your worried expression, I'm not sure that you do." Dr Butler smiled. "I'm pleased to be able to tell you that you have been promoted to the remove from the beginning of the Michaelmas term."

Freddy's face lit up. "I wasn't expecting… Do you mean the remove or lower remove, sir?"

"Oh, the remove, Hall. Where you will be joining your

friend, East."

"Excellent!" Harry beamed.

"Gosh, thank you, sir!"

"There is no need for thanks; it's what you deserve. I was reviewing some of your work with your head of house, and we both agree it is of excellent quality."

"Mr Tallow, sir?" said Freddy, not quite believing that his modern history teacher held him in such high regard.

"Certainly, Mr Tallow. I had him come to my house to look over your work specifically. Of course, your natural philosophy subjects were a highlight. And I've written to your sponsor, Mr Newton, to tell him so."

Freddy took a gulp of the punch, which made his eyes water.

"Excuse me, sir," said Harry. "We haven't seen Mr Topliss for some little while. Is he all right?"

"Mr Topliss is away at the moment visiting his brother Benjamin in Bethnal Green, hence the silence of the bells."

Harry and Freddy exchanged a glance and Dr Butler chuckled. "I shall leave you both to it. And mind you take heed of what Mrs Palmerston tells you about that punch."

The headmaster walked away. His place was immediately taken by Henry Perceval, impeccably dressed in double-breasted tail-coat, a rose in his buttonhole, pin-striped trousers and cravat.

"I say, chaps, I feel dashed left out. Frank Kennedy has invited practically everyone in the school to his birthday party – everyone except me, that is. He's even invited Simon."

"Aren't you going home tomorrow?" asked Freddy.

"Actually, I shall be going up to Laycock with Foxy on Tuesday for a stint. But he's visiting relations in Haversham with his mama until then, so I'm at something of a loose end."

"Could it be that Frank doesn't know you, except by sight?" said Harry.

"You could probably say that about half the people he's invited. In any case, we were introduced at Freddy's do."

"Would you invite him to your party?" asked Freddy.

"You know, that's an altogether awkward question. I've never had a birthday party with friends."

"We can easily change that," said Harry. "When were you born?"

"The 6th October 1811."

"Remember that date, Federico. We'll expect invitations."

Freddy smiled. "If you're at a loose end on Monday, Henry, come up to Linbury and we'll spend the day together."

"I say! That's jolly decent of you, Freddy. I'll take you up on that."

"Federico will be joining us in the remove next term," said Harry.

"That's topping news, chaps. I thought I might scrape through to the fifth, but it was not to be. So, here's to our triumvirate next term."

Freddy and Harry wandered out of the marquee and were surprised to see a small disconsolate figure sitting on a log, his head in his hands. On the ground around him were several envelopes and an open notebook with scrawly writing all over it.

"Why, what have we here?" said Harry, sitting down on Frank's left while Freddy took up position on his right. "Come on, tell your Uncles H. and F. You're not allowed to be unhappy so near to your birthday."

"You haven't fallen out with Carstairs again, have you?" asked Freddy.

Frank shook his head and looked up, wiping his eyes with the back of his hand. "I've made a sewious ewwor."

"What might that be?"

"My mum said I could invite twelve people to my party."

Freddy thought about those he knew were going and couldn't see a problem. "There must be at least ten of us coming."

Frank's head drooped. "Sixty-two."

Harry tried unsuccessfully to stifle a laugh. "You mean

you've invited sixty-two people to your party and you're only allowed twelve?"

"It's not funny, Hawwy East. I shall be in sewious twouble. I gave out sixty-thwee invitations because I thought not many people would want to come to my party…"

"And sixty-two accepted." Freddy laughed. "It shows how popular you are."

"It's not funny, Fweddy Hall."

"All right," said Harry, "leave this to Federico and myself, but first tell us who your top choices are."

Frank counted them off on his fingers. "Carstairs, my best fwend; my fwends, Hawwy and Fweddy, that's you; Wussell Wawwen fwom Linbuwy because he's big and stwong like I'm going to be; Jennings and Darbishire, because they're funny; Berty Wight, because he makes nice tea; Fouwacre because he's my house captain; Gewwy and Gus Gilmore, because they're nice, and Blotwell, because he stabbed that howwid boy in the neck."

"Fair enough. Stay where you are and we'll be back shortly."

By the simple expedient of telling the invitees that there would be no food and, more particularly, no ice cream, they returned in less than fifteen minutes, holding fifty-one invitations. With them was Carstairs, who had been looking for his best friend for some time.

"Done and dusted," said Harry, handing over his share of invitations to Frank, who had been anxiously pacing up and down beside the log.

"There's just the matter of payment now," said Freddy, handing over his share.

"Payment?" said Frank, confused.

"Yes, payment," said Harry. "There's a twelfth man who you've got to invite to your party."

"Henry – Henry Perceval," said Freddy.

Frank's expression became even more confused. "I did invite Henwy."

"Not according to him."

Frank's cheeks went pink and he touched his lips with the tips of his fingers. "Ooo, you're wight. I got sidetwacked."

"He is an unreconstructed scatterbrain," said Carstairs, sticking his nose in the air.

Frank eyed his friend. "Carstairs, have you finished hobnobbing with Lady Chesterfield?"

His nose rose even higher. "I wasn't hobnobbing, my good fellow. We were discussing the crooked spire on the parish church of St Mary and All Saints."

"Stop being supiwior, Carstairs, it doesn't suit you."

"Are you going to give that invitation to Mr Perceval, like you were asked, or am I going to have to do it for you?" said Carstairs with mock testiness.

"Don't wush me..."

"See you tomorrow," called Freddy as he and Harry turned away.

Of course, there was no reply, as the ears of the two younger boys had closed to all but themselves.

On the school side of the road, Mr Hawlings was sitting on a stool smoking a long clay pipe and reading a copy of the *Examiner* dated 4th June. As the two boys approached, he looked over the top of the newspaper.

"Is it that time already?" he said.

"Coach will be here in ten minutes," said Harry, glancing up at the Seekings clock.

"Anything interesting in the paper, Mr Hawlings?" asked Freddy.

The caretaker stood up and tucked it inside his smock. "Well now, funny you should ask that, Freddy Hall, because the king has suggested to Parliament that they suspend the writ of *habeus corpus* during the national emergency. He also suggested that the penalty for seditious libel should be transportation to the colonies, because it's the next worst thing to treason."

"What does that mean?" asked Harry.

Mr Hawlings chuckled. "Why is it that an uneducated caretaker should have to explain to two learned gentlemen, one the son of a magistrate, no less, the meaning of the law?"

"I've read a bit about *habeas corpus*. How you can't imprison someone unlawfully," said Freddy, "but that's the first I've heard of a national emergency."

"It may be the first time that a great many people have heard of it," replied Mr Hawlings. "But there's nothing like declaring a national emergency for people to start believing that there is one. Especially if it's said by the king and printed in the newspapers…"

"They've been saying that the Silesian invasion is imminent for over a year now," said Freddy.

"But what good does it do, trying to frighten people?" said Harry.

Mr Hawlings sat back down on his stool. "Fear is a great manipulator. It makes everything black and white, and presents people with less to think about. Those we look to for strength and resolve can then get away with things they wouldn't otherwise be able to – like, for instance, marrying your half-sister or imprisoning people without trial."

Harry frowned. "Mr Hawlings, you're beginning to sound like a Dorsetshire radical."

The old caretaker took a long draw on his pipe. "Am I, Harry East? And me not even from these parts." A smoke ring appeared from his mouth and floated for several seconds in front of them.

Freddy chuckled. "I wish I could do that."

"But you can't do it unless you smoke," said Harry, "and you don't smoke."

"True," admitted Freddy.

Mr Hawlings pointed his pipe at each of them. "Now, you lads look after yourselves during the holidays and don't get up to too much mischief. You'll need all your fighting spirit for when you return in September."

Before either boy had time to respond, a gossiping cluster

of ladies dressed in their finery and carrying small valises crossed the road to catch the Royal Mail coach to Larkstone and beyond.

"Looks like you'll be on top tonight, with the luggage," said Freddy in a low voice.

"They're still talking about your swimming costume," whispered Harry with a smirk.

"Don't be daft," said Freddy.

Harry stood, hands on hips, his eyes set on the road towards Linbury from where the coach was fast approaching. The post horn sounded. "I'll see you tomorrow at the party, Federico, bright-eyed and bushy-tailed."

With all the passengers on board and Harry sitting cross-legged between their luggage on the roof, the coach moved off at a more stately pace than normal. Freddy watched until it had disappeared over the rise then, with a final farewell to Mr Hawlings, he wended his way back to the village.

In the bar room of the Sailor's Yarn, Daniel was getting ready to open up. He smiled at his son, who had changed into his workwear, including his white apron. "Well, what have you got to say for yourself? Star pupil and swimming champion of Seekings School."

"Dad!" said Freddy, blushing with embarrassment. "I shall never wear that costume again."

"It got nothing but compliments," said Daniel, "as did the handsome lad wearing it."

Freddy's blush deepened, though he couldn't help grinning too.

"Did Dr Butler speak to you?"

Freddy nodded.

"I'm so proud of you," said Daniel.

"Oh, Dad!"

The innkeeper eyed his son and his voice became more serious. "There's a letter come for you, from Greenwich. I hope it's good news." He motioned with his head to the top of the bar.

Freddy's hands were shaking when he opened the sealed sheet. Inside was another paper which he missed in his haste. It fell to the floor. Daniel scooped it up and held it while Freddy read out the letter.

Tuesday 4th July 1826
To: Freddy Hall,
The Sailor's Yarn Inn,
Linbury,
Dorsetshire.

Dear Freddy,

JOB DONE! (Though my sister Jane did most of the legwork.)
I have been assigned to HMS Ajax in Portsmouth and travel on Friday next, but I shan't be lonely as John Fairbrother and Charlie Cooke will be shipmates.
Write to me there when you can, and maybe see you soon?
Thinking of you,
Your old china plate,
Carl Birch

Freddy reread the letter twice to himself. "That's today, Dad – he's actually travelling to Portsmouth, today."
Daniel smiled. "Yes, and he did it, didn't he, as you asked?"
"Of course he did."
"I'm sorry I doubted him, son. He must like you a lot."
"I like him a lot."
"I know you do. Here's the receipt for your money, signed and sealed by the prison governor, no less."

RECEIPT

Received on behalf of Prisoner Thomas White the sum of £5 comprising:

Nine weeks' lodging..................................£4 4s 6d

Prisoners' committee garnish 6s 6d

Victuals and candles 7s 0d

Soap and washing 2s 0d

———————

£5 0s 0d

signed on this day, 2nd July 1826

Joseph Rutland
(Deputy Marshall HM Prison, Marshalsea)

"Nine weeks," said Freddy. "We've got nine weeks to get Tom out of there."

"Now, take it easy," said Daniel. "You need to relax. That's what holidays are about, not taking the weight of the world on your shoulders."

"That's what Mr Hawlings said."

"That man may be just the school caretaker, but he talks a lot of sense."

"I've invited Henry Perceval to spend the day with me on Monday."

"That's good. He's a nice, steady fellow is Henry. Do you know where his family live?"

"Not really. He said he was born in Hampstead, near London."

"Hampstead, hmm? That's a long way up from Limehouse."

"Dad!"

"I know, I know. I'm just ribbing you. Why don't you see if young Carl can get you a visit to *HMS Ajax* in Portsmouth? That'll be of interest to you and will take your mind off other matters."

Freddy smiled conspiratorially. "Maybe Mr Newton could arrange it for me. He knows Mr Pepys, who is high up in the Navy Office."

The outside door opened and the first customer of the evening entered: Zebedee Tring.

"And what are you two gawping at? Haven't you ever seen a thirsty man after an honest day's work?" He sat down in his usual place.

Freddy stepped forward. "A pint of scrumpy, Mr Tring?"

"It might be, but you shouldn't presume, Freddy Hall."

"Would you like me to bring it to your table?"

"You can do that, but don't expect me to pay any extra."

Freddy went behind the bar and fetched down Zebedee's tankard. The door opened again and Doughy Hood and Sam Hingston came in, closely followed by Russell Warren and his father Joseph, chatting breezily about nothing in particular.

Daniel sighed contentedly. He felt more at ease now. The outside world might be talking about war and conflict but here, in his small patch of Albion, peace reigned once again. The community had come together and was getting back to its normal ways.

THE END OF BOOK 1

Dramatis Personae

Complete List: Books 1 to 5

(Names in **Bold Type** are major characters)

Seekings School

Masters

Doctor George Butler (Headmaster) – Teaches divinity (theology) to the 6th form.

Mr. Campbell-Bannerman – Modern Languages.

Mr. Crocker – Classics for the Remove and Upper Remove.

Reverend Croft – Scripture & Swimming.

Mr. Caulton-Harris – Latin Grammar and Athletics.

Mr. S.G. Dearman – Mathematics.

Mr. Robert Hooke – Natural Philosophy.

Mr King – House Master (School House) Classics 6th Form.

Mr. LaValle – House Master (Frobisher) Classics, History.

Mr. Ollerenshaw – House Master (Hawkins) Greek Grammar.

Mr. Ravenshaw – House Master (Raleigh) Classics 5th form.

Mr. Tallow – House Master (Drake) Teaches Modern History.

Mr. Aubrey Topliss – School Librarian, Conjuror. Teaches Alchemy and Archery.

Mr. Francis Williams – Music master.

Assistant Masters

Mr Hunt

Mr. Tatham

Staff

Grizelda Amfortas – Matron

Mrs. Anderson – Drake Housekeeper

Miss Chawner – School Secretary.

Betty Golightly – Nurse.

Mr. Hawlings – Caretaker.

Mrs. Edith Palmerston – Cook, Drake House.

Ellen Palmerston – Under Cook.

Prefects

Cheeseman, Alfred Mayhew – Captain of School House.

Fouracre, George Mark – Captain of Drake House.

Oldham, Theodore – Captain of the School.

Pincher, Jeremy – Tom White's deputy.

Sanderson, Donald – Captain of Frobisher House.

Stevenson Michael – Captain of Hawkins House.

White, Thomas – Captain of Raleigh House.

School House

Blotwell, Simon – (b. Friday, August 13th 1813). Shell pupil.

Darbishire Edwin – Shell pupil. Jennings's best friend.

Fairfax, Hugh – Shell pupil. Quotes lines from the plays of Shakespeare.

Fox Talbot, William Henry – Remove pupil.

Greene, Jack – Remove pupil.

Jennings, John – Shell pupil. Darbishire's best friend.

Kingsley, Lewis – Remove pupil.

Kipling, 'Beetle' – Upper Remove pupil. Part of the triumvirate: Stalky & Co.

Meredith, Samuel – Lower Sixth pupil.

M'Turk (William McTurk) – Upper Remove. Part of the triumvirate: Stalky & Co.

Perceval, Henry – (b. October 6th, 1811). Remove pupil. Shares a study with Blotwell.

Quartermain, Allan – Upper Sixth pupil

Stalky (Arthur Corkran) – Upper Remove. Head of the triumvirate: Stalky & Co.

Templeton-Smith, Victor – Fifth Form pupil.

Raleigh House

Atkins, Humphrey – Shell pupil.

Carstairs, James – (b. March 8th 1815) Shell pupil. Frank Kennedy's soulmate. Known to all, including his family, as Carstairs.

Cholmondeley, Basil – Shell pupil.

Cleave, Rufus – Fifth Form pupil.

Gilmore, Gus – Lower Sixth pupil. Gerry's brother.

Gilmore, Gerald (Gerry) – Shell pupil. Aged 12. Gus's brother.

Jenkins, Clive – Remove pupil.

Wright, Bert (Berty) – Fifth Form pupil and tea maker.

Drake House (for Day Boys)

East, Harry – (b. Tuesday, January 7th 1812). 'Scud'. Lower Remove pupil. Freddy's best friend. Family Lives at Jersey House, Larkstone.

Kennedy, Frank – (b. March 8th 1815) Shell pupil. Carstairs soulmate. A day boy. Family Lives in the Clifftop Lighthouse.

Mortimer, Derek – Lower Sixth pupil.

Redwing, Lance – Upper Remove pupil.

Frobisher House

Archer, Daniel – Lower Remove pupil.

Cox, Laurence – Shell pupil. Nickname 'Apple'.

Ballantyne, Ralph – Shell pupil.

Brownlow, Felix – Remove pupil.

Ferguson Fergus – Oldest member of the Shell, aged 14. Native of Caledonia.

Marriott, Jack – Lower Sixth pupil.

Hawkins House

Bishop, George – Shell pupil.

Carruthers, Oscar – Upper Remove pupil.

Crewe, Gervaise – Shell pupil.

Daniels, Silas – Upper Remove pupil.

Hesilrigge, Phillip – Shell pupil.

Wakefield, Adam – Shell pupil.

Wolseley, Archibald – Shell pupil.

Guests

Thomas Bramwell – G F Handel's servant.

John Carstairs – Carstairs older brother, known as Carstairs.

Mrs Irene Fouracre – Mark Fouracre's mother.

George Frideric Handel – Musician.

Ambrose Kennedy – Frank's father, and Keeper of the Clifftop Lighthouse.

Peggy Kennedy – Frank's mother.

Miss Isabella Perceval – Nathaniel's elder sister.

Alexander Sanderson – Donald's father.

Beatrice Sanderson – Donald's mother.

Trevor Edward Sanderson – Donald Sanderson's younger brother.

Linbury Village

Residents

Miss Beryl Antrobus – School Teacher, and church organist. Lives on the green.

Cyril Barnes – (b May 5th 1798) labourer.

Nora Barnes – Cyril's wife.

Judy Barnes – Cyril's daughter aged 6.

Louis 'Lou' Barnes – (b. November 20th 1823) Cyril's youngest son. Freddy calls him 'Chubs'.

Lucy Cossett – Child aged 6. A member of the Cossett family of labourers.

Mary Evans – Child.

Tom Forrest – Deceased. At one time the long-serving beadle.

Daniel Hall – Widower. Publican of the Sailor's Yarn.

Freddy Hall – (b. Monday, June 11th 1812). The son of Daniel Hall. Lives at the Sailor's Yarn.

Leonora Hall – deceased wife of Daniel.

Ruffy Harris – Butcher and regular at the Sailor's Yarn.

Laura Harris – Ruffy's wife.

Sarah Harris – Ruffy's daughter, aged 15.

Anthony Harris – Ruffy's son, aged 13.

Elias Harville – Journeyman carpenter.

Susan Harville – Elias's wife.

Constance, Rosemary, Rachel, and Stanley Harville – Elias's children.

Sam Hingston – Grocer and regular at the Sailor's Yarn.

Edie Hingston – Sam's wife is Daniel Hall's cousin and helps out at the Sailor's Yarn.

Dorothea Hingston – Sam's daughter, aged 14.

Doughy Hood – Baker and regular at the Sailor's Yarn.

Maisie Hood – Doughy's wife.

Charles and Georgina Hood – (b September 1810) Doughy's children, fraternal twins.

Gabriel Levens – Beadle and parish constable.

Patrick Mason – Builder (roofer and brick layer). Lives in one of the Glebe Cottages.

Brenda Mason – Patrick's wife.

Andrew Mason – (b December 4th 1813) Patrick's son, Michael's twin brother.

Michael Mason – (b December 4th 1813) Patrick's son, Andrew's twin brother.

Eliza May – Owns the dairy.

Clarrie May – Eliza's daughter.

Mrs. Sophie Pattle – Widow. Runs the village shop.

Dolly Peters – Lives down Berry Hill Lane.

Matthew Peters – Dolly Peter's great nephew.

Agnes Pinsent – Gabriel Levens housekeeper,

Luther Pinsent – Agnes's brother, deputy beadle.

Edgar Pitt – Shoemaker (cordwainer plus cobbler). Lives down Big Barn lane.

Mrs Pitt – His wife.

Dick Pitt – The eldest son aged 12.

Mollie Pitt – The eldest daughter aged 16.

Thomas Pitt – Chubs best friend age 6.

Reverend Jeremy Smollett – For many years the vicar of All Souls Church.

Mrs. Snell – Village busybody, lives on the green.

Mr. Snell – Mrs Snell's husband.

Farmer (John) Stadden – the richest man in the district, owner of the labourers cottages in Linbury.

Elizabeth Stadden – Farmer Stadden's wife.

Gavin Stadden – (b January 15th 1809) Farmer Stadden's son.

Albert Tanner – Miller. He is Freddy Hall's uncle on his mother's side.

Emily Tanner – Albert's wife.

Jasper Tanner – Uncle Albert's Sussex spaniel.

Arthur Tree – Glazier, lives on the green.

Duncan Tree – Arthur's son. Aged 20.

Joyce Tree – Arthur's wife.

Zebedee Tring – Itinerant labourer, curmudgeon, and regular at the Sailor's Yarn.

Russell Warren – (b. 26th October 1809) the blacksmith's son and Freddy Hall's longtime friend.

Joseph Warren – Blacksmith, Russell's father.

Charlotte Warren – Russell's sister, known as Lottie, age 14.

Gwen Warren – Joseph's wife.

Reverend Charles Wilson – Calvinist.

Maud Wilson – His wife.

Anne Wilson – (b. 31st August 1809) His daughter.

Guests at the Sailor's Yarn

The Honourable James Brydges – Seekings School governor from Handley Cross.

The Honourable Mrs Constance Brydges – James Brydges wife, also a Seekings School governor.

Charles – Student at Cambridge University. The Reverend Henslow's protégé.

Matthew Dubourg – musician.

Captain Hartwell.

The Reverend John Stevens Henslow – Professor of Botany, Cambridge University.

Harriet Henslow – The Reverend Henslow's wife.

Grace and Ethel Ogilvy – Sisters.

Anthony Salvin – Architect.

Larkstone Village

George Christopher East – Harry East's father. The regional magistrate.

Charlotte Alice East – Harry East's mother. The family home is called Jersey House.

Sir Ronald Farwell – Magistrate.

Mary – The maid at Jersey House.

Monsieur Yves Du Pain – Harry's tutor from Brittany.

Jethro Sowerbutts – The gardener at Jersey house.

Arthur Sowerbutts – Jethro's son.

Dunhambury (County town of Dorsetshire)

John Bowman – A porter at the workhouse.

Mervyn Dumbleton – Chaplain.

Reverend Isambard McKellan – Parish priest, Church of St Nicholas. Simon's vicar.

Dr Skidmore – Doctor of medicine.

Mr Montague Twizzle – Workhouse Master.

Mrs Lilac Twizzle – Workhouse Matron.

Verbena Twizzle – Montague and Lilac's daughter.

Mrs Welbeck – The Reverend's housekeeper.

Blotwell Manor

Bassett – The coachman and rival of Smythe, the coachman at Bruton manor.

Bernice – An upstairs maid.

Billy Binns – (b. 20th December, 1811) Simon's one eyed, coal eating 'friend'.

Squire Hubert Blotwell – Simon's father. High Sheriff and Lord Lieutenant of Dorsetshire. MP for West Dorsetshire.

Lady Mary Blotwell – Simon's mother.

Celeste – An upstairs maid.

Mrs. Cresswell – The cook.

Forbes – The butler.

Mr. Kitching – The under-gardener.

Mrs Kitching – Mr Kitching's wife.

Edwin Kitching – (b. Sept 25th 1816), John Wesley's brother.

John Wesley Kitching – The under gardener's boy aged 17 (1826). Edwin's elder brother.

Mrs Perkins – The housekeeper

Marmaduke Phillips – The head gardener.

Mrs Fanny Winstanley-Meadows – a widow.

Dasher – Lady Mary's horse.

Ferdinand – Simon's colt.

Rachel and Robert – Rabbits.

Bruton Manor

Lady Millicent Bruton – Simon's Aunt (Lady Mary's sister).

Blanchard – The butler.

Dorothy Davies – Senior Lady's Maid.

Thomas Gainsborough – Painter

Gainsborough Dupont – Thomas Gainsborough's assistant and nephew.

Jacob – The second footman, aged 18.

Mrs. Mainwearing – The housekeeper.

Smythe – Coachman and rival of Bassett, the coachman at Blotwell manor.

Mrs. Strout – Cook.

Sox and Box – The rabbits.

Lox, Spotz, Pinx – The baby rabbits.

Greenwich

Royal Observatory

Nicolas Fatio de Duillier – Mr Newton's secretary from the Republic of Geneva.

Isaac Newton – Natural Philosopher, polymath.

Royal Hospital School

Lieutenant Bentley – The Headmaster's assistant.

Carl Birch – (b. November 4th, 1811) Pupil. Brother of Wayneman and Jane.

Chief Petty Officer – Unnamed.

Charlie Cooke – (b. May 19th, 1812) Pupil, Carl's best friend.

John Fairbrother – Pupil. Younger brother of Ellen Lacey.

Commodore Hughes – Headmaster. Teaches Navigation, Nautical Astronomy, Chart Making and Mechanical Drawing.

Pete Walker – Pupil. Used to live up the road from Linbury in Thieves Wood.

London

Royal Family & Members of the Royal Household

King Henry XI

Lady Castlemaine – The Queen Mother.

Prince Charles – The Duke of York (King's brother), Lord High Admiral.

Sir Herbert Taylor KC, the Duke of York's Naval Secretary.

Parliament

Prime Minister – The First Lord of the Treasury.

Henry Addington – The Home Secretary.

George Canning – The President of the Board of Control. Formerly of Gloucester Lodge, Brompton.

Joan Canning – George Canning's wife.

Viscount Castlereagh – MP for County Down. Leader of the House of Commons.

Gerald Cheeseman – MP for Dorset North. Father of Alfred Mayhew Cheeseman.

Sir William Dalrymple – MP for Whitchurch and Lord Lieutenant of Hampshire.

Baron Eldon – Lord Chancellor to the House of Lords.

Robert Jenkinson – The Foreign Secretary and former PM.

2nd Viscount Melville – First Lord of the Admiralty.

F.J. Robinson – The Chancellor of the Exchequer.

Seething Lane

Jane Birch – Samuel Pepys's maid. Elder sister of Carl Birch.

Wayneman Birch – Pepys's boy. Younger brother of Carl Birch.

Will Hewer – Pepys's Clerk.

Mr Pendleton – Elizabeth Pepys's dancing tutor.

Samuel Pepys – The Administrator of the Royal Navy, Secretary to the Admiralty, Fellow of the Royal Society and Master of Trinity House.

Elizabeth Pepys – Samuel Pepys's wife.

The West End and Brompton

Thomas Gale – The proprietor of the Gloucester Hotel and Coffee House, Piccadilly.

Martin – A bellboy at the Gloucester Hotel.

Ned Singleton – (b 23rd September 1813) A bellboy at the Gloucester Hotel. Lives on Thistle Street, Brompton with his Grandmother.

Granny Singleton – Ned's grandmother. Formerly a lady's maid for Joan Canning, wife of George Canning the politician.

Mr Prendergast – Hamleys Toy Shop, Regent Street, store manager.

Miss Price – Hamleys sales assistant.

Marshalsea Prison

Mr Culver – Clerk of the Papers.

Joseph Rutland – Deputy Marshal and Keeper.

Whitechapel Gallery

Dr Arthur Conan Doyle – Visitor.

Ellis Powell – Spiritualist.

Mr Robertson – The Head Printer.

Professor Trimbletown – Curator.

Bethnal Green

Benjamin Franklin – The brother of Mr Aubrey Topliss.

Portsmouth

HMS Ajax

Mr Andrews – The boatswain.

William Bloom – A marine.

Midshipman Robert Dalrymple – Son of Sir William Dalrymple.

Mr. Fielding – The Chaplain.

Captain Stephen FitzRoy.

1st Lieutenant Grimshaw – Officer.

Midshipman Nathaniel Hardy – (b December 1st 1812).

Dick Southern – An ordinary seaman.

Wil Steadman – An ordinary seaman.

Jim Wallis – An ordinary seaman.

3rd Lieutenant Watkins – Officer.

Dockyard

Lieutenant Gerald Byng – Admiralty courier.

Sir George Clerk MP – Member of Admiralty Court of Inquiry.

Vice Admiral Sir George Cockburn – Fellow of the Royal Society. Member of the Admiralty Court of Inquiry.

Mr Collins – Agent Victualler.

Sir William Coventry – Commissioner of the Navy and Privy Councillor.

Mr William Robert Keith Douglas – Dumfries Burghs MCP. Member of the Admiralty Court of Inquiry.

Mr. Gibson – Senior clerk in the Victualling Office.

Viscount Sir Nicholas Hardy – Nathaniel's father.

Vice Admiral Sir William Johnstone Hope – First Naval Lord. Member of the Admiralty Court of Inquiry.

Ellen Lacey (née Fairbrother) – John Fairbrother's sister.

William Lacey – Ellen's husband.

Captain Frederick Marryatt – Prisoner's Friend at the Admiralty Court of Inquiry.

Vice Admiral Sir Thomas Byam Martin – The Comptroller of the Navy. Member of the Admiralty Court of Inquiry.

Admiral Sir George Martin – Commander-in-Chief, Portsmouth. Member of the Admiralty Court of Inquiry.

Admiral Sir Peveril Mornamont – Appointed head of the Admiralty Court of Inquiry.

Captain James Murray – HMS Valorous.

Admiral Sir Edmund Nagle - Groom of the Bedchamber (Henry XI). Member of the Admiralty Court of Inquiry.

Victor Nugent – Helmsman, HMS Revenge.

Captain Shellman – HMS Revenge.

Jeremiah Smith – Bosun's mate, HMS North Star.

William Walker – Dockyard surgeon.

Joseph Wilkins – An ordinary seaman, HMS Achilles.

Town

Moses Greetham – Judge Advocate. Legal supervision of the Admiralty Court of Inquiry.

Mary Greetham – Moses's wife.

John Greetham – Moses's son.

Mrs Mitchell – Owner of the Star and Garter, Portsmouth Point.

Josh Turner – Wine merchant in the High Street.

Henry Vincent - Wine bottler (Whitchurch).

The Military

Major Conway – King's Own Light Dragoons.

Major Danvers – 39th Dorsetshire Regiment of Foot.

Major Foster – King's Regiment of Light Dragoons.

Captain Maunday – King's Regiment of Light Dragoons.

Lieutenant Wroughton – 39th Dorsetshire Regiment of Foot. Major Danvers subaltern.

Frigate Fancy

Pete – Johnny's pet puma.

Aloysius – The albino albatross.

Captain Bartholomew Bonneface – Redbeard the Pirate of the Brigantine Flamingo.

Lieutenant Blenkinsop – The Fancy's first officer.

Johnny Davenport – Johnny the Jungle Boy.

Deidre – The Diabolical Duchess of the Desert.

Femur Fawcett – The evil first mate.

Lucien – The Slow Loris.

Captain Aubrey Lupus – The Fancy's ancient mariner.

Luther – The Lame Lion.

Red Rupert – A cut-throat.

Bimbo St John Stevas – Midshipman, 8 years old.

Steve – The sea eagle.

Tony – The tame tuna.

Wolfram – The weird witchdoctor.

A Map Of Albion

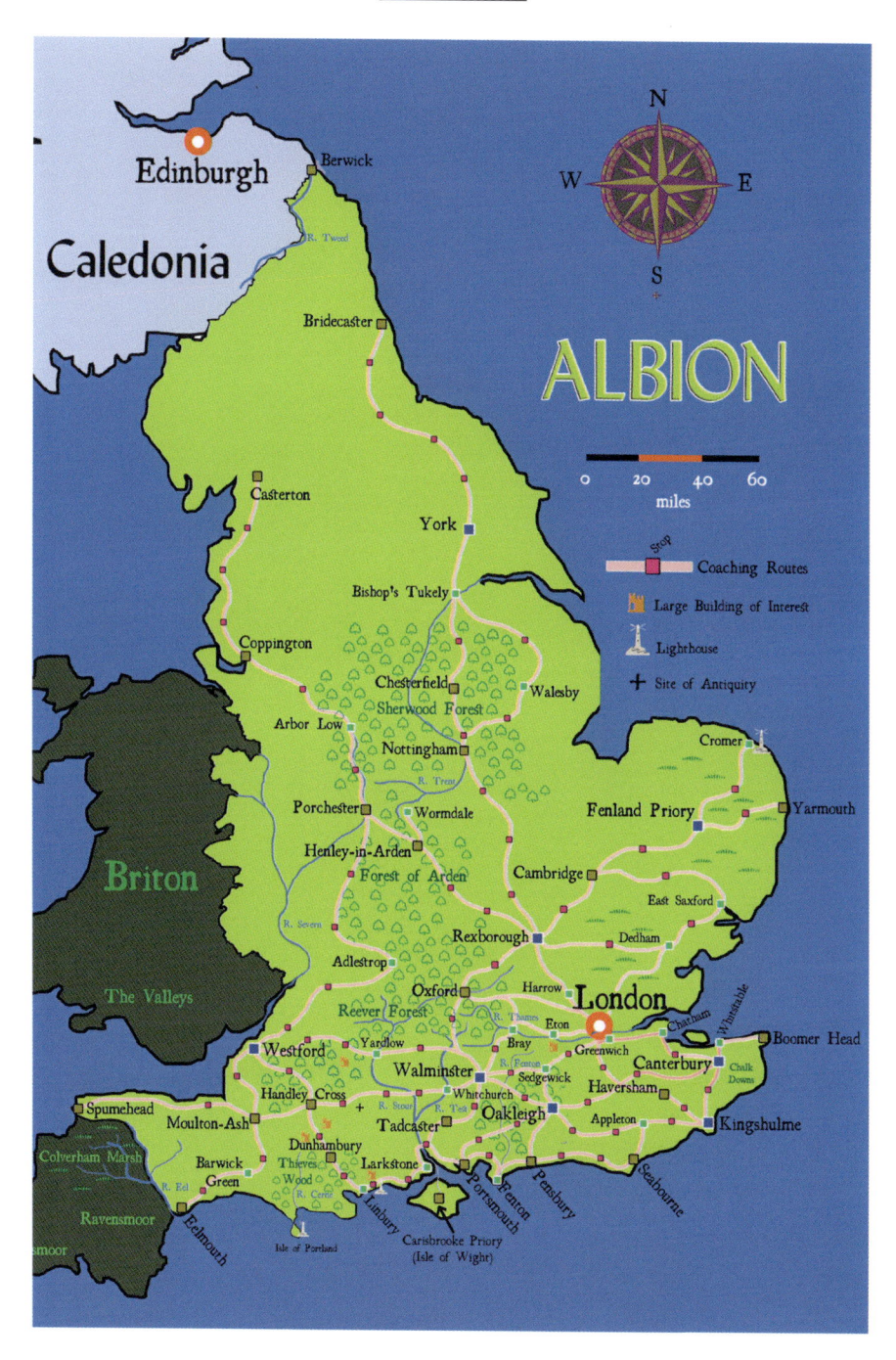

A Map Of Europa

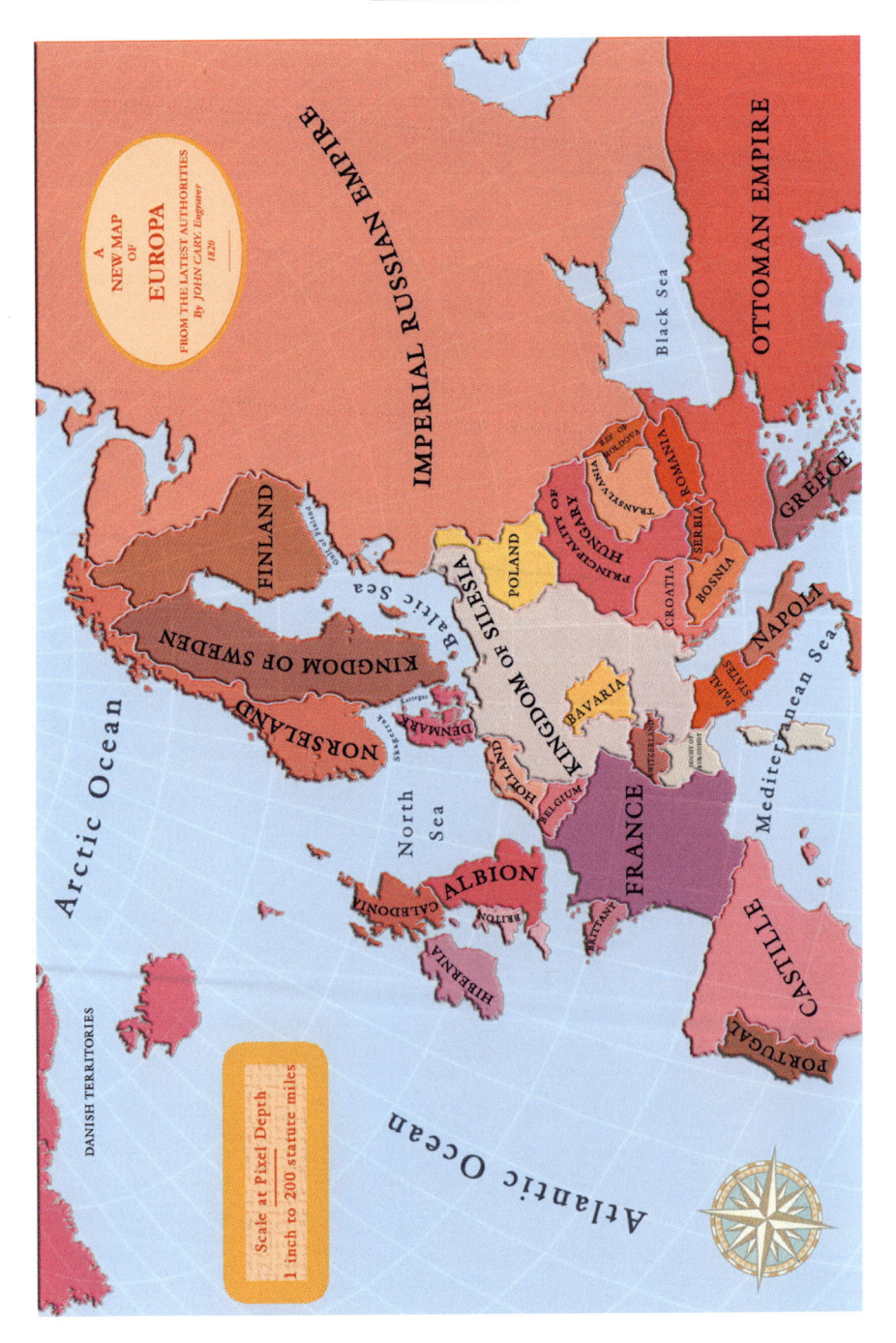

A Royal Family Tree

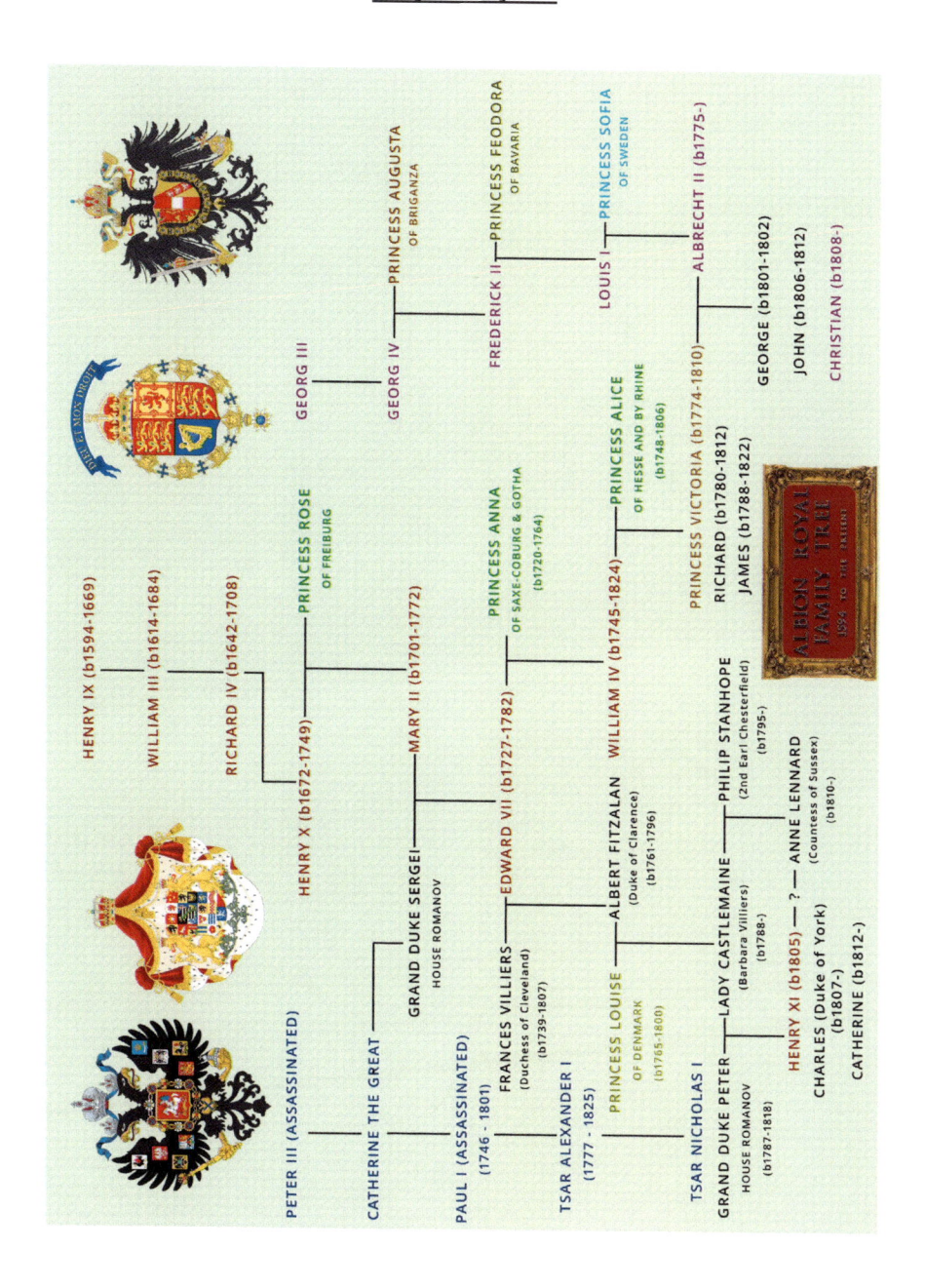

- HENRY IX (b1594-1669)
  - WILLIAM III (b1614-1684)
    - RICHARD IV (b1642-1708)
      - HENRY X (b1672-1749) ── PRINCESS ROSE OF FREIBURG
        - GEORG III
          - GEORG IV ── PRINCESS AUGUSTA OF BRIGANZA
            - FREDERICK II ── PRINCESS FEODORA OF BAVARIA
        - MARY II (b1701-1772)
          - EDWARD VII (b1727-1782) ── PRINCESS ANNA OF SAXE-COBURG & GOTHA (b1720-1764)
            - WILLIAM IV (b1745-1824) ── PRINCESS ALICE OF HESSE AND BY RHINE (b1748-1806)
              - LOUIS I ── PRINCESS SOFIA OF SWEDEN
                - ALBRECHT II (b1775-)
              - PRINCESS VICTORIA (b1774-1810) ── RICHARD (b1780-1812)
                - GEORGE (b1801-1802)
                - JOHN (b1806-1812)
                - CHRISTIAN (b1808-)
              - JAMES (b1788-1822)
            - ALBERT FITZALAN (Duke of Clarence) (b1761-1796)
              - PHILIP STANHOPE (2nd Earl Chesterfield) (b1795-) ── ANNE LENNARD (Countess of Sussex) (b1810-)

- PETER III (ASSASSINATED) ── CATHERINE THE GREAT
  - PAUL I (ASSASSINATED) (1746-1801)
    - TSAR ALEXANDER I (1777-1825)
    - TSAR NICHOLAS I
      - GRAND DUKE PETER (HOUSE ROMANOV) (b1787-1818)
    - GRAND DUKE SERGEI (HOUSE ROMANOV) ── FRANCES VILLIERS (Duchess of Cleveland) (b1739-1807)
      - PRINCESS LOUISE OF DENMARK (b1765-1800) ── (Albert Fitzalan above)
      - LADY CASTLEMAINE (Barbara Villiers) (b1788-) ── ? ── HENRY XI (b1805-)
        - CHARLES (Duke of York) (b1807-)
        - CATHERINE (b1812-)

ALBION ROYAL FAMILY TREE
1594 TO THE PRESENT

Acknowledgement

Some names used for characters and places in these books may be familiar to readers of past children's literature and older listeners to the radio. My purpose was to pay tribute to the stories and writers I read and listened to in my younger years in what to many may seem like a bygone age. There is no benefit to knowing who and what they are, other than as an amusing diversion.

There Are Five Books In This Series

1.

1826: Spring

A bright Spring morning in April. The first day of the new term at Seekings School, and Freddy Hall is on his way there from his home in the village of Linbury, Dorsetshire. Freddy lives at the Sailor's Yarn Inn with his widowed father, Daniel. They are not rich enough to pay the school fees, but Freddy has a scholarship awarded by Mr Isaac Newton for astronomical work he did on the discovery of a moon orbiting the planet Thanatos.

In spite of this good fortune, there is a downside, because the Natural Philosophy master at Seekings is Mr Robert Hooke the sworn enemy of Mr Newton, and Freddy finds himself disadvantaged by their enmity.

With the help of his best friend Harry East, he is intent on rectifying that situation. But on entering the school gates, he is immediately embroiled with another recent arrival: Simon Blotwell, known as a sneak and worse.

Freddy soon finds himself drawn into an unholy alliance with Simon, pitted against the scheming, disreputable Alfred Mayhew Cheeseman, the son of Gerald Cheeseman MP for Dorsetshire North – a staunch ally of King Henry XI.

No deed is too iniquitous for the ambitious Cheeseman whether it be at school or in the wider world.

So, the Summer term is underway, with new friends, new enemies, and new horizons to explore, including a visit to the Royal Hospital School in Greenwich – and at the back of everyone's mind is the ever-present threat of war between Albion and the Kingdom of Silesia.

2.

1826: Summer

The summer holidays and school's out. In Linbury, Freddy and Harry are employed by Russell Warren, the blacksmith's son, to help demolish the remains of the cottage after the fire on the green. Discoveries are made that puts them in danger from the new beadle, Gabriel Levens, who has been appointed to police the area.

However, it comes as no surprise to Freddy that it's the beadle and his assistant who need policing, particularly when a murder occurs and a culprit is soon produced.

Meanwhile, Simon Blotwell is having a hard time at Blotwell Manor, some of it due to his father, Squire Blotwell, a little to the tutor he has been burdened with, but most of it is self-inflicted. His lofty disdain for all his 'inferiors', including the stable boy, Billy, hardly helps him.

Later on in the holidays, he's due to stay at Bruton Manor, a much more conducive environment, but Auntie Millicent – Lady Bruton – insists he bring a friend from school. A suggestion is made that he invites Freddy, but then Freddy is merely a common, country boy...

With the sabres rattling between Albion and Silesia, Freddy wants to visit his friend Carl Birch, who's serving aboard HMS Ajax in Portsmouth and due to sail for the Baltic. But to merely get into the naval dockyard, he needs the influence of someone in a high position in the Admiralty.

3.

1826: Autumn

The new school year at Seekings, and the Michaelmas term is one like no other. Strange portents in the skies and colder than any in living memory.

The fleet carrying Carl Birch has set out from Portsmouth, heading for St Petersburg in the Baltic. The inexperienced Duke of York, Prince Charles, brother of the King, and Lord High Admiral has pinned his colours to the mast of HMS Ajax – a decision which will have far reaching implications for him, the Royal Family and the Kingdoms of Albion and Silesia.

Back home, the village of Linbury is still under a cloud due to the murder. Further disruption occurs when a new vicar and his daughter arrive to replace the old. The beadle, Gabriel

Levens, insinuates himself effectively with the newcomer and continues his ruthless treatment of those who oppose him. As a consequence, Freddy gets a new responsibility, one that he welcomes with open arms.

Far less welcome is the arrival at Seekings of Basil Cholmondeley. Simon Blotwell might even lose his position as the most obnoxious boy in the school, though he is more concerned that he now has a rival in the school choir. His anxiety makes him have wicked thoughts which need the intervention of his vicar the Reverend McKellan, while his study mate, the unflappable Henry Perceval, has to serve innumerable cups of chocolate to calm him down.

Despite being worried about Carl and his other friends in the fleet, Freddy answers the call from Mr Newton to journey to London to give an account of his progress at the school. In the company of Harry and Simon, it's a visit he is unlikely to forget.

4.

1826: Winter

On returning to home, Freddy finds himself in the doghouse with a small member of his family. Russell Warren confides that he is stepping out with the vicar's daughter, but it must remain a deadly secret.

Basil Cholmondeley is using his oily charm to be the soloist in the Christmas concert with the great Mr Handel. Insincere, sincerity is Basil's speciality and causes Simon more than a little anguish. Further anguish is caused when circumstances force him to issue invitations to all his 'friends' for the Christmas revelries at Bruton Manor

The new vicar of Linbury has found a way to prise out Beryl Antrobus from her position as school teacher and church organist in favour of those more biddable to his outlook. Miss Antrobus the indefatigable and staunch ally of Freddy decides to take a holiday, while the beadle and the vicar join forces against the sea of sin in the village.

In the wider world, there has been a disastrous naval encounter in the Baltic which is explained to Freddy in great detail by his friends. The account is sent to the Admiralty, but it is found to be at odds with the official line which blames Captain Fitzroy of the Ajax. As a consequence, Freddy is summoned to Portsmouth where the captain is due to come before a court of inquiry.

By wiles and stratagems at a very high level the inquiry is changed to a Court Martial. Because of his skill at shorthand, Freddy is employed by the Judge Advocate, Moses Greetham to take the minutes of the proceedings, where deceit and treachery are the order of the day.

5.

1826: Full Circle

Freddy returns to Linbury, where news from up north causes a stir in church and leads to many changes in the parish.

London is in foment and revolution is in the air. Things are quieter in the countryside but not by much.

Simon Blotwell has his own worries. Will he or won't he be the soloist in the Christmas concert? Not to mention acting and directing a production of a Christmas Carol which is due to be performed at Bruton Manor over the festive season.

Freddy is left in charge of the Sailor's Yarn, when Daniel goes away for a week. A week where momentous events take place not only in the village, but also at school, where Henry Perceval gets some devastating news and seems inconsolable.

It's December and a new fall of snow heralds the advent season. The school concert and prize giving on the last day of term is a new start for some and the beginning of a healing for others.

Finally, the year is rounded off at Bruton Manor where all is aglow with Christmas cheer, though Simon is still up to his old tricks and causes mischief amongst the guests. There is also the inauguration of a new bishop to add to the festivities, but there is one last throw of the dice by the old guard.

The great play is performed before a large audience and gets a rousing reception, but at the end, much to Simon's chagrin, the production is upstaged by an event which leaves many of those present in Bruton Manor library gasping.